GW00690296

John Cardinal

TRUST THE DAWN

TRUST THE DAWN

John Cardinal

Book Guild Publishing
Sussex, England

First published in Great Britain in 2010 by
The Book Guild Ltd
Pavilion View
19 New Road
Brighton, BN1 1UF

Copyright © John Philip Cardinal 2010

The right of John Philip Cardinal to be identified as the author
of this work has been asserted by him in accordance with the
Copyright, Designs and Patents Act 1988.

All rights reserved.
No part of this publication may be reproduced, transmitted,
or stored in a retrieval system, in any form or by any means,
without permission in writing from the publisher, nor be otherwise
circulated in any form of binding or cover other than that in which
it is published and without a similar condition being imposed
on the subsequent purchaser.

All characters in this publication are fictitious and any resemblance
to real people, alive or dead, is purely coincidental.

As Time Goes By Words and Music by Herman Hupfeld
© 1931 by WARNER BROS. INC (Renewed). All Rights Reserved. Lyric reproduced
by kind permission of REDWOOD MUSIC LTD (Carlin) London NW1 8BD
for the Commonwealth of Nations including Canada, Australasia and
Hong Kong, Germany, Austria, Switzerland, South Africa and Spain.

Typeset in Baskerville by Ellipsis Books Limited, Glasgow

Printed in Great Britain by CPI Antony Rowe

A catalogue record for this book is available from The British Library.

ISBN 978 1 84624 525 1

To my Swedish family and friends

Author's Note

Lammland – despite its resemblance to a real Baltic island – is fictional. So are those who live there, and any similarities to real people are coincidental. I am grateful to everyone I met in Sweden for the unique experiences that sparked this novel, and have striven for accuracy in all aspects of Swedish life; warmest thanks go to my wife Ann for her unfailing support, and to Tricia Wastvedt of The Writers' Workshop for responses that have helped shape the story. I have, however, indulged artistic licence over certain facts. Except on Lammland, *prästkragar* are not among protected species of wild flower; and *Pastorsämbetet* is no longer a key archive for Births, Marriages and Deaths. Curiously, too, it is the only Baltic island to boast crabs . . . All other distortions or errors are likewise solely mine.

Part I

SIDNEY'S WORLD

1

I'm balanced on a bridge over swirling currents; there's a punt drifting toward me. Two girls lounge either side of someone in a straw hat, strumming a banjo: 'Stormy Weather'. It must be Edward. Something tells me I've got to jump. I lean out, judging the distance. They raise their eyes in shock. The river and the boat lurch upwards.

A steward in a white waistcoat slid open the carriage door. 'Tea or coffee, sir?' Trees were hurtling past in the fading light of afternoon; my forehead had hit the window.

It was still hard to believe I was actually doing this. But for Stephen's phone call it wouldn't have crossed my mind to contact Tilly:

'Tilly? It's about Edward – your brother? Stephen seems to think he went to Norway – somewhere like that. He thought you might . . .'

'Guy, is that you? Lovely to hear from you so queckly. Och aye, I'm so lookin' forward to your vesit!' I was seized with panic. The hearing loss had been hardly noticeable at the funeral; now all at once it was an insurmountable barrier.

'No, Tilly,' I yelled, 'I'm not *coming to Scotland*, just trying to get a few facts straight.'

Her octogenarian ears weren't remotely up to it. 'You'll *love* Sco'land, Guy, of *course* you can come. It's by noo means as far as you thenk. Hwhy don't you take the ten thairty sleeper? You'll slumber like a wee bairn all the way – I know I did.'

'Tilly, you don't follow, we've got to track Uncle *Edward. That's why I'm phoning.*'

'And I'm *so* glad you have, Guy, it'll be *great.* If it's Edward you're frettin' over, I can gev you the details – remember we talked about hem at Ben's funeral? We'll have nice wee chats hwhile you're here – stroll on the beaches. The sand's purest hwhite, you wouldn't believe: you can see thengs movin' under-water.'

'No, Tilly, you've got it all wrong. Stephen needs to know by this weekend, so I . . .'

'Noo worries, Guy, this weekend's as good as any to me. Never too busy for vesitors, that's your Aunt Telly. Och, you've made ma day, and noo mistake. Take the train to Abercrombie and you're practically there. You've an airly boat on Saturdays. Gracious me, but it's an age sence I had a youngster comin'!'

A *boat?* I'd not even thought to look up where Tarmain was. In fact it's one of many missable dots off the north-west Scottish coast. Of course it was a cheek asking Georgina in the office to find it on her computer. There's a ferry that plies along the fringe of islands twice a week, linking them with the mainland at Abercrombie. It sounded a complicated expedition, but poor Tilly doesn't get a lot of company. Once she'd got such a firm hold on the wrong end of the stick, I hadn't the heart to disappoint her. Stephen laughed when I rang back:

'Ah, there you go, Guy. Quite a card, our Tilly, ain't she. Never underestimate a Scot. Well, not that she is, strictly speaking – only went up there after that laird chappie, what was his name?'

'Look, Stephen, I might have talked my way round Sidney, God knows how, but this 'Highlands Express' thing doesn't come cheap. Things are a bit . . .'

'It's all right, Guy, didn't I say? We can charge it all up to Ben's estate – 'legitimate search expenses', etc. You go, you'll be fine with Tilly. She'll bake you one of her cakes, I know it!'

*

To be honest, Sidney – that was my boss – had hardly batted an eyelid when I asked for the Friday off. At least it would save him thinking up things for me to do for a little while. June 2008 wasn't a good time for Castle Estates in Wintersham.

'You'll never guess what's up today, Guy.' Trevor and I shared a tiny office. 'D'you want the good or the bad first?'

'Spit it out, Trev, for God's sake.'

'Well you're down to work-shadow Georgina this week. I'm sure she'll *cascade* all over you, you lucky sod. Of course Sidney thinks she can walk on water. Can't be bad, though, can it? Trotting round the county, sizing up the talent – some people get it with jam on!' *Cascade* is the buzz word for when somebody who thinks they know something tells somebody who supposedly doesn't. By *talent*, of course, he wasn't alluding to the broader attractions of Dorset so much as Georgina herself. Trevor obsesses a bit about bottoms. Several times he'd tried to direct my attention to Georgina's shapely behind, convinced I'd be lost without his guidance in these matters.

'OK, so what's the good news?' His recent absence on holiday in Cornwall had made office life disturbingly sweet; now I felt a wicked impulse to make up for lost malice. You have to remember Trevor's a sciatica person, though. His informational balloon punctured by my leaden response, he sat unconsciously rubbing a buttock.

'I'd watch it if I were you, Guy. Let's just say Sidney's on the warpath. You know what they say: last in, first out.' I only came *in* three months earlier. It's true I'd not done much yet. What could you expect? Trevor had been there a year. He made it sound like a lifetime.

But for once I was better briefed than Trevor. The week before, Sidney suddenly wanted me in his office:

'Ah, Guy, glad you could make it. It's about our – you know – long-term plans. Choccy?' Picking himself out an oleaginous Brazil nut, he sat stroking the folds of his neck; Sidney always made me think of a meditating iguana. He pointed at the ceiling with a pseudo-wince: 'They're getting restless up at Head Office, Guy. Can't blame them, can you? We've not shifted more than three or four houses since January.'

He glowered out along the High Street, as if the slump could be blamed on the inhabitants of Wintersham. 'Not that it's about instant results – don't think that. You're new to agency work, and in a flat market like this . . . It struck me this morning, though: if you've no *models*, how are you ever going to learn?' Half a chocolate still melting between podgy fingers, he cleared his gums, leaning forward for an answer. If there was one I couldn't think of it; he flopped back again, sighing. 'Anyway, you know the jargon up top, don't you? It's all about *restructuring* and *cascading* these days. After all, you might want to go forth and multiply somewhere yerself one day.' I got the feeling Sidney despised the bureaucrats at Head Office as much as I did, though he never quite dared say so. Was this a playful prelude to the sack?

'What it is is, it's working alongside Georgina – that's all it is. *Work-shadowing*. What do you think?' I was counting his duplications of *is*, so thinking was tricky. No doubt he thought me too dim to have an opinion, but in an odd way we both seemed like beginners; this was something rather likeable about Sidney, a sort of lifelong professional gormlessness. For a second he stared at my tie, which I'd only put on that morning since he'd scolded me for the lack of one on Friday. A nice blue and pink number – was it a touch too jazzy? 'Point is, is I'd like you to start Monday.' He got up and tried out a spot of louder rhetoric. 'Oh, come on, man, be a bit dynamic for once, can't you? We need to hear something from you!'

'OK, Sidney, if you think it's a good idea.' Who were *we*? At least he didn't seem to expect me to go forth and multiply today.

'Listen, Guy, I don't like to sound mean, but it's not about me having ideas, is it? They're what we're paying you for!' He gave his mock-humorous frown. 'Anyway . . . Georgina's good, Guy. Trained in London and everything – top notch. And if there's tricks we're missing, I want you to pick up on them. "Where angels fear . . .", I s'pose.' He walked across to open the door.

'One thing, Guy, she'll teach you some more advanced techniques, you can bet yer bottom dollar on that.'

*   *   *

'Morning, Guy.' Georgina was standing in the doorway behind me. I'd been taking a long-winded call from a rare new client, not realising she was there. At thirtyish Georgina was a year or two younger than me; she'd been at Castles for weeks, but up to this moment I'd not even dared look at her face properly. She has gorgeous green-blue eyes and a mouth to die for, never mind her rear view. As luck would have it, Trevor was out checking a ramshackle terrace in the High Street.

'Oh, hello. Er, are you . . .?' There was something deeply noncommittal in her smile, but I put that down to ambition. That, or the more advanced techniques, whatever they were – I could hardly wait. Sidney's head reappeared over her shoulder.

'Show Georgina yer books first, Guy. You know, like we said? Haven't really cracked it this month,' he muttered for her benefit.

'No problem.' I backed towards the desk, banging an elbow on the filing cabinet. Georgina crossed the threshold while I swept my lunch-box off a chair. It was an eye-opener the way she pushed the door to, obliging Sidney to slope back to his office; she stood with one toe skewering the scuffed carpet.

'So tell me, Guy, what's your first priority this week?' The flat, Estuary vowels and slightly husky voice carried an undertone of helpfulness, but there was no mistaking the businesslike message. She was wearing a loose white jacket and biscuity skirt that set off her smooth darkish skin as she dangled a hand over the filing cabinet. I was already longing to stroke her slim, tanned wrist.

'Priority? Well of course, we need to sell things,' I began foolishly, then tried to rescue myself with a few specifics. 'There's Ormsdale Court out at Frickleigh, for a start. Nice property, bit overpriced. But there you go – when you're handling somebody else's pride and joy?'

To my surprise her reaction was positive. 'Oh, quite. I think

7

you're so right to look after people's feelings first. Yes.' Her sibi-
lants betrayed the faintest hint of a lisp. She curled an end of
short black hair behind her ear. 'What's it going for?'

'Three fifty. They wanted four hundred grand for it but Sidney
thought the stables were a bit of a liability. We got them to see
some sense.'

'Not a lot, though? Is this it?' She'd picked the blurb off my
in-tray and was scanning the photos. 'So what do *you* think, Guy?'

I caught a whiff of lemony perfume, which meant I couldn't
think. 'Well, it's still expensive,' was my safe answer. 'There's such
a lot out there at the moment – you know, on the market gener-
ally. Can't see them getting that sort of price in a place like
Frickleigh. Not exactly the beaten track, is it?'

'Have you had this out with Sidney?' She gave me a fright-
eningly straight look.

'Well, you know – Sidney's the boss.' This was cowardly, of
course. The trouble was, my brain wouldn't let me just be a
coward and have done with it. I didn't want to think this, but
her idea that you should 'look after people's feelings first' and
then whittle the price down even further struck me as a distinctly
bullying attitude – as if people's affection for something they've
spent a lifetime buying can somehow be 'cured'. No doubt this
was part of the Georgina Method (and right up Sidney Street).
A momentary frown shadowed her nicely full eyebrows. Seeing
them in close-up was a revelation. She moved on, gathering data.

'What about this one?'

This one was more my territory. 'Ah right, yes, nice farmhouse,
wouldn't mind it myself, actually. Five or six acres of secluded
land and a lot of nice views. Needs a bit of work. Four two five.'

'Mm.' Now it sounded as if we weren't asking enough; the
likelihood of ever getting it right felt remote. There was a time-
efficient pause while Georgina thought out the remaining hour
to lunch. 'Why don't we go check it out?'

Despite Trevor's tip-off I hadn't anticipated action quite this
fast. 'OK, you're the boss.'

'Not really.' She was, though.

2

Juggling a cup of scalding coffee, I watched the darkening Yorkshire hills loom and dwindle. In the heated luxury of the 'Highlands Express' I could almost forget the reason for this trip. Uncle Stephen's first call had come right out of the blue the previous week:

'It's about Ben, Guy. Expect you've heard?'

'Ben? Uncle Ben?' Dad's elder brother lived on a diet of cheese and Old Shag tobacco at the edge of Dipsey Marsh, a few miles west of Wintersham. His house had chronic subsidence problems and the damp air did nothing for his asthma, but Ben would laugh it all off, drowning his sorrows in home-brewed cider. Despite a frugal lifestyle he'd always welcome me with that wonderful bony hug and a table piled high with goodies bought in for the occasion.

''Course, Bennie's always kept himself to himself.' Stephen's voice sounded taut. 'Stuck out on them marshes – bit of a recluse, ain't he. Turns out he's been poorly since Christmas, on and off. Bloody good age, mind – eighty-five last birthday, can't argue with that, eh? I'll miss him, though. All very sudden. Just wish I'd . . .' His voice faltered. 'The old tick-tock, you know – he's had a bit of trouble. Packed up on him altogether, last Friday. Tilly rang me lunchtime.'

'Stephen, I'm so sorry.' He was in shock and I felt utterly useless. Guilty, too. Ben had got a new housekeeper in January – she'd ticked me off for treading mud into the carpet; it was pathetic to let a thing like that stop me going, but it had. 'You must be devastated. You and Tilly.' Had I ever met Aunt Tilly? Stephen's breathing whistled in my ear. 'By the way, how's Douglas? And the girls?'

'Doug? Doug's all right; Fliss and Tammie. We all are.' He seemed baffled to be asked. 'It's Ben,' he added, as if I'd not quite twigged who had died. 'Solicitors've asked me to do all the . . . Will you be at the funeral, Guy?' Another quick intake of breath. 'It's this Saturday, you all right with that? Only I'd . . .' He choked a little with emotion. 'It'd mean a lot if you could be there.'

Bereavement's a strange thing. I felt for Stephen's grief, and at some deeper level shared it, but I do tend just to try and get on with life – my way of coping, I suppose. It's true I'd not had all that much to do with Ben; yet to be honest it wasn't only him I was grieving. Dad died the year before last: I could still picture the two of them years ago, at our kitchen sink in Wareham, sparking corny jokes off each other.

'I 'eard yer wife was ill. That 'er coughin'?'
'Nah, just a rabbit 'utch I'm makin' . . .'

At the same time I can't deny, 'trotting round the county' visiting clients with Georgina, I was distracted and excited by her. In the car that first Monday morning she'd given me more of a feel for her ambitions:

'Dunno about you, Guy, but I'm not sitting around in Wintersham for the next hundred years.' She swung us straight into the fast lane between a Mercedes and a Porsche, wiggling a lacquered fingernail at the hollow by the gear lever. 'Here, fancy one of these?' I found an Arctic Mint in there and peeled off the wrapper. It was white and powdery on the outside and soft in the middle. Georgina was bisecting one between strong teeth. 'I always think of my old dad, you know? Ran his own agency in Salisbury. Heart attack, right there at his desk – the one he'd been sat at all his life. Not my idea of fun.'

'No.' Talking was suddenly difficult – the Arctic was generating a lot of juice. 'So what is?'

She threw a canny glance and changed into fifth. 'What I'd call fun? Now you're asking!' I took this to mean she wasn't going to say, but after a minute she turned to me again. 'I'd like to travel, actually. Always fancied Australia. You know, the Big Outdoors? It'd be nice to sell proper hunks of land for once – where people aren't quibbling over a few square inches of driveway or the number of bedrooms or whatever.' Her neat black cap of hair shook with impatience. There was a definite sexiness about her somewhat frost-bound outer shell.

'Me too – Australia's great.' I said it without thinking, enjoying the speed.

'Oh? Didn't know you'd been.'

'Well, no – from pictures, I mean.' Most of my brain-cells were taken up with wondering if I could decently ask her out that weekend. I wasn't too flush for cash; would she fancy a nice long walk along the Treen? Georgina was already helping herself to her next Arctic. As far as I could make out they were her one and only weakness.

Late that same afternoon I caught her in the corridor on her way out and asked if she was free Saturday. It felt like unbelievable luck when she gave her brilliant smile and said yes.

It was unbelievable next morning too, when Stephen rang about the funeral and I had to put her off again.

11

3

At the cemetery a tall, wispy lady swathed in an elderly tartan cloak wobbled across the grass, bright reds and greens setting off her pale features with a touch of elegance.

'You're Graham's bairn,' she told me, as if I completed her stocktaking for the afternoon. 'I'm your Aunt Telly.' Aunt Tilly offered a cold, skinny hand, balancing on the turned earth to which we'd all just committed her elder brother's earthly remains. 'You won't remember, Guy, but you used to set on ma knee back in the auld days. Loved playin' with ma pairl buttons.' Her dove-grey eyes were full of tears; something in her face made me think of Dad again. She gave me a straight, intimate look, reading my thoughts. 'Aye, Graham was a bonnie laddie.'

'You used to come and look after me, didn't you, when we lived in Wareham?'

'That I did.'

'Tilly, can I ask? You and Ben and Dad: you seemed so close back then – what happened?'

'Happened? Well, Ben and I, we were a wee bit aulder, of course . . . Ooh, but it's a long time ago, Guy.'

'You must have known him better than most, surely. Did he ever talk about . . .?'

'If only Graham could have hung on a wee hwhile longer.' I was intrigued to learn more of how the family ticked, but Tilly seemed set in her stocktaking mode. 'He'd have felt the benefit the noow, wouldn't he?'

12

'Benefit? You mean . . .?'

'Och aye, Benjamin'll be wairth a few shellin's.' She gazed back at the chapel. 'Thenk about it. There were five of us. Ben was the eldest – and noo youngsters of his own, as you know – leavin' us four to inherit, you might safely assume. Now Graham's noo longer weth us, of course, his quarter share'll come to you, Guy. A nice wee nest egg! Then there's Stephen and the bairns – it's a blessin' for them, they can do weth some help. I don't doubt I'll get ma share, too, but hwhat defference is it goin' to make at my age? I've all I need, up in Tarmain.' She gave me an appraising look under dusty-grey eyelashes. 'In fact, Guy, make me a nice cup of tea today, and – who knows – I may leave you ma share as well!'

It seemed in doubtful taste to be discussing Ben's fortune literally over his dead body. Drawing back from the clay-lined cavity, it felt like yesterday that I'd stood at Dad's grave. Mum had only wanted a private burial – none of these far-flung relatives. Tilly put out a hand, sensing my grief. 'So sorry, Guy – this is noo time to be thenkin' of money.' Those infant moments on her lap were gone from my memory, but her words made me feel cared for now. Just then Stephen waved from across the path. 'Gev me a second, Guy ma love.' She squeezed my arm and wandered off.

Next to me at the graveside two young workers laboured in shirtsleeves; the soil drummed noisily on the coffin. It was as if I needed to say something to poor old Ben – I wasn't sure what. To me inheritance has always been something that happens to other people. Tilly's laughter tinkled across the grass in the warm summer air: no doubt she and Stephen were sharing some happy memory of their late brother that very minute. If he was, as Tilly surmised, 'wairth a few shellin's', no one could be more deserving of them than Stephen's family, who have never been well off. Doug was trying to set up his own business, and Fliss was getting married soon. Stephen himself still resurrects dead Robin Reliants alongside an old mate from his army days; once in a while they launch one on the second-hand market, more in faith than hope.

It's hard to see what he and Zoë actually live on. 'A nice wee nest egg' certainly wouldn't go amiss there . . .

Little groups of mourners stood around looking clueless, as you do at funerals. Stephen started moving people on. Always intimidated by formal occasions, I followed at a dawdle. Something in Aunt Tilly's stocktaking didn't add up at all. Seeing her turn and smile, I drew level with her again.

'Tilly, you said there were five of you: Ben, you, Dad, Stephen . . . That only makes four, surely?'

'Ah well, now, there was always Edward, wasn't there.' She looked past me with absent eyes, as if this hardly needed mentioning.

'Was there?' I'd never heard of an Edward.

'Well, of course, you won't have met. He was . . . Well, we can talk about hem later, shall we? Och, you were a bonnie wee laddie in those days, Guy. Into everytheng!' This was mystifying; could I really have had another uncle? 'You specially liked ma Madeiras, as I recall. I stell do a good Madeira cake, mind. Come to thenk of it, hwhy don't you pop up and see me sometime? I'll make one special!' Given the remoteness of Tarmain, the idea I might 'pop up' there sounded highly impractical, if appealing. I would never have believed just how soon I'd be doing it.

Back at Stephen's house Felicity and Tamsin, now in their late twenties, greeted us in the garden, where people had started on drinks and nibbles. I hardly recognised them, cool and stylish in black summer dresses. Then a grey-suited Doug appeared, tall and pale, quietly filling glasses. It felt a million miles from those long-lost days playing rounders together up on Ballard Downs, when we were all still 'bairns': to me, as an only child, they'd been precious times. For a second I got that awful spare wheel feeling – when you wonder what you're doing somewhere. Doug spotted me and wandered over to shake hands. We stood a while, silenced by formality.

'Did you know Ben all that well, Doug?'

'Not really.' He crunched a cheeselet. 'Had trips there when we were kids, that's all – out to that bog he lived on.'

'Bog?'

'You know, the Marshes, whatever. Good fun actually – chasing moorhens and things. Used to stalk them with a pea-shooter.' His eyes roved the lawn, as if wondering where else to pay his respects. 'I've been out to see him a few times myself, the last couple of years – you know, since Dad died . . . Not so much lately. They've drained most of the area now, did you know?' It pained me, considering how close Ben had lived, to realise I'd neglected him most of my life.

'Really sorry about your dad, Guy. We all were.' His words were heartfelt; for a second the tears pricked my eyes, so I said:

'By the way – what about Edward?'

'Who?'

'You know, that other uncle of ours? Tilly reckons . . .'

'Search me, Guy.' He looked around as if this Uncle Edward might suddenly appear. 'Never heard of him.' We small-talked a bit more, and he went off to do the rounds with a fresh bottle.

Tilly was now engrossed in conversation with the vicar. I spotted Stephen's head of spiky grey hair at the barbecue; it seemed worth asking after Edward.

'Who? No, don't think so, Guy.' He prodded the embers, staring out over the hedge. 'You know what Tilly's like. Drifting round that funny old croft of hers . . . Ever been up there? You should, you know. Marvellous place. But it's the isolation, ain't it. The silence. Not enough to think about, I don't s'pose. I love Tilly dearly, we all do, but she do get a bit mixed up sometimes. Somebody else from way back, I expect.' He brushed his lips. 'Ah well, that's the Chandlers for you. Tilly should've got married, everybody says so. Can't think why nobody snapped her up – charming, intelligent woman like that, and o' course – well it's pretty obvious, ain't it? – quite a stunner in her younger day.'

Eventually a general drift back to the cars got under way. The riddle of Edward was tantalising; Tilly had sounded so definite about him. Whatever the gap of years, I felt a real connection with Stephen: why would he, or Dad for that matter, deliberately keep quiet about a fourth brother, if there was one? As the guests began their ritual goodbyes in the narrow drive, I caught up with my elusive aunt at last.

'Tilly? It was great meeting you, could we . . .?'

'Pleasure's all mine, Guy ma love. I've so enjoyed our wee talk. Look, Stephen's brought the car, I have to go. I'll be retairnin' to Sco'land straight away through Keng's Cross. They call it the 'Highlands Express' – rather grand, don't you thenk? Not always quite so 'express' as one might wesh, mind . . .' I felt a twinge of dismay. She lifted her bony chin to one side, bringing her shell-like ear with its solitary pearl in tender contact with mine; there was a soft perfume of lavender.

'Tilly, about what you were saying . . .' I found myself practically whispering, but she gave me a quick hug, ducked into the car and wound down her window. 'So lovely to meet again, Guy, after all these years. And don't forget – come and see me! I thenk we understand each other?' She put a confidential finger to her lips, and with a regal wave was gone.

4

Trains always make me hungry. Somewhere north of Grantham – fired by Stephen's promise of expenses – it struck me I might do things in style and book the full 'Highlands Express' three-course dinner. Normally at home this would have been another evening nodding off in front of the television, as happened earlier that week, with dormant Columbus and a half-eaten carrot on the carpet. Columbus is my tortoise.

'Guy?'

'Stephen? Sorry, you've just caught me . . .' I reached groggily for the remote control; after years without contact, this was our third conversation in a week. 'Thanks again for Saturday, by the way. You and Zoë were . . .'

'I wasn't gonna trouble you, Guy, only . . . Chalks & Conroy've been in touch. You know, Ben's solicitors? Well, executors now. They're trying to trace all his beneficiaries. The Will's being checked as we speak – trouble is, Ben was a bit of a Do-It-Yerself man, see, so there could be a few problems. Anyhow, being Without Issue, as they so charmingly put it, the law says if yer Will won't stand up, all yer goods and chattels go to yer blood relatives.' Stephen sounded bored with the whole business. 'Mr Conroy thinks they can sort it out pretty quick – get Turnham's to sell the house at Dipsey, etc. Only there could be a sizeable estate. Reason I'm phoning, actual fact: I wondered if you'd mind helping out?'

Legal matters are my idea of hell on earth; no doubt I owed

it to Stephen – and Ben too – but the prospect filled me with dread.

'It's a bit awkward, Stephen,' I stalled. 'Things are – you know, dodgy at work, and I've not got a lot of time to . . .'

''Course you're busy, Guy, everybody is. I'm not asking you to do a load of legwork nor nothing. Only you seemed sort of interested in Tilly, and I just thought . . .'

'Tilly?'

'Yeah, that stuff about Edward? Really sorry about all that, Guy: I wasn't being quite straight with you.' He paused. 'Eddie was Tilly's baby brother, if you like. It was only Tilly what really understood him – being as they was closest in age. Did you know she'll be eighty-one this year? Eddie was born in '29, two years her junior. That made him fourteen years older than yer Dad, see, and then I come along in '45, the youngest. Graham and me, we was a couple of afterthoughts, as you might say – sort of post-war mates. Ben was the eldest – born '23. Different generation in them days, wasn't it? So the family was pretty much spaced out. In more ways than one, I hear you thinking! Well it's true, we was an odd lot.'

These great gaps of time in Dad's family were news to me. 'Gran must have been quite some lady.'

'Isobel? Yeah, 'course. She had Ben at eighteen and me at forty. Died at seventy-five. Can be done.'

'OK, so what's the big mystery with Edward?'

'No mystery, really. Thing is, I can't say as we knew each other, not properly. Eddie was away at Chapterhouse by the time I come on the scene, and then – well, once he started in the City, we only ever met in the holidays. I know that ain't no excuse. Clever chappie, though, our Eddie, dead musical – amazing on the banjo. "My Blue Heaven", "Stormy Weather", all them old numbers. A real charmer an' all – this great shock of blond hair, always a string of girls after him. Bit too keen on his social life for Dad's taste, actually. Got mixed up with some jazz club crowd in Soho. So they was bound to cross swords, like – Dad pretty much disowned him.'

'Granddad Mark?'

'That's it. Mum, well, she'd play safe, wouldn't say nothing, would she. But we none of us dared mention his name after that. Isobel would turn scarlet if you did, and Dad'd blow a gasket and rant on about discipline and saving money. 'Course, all them things was anathema to our Eddie.'

'So what happened to him?'

'Ah, well, that's the big one, ain't it. All we know is he went abroad. Norway or something? Back in the fifties. As I say, Tilly was closest – if anybody knows what happened to him, she will. Least, could be worth a try. What d'you think?'

'It's not a question of what I think, surely.'

'Right – that's just it, lad – we've gotta be sure, ain't we!' He seemed to be outmanoeuvring me in a verbal chess-game I hadn't realised we were playing. 'Chalks & Conroy won't move on any of this till it's all been checked and rubber-stamped.'

'I see,' I said, not really seeing.

'If Eddie's still around – which we've no cause to think he ain't – or he got married or something, who knows who else might be lurking in the woodwork? I should've pumped Tilly meself last week, but you know how it is – we was all upset. It's all happened so sudden.' Bereavement hung over him. 'Anyhow, Mr Conroy harps on about verifying the facts. What if there's this dirty great branch of the Chandlers hanging around out there what none of us've ever heard of?'

'OK, so where do we go from here?' I could tell what was coming.

'Could you talk to Tilly, Guy?' He let this sink in for a moment. 'Fact is – same as with Eddie – I don't feel as like I really know her. 'Course, we've all been up to our ears lately – sounds funny, I know, right now I can't seem to . . .' He sucked in a lot of air. 'Only you and her seemed to have – well, quite a thing going. You date back a bit, don't you. P'r'aps it's that early bonding thing? Anyhow . . . It's a phone call, Guy, that's all. She won't listen to me – comes the Big Sister, you know, like when we was kids. And she don't hear all that well, to be honest. She'll be all right with you, though, Guy – long as you speak up. I know it's a chore. Hark at me – I'm painting it worse than it is. I bet you're the ideal man for the job!'

For once family duty stared me in the face; it would have been shabby to refuse. 'All right, Stephen, supposing I talk to Tilly. Then what?'

'Good man – I knew we could count on you. Just feed back the info to Mr Conroy, and Bob's yer uncle. Or in your case, Edward!'

By the time I'd stumbled the length of seven carriages to the dining-car, it was all but empty. As the blue of the night deepened beyond the rattling windowpanes, I found myself wondering again about Georgina. Those expressive eyebrows, and the appealing width of that curvaceous mouth – even contorted in anger – were troubling. Perhaps the singleton's existence had begun to weigh a little heavy; apart from her physical attractions, Georgina was someone I could really talk to.

Communing with a lonely piece of lemon sole on a bed of choice vegetables, it came back to me that I should have been having dinner with her that very minute. She hadn't been best pleased to hear I was popping up to Scotland for a long weekend. In an attempt to be open with her I'd admitted, half in jest, there could be a good deal more in it for me than a slice of Tilly's Madeira. George wasn't amused; in fact she was incandescent. Well, she had every reason. I stared at my shamed reflection in the dark window. What would it have felt like the other way round – with her standing me up for the second time in a week?

5

'Guy! You look cold and seaseck – not used to seafarin', I'll be bound! Here, let me.' Tilly moved to take my holdall; I got to it first, then struggled to keep pace as she set off up the narrow track skirting a gorsy hill. Aboard the little Abercrombie ferry I'd been hemmed in at the heaving bows by a deckful of sheep, and was pretty well soaked. Now the stiff westerlies were gusting across a green-black sea straight into our faces.

Once dried out in her tiny crofter's cottage, I settled by the fire while Tilly chatted on about tending chickens or rescuing sheep from rocky crevices around the island. By contrast my office routine in Wintersham – with the odd evening out at the pub or cinema – seemed arid and tedious. I couldn't resist caricaturing Georgina as this snappily dressed career woman with a taste in exotic cooking and fast cars, though it was a callow exaggeration. Georgina always wanted success, but then she was prepared to put in all the hard work to get it; she also happens to be a very nice person.

Sometime after breakfast next day I found Tilly staring out at the margin of low shrubs that shield her kitchen garden from the storms.

'Tilly, I gather Uncle Edward went abroad: when did you last hear from him?'

'Edward was never one for writin' letters. He did send me some flowers once – from Stockholm. Wasn't that a dandy gesture! Would you credit it, I've kept them.' She pointed to a bunch of

21

dried anemones hanging from the dusty beam. 'Edward could have his romantic moments.'

'Stockholm?'

'Aye, his shep sailed to Sweden in – ooh, the airly fefties, it must have been. He was – hwhat – twenty-two? No doubt he was after a job, hopin' to make a go of it. And I thenk he knew a gairl there. Well, Edward knew a gairl everyhwhere, didn't he. We none of us had any news after that, notheng at all. Aside from . . .'

'Yes?'

'Well, I thenk Edward had more of a conscience than most people would have credited. He'd post money to Isobel and Mark from time to time – noo large amounts, mind. A kind of a peace offerin', as you might say. And a farewell too.'

'Why farewell?'

'Well – hwhen the payments petered out, the family lost contact. He'd geven noo address, you see. Didn't want anyone runnin' after hem, noo doubt. That was deffcult for Isobel – you can see it from our mother's viewpoint? But it was Edward's way. The money was a recognition of hwhat she'd geven hem. He couldn't face Father. It never was good betwixt them. Tairible, really. Mark hoped he'd go into the Army like Ben – Stephen too, much later. But Edward was noo soldier, never in a thousand years. And not good at forgivin', to be pairfectly honest.'

'So that was the last you heard?'

'He could be stell there, for all I know. I *hope* he's there.' There was a catch in her voice. We shared a moment of concentration and grief. 'All these years – the selly boy!' She dabbed her eyes, beside herself with love and annoyance.

For those two days Tilly and I tramped the dazzling beaches and rugged hillocks of Tarmain. Of course her talk of a 'nice wee nest egg' had had a certain appeal – who wouldn't have thought so? But in the long hours of reflection it wasn't money that preyed on my mind. As if released by the crisp air and sunshine, my thoughts ranged over the past – with sharp regret for not having done far more about Dad's family a long time ago. Ben, Tilly and Stephen had been a major part of his life, yet up until he died I'd seen precious little of them. Now Ben had followed him to the grave, I felt – with something akin to panic – the clues to their world fast receding. My hopes of reconnecting with it began to focus on the shadowy figure of Edward. It would be fantastic to meet him in the flesh and ask all the questions I should have asked Dad.

In those special hours together, Tilly and I shared something difficult to define. The sheep made discreet way for us as we went, treading our careful path between neat black droppings. Toward dusk, as the sun withdrew its scant warmth and we turned back into a freshening wind, the island seemed to brace itself once more against the ferocious elements. Tilly's defiance and flinty good humour would likewise endure, as stable and sharp as the rocks below us where the waves surged and foamed.

On my last evening we sat long over her excellent Scotch broth, followed by a 'wee dram of hwhisky' (in Tilly's case, 'for purely medicinal pairposes'). Around ten she brought out one of her famous Madeira cakes. Who could resist? On the mantleshelf a grinning face watched me eat. The faded sepia snapshot had caught a sandy-haired, moustached young man with tender grey eyes like Tilly's, one foot planted on white sand and the other on the prow of a rowing-boat.

'Who's that, Tilly?'

'Och, Guy. Can ye nae guess?' I'd not quite imagined such a muscular, energetic Uncle Edward.

'I was wondering, how did he get to Sweden?'

'Everyone travelled by shep in those days. Edward embarked at Harwich, that much I recall. Contacted me hwhen he arrived – the only time. It'd been a rough crossin', by his account. He was like you, Guy – not the best of sailors!'

'You wouldn't know which port he rang from?'

She stroked her chin, head cocked. 'That's more defficult. I know he said he'd look for a cheap hotel – get his head down for an airly start next day.'

23

'Nothing else?'

'Nae, I don't thenk . . . Well, only that he'd not guessed he'd be so close to Denmark – the opposite coast was clearly vesible from the dockside.'

'And which way was he heading from there?'

'Well if we knew that there'd be noo mystery, would there? It's fefty years ago, Guy!'

'You didn't talk again?'

'He never planned thengs, you see. He could have hetchhiked, he was fond of that. Eddie wasn'a one for wastin' money.' She sat musing. 'Wait a menute, though. He did send a postcard. I may stell have it.' Plucking forth a large shoebox, she flipped through the neat bundles. 'Och, would you credit it?' She held a card to the lamp. '8 December 1951. Looks like Kalimar – Kalmar?'

I studied the monochrome elegance of an imposing castle built, it seemed, almost on the sea. 'May I read this, Tilly?'

'Be ma guest.'

Dear Tilly,
    A line to say I'm all right and on my travels again. Will let you know where I end up.
    Sweden is *beautiful*. Look at this fantastic castle!
    Give my love to Tarmain – and THANKS for everything.
    Say hello to Bennie, Graham, Stephen and all the family.
Love Ed.

'Hwhere's Kalmar, Guy? Some place weth a fine castle, that's for sure.'

'Tilly, this is marvellous!'

'You thenk so?' Her frail face lit up. 'Well, if it's of any use . . .'

The ferry back to Abercrombie was due early next day. Having subsided one last time on my heather-scented bunk next to the fire, I watched the flickering shadows as Tilly made her candlelit way to her own in the little back bedroom. Against the wind's steady moan outside, the deep tranquillity of the house seemed to embrace me. In a place like Tarmain you're not always aware of sleeping at all. There's refreshment in the sheer necessity of focussing on the present – the spirit of survival, the centuries of simple, rigorous life.

'Guy, here's sometheng you may wesh to peruse?' She dropped a little black notebook next to my breakfast porridge. 'Who'd have credited – Edward's diary for nineteen fefty-one.' I didn't ask why she'd not produced it the previous evening. 'You know, Guy, you're not unlike Edward yourself. I remember hem comin' to see me before he left – much like you're doin' now. Hwhen he'd gone I phoned hem in London about the notebook, but he said it was noo matter – I should keep it as a souvenir. Now hwhy should he say a theng like that?'

'You think . . .?'

'Vairy odd. I've noo occasion for souvenirs these days, Guy. I shall leave this wairld as empty-handed as I entered it. But – who knows? You may find sometheng in there to help you trace hem. I'd like the truth, if ever you do. Take it.'

'Tilly, you've been so kind, I . . .'

'And make sure *you* don't leave anytheng on Tarmain!'

In a way, though, I did.

Tilly gave me the warmest hug at the quayside. None of us is here forever. Perhaps the rest of her life's journey could be as good as the hopes I had for my own. Slipping Edward's little diary in my pocket, I resisted the temptation to open it until Tilly's waving figure across the water was too small to see any more.

6

I never made it back to Castles on the Monday. Sidney took it quite well. By the time I turned up on Tuesday morning (an hour late), Georgina had taken over Trevor's desk – he was on sick leave again. We all knew she had a perfectly good one of her own up the corridor near Sidney's, but it was a lot easier keeping an eye on me in here. Almost nothing at all was happening on the local housing market, so there was little excuse to go out. After the freedom of Scotland and the loveliness of the west coast islands, I felt grounded.

'OK, Guy, I thought you could show me your filing system today and we can get these in-trays emptied.' Slump or no slump, there was never any let-up in the amount landing in them. Having cleared her own post, Georgina was now eyeing Trevor's and mine with undiminished appetite. She favoured ruthless use of the wastepaper basket; no doubt Sidney was relying on her to show us the error of our ways. In an effort to assuage her work ethic I dredged up a few old files that were lying fallow, so we could discuss dynamic strategies for resurrecting them. She'd slip a glossy fingernail under the front cover and smile sideways, breathing mintily on my cheek. Her unusual low voice was obscurely alluring. 'So what would you suggest, Guy?'

On Thursday I suggested dinner again. This took a lot of what Georgina would call 'mind-setting'. There was no reason why she should have forgiven me for standing her up twice, but she accepted, which was more than gracious. We drove out to the Hog's Head in Frickleigh: being a Saturday night, the place was packed – you had to breathe in to let people pass. Georgina picked out a stick of that stale bready stuff and nibbled the end off.

'So anyway, you haven't told me anything, what was it like up in Scotland?'

'Oh, you know – sea, sky and Sassenachs,' I said at random.

'And there were lots of them up there?'

'Sassenachs? As many as you'd expect, I suppose. In Edinburgh, anyway. Crammed with visitors – always is. Not Tarmain, though. On Tarmain it was just Tilly and me.' She looked as if she didn't believe this; I stared out over the pristine tablecloths. 'Apart from a few sheep, that is.' The impossibility of conveying the magnificence, the inspired, turbulent peace of Tarmain was depressing.

'Sheep? I bet *they're* not too keen on Sassenachs.' Georgina looked round the room with the ghost of a smile. She had a lovely sense of humour when she was off duty. Most of the time at work, unfortunately, her professional persona seemed to forbid it. 'I wish I could make soup like this.' She slid her spoon around the last drops and breathed in the aroma of asparagus and radish, eyes closed, affecting a theatrical trance. 'Mm, beautiful blending, beautiful proportions, it's all lovely, isn't it. Do you cook at all, Guy?' She fixed me with her glazed pupils.

I didn't like to say too much about my cooking. 'A bit.' Georgina inclined her head comically to one side, waiting for more. 'Nothing grand like this, of course. Normal things.' What was the matter with me? I was having this superb dinner in a cosy dining-room with this sweet, quick-witted and extremely good-looking girl – yet part of me wasn't there at all. Scotland and Tarmain had captured my heart. Tilly's presence in that marvellous setting, and the mystery surrounding Edward, must have stirred a certain wanderlust. I was already working out how to tell Sidney I'd got to go to Sweden next.

The following Monday Stephen rang again.

'Guy, something's cropped up at Chalks & Conroy. They're

round the corner from you, ain't they – d'you think you could drop by? Only I'm a bit tied up at the workshop this week. Most of Bennie's stuff's at the house, but there was one or two bits 'n' bobs in with the Will. Mr Conroy says it's something we might as well pick up now, I dunno what.'

Mr Conroy straightened a fine silk tie as I entered. 'Good of you to call, Mr Chandler. Your uncle's personal effects included a few minor items that we . . .' He pulled out a handful of stout A4 envelopes and passed one across the desk. It bulged with some largish object. 'If you wouldn't mind signing? I don't know if your uncle left any note of explanation, but these are really family matters, not ours. I'm sure you'll know what to do with it.'

Back at the flat that evening I broke the seal and slid out a long leather-bound box with *HOHNER* in gold letters scrolled across the lid. The German harmonica factory? The catch sprang open at a touch; nestling in deep red velvet lay a smooth, silvery instrument, its row of neat round holes set in lustrous pearwood, a shining chromatic button at one end. It felt heavier than you'd expect, with a faint metallic smell. An ancient childhood memory surfaced: kindly, pungent Uncle Ben taking me on his knee; the trembling, tobaccoed lips squeezing out 'Three Blind Mice' . . . As I raised the harmonica to blow, a scrap of paper dropped to the floor.

Edward's. He'll want this.

In Ben's deliberate writing, large and sloping with an odd, backward capital E, it might have been no more than a scribbled reminder to himself. And yet at that moment, reliving a young boy's proud initiation into musical mysteries, it felt like an intimate instruction to me, spoken by a much-loved uncle in that familiar, slightly hoarse military voice.

Neither Stephen nor Tilly had mentioned a harmonica; Edward must have been a most versatile musician. If this was his, why had he left it with Ben? Tilly had hinted at absentmindedness – in all likelihood he'd simply forgotten it. Perhaps before leaving the country he'd have done the rounds of other relatives beside her; why wouldn't he call on Ben to regale him with his latest tunes?

On second thoughts I stowed the harmonica unplayed back in its box.

Castles had a set policy on leave of absence, and I was still the new kid on the block. Having engineered a day off for the Scotland trip (and ended up taking two), I could hardly ask Sidney for another fortnight to go haring off abroad in search of an uncle who disappeared half a century ago. It was a piece of luck, therefore, that my statutory two-week summer vacation was due in little over a month. The next morning – Georgina was out at a meeting in Salisbury – I went cap in hand to Sidney and pleaded with him to let me move it forward. It would have been pointless trying to explain the deeper family reasons for going, but inheritance seemed to be something he could relate to. He huffed and puffed for a while, then agreed to my leaving a week early. It was hard to see what actual difference it would make, but Sidney had his principles; he made me feel like a schoolboy bunking off.

That still left a good three weeks before I could actually bunk. Relations with Georgina were definitely growing warmer, although it wasn't exactly serious. We'd kissed a few times; past experience told me not to take things too fast. She loves driving, so we started heading out to the coast of a Friday evening, or taking the odd day-trip at weekends, sometimes as far as Devon. The weather was hot; we even swam in the sea once. Late one afternoon, on the long drive back from Budleigh Salterton, we pulled into a service station on the A35. In the washroom I freshened up with some cold water and flicked a comb through my hair. Water tends to darken it, but it's darkish anyway, with a slight wave that seems to come and go; on a good day, if it's not too long, I can look presentable enough.

It struck me George and I made quite a good-looking couple (though whether she was a little out of my league is another question). At any rate being out with her made me feel good about myself. Men looked at her a lot, I'd noticed – well, who wouldn't? The striking face, that lovely skin, and in her swimsuit she's a very nice, generous-breasted woman – though for the office it would normally be the smart, loose-fit mini-jacket, with a single top button left undone to keep you guessing. At the same time she had that engaging, strong voice, with a tigerish intelligence behind it that meant you had to think to keep up.

'You don't talk a lot, Guy, do you.' She slid her cobwebby fleece over the back of a chair and stared out at the carpark while I manoeuvred our tray of goodies to the table.

'Don't I? Not when there's nothing to say, I suppose. Can't talk about Castles all the time, can you.'

'I *don't* talk about it all the time!' This was becoming one of our standard skirmishes. 'You seem sort of broody today: what's on your mind?' The elusive lisp, like a small escape of vulnerability, drew my gaze to her mouth again. 'Guy?' Up till then it hadn't felt worth mentioning, but – being asked like that – I went ahead and explained all about the harmonica. 'That's nice. So – it's yours to keep now, is it?'

'George, you're not listening: it's Edward's. Rather a good one, actually. Ben thought he ought to have it back, that's all.'

'Right. And who's Edward?'

'I've told you! That other uncle of mine – Ben's brother? Well, and Dad's and Stephen's, not surprisingly. And Tilly's.'

'OK. So it's up to you to see he gets it?'

'Except nobody knows where he's got to. Went abroad in the fifties.' The topic of Edward was a new danger zone. Our relationship had reached a delicate stage; it felt a little premature to mention the idea of going hunting for him yet a while.

'Well in that case he won't, will he?' She shrugged. 'You'll just have to keep it.'

'If it's his I can't, can I.'

'Can't you? It's a mouth-organ, right?'

'That's the popular word for it, yes.' These feelings were difficult to express. Ben's cryptic message had begun to make finding

Edward seem like something of a duty of honour. 'Anyway, it's
a proper concert instrument these days. You've heard of Larry
Adler?'

'No.' She looked bemused. 'I wouldn't know, Guy, but it's not
as if it's worth a lot of money, is it?'

Trying to explain further would risk exposing my wanderlust.
The rows of empty cars stared in at us. 'What about you, George
– have you ever played anything?'

Her eyelids fluttered in slight embarrassment. 'You won't believe
this. I tried the violin once.'

'No!' This earned me a playful slap on the wrist. Her violin
teacher at school had said she had talent; she'd even joined a
chamber group for a short while. 'So what happened?'

'Oh, you know. Other things came along.'

'Boys, you mean?'

She gifted me one of her dazzling smiles. 'Let's drink this and
get out of here.'

When I wasn't out with Georgina there was a lot to do getting
ready for the trip, which would have to count as this year's summer
holiday as well. A quick scan of Edward's diary for 1951 had
revealed no actual destination. The style was somewhat staccato
and not much given to specifics, so apart from the card to Tilly
from Kalmar Castle on the east coast, her verbal account was
still my best clue to his point of entry to Sweden: . . . *so close to
Denmark – the opposite coast was clearly vesible from the dockside.* This
could only mean Malmö, from where there is now a modern
bridge to Copenhagen.

I rang the Danish ferry terminal and waited forever to be told
they used to run services to two Swedish ports during the fifties,
Gothenburg and Malmö, but had dropped the latter sometime
around the turn of the millennium. My best bet would be the
overnight crossing from Harwich to Gothenburg in the west,
catching the train south from there.

Part II

EDWARD'S WORLD

7

I left Wintersham on the last Tuesday in July, still not having managed a proper talk with Georgina – which was terrible, I know. It felt extravagant to be taking the more expensive route by train and ship when British Air did a perfectly reasonable flight straight from Heathrow to Arlanda, but it was the closest I could get to treading in Edward's footsteps. Towards dawn the wind got up, and for a while my balance organs took issue with the heaving bunk in a narrow cabin, far too close to the engine-room. Eventually I slipped into dream-ridden sleep – playing uphill tennis with Trevor and arguing about house prices while Georgina sat keeping the score.

Next morning we were greeted by brilliant sunshine on a deck awash with salty spray. To escape the clanking cabin I tucked myself up in a deckchair behind the funnel, ignoring the evil odours; in my minimal rucksack Edward's little diary was the only reading matter to hand. Stephen had already filled me in on his early years: thrown out of Cambridge for hoisting a punt onto the college roof, he'd 'temped' for a while in London, frequenting various nightclubs to hear the likes of Ronnie Scott and Humphrey Lyttelton. Their father, Mark, had never accepted Edward's rather broad taste in women; and yet I couldn't see anything all that wicked in what he'd actually done. The last straw, apparently, came when he 'borrowed' one of Mark's suits without permission for some posh do in town, returning it next morning spattered with wine. After a brief apprenticeship as a banker's clerk on Throgmorton Street, he just left one day without a word to anybody. No one was greatly surprised – it seems people expected Edward to be unpredictable.

The diary records his next move, in February 1951, to Billingsgate Market, where he would set up the stall among fast-talking traders in the dark freezing hours before dawn. He even jots down one or two of their cockney witticisms with some affection, though the work itself – loading and unloading boxes of fish – must have been physically hard as well as brain-numbingly boring. No hint here of any plans to go abroad. I flipped forward to the final pages. Apart from a note at the tail end of June – *DFDS Crossing booked: Harwich midday 29 July* – again, nothing useful. The diary comes to an abrupt end with his last entry on Tarmain, the day he left the thing behind in Tilly's little parlour:

> Good old Tilly – made me porridge for breakfast again, the way she used to with a dollop of hot treacle. Another hike round north perimeter this morning. Where does she get her energy? I'm due for the midday boat, worse luck. If only I could stay here and forget fish!

Still no fat clue about Sweden. I ploughed through systematically now from March to the summer. On 16 June he buys a map and is boning up on the geography; it's clear he's made up his mind to go by this time, but there's no sign of realistic planning – nothing about getting work, for instance, let alone settling down there. In spite of an up-beat, often facetious tone, the mood feels somewhat depressed, as if this trip is a leap in the dark – a last resort to lift his spirits.

Nor could I find any reference to knowing anyone there. I was with Tilly on this, though: we both suspected he had some perfectly good reason (probably female) for going to Sweden.

The ship docked in Gothenburg shortly after midday. Within an hour I was on a fast train to the southern tip of the country.

Malmö's airy Central Station lies close to the quay; in the late afternoon vessels were being unloaded, porters and crane drivers shouting in their angular, oddly imperious language. Across the Sound with its futuristic new bridge, ships floated in a sea of molten silver. Beyond them, against a vast tapering strip of gauzy white cloud, the dove-grey outlines of Copenhagen's rooftops on the opposite coast stood in delicate silhouette. I could almost see keen-eyed Edward standing at this very spot, back in 1951, the breeze catching his long fair hair as he gazes toward Denmark. Today was 30 July – the exact same date on which he must have arrived here all those years ago.

Putting my watch on the extra hour by the station clock, I strolled down Storgatan in the sunshine; its rather grand architecture gives the wide street a self-important feel. The modest *Krogen* hotel squats between a baker's and a hot-dog stall: up on the sunny first floor a large bed welcomed me with the smell of fresh rose-water. In moments I was asleep again.

Much later, in the downstairs dining-room, two or three unattached American women sat talking in loud voices; there were a few Swedish businessmen, and a chatty family from somewhere like Poland or Estonia. I found a vacant table crammed into a recess near the window overlooking the harbour; it was pleasant to watch the ships and the other guests, waiting to be served. What would Georgina be doing right now? That funny sense of familiarity and distance came over me again. Perhaps it was just homesickness.

8

Picking up Edward's trail at his Scandinavian point of departure had seemed a smart idea back in England; now I was here it felt a little daft. How much of a trail did anybody leave behind after (I did the arithmetic for the first time) fifty-seven years? There was no time to get anywhere on this before a smart-suited businessman strode in and sat down opposite me without so much as a word or glance in my direction. Had I taken his *stambord*? The clean-shaven chin and short fair hair, though, along with the gently closed mouth below a straight Nordic nose, were rather reassuring. Now he made eye contact, holding out a manicured hand.

'Svensson.'

'Oh. I'm Guy. You – stay here a lot?'

'It's the route to Europe. Everybody travels through Malmö.' He gave a tolerant smile; his English was clipped and unhesitating.

'So you'd be – a commercial traveller of some sort?'

'I'm in cardboard boxes.' I daren't laugh at this. 'And yourself – on the tourist trail? Your first visit in Sweden?'

'I've just arrived. To tell the truth I'm not really a tourist, though.'

'Ah, the truth. One should always tell it.' There was the shadow of a smile again. 'Well, at least pretend to. So you've yust arrived, but you're not a tourist. And what d'you like Sweden?'

'Fine, so far.' My mind lurched a little at his idiom. 'The thing

38

is, I am on holiday, in a way, but I've also come looking for somebody.'

'A girlfriend?' Mr Svensson's comfortable, fact-gathering manner showed he wasn't a man to waste time on small talk.

'As a matter of fact it's my uncle.'

'You've come to Sweden for find your uncle. And where is he, this uncle?'

'That's the problem. I've no idea. He came here fifty years ago.'

'Fifty *years*? You can't be serious.' He leaned back in his chair to enjoy this. 'All right, so your uncle comes here for fifty years ago . . .'

'Fifty-seven, to be exact.'

'Fifty-*seven* years. Mm, let's see: 1951. The *Festival of Britain*?' His knowledge of English culture was impressive. 'And what does he come for?'

'In his case it probably *was* a girlfriend.'

'Ah-ha, OK. That figures.' He sat thinking again. 'All right then. This uncle of yours, he's coming to Sweden for find a girlfriend. Do we know it's his real reason, or are we . . .' (he frowned, reviewing some inner vocabulary list) 'are we yust *surmising*?'

'It's only hearsay, but it seems likely.' I liked *we*; Mr Svensson seemed keen to engage with the problem.

'Hearsay? Where from? I'm sorry, I shouldn't ask. Curiosity, I'm afraid. You must say if I . . .'

'No, go ahead. From an aunt, as a matter of fact. Aunt Tilly.'

'Aha!' Again the sardonic twist to the eyebrows. 'Auntie Tilly. Now there's a thickening plot, isn't it? We're come to the nub, I think. Your aunt suspects her husband of a fling abroad. In Sweden, yes of course. And it's for fifty-seven years ago. The English romantic! Blonde women and free love?'

'No, not husband – nothing like that. Her brother.'

'*Brother.* So sorry. And is it allowed to ask his name also, this brother?'

'Edward. Edward Chandler.'

'Uncle Edward and Aunt Tilly. The Chandlers. So it's mean you're a Chandler also?'

'Guy Chandler. Pleased to meet you.'

'Bo-Göran Svensson.' We seemed to have done the introductions twice now. 'Bo-Göran, it's a mouthful, especially for foreigners. My friends, they say only Bo.'

He liked to talk with foreigners, he hoped I didn't mind? The dish of the day was good value – he'd recommend it. He was starving. Was I ready to eat?

We ordered the staple meatballs with boiled potatoes and cranberry sauce. Everything tasted a little sweet to me, and the table still swayed a little after the long sea voyage, but I was beginning to feel better. Bo Svensson might be very useful.

'OK, so Uncle Eddie arrives in Malmö, 1951. He may already know a girl here – or not. Let's guess she's around his age, shall we . . .?'

'He was born in '29.'

'So . . . Twenty-two, twenty-three. He won't speak Swedish – or only a few phrases. Maybe he prefer the language of love – it's possible he's been unlucky in love before? He's heard about Swedish women . . . Though where this country get her reputation, it's a mystery.' Bo shook his head at a forkful of potato. 'Eddie's had a bad time at home also – trouble with his father, you say? He'll want to make a fresh start, earn a living, settle himself here.'

'Where would you go first – in his shoes?'

'For start a new life? He must register with the police. And for that he need a work, and so on. It's chicken and egg here in Sweden. At least the offer of one – a letter of introduction, something in that way. Does he . . .?'

'Not that I'm aware of.'

'Oh. Well then it's more difficult. What have he done in UK? Some work – a trade?'

'He started out in a London bank, by all accounts.'

'It's his choice for career, then – banking?'

'Ah, no. Seems he only lasted a few months. Ended up as a porter at the fish-market, according to his diary.'

'Mm. Billingsgate?'

'Yes!'

'So we have someone more like – more a yack-of-all-trades?'

'Sounds right. Mind you, Stephen – he's another uncle says he went to quite an up-market school. Have you heard of Chapterhouse? He could have had some sort of accountancy qualification later, too.'

'Right. So Uncle Eddie's good with figures. But he can't go into finance, can he? Not from the beginning anyway – the language will make it impossible. That leaves manual works, I guess. He's been on Chapterhouse, so he'll be physical fit . . . The prospects aren't great, are they? Isn't it something else he can do?'

'He played the banjo, apparently. Rather well, according to Stephen. And the harmonica, as it happens – many years ago.'

'Ah, now that could be something. I can't see Uncle Eddie packing fish all his life, can you? In the first weeks – a young man – maybe he get something like that in Malmö. *Footloose and fancy-free?* But – a clever man, also. Clever, musician – he'll want something more. Perform music? Maybe teach?'

It all sounded cogent enough. Some of Bo's guesswork may have been a little wild, but he seemed to bring me a step closer to the reality of *Uncle Eddie*. 'So, let's say he's get a job. He's registering with the police, it's legal. OK, now he's need somewhere to live. If he don't share with the girlfriend – it's also possible. A small place: somewhere to cook, sleep, and so on. One, two room with kitchen? It's plenty in Malmö – not so expensive. Eddie won't have so much money, probably. For all this, he must register himself at *Skattemyndigheten.*'

'Scatter what?'

Bo laughed out loud for the first time. '*Skatt*, it's tax. The Tax Office. National regulations – here in Sweden we keep track of our foreigners. Can't have you grabbing the country like last time.'

'Last time?'

'You know – the Danes? Germans also, a few times. For many years ago.'

Being lumped in with the Danes and Germans was a novelty; I wanted to give as good as I got. 'You grabbed ours first.'

'Did we?' He looked up sharply.

'The Anglo-Saxons. Well, Angles, anyway. Weren't they from Scandinavia?'

'Ah. But you needed the blood. A stronger gene pool?'

I let this go. 'So do you think there could be records? Even back to 1951?'

'Sure it's records. You can get 1851 if you want. I'm serious.'

There was a lot to think about in the night. Next morning, reaching the breakfast table with its crisp linen cloth and sprig of freesias, I found Bo already well into rolls and cheese. By profession he sold machines that cut and glued every conceivable shape and size of cardboard box; today he was due to drive over that great bridge for a meeting with a colleague in Copenhagen.

'Guy. Too early for you? Here in Sweden we like to crack the dawn.' He lifted a jug of coffee. 'What's up today – "fresh woods and pastures new"?'

'I've got to get a handle on Uncle Edward somehow.'

'Ha! Handle – I like handle.' He savoured it with a fresh mouthful of roll and jam. 'Well, the Tax Office may have the best *handles*. Why don't I give you a lift to *Skattemyndigheten*? You British, you love your *Births, Marriages and Deaths*, don't you. We do all this of course, but here in Sweden it's *residence* first – where people live, when and where they move on. We like to keep' – he smiled knowingly – 'a *handle* on them. Maybe you Brits aren't so fussy about where everybody *is*?'

Outside the Tax Office we shook hands again. I was sad to say goodbye to Bo Svensson. He flipped out a card and declared himself happy for me to call, perhaps en route back to England.

With that he ducked his short-cropped head into the sleek Saab and slipped away to join the morning rush for the harbour.

The woman on duty fetched a large register. There were a remarkable number of Edwards, but only one Chandler. Already missing Bo's good-humoured guidance, I caught the duty officer's eye again. She leant over my shoulder, translating with dour accuracy:

Shandler, Edward. Immigration: 30 July 1951. Civic Registration: 31 August. Nationality: British/English. Residence: Lundavägen 15. Profession: Accountant . . . Deregistration: 25 November.

'Deregistration?'

'It's deregistration when you transfer to a new administration commune.' She addressed herself to my left ear with faintly curried breath. 'Registration occur in the new commune, but date of departure is recorded also in the old commune. Here in Sweden we do the administration by communes.' The voice carried a controlled impatience, as if I were insufficiently briefed on Swedish bureaucratic virtues. I peered through her glasses at her strongly magnified pupils, awaiting enlightenment on how things were done *here in Sweden.* 'We can watch people's movements better this way. Especially ones in the Undesirables category.' Had she already put me in it?

'So he moved elsewhere? Could he have returned to England?'

'No, Mr Shandler have remained resident here in Sweden.' She scanned the entry again. 'We have no record of an Emigration for Mr Shandler.' Her tone made it sound regrettable.

'Is there some way of finding out where he went?'

Looking a little insulted, she adjusted her glasses and checked the dossier again. 'Destination Commune: Valstad. It's the new commune – on Lammland.'

'On . . .?'

'It's many islands in the Swedish archipelagos.' The language error glitsched solemnly by; now I was in for a geography lesson. 'An archipelago are a collection of islands. Some is very small, but of course we have bigger ones also.' She closed the tome with a thud, punctuating the end of the time at her disposal. 'Lammland, it's big.'

I thanked her and beat a hasty retreat, scribbling the details on a card from the *Krogen*. What were the chances of finding the right archipelago, locating the correct island and getting to Valstad? Experience would shortly confirm you have only to take out a map in Sweden for passers-by to stop and offer help; Bo had kindly left me his. Outside on the sunny pavement a wiry lady with a shopping bag blinked into my face.

'Are you look after the station?'

'No, I – I need the tourist office, I think. Valstad? Are there boats from here?'

She gave a sympathetic smile. 'Take train from Central Station till Vyborgshamn. There can you take ferry – it's go two times a day.'

9

Vyborgshamn turned out to be another three hours north of Malmö, up the east coast this time; by 1.30 pm my train was gliding noiselessly out of Central Station. The ferry to the island was due to leave at midnight, a further four-hour crossing. I dozed in the waiting area, surfacing from time to time to stare in gathering darkness at a succession of quayside dockings and departures. The whole task of finding Edward could take a great deal longer than the strict leave meted out to me by Sidney. Knowing he worked all hours at the office, it occurred to me to ring straight away in the hope of a modest extension. There was a phone booth in the restaurant.

'Guy? Is that you?' The warm intimacy of her voice in my ear, with that overlay of huskiness that always aroused baser instincts, caught me unawares. Georgina must have taken on the functions of personal assistant to Sidney. I swallowed guiltily, anchoring myself against the glass.

'George? I've tried to phone,' I lied. 'Things have moved on, it's – been a bit complicated here . . .'

'Oh, and where might *here* be?' She'd known there was holiday time due to me, but nothing about bringing the date forward, let alone any plans to leave the country. What was even more unforgivable – having pencilled in another dinner date: I'd let her down a third time. It was typical of me – acting as if my life had no bearing on anyone else's.

'George, I know it's late in the day, and I'm truly sorry about . . .'

'*Sorry!* You're *sorry?* That's s'posed to cheer me up, then, is it?'

'Honestly, George, I meant to . . . God knows what you must think of me.' I hardly needed God to work it out.

'Where the hell *are* you? What are you up to, for goodness' sake?'

'There's this problem over the Will, you see. You know, Ben's estate – we talked about it? Someone had to dig around and get some information, so Stephen thought . . . There's certain questions need answering, Ben's money's got to be . . .'

'Oh, great. So you've got yourself a nice little excuse to go bombing off again. That's all I need! Have you got any idea what life's *like* in this place – what sort of a *week* I've had? Sidney's trying to launch this new 'Fast Turn-Around' policy, and you're out on one of your jaunts. Why can't somebody else do a bit of digging for a change? In any case, how can you just stand me up like this? Not just once but *twice*.' To my deep shame, she'd lost count; her fury cranked up a gear. 'You fix me up on these charming dinner dates and then don't even bother to mention when His Lordship can't make it. What am I supposed to think? Don't you have any feelings at all for what it's like to be somebody *else?*'

It was richly deserved, every word of it; she wasn't finished yet. 'And another thing: you know Sidney likes this line kept free. What makes you think it's OK to ring me at work? He's out at Limmingham tonight – trouble-shooting on some hop-farm deal. I'm supposed to hold the fort here till he gets back, God knows when that'll be, and I don't need *this*.' My watch said 10.30 pm; even subtracting the extra hour, it meant serious overtime. I daren't tell her I'd really rung to speak to Sidney. Despite the blazing row, Georgina's anger betrayed a vulnerable centre – the implicit belief that any communication from me would, as a matter of course, be intended for her. 'Anyway, you still haven't told me where you are.'

'You're right, George, of course you are, I've been awful to you, and *please* believe me, I'm so sorry . . .' This was the heart-felt truth – but at that same moment it dawned on me I was not actually going to tell her about Sweden. Not yet, that is. 'It's just that – you know, what with the funeral . . . Stephen needed a bit of support, and then all this trouble-shooting on the Will for poor old Ben . . .' *Trouble-shooting*: it was an unconscious echo of her words. Mentioning Stephen might make her assume I was at his place, or perhaps even Ben's.

This was anything but my finest hour; and yet – though genuinely shocked and depressed over my own behaviour – I daren't go into more detail for fear of prompting all sorts of unanswerable questions. Ben's death had probably shaken me far more than I'd realised. Somehow it had brought so much else to the surface: as if restarting a process of grieving that stalled when Dad died. Later, surely – once matters were clearer – there'd be a chance to talk everything through, make it up to her for all my shortcomings. 'Ben was such a nice man, I . . .' At that point she must have heard something in my voice.

'OK, listen, Guy, I know you've been through the mill and I'm sorry about your uncle, really I am.' The phone clicked at her end, there was a rustle of papers. 'Sorry, Guy, it's . . . I'll have to go. Sidney's downstairs, he's just got back. Talk to you later?'

I'd got a ticket for the ferry but was too late to book a berth. Grappling the rucksack onto a shelf next to a chaos of holdalls, I stretched out in the rear lounge near the bar, having ceded to the temptation of a small Scotch. *Medicinal pairposes.* The holdalls belonged to a mixed choir of teenagers from Swansea; now and then they'd rise to a chorus of 'Land Of Our Fathers' or 'All Through The Night', with background titters. Knowing the tunes, it crossed my mind to whip out Edward's harmonica and try playing along. Edward had obviously been the real musician in our family, but I've got a reasonable ear for melody; it would be nice to think we had something in common. He and Ben hovered in my whisky-numbed brain now like benign ghosts.

In the event, though, the moment passed and a multitude of bodies were soon jostling for space on the carpeted floor. One or two wanted to bicker a little before settling down.

'You're like a cow giving *birth*.' His tone was amiable. 'I know you *fancy* yourself at the Cardiff Eisteddfod or whatever, but we've all to muck in when it's the choir, isn't it?'

'Shut your face, David Morgan. You're not *exactly* Robbie Williams yourself, are you?' She sat up, pigtails bristling.

'Don't take no notice, Betsy, he's jealous, that's all.'

'Well,' declared Betsy for everyone's benefit including David Morgan's, 'if that's his idea of *attractive*, then he's another think coming.' She wriggled onto her side, eyes shut tight. Later a scattering of snores told of successful contact with the world of dreams.

Much later again, I'm tracking Edward through a wood. His silhouette glides forward in moonlight, but the face is obscured. There's a rifle range nearby. Shots whistle through the air, making me duck low between trees and mossy banks. Dad is propped up against one, reading Edward's diary. He half-turns to me: *You know, Guy, Georgina's a nice girl, isn't she*. He knows how I've treated her, thinks I should *do the decent thing*. My feet burrow in dead leaves; why am I wearing children's sandals? Another deafening shot: it seems impossible to tell whether it's hit Edward or me.

I woke with a racing pulse, my watchstrap cutting into me; it was a quarter to three. The hours of darkness inched past.

It was still dark the next time I came to; stewards navigated around us, keeping an eye on things. Avoiding recumbent bodies, I crept to the stairs and climbed two flights out onto the deck. The ship buzzed ruminatively, rocking itself in slumber, the sea breathing and whispering beneath. Ahead of us to the east a glimmer of impending light hung at the edge of blackness. A few spectacular stars lingered in the sky. My head full of strange landscapes and languages, I leaned into the breeze at the south-facing rail; the black contours of an island glided past, remote and self-contained. Further on we passed its partner, larger than the first, tinged now with the earliest glow of sunrise. Touches of darkest green were filtering in, brushstrokes in a tentative watercolour.

All at once a coastline stretched before us – a mainland of sorts (though the real Swedish coast had fallen far behind), its trees and rocky hillsides finally visible. Amber rays caught the ship's masts and white paintwork. A windmill stood sentinel, dark silhouetted arms heavily diagonal against the pink-flecked dawn. The ship seemed to drift into the port with its encircling wall of stone, fortified by medieval towers and gateways.

Valstad.

Among the jostling holiday-makers and returning locals a murmur of conversation went on in Swedish and English; we edged our way down the gangway to feel the solidity of land underfoot again. The choir huddled together, sleep-starved and wordless.

Straight ahead, a steep, cobbled street led up to the town centre; nothing would be open at this hour. Past the quay to my right, yachts lay at their berths in the marina, sails blinding white in the morning sun; if they were occupied, no one had yet stirred. The rucksack felt heavier than yesterday. In clothes more geared to the brisk Dorset breezes it already felt too warm; the day promised serious heat later on. Sleeplessness dragging at my legs, I headed up onto a stretch of grassland skirting the ancient wall, and found a shady spot near one of the great arches. Curled up on the grass, I was soon in my dreams again.

10

I wake this time in direct sunlight, hot and insistent; bits of grass have stuck to my sleeves. The sea gleams a delicate turquoise beyond the marina. Within the limestone walls, medieval buildings are jumbled on the hillside around an onion-tower cathedral. I slip through the gateway, climb the aching hill. The main square is enclosed on all sides by timber-and-stone buildings; at a café, the *Musica*, parasols shade neat round tables. It's a relief to shed the rucksack and sit.

Baskets of cornflowers and daisies hang motionless on the terrace. The heat is intense in the still air, though it's not yet ten o'clock. The skeleton of a roofless church, its arched stonework like the whitened bones of a slain mammoth, rises above *Stortorget* against a fairy-tale blue sky.

As I browse the drinks list a tall girl, her dark hair tied with a simple ribbon, steps out of the shaded interior dangling a tray, and picks her way around the muddle of chairs and empty tables. White sleeves tucked loosely back from her downy forearms, she's wearing an oat-coloured skirt above smooth, tanned legs. She begins clearing a mass of glasses and crockery. Someone has left a full milk shake, which she balances on the tray before dusting the table with a deft flick. Her clogs graze the flagstones; from behind I catch the brief gleam of slim ankles in sunlight.

'That looks heavy.'

She turns quickly. 'Förlåt? I'm sorry, I didn't see you. Coffee?'

It's disarming the way everyone responds in fluent English. I ask for rolls and jam with the coffee.

The square grows busier. Tourists stop by and leave again; during a lull the girl does another circuit, clearing away.

'I wonder if you could tell me – the Town Hall? I need to check some records – someone who lived here, years ago.'

Putting down her tray, she shields her eyes from the sun, dark brows drawn upward, and points across the square. 'Round the corner, up a level, on your right.' The slight questioning intonation gives her voice a gentle energy; perhaps it's an effect of her accent.

'I'm new to Lammland – what's to see here?'

'Plenty for tourists in Valstad – August, it's the busy time. But you can find other places, much quieter, you know? Small villages, some lakes, beaches of course, and woods, places like that.' Her smile briefly lights the space between us; she's so pretty I can't think what else to say. 'You can get brochures on the tourist office. Enjoy your vacation.' She moves on.

A group of elderly ladies are sitting down at the front of the terrace. The girl has picked up her tray and gone over to take their orders. By the time I get up to leave she's nowhere to be seen.

The Town Hall echoed with a hush of soft shoes on cold stone floors; a queue of people were waiting to speak to a girl who looked as if she rarely saw the light of day. When my turn came she listened with undisguised boredom, fiddling with an earring.

'Chandler? It's certain he came to Valstad?'

'So they told me in Malmö.'

She consulted a giant register, her wan face screened by mousy hair. 'Chandler – yes, here. Edward.' Fleeting eye contact suggested a fragile spark of interest. 'January '52. Vandringe. The parish register, it's in Segelholm – Saint Olof's Church. It should tell you more.'

'Saint . . .? Could you write that down, please?'

'It's in the near of the coast. You can take bus. The Låtby

route? Of course a lot of people goes with bicycle on the summer. You can hire one at Riegers if you want. Shall you have the address also?'

The thought of hunting Edward down on a bike rather appealed. At the shop I found an old but serviceable one with panniers and a rack to prop the rucksack on. The tourist office provided a free map; over a picnic lunch by a fountain I spread it out and located Segelholm, an inch or so above Valstad on the west coast; it looked like no distance at all.

Opposite the fountain I wandered into a museum of Lammland's prehistory. It was clear fishing had loomed large in the early years of human habitation. Next to massive rune-stones set in whitewashed alcoves, there were blown-up photographs of neolithic remains along the coasts, including curious ridges of stone just below sea level. Some archeologists believed these to be primitive jetties that once sheltered the light, coracle-style boats; a more sceptical view saw them as natural accumulations of rock that had merely subsided into the sea – perhaps before the silting-up of the Baltic, when it was still strongly tidal. My money was on the man-made theory.

After half an hour I'd had enough; lack of sleep weighed on me again. It felt pointless to rush off to Segelholm just yet: I'd have more energy in the morning. This was supposed to be leisure as well as business, wasn't it?

11

Saturday morning dawned heavily overcast. I'd settled for a small family-run guesthouse outside the old city wall, with a westward view of the coastline. Today there was little to see beyond the windless beach, hemmed by fog and ghostly white under a leaden sky.

Steady drizzle glazed the cobbles as I headed north out of town. On the coastal road the occasional Saab or Volvo would swish by, with a heavier stream of cars in the opposite direction; the roadway glittered with headlights. A group of fast-cycling Americans passed me, flicking water from their eyes and calling 'Hi!' like old comrades; they were soon out of sight. You get used to rain; once in open countryside, pedalling doggedly on, I could keep dry enough under a billowing yellow rain-cape from Riegers.

Before long almost all traffic petered out. The road led between stony fields and straggling fringes of juniper, emerging occasionally to skirt the bleak beaches for a kilometre or two. The sea lay still and opaque behind curtains of diaphanous mist. I stopped once at the roadside to eat some black bread with acrid coffee from a flask. Later, as daylight drained from the sky, I pulled over again to check the map; within seconds a bald cyclist in shorts, cheerfully soaked, slid alongside.

'Need you help?'

'Is it much further to Segelholm?'

'A few kilometre to push.' He glance doubtfully at the bike.

53

'But it's a campsite at Emsäde – over the next hill. It's clean and it's sheap. Good holidays!'

'Ems . . .?' But he'd gone.

The island was a good deal bigger than I'd realised, and the turn-off to Emsäde rather too tempting to resist. The muddy track led between dense thickets; in a clearing some dozen or so campers sat at two long tables by a stream enjoying what looked like an impromptu party in the rain, a celebratory bottle passing from hand to hand. Several children were throwing remnants of bread to a squabble of ducks.

Seeing my drenched form stumble into view, they called me to join them for baguettes and tinned tuna. Being tentless, it was good to hear you could rent a small *stuga* for the night; I sat listening to anecdotes about travel and lost luggage, my throat warmed by the tingle of *brännvin*. Tomorrow could take care of itself.

*   *   *

The drizzle still persisted next morning with no sign of a break. After breakfast I rang Castles again, then remembered this was Sunday. Leaving the campsite number on Sidney's answerphone I set off, happily liberated from the rucksack, to cycle the last few windswept kilometres to Segelholm.

When you get there the road all but merges with the beach, deserted today apart from a few gulls wheeling and calling soulfully over the rain-pocked sea. Tyres skidding on the mud, I followed the bend of the road and came at once to the village church. Headstones dotted the graveyard between hedges of yew; you could almost hear the snails gliding about in search of nourishment.

A dismal bell tolled as I crunched up the path. From the doorway emanated the clear, deep voice of a vicar in mid-sermon. Inside there was a whiff of lilac and furniture polish; forty or fifty pairs of eyes swivelled round to watch me pull the massive portal shut. People sat or stood in shorts and T-shirts, their necks and faces red with sunburn.

'So you see, the world is unfolding as it always done, and in this meaning we can do nothing for it.' No doubt the English sermon was prompted by the influx of tourists; the vicar paused, smoothing his crisp white collar. 'But in another way – think on our Lesson? – it's many things we can do. We can make that difference, because we're not simple observers which look at all these wonderful and awful happenings in the world, are we? No,' he answered himself, 'we can have influence on those happenings – influence in the good way. We're a *part* of the world, of this things which happen in it.' He watched me creep to a noisy pew. 'Jesus, He was doing something for the people. He talk with them of course. But He could give them comfort also. In that way He cured them – which is a cure not only in the body.'

People shifted in the pews, as if unsure what kind of cure he had in mind. 'Later, he get away to the fishing-boat, for escape. But we must do it sometimes also, don't we? Escape from the crowd? Jesus, He was human, like us. He must recharge His batteries – like us. And then come the storm. Jesus was ready. He could calm it, that storm. He could even walk on the water – it's call a miracle.' The sunburnt visitors had a faraway look; the vicar waved his palms in what seemed a gesture of frustration. 'Now of course, *we* can't make miracles. Unless, that is – unless we have a special talent, hidden among us here today, what I don't know about?' There was a polite release of *sotto voce* mirth.

'No, because we're human only. Miracles, it's not possible for us. Or is it? Let's think. When we talk with someone – really *talk* with him – isn't that a kind of a miracle? And when people talk with us, isn't it a miracle, that also? Where would we be without those people?' The restlessness was palpable; his visitors, whoever they were, seemed to have their minds on other things. The vicar clutched at the air, as if for moral leverage. 'So: do this today. Talk with someone. Yes, talk – and listen. Really *listen*. Someone have a problem. We can put our own problem in the background. Listen to him instead. Or her, of course. Let's try talk with someone today – and tomorrow?' He stopped, quite still for a moment.

'This can change our life.' Crossing himself, he stepped from the pulpit to join in the singing.

The organ lurched into life with a few jabs of uncertain harmony; the congregation rushed to catch up with 'O God, Our Help In Ages Past'. Most sang from an English word-sheet; a few locals stayed with the Swedish version. Afterwards the organist attempted a Bach fugue while people fumbled for their money. I sat wondering what to do about my five hundred *kronor* note.

As the vicar exchanged a word with each of his unusual flock at the open door, I noticed their prevalent Australian accent. Outside, a yellow bus was backing up to the gate through the rain. When everyone had gone he strode past me to the altar. *Put our own problem in the background.* He stood in his black cloak, stacking hymn-books and scraping burnt-out candles from their holders.

12

At my approach the priest swung round; in his late thirties or early forties, the animated face and springy hair suggested a zest for life not easily contained.

'Välkommen!' Realising my Swedish would carry me no further, he reverted to English. 'You're not in the group? They're from Sydney – doing Europe with coach.'

'A lot of work for you.'

'Are you – just look around? Take your time. We're obliged to keep the church locked, except for services. A pity, in my opinion – but it's that way, these days. A church should have permanent open, don't you think? What good is it if you can't go in when you want?' He dropped the guttered candle-ends into a tin. 'A lot of people is like you – they want to look. Some, local ones, they say foreigners don't help to the maintenance. But we don't pay the Queen for look at Buckingham Palace, do we!'

He dusted off waxy fingers to extend a supple hand. 'Mats Carlsson.'

'Guy Chandler.'

'From England?'

'Dorset, actually.'

'Ah, beautiful Dorset – unbelievable churches. Are you inter-ested of old buildings, Mr Chandler?' He glanced up at the vaulted roof. 'Do you know, when the Danes first came in the 1200s they'd never seen craftsmanship like we have here on Lammland. Bronze and silverware, goblets, and so on. They grabbed all they could and ran, as far as we know. But if you go in the museum in Valstad . . .'

'I'm sorry, d'you mind if I ask you something?' The bushy eyebrows lifted; I told him of my search.

'Well, all records are in our *Pastorsämbete* – that's the pastor's office. You're make a family tree, something like that?' While I explained in briefest terms about Edward, Mats Carlsson led the way outside, rain blowing in our eyes, before ducking under a porch and down a flight of stone steps to unlock a small door.

The place felt damp and somewhat subterranean, with a musty smell of paper; there appeared to be no electric light. 'It's not so often we open here. I have charge of six parishes, you see. Six! Can you imagine it? Be a vicar these days, it's be everywhere at once. Now I know how God must feel . . .' He lit a row of four candles; the flickering arcs revealed a shelf lined with heavy tomes. 'Some early records are missing – it's get better as we go. Edward Chandler: have he a middle name?' I realised I'd never asked. He manoeuvred one of the books down.

'Here, we're lucky! Edward Chandler: he's take up residence February 1952. Was he plan to stay permanent, you think?'

'It seems likely.'

'Interesting. From England. What would he do for support himself in such a village? In middle of winter?' His lips puckered. 'Freezing cold, and a foreign country . . . Have he a trade before this?' I gave a brief résumé of Edward's accountancy days, and his musical talents. 'Hmm. Find work around here, it's not so easy, is it? An Englishman . . .' He tugged at his white collar. 'If he registered as resident, and wasn't plan to return till England . . . I wonder: could he have became a teacher?'

The similarity to Bo Svensson's conclusions was striking. 'You think so?'

'It's happen with many visitors from UK. Or the States. Everybody need English. You should know, it's your most valuable export!'

'So he might have taught at a local school?'

'Or in Valstad. Somewhere on the island, anyway: he couldn't be every day hopping over to the mainland. Although people do it these days – fly to Stockholm two, three times a week; the airport's forty minutes with car. But back then, on the fifties . . .? Of course it was a big demand for English after the war. Some Swedes, they had a bad conscience – you know, Hitler's march into Norway, all that? It's a couple of English schools in Valstad, and one in Lindhem, that's on the east coast. In the first place Mr Chandler would need money, unless he can find someone to . . .' He left the sentence unfinished.

'And in the second place?'

'Well, you must have a job for get a residence permit – and a place to live for get a work permit. It's a Swedish Catch 22, if you want – very boring. But it's the law.'

He skimmed the remaining pages; moments later his broad forefinger thudded on the yellowing page. 'Ah, look here. You see: married! Vandringe, April 1953 – long before I came. Vandringe, it's the next village. And look: Charlotte Löwensten. Now the Löwenstens we *did* know. For many years ago, but . . .' He mused for a minute. 'It's – a close relative?'

'He's my uncle.'

'*Uncle.*' Mats Carlsson gave me a canny look, but he was nothing if not diplomatic. 'Have you – any recent communication?'

'I'm afraid not.' I peered at the scrolled letters meandering across the creamy paper. 'Does it say where they lived?'

'It's give only Charlotte's original address. Her parents, that is. Holger and Berit Löwensten. You can ask there.' He smiled wryly. 'We may be out in the wilds, Mr Chandler, but everybody know everybody around here – or know someone who does. People often know far too much . . .'

He stared across at a tiny stained glass window. Jesus was skimming over neatly packed waves on a vast lake.

'Would there be anything else on him? Children, for instance?'

He pored through another volume. 'Well, what do you know! It was a Philip Chandler. Born Vandringe 8 November 1953.'

He scoured the rest of the entries before replacing the book. 'I doubt we'll come much further down here, though. Is it something else I can help with?'

Edward's identity was assuming more personal dimensions; for the first time I imagined a family man, settling and leading a full life in a foreign village almost six decades earlier. 'I can't thank you enough, Mr Carlsson, you've . . .'

'Mats, please! May I ask – where do you stay?'

'Oh, I cycle around. I'm at Emsäde at the moment.'

'Well then. You must call in, meet with my family? We're right here, behind the church. Let me think: Monday is always busy – I drive to Klosterbo tomorrow, but . . .'

'It's very kind, I wouldn't want to . . .'

'Are you free Tuesday? It should be interesting to hear what more you've succeeded to find about your uncle. You can meet our youngsters – Annalena, she's teach in Kalmar now, but Inge and Erik, they're still on school. And we have a large dog!'

Why he'd want to invite a complete stranger was beyond me. Perhaps he felt it went with the job – or could running even six parishes not be quite enough to occupy such a dynamic man as Mats Carlsson? 'Come to lunch, then. If you have no other plans?' My only plan now was to visit Vandringe. 'I can give you a lift if you want. Oh, but of course, you have own transport. Good luck, then! And don't forget – midday Tuesday.'

Vandringe was a short ride to the south-east. Soft rain bathed my face; the wind had dropped. Minutes later the sun glinted through the clouds, creating a transient rainbow; there was a heavy sweetness of blossom in the air. Along the wayside clusters of wild flowers brushed my legs with a moist kiss.

The village was little more than a scattering of cottages around another fine old church; the island seemed awash with them. Opposite stood the Löwensten house, its outer porch covered in white roses threaded with veins of pink; raindrops balanced on each petal.

A young girl of ten or eleven opened the door.

'Ja?' She looked up, confident and unsmiling, brushing blonde strands from her eyes.

'Oh, hello. Could I speak to – your mother or father?' She stared, turned to call 'Mamma!', then resumed her unabashed scrutiny. 'So what's your name?'

'Angelica.'

'That's nice. And are you an angel?'

'No.' She stood unmoved, though without hostility. 'But I've seen one, if you want to know.'

'Have you now!'

'I *have*. Coming out of the sea.' The revelation seemed as startling as her English, which was articulate despite the marked Swedish accent.

'When was . . .?'

'What's *your* name?'

'I'm Guy.'

'Guy.' She tried it out, frowning. 'And are you a Nice Guy?'

'I try to be!' I was just thinking Angelica was a force to be reckoned with when a tall woman appeared, drying her hands on a cloth. 'Sorry to disturb, do you speak English? Angelica here was just . . . The Löwenstens – would you . . .?'

'Gå in nu, Angelica.' The girl gave a parting scowl and disappeared. Her mother appraised me with quick eyes; there was a brief hesitation. 'Löwenstens – they lived here once. It's your family?'

'I'm a distant relative.'

She gave a small frown of curiosity, not unlike Angelica's. 'The old man – he died here. But his wife, she stayed many years after. At the end she couldn't take care of the house. When we first came here my husband, he . . .' She sighed. 'This place was in a terrible state. Poor Berit, she must move till Valstad – a little apartment, it's on the harbour. 1984. She's long dead now, of course.'

'It's their daughter I need to trace – Charlotte.'

'That's right – a daughter. Charlotte?' She stared across at the church, repeating the name. 'I talked with Berit only a few times, you see – we must organise carpets, and so – she left so many things to us here. But she showed me photos one day: the family, her daughter's wedding. The young woman, she was looking so happy – Charlotte. And her tall Englishman, so smart – with suit, and a fine moustache. A lovely wedding – here in the church. But they haven't live here since many, many years.' Her eyes darted around my face. 'You're from England?'

'I'm Edward Chandler's nephew.'

She thought hard again. 'Chandler, yes – that was him, I'm sure.'

'Did they settle locally, do you know?'

'Sorry. You can ask in the village. Or maybe . . . Is it possible he's bring her back till England?'

We looked at each other.

'Well, you've been most helpful.'

'I hope you have success to find him.' As I walked down the path the front window swung open and a small blonde head appeared.

'Goodbye, Mister Nice Guy.'

13

Dusk had fallen by the time I got back to Emsäde. Unused to all the cycling, it was a relief to while away an evening in the cosy *stuga* messing about on Edward's harmonica. The knack of using the semitone button while either blowing or drawing air clearly wasn't something to be mastered overnight. On the point of giving up and going to bed, I noticed a message by the hurricane lamp in the warden's spidery handwriting:

Gy. Plees ring ASAP. Gorgina.

At reception Herr Wittberg stood sifting through a heap of old keys.

'Have you a nice day?' The only phone was on his desk: again the monotonous English tone ringing unanswered in my ear. Herr Wittberg scratched his close-cropped head. 'Better luck another time! Shall you staying one day more?'

'Till Wednesday, if that's all right.'

'Welcome. You can phone always, here on reception. We should have sunny tomorrow.' He seemed in a chatty mood.

'Have you – worked here long?'

'You can say! I live sixty year in Segelholm – it's big shanges.' Like many Swedes, Herr Wittberg could well be a lot older than he looked.

'In what way?'

'I mean in the tourist way. On the sixties, seventies, the big ships, they dock always in Låtby. Today they doesn't come any

longer so far north. Now it's people come with car from Valstad.
Or like you, with cycle.'

'You didn't know someone called Chandler, by any chance?'

'Family Shandler, ja.' His quick glance of recognition wasn't
altogether comfortable. 'They was well known here about.'

'You *knew* them?'

'Ja ja, of course. Everybody know. Charlotte – she was a good
woman. Good with the shildren, very popular. She know the way
to the heart. Of course was through the stomach!'

'She was a cook of some sort?'

'Cook, ja, nurse – all things. She make dinners on the junior
school – in Sömninge. It's a village. The shildren was hungry
when her man finish with them!'

'You mean – Edward Chandler worked there too?'

'Oh ja, everybody know Mister Shandler. He was take care of
the young ones. He play guitar – a clever man. Teach very good
– people say it. Torsten also. Get good teachers in such a place,
it's hard. He snap him up – you can say it so?'

'Torsten? He'd be the headteacher?'

'Torsten Gellerstedt, ja.'

'And he gave Edward the job?'

'Of course. Mister Shandler, he was teach all the courses. In
the beginning he speak only English. Was hard for him – and
for the shildren, of course. But they love him – the music, the
England life. He have *känsla.*' Herr Wittberg tapped his chest.

'Feeling?'

'Ja ja, feeling. The language, it's important, but not so important like the feeling! He learn also Swedish later – speak very
good. He was many, many year on the school.'

'So what happened to him?'

'He go away. Many people was sad, of course. Was a big gap,
after he was away – the music, you see. Always he was make
concerts – on the schools, the shurches – sometimes he go on the
mainland, other places. I can say it, he have energy, your Mister
Shandler! After, we hear nothing. Nothing of him, nothing of

Charlotte. They go both another way.' He fiddled bleakly with the keys.

'They separated? You don't mean a divorce?'

'Divorce.' He gave a sombre nod, as if learning the word.

'When would that have been?'

'The seventies – about. On the school it's build new class-rooms, after they was away.'

'You've no idea where they went?'

'Charlotte, she have a sister – she go on the mainland.'

'And Edward? Could he have gone back to England, do you think?'

'Why not?' he answered brightly. 'He disappear.' He twiddled his fingers like a conjuror. 'Maybe he go till England, maybe no. Nobody know. It's for everybody a big shock in that time. They was so long time together – man and wife. In the beginning they was happy, I think. But who can say it?'

'You've no idea what went wrong?'

He perused one of the keys as if wondering where it belonged. 'Of course . . . Mister Shandler he have always the eye for the ladies. It's no secret. If he find another woman? It's maybe. Nobody know. But the young boy, he can be still on Lammland – it's possible. Where he is?' He shrugged gloomily. 'I have my two boys – they has family now, of course. Björn och Ivan. Junior school, it's the past for them. For me also.'

'Yes of course. But you're talking about Edward and Charlotte's son – Philip?'

'Philip, ja. Philip.'

This was more than I'd dared hope for. 'So could he still be around somewhere – in this part of the island?'

Herr Wittberg frowned. 'I can't say you. Philip, he was maybe twenty, twenty-one when they go away – mother, father. He can be now – fifty maybe? It's a lifetime, isn't?' He scratched at the key with his fingernail.

'What was he like?'

'Philip, he was a good boy. Clever also, like the father. With the hands – technics things. From eleven year he travel every day with bus till the boys' school, in Valstad. Björn, Ivan – my boys – they go in Lindhem, it's near. For Philip, Valstad – it's the better way.'

'What, an hour on the bus every day? An hour back again? Why do you say that?'

Herr Wittberg avoided my glance. 'Oh ja, better he go in Valstad. Away from the father.'

'To get away from Edward? Why on earth would he . . .?'

He looked pained. 'Mister Shandler, he could be – not for everybody good news, you understand me?'

'You mean he fell out with people? Did he get into fights or something?'

Herr Wittberg's gnarled hand hovered in a cautionary wobble above the desk, as if I'd missed some subtlety here. 'He was – in the head very strong, you know? He was . . . How you say this?'

'Hot-headed? Determined?'

'Determined, ja. Edward Shandler, he was a determined man. He do things . . .' He scooped up the keys and flung them in a drawer. 'He do them his way. Why not ask on the school? Somebody maybe know. Somebody maybe know something.'

'Ah, so the school is still running?'

'It's many shanges of course. Very bigger – many teachers. In the beginning was yust two classes – Mister Shandler and old Torsten. Torsten Gellerstedt, he retire many year now, of course. If he can be still live – who can say?'

14

Waking in the small hours next morning, my mind was full of Edward's life on the island. With his banjo – or guitar, possibly – and his quick rapport with children, I sensed something of the wandering minstrel, a sort of happy-go-lucky, Pied Piper waywardness. At the moment his trail seemed to fizzle out some time in the early seventies; it might be worth checking at the primary school where he once worked.

Sömninge lies on a convoluted route inland about midway between Vandringe and the district town of Klosterbo. The forecast upturn in the weather still hadn't materialised. Segelholm beach, lashed by stinging squalls, was cold and deserted; a straggly offshore reef flung up showers of spray from a black, menacing sea. Pedalling on through the deluge, I reached Sömninge around midday. To an outsider one cluster of houses can look much like another in this part of the globe; on the neat village green a silent couple watched me pass, huddled under an umbrella.

Crossing to the school beyond, the sound of children's shouts and laughter – in what must have been prime holiday time – came as a surprise. In the classrooms excited boys and girls, coached by local artists, were painting Lammland's flora and fauna. Two very small boys helped me off with my wet things and whisked me to the staffroom where a tall, smartly dressed woman was masterminding today's special activities.

'Larsson. You've caught us in the long break, so that's lucky.' Fru Larsson waved me to a seat by the double-glazed windows, and continued a wordless dialogue of glances and signals with colleagues while listening to the honed-down version of my quest. 'Well, why don't we ask Solveig here? She remembers everyone from way back, don't you, Solveig. Including Mr Chandler, I dare say.' In an armchair the frail, white-haired lady was at once alert to the voice. As she extended a bony hand I noticed the white stick at her feet.

'Edward?' She lifted her tremulous head sideways, smiling significantly and casting restless eyes at the ceiling. 'I knew him, yes.'

'Solveig, *this* Mr Chandler is Edward's nephew. He's come all the way from England to find out if *our* Mr Chandler's still alive. That's right isn't it, Mr Chandler? How old did you say your uncle was?'

'Born 1929. So he'd be – what? – seventy-nine.' Fru Larsson's eyebrow twitched; the fact was I'd hardly considered the very real possibility of Edward's death.

Solveig, however, seemed – like me – to find her colleague's approach a shade too cut-and-dried. 'Well, we never can tell, can we? We never can tell.' There was something prescient in her unseeing gaze; I couldn't help wondering how old she might be herself.

'I'll leave you two to chat while I check at the office, shall I?'

Solveig turned out to have been a considerable fan of Edward's: 'So good with the children. And such a man of music, wasn't he? Always a tune in his head. That banjo! He'd even play here in the staffroom, when the colleagues were tired or depressed. I can still hear "Stormy Weather" and "As Time Goes By", can't you?'

'Do you remember what happened to him?'

'Everybody *knew* they had problems. Charlotte wasn't at all Edward's type of woman, in my opinion. Even if I can't *see*, Mr Chandler, I can *feel* when a person is unhappy inside . . . But goodness me, she was a good cooker! *Lovely* lunches – I can taste her stewed beef and broccoli now. We don't get food like that any more.' For a moment Solveig's nostalgia for long-lost school dinners quite carried her away.

'The marriage didn't work out?'

'Ah, no. No, not really. Of course Edward, he needed excitement, you understand what I mean?' She sighed, as if it were a fatal flaw in a man. 'Charlotte was not a woman to accept adultery.'

I nodded at her directness, then remembered she couldn't see me. 'So she left him?'

'In the end, yes. Edward was a very active man, you see. Not only for the music. He had his skiing also. Always away on this trip or that, with the children – and sometimes without. It was his passion, really. Wasn't that strange, for an Englishman?'

'Where did he go?'

'To ski? Well he'd have to go to the mainland, wouldn't he? We have no mountains here on Lammland . . .' She gave a crooked smile. 'I went with them once, to Åreskutan, on the Norway border. Ah – the snow, the log cabins, the mountain air!' She sniffed in ecstasy, eyelids flickering. 'Not that I skied, of course. But I did all right, on my tea tray . . . If you find out what became of him, please let me know.' With that she stood up, her lunchbreak evidently at an end. For a second her quivering hand clasped mine. Then she grabbed the white stick and was off on the hazardous journey back to her classroom. Beyond the glass partition children circulated around her like pilot-fish, opening doors.

'I'm afraid it's not much on record in the office, Mr Chandler.' Fru Larsson reappeared thumbing her notepad. 'Your uncle left January '75. We have nothing after that. But then, when you think of it, why would we? Speak to Mr Gellerstedt, though – he was Head then. Here: the address.'

'You've been most kind.' I took the note, guilty of spending her valuable time.

'Would you like a lift? You're in luck – Harald goes that way.'

Portly Harald stood by the entrance stubbing out a cigarette. Winking at me, he made a wheezy dash through the rain to a battered Volkswagen. Inside, the reek of stale nicotine caught my breath as Harald worked through a strenuous coughing fit. The sudden cloudburst had turned the road to a coursing stream in seconds. Squinting between the beleaguered windscreen wipers, he wrenched us round a series of tight bends, lighting another cigarette. Comic gestures at the downpour and the corkscrew lanes made up for his apparent lack of English.

Herr Gellerstedt's converted farmhouse lay at the end of a waterlogged track. Harald introduced me in rapid Swedish, then held out a genial hand, wished me 'Lycka till!' and slithered back to the car under a sodden copy of *Klosterbos Allahanda*. He'd be back to his geometry project again in fifteen minutes.

Clouds of sweet pipe tobacco drifted after Herr Gellerstedt as he led me down a dark passage, his bald pate carried with a certain *hauteur*.

'So, you are Edward's nephew?'

By the crackling wood fire he relit the briar stem, sucking noisily and prodding back a stray wisp of tobacco. 'I hate to be the bearer of bad news, Mr Chandler.' The sombre pause emphasised the elegance of his English. 'I'm afraid your uncle passed away – let me see, two or three summers ago.'

For a minute or two I couldn't speak. It was as if my whole purpose in coming to Sweden had foundered: however remote the prospect, I'd so much wanted to bring dear old Tilly joyous word of her younger brother – see those sensitive grey eyes light up in gladness once more. At the same time my grief was for what seemed a true creative spirit, someone with whom – across the gap of time – I'd begun to feel an unexpected empathy. Ben's funeral passed before me again; how could he and Dad have gone to their graves without ever having talked of brother Edward?

In head-magisterial discretion Herr Gellerstedt waited silently for me to absorb the news. 'I'm sorry for your loss, Mr Chandler,' he ventured. 'I tell a lie, though – heavens, but the time flies. It must be *four* years ago. Yes, June 2004 – the year I lost my Deputy and my Finance Officer, all in the same term. We were rushed off our feet with timetables and invoices. But I did go to your uncle's funeral.'

'You were there? Did you know him well, then?'

'The school owed it to him, in many ways – although it's true I'd have gone on my own account. Edward was a competent teacher and a fine colleague. Always he'd come to lessons with his music and his banjo. It could be geography, English, anything – he'd find a way to bring things alive with a tune or a song. This kind of teacher is gold-dust, Mr Chandler! Are you – in education yourself?'

'I'm afraid not. Edward's life has always been a closed book to us in England. He left a family, didn't he?'

'Edward was married, of course. But Charlotte, his wife – well, we can say she was out of the picture many years by then. The split was a very public affair – bound to be, in a place like this. She stayed with him, at the school, year after year, but it was common knowledge Edward had someone else. Charlotte had perfectly good grounds for divorce.' Herr Gellerstedt seemed keen to put the record straight; I had no great desire to hear about Edward's infidelities, if that's what they were. 'Edward was at the school twelve years. A young, vibrant teacher like that – we were lucky to get him. Of course I'd have welcomed a longer stay. What headteacher wouldn't? Good teachers – and good caterers like Charlotte, for that matter – are not easy to find. But in fact he and I also became good friends.' There was a hint of tearfulness in Herr Gellerstedt's otherwise stern eyes. 'Unfortunately – man and wife, working at the same school – it was clear to everyone how things stood. Afterwards Charlotte moved to her sister in Vyborgshamn. Edward, he went to Kiruna.'

'To . . .?'

'That's far up in the north, inside the Arctic Circle. Good for skiing, of course. But it's not a place he'd have gone to, I don't think, if it hadn't been for that woman – whoever she was.'

'His second wife?'

'Well, that begs the question, doesn't it? I don't know that they ever were married.' He stared into the fire. 'As things turned out, I didn't meet her till Edward's funeral. We didn't really talk. To be honest with you, I had no wish.'

'Was she not – not the kind of person you'd have imagined him marrying?'

He looked up sharply. 'Imagined? That's not for me to say, is it? I don't claim to be a great judge of character. Edward always sounded happy enough with her to me. But I did learn for a fact they couldn't have children. Otherwise they might well have married eventually.'

'So – would it be right to assume Philip was his only child?'

'Just the one son. They did their best for him.'

'You met Philip? You know him?'

'I believe it was for his sake Edward and Charlotte stayed together so long. We all knew him as a young lad, of course – spent a term with us here in Sömninge. Nice enough boy. We've met only once since then – at the funeral, in fact, up in Kiruna. Philip must have been at least twenty at the time of the divorce – that would put him in his early fifties when Edward died. I've no doubt he loved his father dearly.' For such a personal comment the tone sounded curiously detached.

'And did you talk to him?'

'It happened that Philip and I travelled back from Kiruna together.'

'Ah, you did?' He looked at me blankly. 'I'm told Philip went to secondary school in Valstad. Where did he go after he left?'

Herr Gellerstedt sighed with a slight show of impatience. 'I'm not sure he went anywhere. He may have got a job of some sort in Valstad. You'd have to make enquiries in the town.'

'So he stayed on the island after his parents moved away?' Another blank look; this was becoming hard going. 'Herr Gellerstedt, the Chandlers in Dorset will need me to find Philip now. Does he have a family at all? I'd be most grateful for any information.'

There was a conspicuous silence. 'It's not so easy, Mr Chandler. In the first place I had no word from him at all after the funeral. And I'm afraid the school will have no record of his address.' This struck me as downright evasive. Considering the one-time friendship between Torsten Gellerstedt and Edward, one might expect him to have kept up at least some contact with Edward's son; I couldn't see that it was particularly a school matter, either. 'I believe he lives somewhere in the southern part of the island.' This was as far as he was prepared to go; I felt the atmosphere of commiscration with me cooling.

'I've heard Edward was a determined sort of man. Perhaps not altogether liked by everyone? Were there people against him for some reason?' Silence again – even longer this time.

'Nobody is liked by everyone, Mr Chandler,' was his oblique reply. 'Edward and I stayed in touch – one or two long phone calls every year. He liked to know how things were in Sömninge – asked after some of the children. He may have come over from the mainland to see Philip sometimes, but that was his own affair. As it happened he never came back to visit us here, and I wasn't going to try and persuade him. People sometimes prefer a clean break. I myself always liked Edward, as I've said. I can even say I loved him.'

The angular chin twitched forward, as if he expected to be challenged. 'But yes, he knew his own mind. Some people could find that difficult. In my opinion, teachers need their own strong, clear views; it's part of what used to be called a teacher's voca-tion. When I was a young teacher starting out, it was the norm. Nowadays people think you can send teachers on a course and teach them to have opinions and "personality".'

It sounded like a well-worn hobbyhorse. He gave another weary sigh, levering himself up. 'Today's brave new world! Well, I've enjoyed our talk, Mr Chandler. Can I do anything else for you?' The sharp tap-tap of his pipe on the hot fender signalled an end to our conversation.

15

Wheeling the bike back across the empty school playground, a stunning mosaic caught my eye: the swirl of white pebbles traced an angel with outstretched wings, hovering above what could have been a mountain range, or perhaps a stormy sea.

I set off through driving rain, the wind behind me now. Finally knowing Edward had died, it was time for some fresh thinking. The woman he'd gone to live with in the snowy wastes of Kiruna was of no interest to me. Torsten Gellerstedt's account seemed authoritative enough: if he knew *for a fact* Edward had no other children, this brought the spotlight squarely onto Philip as Ben's remaining beneficiary. The resistance I'd met only strengthened my resolve: given that old Torsten couldn't, or wouldn't, help me any further, there had to be some other way of tracking down cousin Philip.

At Segelholm I dismounted for a minute under a panoply of dripping trees. As I squelched in soggy trainers onto the shingle, gulls circled overhead with mournful shrieks. The sea was pitted darkly with rain, clouds hanging over it in shreds. Across windswept shores the yellowy daylight had dimmed; a lighthouse began flashing its solemn beacon beyond an outcrop of rocks to the south.

Retrieving the bike, it was obvious the rear tyre had gone flat, but to my exasperation the pump wouldn't fit – there seemed no way of shutting off the hissing air.

'Problems?' Her voice, right behind me: the girl from the café in Valstad.

'Oh, hi – never expected you here!'

She stood in a white rain-cape and sandals, her head tilted sideways, brushing a thread of wet hair from her eyes. 'My bike's along there too.' She gestured towards a boathouse higher up. 'You need a proper pump. Shall I get mine?' Without waiting for an answer she set off up the beach again, bare legs lashed by the rain.

Within a minute or two she'd bumped her bicycle across the shingle and was crouching next to mine with the pump.

'Thanks. Am I glad you turned up!' I looked down at her rain-darkened hair.

'You must fix it really tight, that's the main thing. Look, like this.' She fitted the valve with quick fingers, pushed up her sleeves and began pumping. 'I don't even know your name.' The rain steamed slightly on her arms.

'It's Guy. Here, let me do that.'

'I'm Helena.' She stressed the long second syllable. Her energy made me feel clumsy and tongue-tied; not looking up, she was concentrating on the tyre. 'You should get this type of pump – the one they've given you is useless. Is it from Riegers? There, that's fixed.' She stood up. 'Where are you staying?'

Her nose wrinkled comically when I mentioned Emsäde: 'No, honestly, it's perfectly all right, I've got a nice little *stuga*! What about you – you live near here?'

'I'm on the east coast. I like it at Segelholm, that's all. The beaches are different this side of the island. Not so rocky.'

'You've cycled all that way?'

'Not quite! I cheat most times.' She gave a mischievous chuckle, her full white teeth showing briefly. 'I've left the car at Klosterbo. It's easy, the bike hangs on the back. So I can go a little bit further.'

'Pretty awful weather for it.'

'I don't mind the rain. Don't you think it's refreshing?' She looked up at the heavy grey sky as if to taste it, dark brows and lashes misted with rain. 'I'd better go, it's getting late. Maybe see you again?' She stepped away, lifting a palm in neutral farewell, and bounced the bike onto the roadway. At the turn of the lane she stood up on the pedals, hair blown across her mouth. 'Don't stay too long,' she called. 'You can catch cold.' She waved again and disappeared round the corner.

16

'I thought you cared about me.'

'I do care about you.'

'You've got a nice way of showing it.'

'I'm trying to, it's just . . .'

'Right, well *thanks* for ringing back *asap*!'

'I'm really sorry about that, it was . . .'

'So when are you coming home?'

'Coming home?'

'Yes *home* – you know, like as in – where you live?' Her nasal tones twanged in the earpiece.

'I don't know yet.'

'Don't *know*? What is this – some kind of guessing game? Anyway, where *are* you, for goodness' sake?'

It was time to come clean. 'I'm in Sweden, as it happens.'

'*Sweden*? What the hell are you doing in Sweden?'

'George, the thing is . . .' It was bad enough having temporised for days over my current whereabouts: she now deserved nothing short of the full, honest truth. In itself it wasn't the Will business that was hard to explain so much as the whole tangle of emotions that surrounded it. In the few weeks she and I had spent together some sort of communication had started to develop, but I had yet to open up with anything like my true feelings.

The trouble as well – this sounds pathetic, I know – was that phones have never been a good medium for me. I can only say, at that distance, over a very bad telephone line, it felt hopeless trying to convey all the implications of what had happened. 'We'll go through it all together very soon, George – that's a promise. I want us to be totally straight with each other.'

'Oh *do* you. Go through all *what*?'

'Honestly, I do understand, George, this must seem crazy from your angle – disappearing like that, taking all this time off, especially being new to Castles and everything. But – well, we've all got a right to annual leave, haven't we – Sidney's not going to offer another lot later on, is he?'

'Yes, but – Sweden? It's not as if you know anybody out there, is it? Not to mention swanning off without so much as a word – and here's me thinking you *liked* me!'

'George, that was terrible – truly, I'm sorry. These last few weeks, we've been great together, you're really special to me, you know you are, but this business with Ben and Edward . . .'

'What are you *on* about? What's Sweden got to do with . . .'

'Trust me, George – can you?' Saying this, it was obvious trust was the last thing my recent actions were likely to inspire; at that moment, unfortunately, I could see no other way out. 'I *promise* I'll tell you everything the minute it's all finished. There's one or two things need buttoning up here first, it's not much, once that's done I'll be . . .'

'Yeah, right. Well you're not the only one.' Her mud-flat glottals tautened. 'I've got a few odd jobs on here too, in case you hadn't noticed – like becking and calling for Sidney, for a start. *And* keeping on top of all this paper rubbish – including yours, by the way. Funnily enough your in-tray doesn't empty itself! Oh, and Trevor's on sick leave again this week, so guess who's lumbered with feeding His Lordship's flipping *tortoise*?'

'Columbus? Oh, George, I had no idea you . . .'

'No, well of course you wouldn't, would you. There's a whole lot of things you've got no idea about. Like that Work-shadow business, while we're on it – you know Sidney wanted feedback? So it's muggins here who's been talking up all your glittering talents and techniques. Why do I bother? Don't mind me, though,

Big Guy – not if you're busy. I'll see you when you get back if that's how you feel.' She banged the phone down.

Not for the first time in my life, relations with a kind and caring member of the opposite sex had plunged to the very depths.

Back in the *stuga*, Edward's harmonica lay untouched in its box by the lamp. *A clean break*; his lone spirit hovered in my downcast heart.

*   *   *

Herr Wittberg's forecast of sunny skies was at last fulfilled next morning. It found me in no mood for social life; nevertheless, this was the day of the promised lunch with the Carlssons. Not wanting to let them down I set off before 10 am planning to make it in good time on foot. When I got to Segelholm the beach was transformed to a dazzling desert of white stones and sand, baking under a deep blue sky with its distant cargo of drifting cloud. There was almost an hour to spare. Strolling down to the lapping sea in shorts and a loose shirt, it came to me that Georgina would be beavering away at her desk. I breathed in the guilty luxury of tepid oxygen and untrammelled leisure.

Our conversation the previous evening had been a ghastly mess for which the whole blame rested with me. It was clear her comments to Sidney on the Work-shadowing week had been far more flattering than my actual efforts could possibly warrant. If she was prepared to do all that – not to mention feeding Columbus – surely it said something for what she must feel for me? So many kindnesses made my abrupt departure all the more despicable.

And if, as seemed certain after last night, our latest altercation meant she wouldn't want to see me any more, her reasons were clear as daylight: it served me absolutely right. The thought of losing her altogether filled me with alarm; for the first time I began to brood on just how empty life would feel without her. The number one priority now was to trace Edward's offspring and get home as fast as possible; if I could do that, then perhaps

– if I was very lucky – she might still find it in herself to forgive me. Whatever happened, once this whole business was over I'd need to find some proper way of thanking her for all her loyal support.

For this morning, though, there was still time to kill. I strayed in among the chalky outcrops to the south. Embedded in the rocks lay bits of fossilised shellfish and other calceous remains; a child had stuck a row of seagull feathers into a crevice. The sun's movement was almost perceptible minute by minute, climbing towards its searing zenith. Craning my neck I could squint into it at the overhang of cliffs above me, wondering what the chances were of being buried under some fatal rockfall of the kind that must have happened here countless times in the past.

Out to sea a soft haze fuzzed the horizon; the low weed-covered reef seemed to hover above the surface. Up the coast to the north a distant figure was wandering along the beach away from me. Wasn't that Helena again from the café? She stopped to look out at the reef, shielding her eyes, and I was sure. What could it be about Segelholm that drew her back here? It's a fine beach, but there had to be dozens of others to choose from around the island.

After a minute or two she turned away without looking in my direction and continued towards where the beach recedes round the headland. For a moment, standing there rehearsing her name, I thought of going after her, but something told me she ought not to be approached.

17

'How goes it, then, Guy? Found your uncle yet?' A cordial hand on my shoulder, Mats Carlsson led me round to a table on the lawn, laid with tasteful salads and cold hams. Leaning back in his wicker chair, today's casual slacks and open-neck shirt made a striking contrast to the black robe of his profession. He seemed genuinely saddened when I told him Edward had died, and wanted to know more.

Having to retell the story of Edward's unexplained departure all those years ago, and his severing of contact with the family, stirred the sense of loss again. As if in sympathy, a full-bodied Great Dane came lumbering up and buried his muzzle in my abdomen, waiting to have his ears rubbed.

'But your father and his siblings – they'd have had an idea why he went, wouldn't they?'

I shook my head, as mystified as he was at the dearth of information about their black sheep of a brother.

'So where do you go from here?' Mats served out some ham.

'Edward's son, Philip Chandler, apparently lives on the island, though no one seems able or willing to say where. It's him I need to find now.'

'Mm. Can't help there, I'm afraid.' He lifted the water-jug; a slice of lemon dived into my glass.

'Perhaps I can.' Mats's wife was coming down the steps from the house. 'You're talking of the Chandlers?'

'Gudrun, this is Guy.' She crossed the grass and shook hands, an attractive woman with black, shoulder-length hair in loose ringlets. Her husband shifted to make room. 'Have you come across the family, then, love? Gudrun know everybody on the island.' Mats's weary gesture implied his wife was a fount of information way too copious for him to handle.

She held out her glass while Mats poured. 'I don't know everybody, Mats. I only pretend . . .' Taking an unhurried mouthful, she threw me an impish smile; they seemed as much at home in English as Swedish. 'But as a matter of fact I *can* offer you a Chandler – if she's any use. Sofi. She and Annalena were in the same class at Lindhem. Sofi was the apple of all the boys' eyes! So lovely to look at, and such a positive personality. You remember her, Mats?'

Her husband's eyes narrowed. 'Well, now that is something. Have I meet her? Sofi Chandler – it's bound to be a connection, isn't it? Our Annalena have so many friends,' he smiled at me, 'it's impossible to keep track.' Turning back to Gudrun, he asked: 'OK, what about the parents?'

'I talked quite often with her mother. What was her name? Märta, something like that. Nice woman, always smart dressed. They lived in Vätshamn – that's on the Fensborg road, twenty kilometre south from Valstad. No, Maja – that's it! Very cultured – into films and plays and things; she have a subscription to that film studio on Älvatrappan. The Big City it's not, Guy, but we have a cultural life, of a sort. They seemed rather well off. Maja, she was a elegant woman – expensive clothes, sports car . . . A little childish in her way, maybe, but very sweet.

'She liked to drive out and fetch Sofi on weekends – they'd hired a room for her in Lindhem. It's a long drive – and it's a perfectly good grammar school in Valstad: really I can't think why they haven't send her there. Maja, she had an idea to "correct" Sofi's towny education – as if too much culture should be bad for your health! She was waiting often for her when I came to meet Annalena; we'd go for coffee sometimes. Maja was my age, about. It was nice to talk; once or twice we'd get into more personal things.'

'Like Sofi's father?' Mats put in.

'Never much involved in the school, as far as I could see. I never met him.'

'Haven't Maja talked of him?'

'Only to say how busy he was always. Had a small computer business in Valstad. It must have some success because they opened another later, in Vätshamn. Maja mentioned he was older – I think it could be fifteen, twenty years between them. We've lost contact now. I have a feeling it was no easy marriage. The age gap maybe?'

Just then a girl and her brother, about thirteen, came out carrying croquet sticks. After polite handshakes they began hacking round an improvised course, somewhat hampered by the family dog – and the six-inch grass which no one had got round to mowing.

'Well, I can't think we'll find another family of that name on the island, shall we?' Mats watched the croquet for a moment. 'Sofi *must* be Philip's daughter, surely. I mean, Chandler's very English, isn't it. I expect Annalena could confirm it, Guy. It's a pity, this summer she's on a teaching programme in Sri Lanka, so it'll be end of August before . . .'

'Yes, of course.' The promising lead appeared to be slipping away. He drained his glass and leaned forward. 'Have you searched in Vandringe churchyard? One never know – sometimes a tomb-stone can give a clue.'

The prospects of finding anything useful among the graves at Vandringe were not good; it seemed unlikely Edward's actual remains would have been returned to the island. Nevertheless it was something tangible to do; again Mats wanted to run me there in the car, being bikeless that day, but – feeling he'd done rather a lot already – I thanked them both and set off on foot.

By the time I reached the sleepy village, the heat had grown intense. Inside the churchyard a woman in a black headscarf was filling a watering-can. There was no sign of Edward among the generations of well-kept graves, though several Löwenstens cropped up, including a Holger – departed 1981 – and his wife Berit who followed him in 1986.

Then, a row further on, I found Charlotte: 1932–2003. This had to be Edward's wife. That she should have wanted to return to her home village was natural, but it seemed very odd the family had seen fit to bury her under her maiden name – perhaps on Charlotte's own last wishes. The headstone made no reference whatever to her marriage, reinforcing the impression of Edward as a difficult man.

Beyond the gate an elderly gent was shuffling by with a mangy dog; in desperation I approached him and asked after the family. He stood pinching a fleshy lower lip, his breathing wheezy and truncated.

'Shanler?' The tremulous mouth wrapped itself round the awkward word. 'It's Shanler here, ja. For many years ago.' His opaque eyes quizzed the sky, then searched my face for support. 'Schoolman. Is blond hair. Very big?'

'That's the one. You remember him?'

'Remember him, remember he wife, she live here about.' He pointed in the direction of the house I'd visited on Sunday.

'The Löwenstens and their daughter, Charlotte, I've got that bit. Do you know where they lived after he married her?'

His eyes glinted keenly. 'Löwensten. OK. Löwensten.'

'Where was their house?' He stared again, pointing back the same way. 'No, it's the young couple I'm after – Edward and Charlotte?' As I spoke, I remembered Torsten Gellerstedt saying Edward had spent twelve years at Sömninge. Since the school records proved he left the island in January 1975, Edward couldn't have started work there before 1963. Yet he'd married Charlotte in 1953 – which tallied with the twenty-odd years they would have cared for Philip. This left that first decade of their marriage unaccounted for. Where might they have spent it?

'Zey away now. Maybe . . . ?' The old man sliced the air at his neck with a nicotined finger.

84

'Yes. Both dead now.'

He nodded grimly. 'Shanler skis. Very good skis.'

'Right, yes, I heard about that. But it would help to know where they lived earlier.'

Sudden clarity lit up his face. 'Where zey live? Before? Oh ja, live in Valstad.'

'Ah – would you know where? An address?'

'Sorry.'

With no more clues locally – and pending any enlightenment from Annalena Carlsson – the trail had gone cold for now. Time was short; perhaps tracing Edward's earlier career offered the best chance of locating Philip. The island 'capital' beckoned.

18

There was a bus from Emsäde at 10.15 next morning. The local company, as if in a fit of anglophilia, were experimenting that summer with double-deckers – like those big red London Transport efforts, only in olive green. Hearing the engine climb to boiling-point on every hill, you'd think they'd snapped up a few of London's cast-offs and given them a lick of paint. The tortoiselike pace only deepened my frustrations: seven whole days in Sweden had brought me scarcely any closer to tracing Edward's family. My return voyage was booked for the following Wednesday: as things stood, there seemed little hope of a breakthrough inside another week.

From the bus station I made straight for the tourist office again and asked to be put through to the ferry terminal. A charming female voice apologised: the first alternative crossing they could now offer me was on 27 August.

Three weeks from today! What on earth would Sidney think – let alone Georgina? The horror of discovering she'd been landed with feeding Columbus, on top of everything else, hit me once more. Knowing his weakness for dandelions, Trevor had promised to get fresh ones from Frickleigh Common: would George end up doing that too (and clearing up if they made him pee on the carpet)?

Seeing no alternative, I carried my shame and accepted the booking. Afterwards, light-headed from the vast new tract of time, I bought a straw hat: it gave a distinct 'Edward' feeling of illicit freedom. Across *Stortorget*, the terrace at *Musica* was empty. I sat down at the same table as before, but a different girl came out to take my order this time. Someone had left a leaflet. *Learn English and Talk to the World – Studiecirkel.* Then it came to me: *You should know, it's your most valuable export!* If language teaching was Mats Carlsson's best guess at Edward's first job, it would be foolish not to look into it. I checked the town map and pointed myself in the right direction.

Studiecirkel was off the high street at the head of a covered stairway. A dark-suited receptionist received my every syllable with reverence; English seemed to be the *lingua franca.*

'We have everything on computer, sir. Is that "Chandler" with CH?' He prodded the keys. 'Sorry, it's bad news, I'm afraid. We've nobody on file by that name.' At that moment a very tall gentleman in a white jacket strolled towards us. 'Have you met our Principal, Mr Samt?'

Mr Samt shook hands with a grave nod. 'Why don't we try upstairs? It's many older records to consult. Will you follow with me?' He smoothed the creamy jacket as if to expunge obtrusive idioms, and led the way up a narrow spiral. 'Mind your head.'

The sunny loft was crammed with filing cabinets. 'It exist two types of people, Mr Chandler: hoarders and tippers. I'm a hoarder. Which are you?' To cheer him up I declared myself a hoarder. He gave a painful laugh and let me riffle through the files with him, but in less than a minute he was hovering behind me, beaming. 'What do you know? Look, Edward Chandler, 1954 through '59. How's that for efficient?'

'Marvellous!'

'There's an address on Holmgatan. It looks as if your Mr Chandler worked here part-time all those years – mornings only.' He paused playfully. 'I wonder what he did in the afternoons?'

19

Down a level from the English school, Holmgatan led to a somewhat missable boutique under the sign *Janssons Antikvariat*; it seemed unable to make up its mind between souvenirs and furniture. On assorted tables and shelves lay ceramic pots, breadboards, glass knick-knacks – anything to catch a tourist's eye. I stepped between large earthenware jars to the counter and began fiddling with a stand of necklaces. Moments later an unshaven man in his late seventies emerged from the gloomy hinterland.

'Pretty things, isn't?' His consonants hissed encouragingly.

'These are lovely. You've got quite a collection.'

'It's many differents. I make a big mix. Was you – look for somethink special?' A monocle on a chain dropped from his eye.

'Actually I'm trying to trace someone. Edward Chandler?'

'Oh, ja. Of course. Edvard Shanler.' He seemed to be correcting my pronunciation. 'It's for many years and years ago. He live here, with he wife. Charlotte. They live on the apartment, it's upstair.'

'Ah, they rented rooms over the shop?'

'They was new-marrieds – we was neighbours. I live on other side the street: Ironmonger Pålsson. Pålsson, it's me. The shop – it's go bankrot! Nineteen hundra sixty-tree.' He pointed at a half-timbered house in shadow across the way, smiling. Life seemed better since he'd moved to the sunny side – good enough, indeed, to have stayed forty-five years. 'You interest of Edvard?' The restless eyes sized me up as I outlined the story. 'Charlotte, she make a pretty home. The rooms – I live now, it's my.' He pointed at the ceiling.

'I gather my uncle had a job in Valstad. Did Charlotte work too?'

Herr Pålsson spread his hands. 'They arrive with nothink. What they can do? Your oncle, he was come from England – no money. And Charlotte, she – well, Vandringe.' He shrugged. 'In the country, the villages, is no work of course. A poor village – like the all villages, on that time. They must work in town, the both. Charlotte, she was clip hair – on the barber's. You say this way?'

'A hairdresser?'

'It's on the corner. Edvard, he was teacher on the English school. But he like also everythinks what old – the furnitures, the anti-cues. It's good for make money, no? Money, it's problem when they was arrive – and bigger problem when baby was arrive!'

'They had a baby while they were here?'

'Charlotte, she stop work – it's normal, ja? Babies, it's very much cost – of course. But Edvard, he hear what is happen every day here – under they feet. The shop was own of Isak Jansson. It's get bigger – the anti-cues, always more. Good business – but for one man is too much. Old Isak – how he can make so much work?' Herr Pålsson polished the monocle on a filthy rag and squashed it back under his white-tufted eyebrow. 'Edvard, he help with pack, unpack the things – the pictures, the anti-cues. I see it, from other side the street. Isak pay Edvard, pay him good. Isak, he was happy – of course. In the beginning.'

'Oh? So – later on . . .?'

'Ja, later . . . In the first days was only the anti-cues. For Isak, always the good ones. No rubbish.' I avoided eyeing his present stock. 'For Edvard, it's different: he was interest of the furnitures. Oh ja, and he was *know* them! So of course, he have ideas.'

'What sort of ideas?'

A bell jangled. 'A moment, please.'

At the door Herr Pålsson redirected a woman up the street.

'She want candles – people think I sell, but it's not.' He shuf-

fled back through the clutter. 'Edvard, he start buy furnitures, ja
– second-hand. Small pieces – a shair, sometimes a stool, like
that. He fix in the workshop – it's here, on the backside. A table-
leg, it's loose – Edvard, he can fix. A joint – he do it good. He
can make with hands, with the glueing, everythinks – *very* good.
He was – ' the old man frowned, searching for the word.

'A real craftsman?'

'Ja, craftman. Isak, he can't do so good – he say it heself.
Edvard, he make everythinks like new – so can Isak sell on a
better price. He's happy – it's business, no? And Isak's word, he
keep it: he pay Edvard what work he done. But was always Edvard
which have the eye for bargain, for make money. And the nose!
You say this?' He tapped his own, glancing down. 'You like the
silver ones. It's pretty, isn't?'

'Oh. Yes, they're beautiful . . .' I'd hardly been aware of sifting
through the jumble of trinkets.

'I give you good price today. Somethink for a young lady –
you have a fancy?'

A droplet of translucent amber, one tiny primeval fly glinting
inside, lay threaded on a silver chain in my palm. It would look
stunning against Georgina's long milky neck. 'This one's very
fine. How much?'

He studied his grimy fingernails. 'Four fifty. Svedish crones. Is
very good the quality. But I give you today: four hundra. It's very
sheap.'

This was rather more than I'd thought of spending. 'So . . .
There was friction of some sort, was there, between Edward and
Isak? Surprising, if Edward could get things at knockdown prices
and do them up – you'd think that would have pleased Isak?'

Herr Pålsson was already rooting out a clot of cotton wool
and a box for the necklace. 'You like the bargains. It's was the
same with your oncle.' Putting me in the same category as Edward
was a neat way of pressing the decision.

'All right, then. I'll take it.'

The sale seemed to release a fresh wave of information. 'Edvard, he was make many contacts – right place, right time, always! Auctions of course. But likewise houses.'

'Houses? Ah, you mean when people die? House clearances, that kind of thing?'

'Clearance, ja. But your oncle stir also the feathers of the living!' He wagged a finger, clucking through tar-stained teeth. 'Edvard, he was Englishman. In fifties time – not so good.'

'You mean – being a foreigner?' I'd not imagined the model democracy on display *here in Sweden* ever harbouring xenophobic tendencies.

'The youngs today, it's different. But for Isak, the foreigners – they not so welcome maybe. Edvard, he say me one day: he come till Sveden for make fortune. Ja, he say! The tourists, they come with money. Here on Lammland it's need the dollar. The pound.'

'So he made himself rather unpopular?'

'Unpopular, popular, it's depend.' He took my cash and pushed the little package across the counter.

'I'm sorry – depends on what?'

He shrugged. 'Me, I get on always good with Edvard, Charlotte – the both. No problems. And the little boy, of course.'

'Would that be Philip Chandler?'

'Philip. Ja, of course.'

'You knew him as well?'

Herr Pålsson fell into gloomy silence; my credit seemed to be running out again – or was this the same reluctance I'd stumbled on with Torsten Gellerstedt?

'These are nice.' Behind me a stand of colourful postcards displayed Valstad in all its seasonal moods; Herr Pålsson's brightened at once. 'You talked about moving across from the ironmonger's: was Edward still here then?'

'Isak, he give me a work. I was need it bad – same like Edvard. We make together in the workshop – six, seven month. Edvard, he learn me many things – fix the furnitures, the anti-cues. But he have big ideas, you see. For Isak was problem.'

'You mean – he tried to take control somehow? A bit on the bossy side?'

'Bossy, ja. Edvard, he was a bossy man.' Herr Pålsson glared as if suspecting the same fault in me. 'I say you before: he was teacher. For teach the shildren, bossy, it's good maybe? For sell things, it's problem. Isak, he was a good man, but in the long time he was get tired.'

'From working with Edward?'

'You see, after the first years was the music instruments also.'

'Musical instruments? Sorry, I'm lost. They sold them as well?'

'Edvard, he start sell – what you call them, block flutes?'

'Recorders?'

'Recorders, viols, some banjos. He can play good – everythinks. Accordion; sometimes a harmonium, like that. For Isak it's a big shock. He know nothink in this business, *nothink.* It's crazy – the harmoniums and so, it's take too much place. One day Edvard, he buy a *piano.* Business man dies, the house is clear . . .'

'Another house clearance?'

'Of course Edvard, he buy on a good price. Always. But I can say this was the end for Isak.'

'Edward got the sack?'

'Ja, sack – he must find another work, another place for live – with Charlotte. And the boy of course. A piano, it's big.' Herr Pålsson stretched his arms wide. 'Stand many month, here in the shop. Six month, a year. It's make big trouble between Shanlers and Janssons – even today.'

'Really? You mean – like a family feud?' I knew incidents like this could cause ructions lasting decades. Herr Pålsson didn't seem to know *feud.*

'Later, Isak, he sell. Till cinema *Filmstudio* – the piano, it's for the silents films. The people, they seeing the film, somebody is playing – for mood music? It's name *Inblick* today – you can go in, here on the corner. Of course it's no more the silents films.'

'So the Chandlers, where did they . . .?'

'Sömninge – the ground school. It's need teachers.' (Herr

92

Wittberg had mentioned *grundskola.*) 'They both was get a work – lucky, isn't? One more time, you see – right place, right time! But me, I work many years more for Isak. And for Nils – it's Isak's son. Nineteen hundra ninety-four, I buy from Nils.'

'You bought the business?'

Herr Pålsson raised a cagey finger. 'The shop only – I buy empty. This way can I start again. Always it's business, isn't?' He surveyed his motley empire with pride. 'But no more pianos!'

'Herr Pålsson, it's been fascinating. Have you any idea where I could find Philip Chandler?'

He developed a sudden itch between the shoulder-blades. 'Philip, he was live in Vätshamn. *Was.*' His stare emphasised the obsolescence of the information.

'Ah.' I picked out a handful of postcards for one more charm offensive. 'You wouldn't have a phone number, by any chance? An address? He'd be my cousin, you see. We've never met. Seems a pity not to look him up – while I'm here?' I pushed a hundred *kronor* note across the counter.

After a brief hesitation he fished up an accounts book, flicked through the thumb index and swivelled it my way. 'An hour with bus. Go Södergatan.'

'You've been very kind.'

'Welcome to back.'

20

The talk with Herr Pålsson left me hungry; grabbing a hot dog at a stall outside the city wall, I noticed a car hire firm across the road. Driving would save a lot of time. Soon after two I was at the wheel of a small Fiat, weaving back through the medieval centre on Södergatan and out through the south gateway. Along the main coastal highway to Vätshamn the blue sea glittered; welcome sea breezes wafted in at the open windows.

The large, elegant house lay in a becalmed backstreet, its balcony and trellises supporting an abundance of roses; rampant branches overhung the driveway, their blossom dropping silken petals. To my dismay the place was empty and locked up; concerned not to scratch the car, I'd missed the large *For Sale* sign. Having noted the estate agent's address, it was no more than a two-minute drive back to Vätshamn's high street.

'Rosengatan 11? Yes, sir, we're make the sale here at Gustavssons, on owners' instructions. Lindell.' He held out a business card. 'If you're interested of the property, sir? We can arrange an appointment for view the house. Which day is good for you?'

'No, no, sorry, I didn't mean . . . Would it be possible to speak to the owners – the Chandlers? It's about – a business matter.'

'I'm sorry, sir. The family left for two or three years ago.' Herr Lindell pulled at his smart shirtsleeves and closed the diary.

'Do you have an address at all? A phone number? It's quite important.'

'Sorry,' was the predictable reply again. 'Here in Sveden it's not allowed we give out client information. Protection of privacy, and so on. But of course, I can give on a message, if it help you? You are Mr . . .?'

There was a moment's pause when he heard my surname, but he wrote it down.

On the way back through Valstad I wondered how Philip and his family might react to hearing from an unknown Chandler after all these years. I'd given the campsite details: what were the chances he'd ring before I left? Unless he did, my current line of enquiry wasn't going anywhere.

21

'So why stay?'

'Sorry?'

'Why stay if you hate the work and your boss thinks you're useless?'

'Ah, well . . . I've probably painted it blacker than it is.' Sidney didn't think that, exactly – did he?

From the beach the horizon gleamed silver in brilliant morning sunlight. Following yesterday's abortive trip to Vätshamn there seemed little choice but to hang on at the campsite in the hope Philip would call – not that I planned to sit in my room all day. It had crossed my mind that staying put in Emsäde might increase the chances of meeting Helena again, but I'd never expected it to happen quite this soon. For whatever reason, the beach at Segelholm evidently exerted a powerful draw.

'Sounds black enough to me. Why don't you look for something else?' She stood thoughtfully in her pale blue swimsuit a little way up the sandy shingle, the dark mass of her hair dancing and shining in the sun. I squatted at the water's edge, bringing the microcosm of the seashore into close-up. Helena strolled down to squat close by; between us a delicate spiral protruded from the wet sand, sculpted by an unseen mollusc.

'Sidney's not that bad, really. He's reliable – well, you know, predictable. There must be worse bosses.' My scant description of life at Castles had so far left out any mention of Georgina.

'In any case, you've not said why you think the work's so meaningless. Selling houses makes sense, doesn't it? Everyone need somewhere to live.' She prodded the sandy whirl to see if its proprietor was in.

'Ah, but most people couldn't pay out the kind of money some of our clients flash around.' It was the first time I'd called them 'our'. Might there be a part of me that belonged at Castles after all?

'I don't see what difference that makes. What's the point of earning money if you can't spend it on something you want?' For a moment I was lost in her speckled brown irises. Having found the little bump of sand inert, she got up and surveyed the horizon, shading her eyes.

Helena's reactions weren't quite what I'd expected of a young woman living in a mature, scrupulous democracy like Sweden, especially when she appeared to uphold the inalienable rights of man to happiness, a good salary and a big house to live in. I stood up to meet her direct look. 'Yes, but all men are supposed to be equal, aren't they? Going back to first principles, wealth ought to be distributed a bit more evenly. Why should one man be able to afford a big house when his neighbour can't?' Perhaps I still hankered after the leftist certainties of my student days; they sat less easily, though, with an inheritance that could soon mean a big improvement to my own fortunes. These were contradictions I'd not yet got round to addressing.

'Oh, right. So you'd screw the rich and dish out their money to the poor, would you?' The toughness of this seemed in sharp contrast to her easy presence, standing there hand on hip in her washed-out bikini. It was clear she'd wasted no time getting out in the sun since the weather changed; the smooth glowing skin exuded a fragrant saltiness. Had she been for a swim already?

'That's not what I'm saying. Some people are going to have more money than others, that's in the nature of things. If you've got special talents, good luck to you, I'm not trying to . . .'

'Anyway, aren't you being rather deterministic? All this talk of

97

equality comes in conflict with what you were saying about individual freedom.'

'Was I?'

She gave a scornful laugh. 'I've noticed it before: you British, you love to talk of freedom, but in reality you don't believe in it. I don't think any of you honestly believe it exists.'

'Now that's not fair! There can't be any real difference between Brits and Swedes over this. It's the same for any other developed nation, come to that.' Who were all these British people she knew?

'So everyone's the same now, are they? That's great.'

'I didn't say that either. I take a little pride in being British, that's all.' Her smile told me how antediluvian it sounded.

Helena picked up a flat stone and spun it across the water: five distinct bounces on the silky surface. Her arguments were as facile as they were hard to refute; it would have been nice to find a topic on which we could agree a little more. I wanted to reach out and touch her shoulder, but she moved away, choosing another pebble.

'Well, we're not going to get much further today putting the world right. I know, let's cycle to Nordspetsen.'

'Nord what?' Instead of answering she dropped the stone and raced up the noisy shingle. She was already whizzing off along a dusty track before I could get my feet on the pedals.

I had no idea where Nordspetsen was or what we'd find there. The track led north-east along the shoreline for a couple of kilometres, the soft breeze doing little to lessen the searing heat on arms and shoulders. In a fit of bravado I'd taken off my shirt and was disporting a pale British torso, hoping it might turn a more appetising colour in the foreseeable future. Helena took everything in her practical stride, offering lotion from her saddlebag and warning against too much sun in the first few days.

We were soon bumping along between conifers over ridges of dried mud, the occasional tree root fingering its way across the path. The lower branches flailed my skin, but at least they offered a little dappled shade. A warm smell of earth and leaves hung in the air, and something sweeter, hard to identify. Could those red smudges really be wild strawberries? All at once we were at a large deep pool; Helena threw down her bicycle among the tall grasses.

'We should find freshwater fish in here. Look, can you see those tiny ones over there, in the shade?' A spindly pine overhung the glittering surface, sheltering a constellation of minnows; they darted in all directions as we leaned out. 'Can't see any big ones, can you? I'm sure they're in there somewhere.' She stretched her neck an inch further, grabbing my wrist for balance. I'd hardly registered the contact before she stood upright, letting go. 'I think they must be round on the other side. Come on.'

Kicking off her sandals, Helena padded barefoot along the muddy verge; I did likewise, twigs and small stones cutting into my toes. She scoured the mirroring surface for signs of movement. 'I've always thought it'd be nice to be a fish. All that water, and just you, skimming along, you know? Like flying – only in slow motion. What would you like to be?'

'Not a fish, anyway. Too many things trying to gobble you up.' Privately I could think of a lot of worse things to be than a fish skimming through the water with Helena.

'Ah, but you'd be quick, you'd get away nine times out of ten.' She wiggled a flat hand fishily through the air.

'What about the tenth?'

'What? Oh, you're such a scaredy cat!' The gentle mouth twitched mockingly 'We've all got to die, haven't we?' It would have been too niggling to say I'd rather not die in another fish's stomach, or suffocate in the grass with a hook through the gullet.

We'd walked the full circumference of the pond without finding any bigger fish, and were back at the pine tree, still chancing its luck at forty-five degrees to the water. It seemed a good place to flop down and pick pine needles out of toes. Helena sauntered back to her luggage rack and dug out a sketch-pad.

'I didn't know you were an artist?'

'Don't move.' She scanned the little composition for a long

moment, with the tree at its precarious angle to the bright water and me leaning against it, pruning a foot.

'You can't do me like this.'

'Just watch me.' Now she sketched quickly, undeterred. I toppled back, laughing.

'Guy!' Her sternness surprised me. 'I told you, keep still.'

I've kept that sketch – like the fixative that makes those hours permanent. Looking at it I can smell the resinous pine, see the dark seriousness in Helena's eyes as she concentrates. We walk on with our bikes. Occasionally she'll linger a few minutes and sketch a flower, or a vibrant green beetle, or a cluster of trees against the skyline. When it's done she leads the way again without speaking.

Not long afterwards we'd left the wooded undergrowth and come out into a lovely open space of lush sheep-nibbled grassland between clumps of prickly gorse. From here you start to climb toward the cliffs at Nordspetsen – the northernmost tip of the island that overlooks the Sound near a wide estuary. On the soft, springy grass the little pellets of sheep droppings made me think of Tarmain.

'What a place – it's Treasure Island!' I wanted to run ahead and look over the edge, only another fifty yards further up, but Helena stopped. The sun was misting over behind a bank of flimsy cloud. Somehow the serenity that was ours moments earlier had evaporated. 'Helena? Are you all right?'

'Mm? I'm all right.' Glancing at her watch, she wheeled the bike round. 'You go on if you like, Guy. I'd better be getting back.' She was already standing on the pedals, jolting her way downhill among the trees; I scrambled to catch her up.

We cycled in silence for a few minutes. The track emerged again at the west-facing shore.

'What is it, Helena?'

'It isn't anything. I'm all right. Don't be a fusspot.'

'Where did you learn that?'

'What? Fusspot? Oh, Mrs Potter, I expect.'

'Who's Mrs Potter? Is she a fusspot?'

'No, not at all. Mrs Potter was great. My host family in Streatham – didn't I mention being *au pair* for three months? That was the idea, anyway. My last year in school. Let's just say I wasn't cut out to mend dungarees and get the coal in.'

'Dungarees?'

Helena gave her innocent, rippling laugh. 'The children – they both wore them. Claude was five, Jill was seven. They were always getting filthy and torn. Mrs Potter showed me how to darn. Well, she tried. She was very kind, but they couldn't really afford me. The sewing was hopeless. It was bad enough trying to stop the kids break their necks at the playground. Claude liked to go down the slide on his back, head first.'

She stopped her bike for a moment. 'I'm talking a lot of me. What about you?'

'What about me?'

'What made you come to Sweden? Most English people don't come here without a reason, I know that.'

'I read something in a magazine. You know, all that Nature – forests and lakes and things. Sounded fantastic.' If this trip was going to be a wild goose chase – as seemed more than likely at that point – it felt simpler not to go into too much detail.

The afternoon was all but over; the only thing clear to me was that I wanted to see her again. 'You come up here a lot?'

'Sometimes. It's depend.' The grammatical slip told me her mind was elsewhere.

22

Back at Emsäde that evening there was a call for me at reception. Would this be Georgina again, ringing to break it off for good? That's what other girls before her had done; they'd made it perfectly clear why, too. Picking up the phone in dread of what she might say, it struck me how direct and honest George always was – all the things I'd so miserably failed to be with her, in fact. I didn't deserve her. I didn't really deserve anybody.

'Mr Chandler?' A woman's mature voice spoke very quietly. 'You left a message at Bengt Gustavssons. For my husband?'

'Fru Chandler?'

'Herr Lindell said you'd given the same name as ours. You're related to – Philip's family?' She listened patiently as I tried to outline in brief my mission to trace Edward's descendants. 'Edward? Philip's father? I'm sorry, Herr Lindell didn't mention your first name.' Her English was clear and seamless.

'I should have explained: Guy Chandler – Graham's son. My father died the year before last, you see, rather prematurely in fact, and now their elder brother, Ben, has died. Tilly was at the funeral, and we . . .' Suddenly I couldn't go on. It felt ridiculous to be getting emotional again at a moment like this, but all I could see was Dad with Uncle Ben at the kitchen table in Wareham, drinking tea out of a saucer. I tried to slow my breathing. 'In actual fact it's to do with Ben's estate.'

'So you're . . .?'

'Philip's cousin.'

'I'm sorry, Mr Chandler – Guy, is it? I can understand this is hard for you. Unfortunately, it's not so easy for me either.' There was a long silence. 'My home is in Hälsingborg, you see; that's on the mainland – the west coast. It's a day's journey to Lammland, I'm afraid.'

'I see. You know, Fru Chandler, it's so good to talk to you . . .'

'Maja, Won't you call me Maja?'

'Maja, this must be . . .'

'It's all right. So if you're Philip's cousin . . . You must have things you need to know; I understand that.' Despite the remoteness she conveyed a sense of sympathy and caring. 'This is so difficult on the phone. I can't travel this week, but I have some business in Vätshamn . . .' Another pause. 'Mr Chandler . . . Guy, would next week do? Thursday is possible, I think. Will you be still at Emsäde?'

*　　*　　*

Maja's phonecall gave me a definite lift: it was progress, anyway. By breakfast-time next day, though, it felt a very long wait till Thursday of the following week for further developments. Then I remembered about the Carlssons' daughter, Annalena, having been Sofi Chandler's classmate at secondary school in Lindhem. Might they still have some record of Sofi's father? Not that I needed a particular reason for going anywhere – this was my one summer holiday, wasn't it, to do what I liked with?

The trip would take me right across the island this time, albeit at one of its narrower points. In the cool air of early morning it required a little more *mind-setting* to cycle straight past the beach at Segelholm; I didn't want to seem to be hanging around for Helena. The temperature was on the rise. Outside Klosterbo I stopped near a stream and opened a tin of lager in the baking sun, then set off again on sluggish legs, regretting the beer. It was a relief to reach Lindhem at last, perched on a hill with a fine view eastwards over the harbour.

The school was closed: absurd of me to have expected otherwise. The only place open was the library. I wandered into the reference section and sat leafing through the local *Lindhemsbladet*, dependent on the pictures for enlightenment. Scenes of school-children on summer camp, children at a choral concert in Stockholm, and children feeding orphaned hedgehogs put me in mind of Edward's trips described by Solveig, the blind teacher. Libraries keep back numbers. Edward's own exploits were far too ancient to hope for anything about him, but people often pass on their passions; it seemed feasible this or that member of his family might turn up among the sports pages.

At the desk an elderly librarian with a whistling hearing aid flashed an eager smile.

'*Kan jag hjälpa dej? Fru Tegens.*' She gave a slight bob of the head, like a courtesy left over from a bygone era; the prospect of helping me appeared the highlight of a long, stuffy afternoon. It was clear substantial funds had been invested in transferring the entire collection of microfiches onto computer, including news articles dating back to the early 1980s. Sliding the mouse under my hand, she sat and watched me play around with the database, getting nowhere.

'Is there a quick way to do a search?'

'Of course. Which name?' It was dim of me: why limit myself to the sports pages? Her search brought instant results racing across the screen. 'Yes, here we have: Sofia Chandler. She was *Lucia* in 2000.'

'*Lucia?*'

'It's tradition here in Sweden. Some days before Christmas – look: written 14 December. The festival itself, it's on 13 December. We have every year. *Lucia*, she's a kind of goddess of Light, so she wear candles in her hair. Of course it's a little bit dangerous with real candles. It's therefore they take electric ones now – in many schools. Not all – it's different.' It certainly was; Swedish Christmas was unknown territory to me.

'So does she just – turn up and shine her light on everybody?'

'You can say so! She have also many maids. And it's a star-boy with her.'

'*Star-boy?*'

'He wear a special hat. And *Lucia* have always long blonde hair. I think it's a picture here somewhere.' She reached across and tapped at the keyboard again. 'You see? Mm, very pretty.' A line of smiling fourteen-year-old girls were crossing the stage led by a queenly figure in a trailing white robe, a crown of lighted candles tremulously balanced on shining blonde tresses. Seeing a photograph of Edward's rather stunning granddaughter for the first time was a thrill. 'She's – a part of your family?'

'She'd be my . . . I wonder: can this be magnified a bit?' As we zoomed in on Sofi, her attendant also came into focus: much younger, he wore a vast cloak and what looked like a very large star-studded dunce's cap.

'So he's the star-boy.'

'He go everywhere with *Lucia*.'

'And what does this caption say?'

'*Sofia Shandler, 14, is in eighth grade at Lindhems school. She play a photogene Lucia on yesterday's festival in Main Auditorium.*'

'Photogenic *Lucia?*'

'OK, photogenic.'

'Sorry. I'm so sorry – your English is great.' The picture of *Lucia* and her entourage was a wide-angled shot taken from the side of the stage; behind Sofi and her 'star-boy' helper a small segment of the audience was visible. 'And would those be parents, do you suppose?'

'It's possible.'

It was intriguing to think Maja, and perhaps Philip, could be somewhere among them. 'Fru Tegens, you've been a tremendous help. One more thing: is it possible to get a copy of this?'

Another keystroke brought the copy snaking out in magnified format.

'The newsprint don't enlarge so good.'

'That's perfect.' I was about to take out some money, but Fru Tegens held my wrist.

'It's no charge. Our supervisor, she want we make a profit of everything – but what's a library for if it's not for help people?'

23

'Clockwise.'

'What?'

'Round the island. We're heading clockwise. Hey, look at this.' As my front wheel draws level, Helena points at her left thigh, pounding steadily up and down. Improbably, a dragonfly has landed on the bronzed skin. Green-blue filigree wings tremble for a second before carrying it off again on the flapping wind.

'Fabulous!' I'm stirred more by her glowing legs than by the dragonfly.

'They breed in the big lake – it's not far.' Helena is tireless. Squinting into the sun, we engage a lengthy gradient that demands yogic breathing.

'Is that why you come this way?'

'Not specially. My right side needs more sun, that's all – I always seem to cook down the left. Anyway, can't spend all day making up your mind, can you.'

'Impulsive.'

'Maybe. You're not?' She flashes her smile as I fumble with the gears.

'Sometimes. Can't say it's got me far lately, though.'

'OK. So what are we really talking about?'

There was never a time when Helena didn't give me that dizzy sense of moving too fast over uncharted ground. Another lovely day with her had been bestowed on me unannounced; premature revelations could spell disaster. This was Saturday: much earlier she'd come bumping onto the grass in her battered Volvo to find me lingering over muesli and rolls outside the *stuga*.

'Still eating?'

'Helena! There's plenty here, have you . . .?'

'I thought we could do the Tourist Bit today.' Cool in frayed shorts and light blouse, she shaded her eyes, looking out across the river. 'If you want to, that is.'

'Of course!'

'Where shall we go?'

'You decide.'

'I've seen everything, so it makes no difference.' She stood unhooking her bike from the car. 'D'you fancy a museum or something? Or we can drop in on pottery workshops, things like that. It's lots around the island, you can't miss them. I tried to make pots once. Have you done it? The wheel's a lot harder than it looks. Nothing stands up straight.' Perching on the saddle, she jiggled up and down, waiting. 'Why don't we head north and see how far we get?'

By now we've long passed the beach; Helena has taken a right through the village towards Vandringe, then veered north again onto a broad peninsula. We skirt the east side of the estuary this time, with Låtby's disused harbour and the rocks of Nordspetsen more distantly visible on its opposite flank. Reaching the inland lake – an old limestone quarry – we squat on the flower-strewn verge.

'Not Segelholm today?'

'I cycle all over.' Helena pours steaming coffee; she sounds a touch defensive. 'Segelholm makes a nice change, of course. More flat shingle and sand than where I live – easier for swimming. More protected from the wind most days, too. You've been in Lindhem? Hörnvik's not far from there. I can show you.'

She takes out the sketch-book and turns up a fine drawing of what looks like a large mansion nestling below a long ridge. To the right, behind the house with its undulating roof of quarried tiles, the escarpment juts straight out into the sea, the lower slopes dashed by foaming waves. Two windswept figures are making their way inland. 'You see? It's much more big rocks on the east coast – quite sharp for your feet. But you can dive from them – it's deep, even close to the shore.'

'Did you draw this?' I sit admiring the pencilled cross-hatching by which she's captured the multifaceted rocks. They contrast with the softer textures of hillside and sea, and with the firmly etched house in the foreground. The building itself has old-fashioned shutters to either side of unusual curved windows, and a sweeping flight of steps up to the central door. Some distance in front, a shallow river runs seawards from left to right at the foot of the picture. I'm visualising myself walking along it. 'Is this your house?'

'You're full of questions, aren't you.' She pushes the sketch-book back in the pannier.

Energised by coffee, we settle into a smooth rhythm; soft breezes blow from the estuary on our left. At its north-western extremity, a few hundred yards across the water, rises the dramatic rocky outcrop of Nordspetsen, but this side there are no cliffs, only a steady upward incline to a cluster of grassy hillocks and dunes. Helena's stamina has long since outstripped mine, yet as we approach the headland she seems to press the pace even more, as if overcoming a resistance beyond that of the hill.

At the top she stands triumphant astride her bike, pointing downwards. 'Guldstranden!'

The landscape has opened out below us, a vast sandy beach far more spectacular than Segelholm. For the last half kilometre we follow the downward slope, which leads us in a delightful free-wheeling spin off the road straight onto the smooth flat surface, firm as a drum. The endless expanse of finest sand, a shade duskier than the gold of its name, recalls that harrowing rescue scene in *Dark Forces* shot here by Yngve Feldman.

Helena has whizzed ahead. Now we're flying eastwards close to the water, carried along by the lukewarm wind. Rolling waves crash white-crested onto the sand, iridescent spray flung up. Midway round the bay, the coastline projects a short distance out to sea in a narrow tongue of sand. Helena turns, zigzagging new marks on the moist surface. She skids to a halt and points toward the horizon.

Across the Sound lies another, much smaller, island, isolated and somewhat indistinct, though perhaps little more than three or four hundred yards from where we stand.

'Stenö.' The wind snatches her voice away. Seeing the tiny island, it occurs to me to try swimming over to it. I'm not a bad swimmer; the water doesn't look at all dangerous. When I catch her up, though, Helena is quick to discourage me. 'No, you shouldn't swim here. It's lots of funny currents, especially around Stenö. It's mean Stone Island.' There's something odd about her commanding tone – almost like someone else talking. She stares across, shading her eyes; the sudden cautiousness feels out of character – not her normal energetic approach. She's withdrawn somewhere, into a tighter, more Swedish identity.

A second later her voice has resumed its natural cadences. 'The geology's special up here. Did you know it used to be a complete causeway over to Stenö, only a few million years ago? That's nothing, in geological time. Still there, of course, under water. Pity. If we'd been around then we could have walked it.'

'Well there must still be a good chunk to walk on, surely. We could get a good way out on that, couldn't we?' I drop the bike and sprint across the wet sand in my shorts. From the water's edge her slim figure looks apprehensive, vulnerable; she hasn't moved. 'Aren't you coming in, Helena? It's not cold – the headland cuts the worst of the wind. How can you resist?'

'You go in if you must, Guy,' she calls. 'I'll stay and watch.' I venture a few yards out on the submerged sandbank, then think better of it and race back, stamping the glittering spray in all directions.

'Oh, come on, Helena! We can swim in this bit, surely?' But nothing is going to persuade her. Stenö shimmers hazily across the water. Perhaps the closeness is deceptive; seeing she won't join me, I hold back. The water does feel cold. What are these currents she's talked about – can they really be that much of a danger? Real or imagined, Helena's not prepared to discuss it.

24

In the following days there were no further impromptu visits from Helena. She had her work, of course – three days a week at *Musica*. In any case, why should she spend more of her leisure time with me? I walked or cycled alone, exploring the forested inlets around Emsäde and taking the odd dip in the sea. The campsite was well placed for doing what Helena called the Tourist Bit, though the evenings could be rather long. With Edward's death now an unalterable reality, it would have felt disrespectful at first to think of playing on his harmonica, but as time went by the urge took me to keep it warm, so to speak, in his honour. Musical instruments are, after all, meant to be played – a view I was sure he'd have approved. Experimenting with its plaintive strains was becoming a nice way to wind down before turning in; there wasn't much else to do.

To save time Maja had arranged to fly via Stockholm to Valstad first thing on Thursday. The previous evening I'd rung to book a car again, planning to pick her up at the airport, and was rather looking forward to it; we might go to lunch together. Then halfway through breakfast that morning Herr Wittberg put his head round the door to say there was another call for me.

'I'm terribly sorry, Guy, something's cropped up here.' Maja's voice sounded strained. 'I can't come across this week – someone's ill at work. Thursday's our worst day in the office. This must be so frustrating for you – and I really wanted that we talk personally.' She took a long breath. 'Guy, this is a bad time for telling

111

you, but I don't suppose it's going to be a better one. I'm afraid
Philip – he died, you see. For two years ago – almost three. This
is awful, to pass it on this way, you must feel you've had a wasted
journey – and now waiting for me these last days . . .' I leaned
against the reception desk, staring out across the river; there'd
been a lot of death to absorb lately. 'It all happened so quickly.
He was away on one of his competitions – December 2005.
Sometimes I can't believe . . .'

'I'm really sorry, Maja, I . . .'

'Philip was fanatic for his skiing, did you know?'

'Skiing? I knew Edward skied.'

'Philip always wanted to be the best. Of course he took after
Edward in that way – and other ways. Edward was an adventurer, wasn't he? And a strong skier, for someone not born to it.
But for Philip it was more professional. He was very good, you
see. He won competitions – prizes. Edward never bothered with
all that. Philip went often up to Jämtland, close to Norway – one
of Edward's favourite resorts. The week before, it was a small
avalanche, on one of the high peaks – Åreskutan. We didn't think
about it; it's not so unusual. But it was one slope, a black run,
Philip loved it – obviously it was unstable. He was skiing alone
all day. Bad luck, really. It's that way some days – nobody know
what can happen, one minute you're skiing straight down, lovely,
and then . . . Philip, he would joke sometimes about when his
number should come up! They took two weeks to find him.'

'Two weeks?'

'You won't want to hear all this, Guy, it's . . .'

'No, please. I need to hear.' I watched bemused as a large
tabby cat dropped out of nowhere onto the terrace wall outside
and began washing himself.

'The main thing for me, Guy – I must explain – is to get Sofi
back.'

'Sofi's gone away?'

'This is hard for you, Guy. How could you know any of it?
She'd already left the island that summer – the same year. Of

course she's in touch: we talk, on the weekends. But for people in Vätshamn – well, she was here one day and gone the next. When we lost Philip, so soon after, I didn't know what to do. Sofi says she must get on with her new life. It's natural. I think she's with someone, you see – it's only a mother's feeling . . . I hope she's happy. I *think* she's happy. But I worry for her – can you understand? Until she's . . .'

'Of course. So when she phones, where does she . . .?'

'It's a pity, Guy, I can't say you where she is. She's given her instructions, you see. Sofi can be very determined – I can say quite bossy, even. And to lose her father in that way – it had a strong effect, I'm afraid. She don't want that anyone shall know where she's living. It's her way to deal with what's happened. Sofi was close to Philip – very close. The house in Vätshamn, it was important too – to have a home you can come back to . . . But Guy, it was too big, all those rooms, even before she went, and when Philip have his accident . . . I waited, I waited two years, but it was no choice, I must do something. So I put it on the market. Well, you know, of course, Gustavssons . . .'

'I understand. Once you were alone in the house, you must have . . .'

'Well no, that's not all. Philip wasn't so much at home any more, you see.' Maja was plainly set on telling the whole story. 'We divorced, in fact – two years before. Of course we stayed friends. Philip, he have his apartment, near the harbour. So for a long time it was Sofi and me only, in the house. My parents are here in Hälsingborg, but I have friends still on the island. Sofi too, naturally. She says she's wandering in her wilderness. She know she can't live in it forever. One day – not yet – I think she must return and face all that's happened. She'll manage it, I think.'

My own griefs felt petty compared to Maja's. The cat stared in at me, green-eyed; I envied him his simple universe.

'Maja, it's good we've talked, and I'm so sorry you can't come today. Perhaps I could get over to . . .'

'To Hälsingborg? I'd like that. Sorry to talk so long, Guy – it's nice to have someone to . . . Goodness, is it so late? I must go. We'll talk soon. Take care, and sorry again for today. Bye-bye.'

The moment Maja rang off, my head was crowded with all the things I should have said but hadn't. In fact the call ended in such a rush, I'd not even raised the inheritance issue – although from my earlier mention of Ben's estate she must have guessed there was something in the offing. I thought of Edward's divorce: weren't they supposed to run in families?

Not that Maja herself could inherit, of course. The consequences of Philip's death were slowly dawning. Stephen had been quite clear about *blood relatives:* it was Sofi we needed to contact now, as Edward's direct descendant – the only surviving one, in fact. If Sofi's secretiveness about her whereabouts seemed a little strange, Maja's concern not to disclose them was understandable; but it would be essential to get back to her very soon and pass on the details of Ben's executors for Sofi. Then it hit me: after all that, I hadn't even asked Maja's phone number! Was it worth trying the Carlssons again in the hope of tracking it through Annalena?

The morning chill had long thawed by the time I'd pedalled the eight kilometres to Segelholm once more and slipped through the churchyard to the vicarage door. They were out. No doubt Gudrun led a busy life; as for Mats, he was bound to be out ministering to one of his other numerous parishes.

On the face of it there was nothing to stop me contacting Maja again through Gustavssons. Herr Lindell's slightly antiseptic manner, though, had made it plain he knew – no matter how impressive the properties on display – I wasn't going to buy one. Where someone else might have persuaded him to disclose her number, I don't have that kind of assertiveness. Leaving another message felt like a waste of time – I needed to speak to her personally now.

The remaining option was to sit it out at the campsite till Maja rang back. I'd been there almost a week; its attractions were beginning to pall. There could still be an outside chance, once her mother had spoken with her, that Sofi would feel moved to get in touch with me herself. Few of us are immune to the appeal of personal gain: might this be enough to coax her out of whatever wilderness she currently occupied?

Since Philip had died, Edward's harmonica should also rightfully pass to Sofi. When the time came, no doubt, I'd miss it. My departure from Sweden, meanwhile – even with the extension – was scheduled in just under a fortnight's time. In the darker recesses of my mind ran a silent hourglass, unseen and inexorable; the sand was rapidly dwindling.

25

As I emerged across the Carlssons' copious lawn, one of the green double-deckers slid into view beyond the yew trees. It was only a short sprint to the road.

'*Hörnvik, tack.*'

We threaded our way between sunny fields and deserted chalk quarries. It was all very well acting on impulse, but – even supposing she was in – what grounds were there for supposing Helena would welcome an unannounced visit from me today? Her sketch of the house on the rocky east coast floated in my mind's eye; the uneasy fact remained she'd avoided giving its actual address. The few hours we'd spent together were delightful, but why should she see me other than as just one more tourist among thousands streaming through Valstad every summer?

None of these reflections, however, were going to deter me. At Hörnvik the bus stops half a mile short of the river Helena had sketched – the road too twisting and pitted for larger vehicles – before heading south again to Lindhem. On this side of the shallow, widening stream a narrow track leads eastwards to the beach, with a smell of sun-warmed water and steam rising off wet grass. Leaving the stony path I picked my way between tangles of pine and silver birch up onto a wooded hill – doubtless a familiar walk for Helena.

From the headland you can look back over the full length of

the small estuary. The solitary house was visible at once in clinging mist, huddled against the cliffs opposite, its unmistakable stone-tiled roof running to tall gables at either end. The chalky crags, topped by a rough walkway, fall sheer behind it and, at the seaward end, straight into the swirling water.

The midday heat was on me by the time I'd retraced my steps. Beneath the little bridge fast currents gurgled over the pebbles; a silvery fish plopped near one of the wooden supports. From here the house stands no more than a hundred yards or so along the far bank. Three stylish dormer skylights offset the rather grand windows on two floors below them, with a curving stone stair-case that leads up to the central portico. Could Helena really be living alone in such a spacious residence?

At the top of the steps I found an ancient bell-pull; a dog barked. Helena was there at once, bending to hold his collar, looking up at me with her dark, beautiful eyes. The full-grown golden Labrador rushed to lick my hand.

'Sorry, this is Snuffi. He gets a bit excited. We don't get so many visitors. What are you doing here?' Her voice sounded a downbeat note; she'd not used my name. The grey smock, pulled up loosely at the elbows, gave her an artistic air as she drew Snuffi back to let me in. Helena never used make-up; she had a paler, more susceptible look today.

'Hope you don't mind too much? That sketch of yours – curiosity got the better of me.'

'Mind those.' Along a whitewashed passage an assortment of bric-à-brac vied for floor-space: brass coal-scuttles, pokers, tarnished copper kettles. On the darker, cliff-facing side of the house Snuffi led us into the kitchen, claws clicking on the rough pine boards, and started drinking noisily from a bowl. It was cool and shady in here, though no less cluttered, most of the floor occupied by ceramic pots and ornate mirrors.

'It's a lot of stuff, isn't it. We can sit over by the window. Coffee?' Why did she surround herself with all this? No doubt she had a thousand things to do on her day off – I shouldn't have come. She filled a kettle at the sink, gazing across the rear yard past a glass-fronted conservatory. 'Or – second thoughts – if you're so curious: maybe you'd like to look around first?'

Out in the hallway I peered up at the finely crafted stairwell. 'What a marvellous place! These old properties have such a lot of history, don't they – and life, somehow.'

'I love this house.' She went up the stairs, drawing a finger along the swirled banister. 'People tell me it's quite special. Oh, but of course: the Estate Agent casts a professional eye.' She glanced impishly.

'Not at all! Not sure I can make you an offer today, though. Have you had this all checked for woodworm?' I pretended to test the banisters; they were solid as a rock. 'You know, there are lots of places like this around Wintersham. Different sort of style, of course. This is more . . .'

'More what?'

At Castles we'd have had it down as *suitable for modernisation*, which in our part of Dorset goes for almost anything over twenty years old. 'Ooh, I don't know. Continental, maybe. Have you lived here long?' I joined her on the top step.

'Most of my life, actually – on and off. Shall we? *No*, Snuffi, stay.' He knew not to cross her, flopping on the threadbare carpet with a whistling snort.

The rectangular landing, lit by a skylight through which sunshine now streamed, gave onto the entrance-hall below. We stood in front of the large east window.

'This is the best side of the house. Especially in the mornings – gets most of the sun.' Rows of antique-looking kitchen chairs and faded chintz sofas were marshalled along the walls; it felt like an improvised stage set. On a narrow corridor to the rear we passed several bedrooms crammed with furniture and relics; some suggested the nineteenth century, or in one or two cases perhaps even the eighteenth. A couple of the dressing-tables were adorned with silver-backed hairbrushes and collections of amber. Peeping into this room and that, the colourful quilted bedspreads, scalloped wardrobes and mirrors seemed to conjure something like a cameo of Swedish country life in various forgotten eras.

At the end we stepped inside the tiniest bedroom, sunlight glowing through linen curtains. By the bed a small painted cradle was hung with a mobile of birds and fish; a black-faced rag doll sprawled on the coverlet.

'Your room as a child?'

'It's so far out of the way – I could do what I liked in here.' Helena flashed dark, mischievous eyes. 'This is still my favourite room, above all in winter. The main bedroom, it's not so *gemütlich*. Warmer here, too. The boiler's as old as some of the antiques.'

Turning in the passage I happened to glance out through the tiny back window. Across the yard a young worker, sweating and stripped to the waist, was balanced high on a ladder in the baking sun, nails bristling between his teeth, hammering the outhouse roof. I ducked out of sight before he could look up.

We returned to where a wide, mahogany hall-stand presided over the landing, leaving hardly space to squeeze past. From the centre of the ceiling a brass candelabrum primed with fresh candles hung over the hallway below.

'You've got plenty of furniture! Would some of these be family heirlooms?'

She caressed the top of a velvet chaise longue; on it a mottled cat lay curled up, two battle-torn ears twitching at our voices. 'Pappa was in antiques. *His* father also.' Her tone was factual but there was a twist of irony in her smile. 'You haven't seen the attic yet! We might as well do the full tour while we're up here – or have you had enough?'

Beyond the hall-stand another, much narrower staircase branched improbably upwards again; a low door gave access to the roof-space. It was hard to believe there could be more. Halfway up she stopped and turned.

'Do you like art?' A faint fragrance of herbal soap wafted down to me.

'Of course – well, some. What do you like?'

'I'm not fussy. Anything related to the sea, though – that's something that touches me.' We ducked under the lintel into a twilit attic. 'Pappa was in the merchant navy. A long time ago – before he had the shop.' Her father seemed to figure large in her thoughts, though it sounded as if he belonged to the past tense. It felt cool and secluded in here, slim arrows of sunlight from the shuttered dormers piercing the shadows. Adjusting to the gloom, my eye was caught by a row of seascapes propped against the rough plaster.

'Look at these! Watercolours, aren't they?' I walked over and turned a small frame.

'Those are. It's more oils that end – and drawings.' I blew dust off the picture and moved nearer the window. This was a view of Valstad, perhaps at dawn; the towers of the old city wall were picked out in deep red highlights, toning in with a pinkish wash of morning sky. In another, swirls of cloud were scudding across a windswept beach. She stood waiting, head on one side.

'What do you think?'

'Helena, these are great. Are they yours?' Her slight smile confirmed it. 'I mean, you're really talented. You could sell some of them. Oh, sorry – trust me to put my foot in it. You must have done already.'

'No, it's OK. I have sold the odd one, if you want to know. Not recently.' There was a faint resonance under our feet; Snuffi barked once downstairs. 'Are you OK to browse a bit more up here? Someone's at the door. I'll be right back.'

26

Maybe the roof chap wanted paying, or something; it was none of my business. I began sifting through the stacked frames. Beside seascapes there were rural scenes from around the island – several sketches of ruined churches, with lights and shades felicitously done in gradations of grey and black pencil or charcoal. I recognised the wooden bridge at Hörnvik with a man fishing from it, and a woman walking a dog in the vast sandy wilderness of Guldstranden.

Helena seemed to favour solitary figures, accentuating a mood of loneliness, yet giving movement to scenes that might otherwise have been static. Some of the drawings were partially toned with watercolour, others left untouched. I moved along the row, tipping forward frame after frame. These larger ones were more sumptuous landscapes in oil, though painted in a sparing range of washed-out greens, blues and dark browns.

One small watercolour, of a sleek light-blue yacht being winched up a beach, had a magnetic charm that drew me back. I once learned – it was on a sketching course – that we read pictures from left to right, like a book. To the left of Helena's beach a girl's headscarf blows wildly in the wind as she tries to help her male companion with the winching cable. This side of the scene is a vigorous black-pencilled sketch, left unpainted apart from the bold mauve dab of her scarf, giving it a fast, impromptu feel. The vibrant ultramarine boat draws the eye strongly to the centre, but the tones all around are soft and muted, like a halo of yellowish light. Near the top right-hand corner the sky above a choppy sea carries shadowy omens that seem to reach beyond the frame – a swirling wash of black, suggestive of an imminent squall. The whole scene is one of passion and foreboding all at the same time.

'A bit ragged, don't you think?'

'No, that's the beauty!' Lost in the picture, I'd not heard her come back up. 'You've captured the wind and the movement to perfection.'

'That's nice of you. Really I don't think any of them are anything special. I enjoy painting, that's all.' Her rather clipped comment seemed to mask something painful. The stillness of the attic hung around us. In contrast to her art, the house had a static aura, as if frozen in time.

'Helena, this house, all these things: did you inherit them?'

'It's a complicated story. Pappa died in February '99. We were three children. You'd think it could be straightforward, wouldn't you? I can't believe it's over nine years ago. Completely unex-pected – he had a stroke, at fifty-three. It was a big shock, of course. And of course we miss him still.'

'I'm sorry, it was thoughtless to ask. You must . . .'

'No, it's all right, I can talk of it now. Have you seen all these?' She was picking through a jumble of sculpted elephants and other animals. Piled near the door lay bamboo rattles, thumb pianos and what looked like a handmade musical bow spanned by a single string. A rough-hewn xylophone with gourd resonators stood in the corner. Everything suggested some form of native art. 'Pappa spent time on the Ivory Coast, Madagascar, places like that. He loved to collect things – went all over Africa on different voyages. And yet he was always so happy to come home. Cecilia's theory is he travelled only to find things for the shop!'

'Cecilia?'

'My sister. So much stuff he couldn't sell. Or wouldn't – I'm not sure.' Pushed into a recess were several carved stools, a couple of coffee-tables in lustrous black wood, and two beautiful ebony statuettes of black women with elongated necks. On the other side of the attic three dust-laden grandfather clocks stood sentinel over a whole battalion of smaller timepieces ranked at their feet.

'And all those? Your father was a remarkable man.'

'Ah, clocks! They came from *his* father: Grandpa started the original clockmaker business in Valstad after the war. When Pappa came ashore for good, he got a similar job in Lindhem, 1973 fixing wrist-watches, and those big old pocket-watch things, you know? That's where he met Mamma. It's not unusual around here for people to marry someone in the next village.'

'And the antiques?'

'That was later. From the early '50s it was lots more tourists in Valstad – grandpa was branching out from clocks into everything else. Old things came in demand – it's where the money was. Eventually he couldn't manage alone, so Pappa would drive into Valstad to help. They worked together eight years. Good years, I think. Grandpa taught him so much. You could see they were happy, father and son. But it became difficult when Grandpa died. Styles were changing . . .'

'Your father took over the business?'

'The business, this old house of Grandpa's . . . Everything happened at once. And then it was Peter, all in a few months.'

'A brother?'

'He was the youngest. The only one of us born here, as it happens. Doris, my mother – she would have loved it. So much space – that was before we had all this stuff.'

'So you mean – didn't your mother . . .?'

'Sadly she died only a few months after the birth.' Helena spoke slowly and carefully, as if to control her pain. 'Quite suddenly, in fact. A brain aneurysm. She'd been walking in the woods, beyond the river – they found her some hours later. No one could do anything. November '85, same year as Grandpa. We'd hardly moved in.'

'I'm so sorry, Helena. What a sad story. She would still have been a young woman, then?'

'Thirty-eight. She was only thirty-eight. It was an awful time – for all of us. But you get through, somehow. Pappa, he was heart-broken. I don't know how he kept going. He just did.'

'I don't know how any of you did.'

'It's a long time ago. Are you ready for that coffee?'

27

Down at the kitchen table I sat watching Helena potter about. It moved me that, whatever the pain of those early years, she'd been able to talk with such calmness and candour. Snuffi padded over and lay down close by, waiting to be stroked.

'Can I ask, Helena – how old were you when your mother died?'

'I was seven. Seven and a few months.' She brought cups to the table. 'Milk?'

'You've had more than your share of sadness.'

'We had this house, of course – a big change from the apartment in Lindhem. A stable centre: I realise now how important that was. And Pappa had the business in Valstad to run. That kept him sane, in a way. He worked and worked. We were all working through the grief. But it also meant Pappa was away a lot. He'd leave each morning very early and come home late at night. He worked too hard. Always.'

'It must have been dreadful for you.'

'It was hardest for Pappa. And Cecilia – she was four years older than me. That made it worse for her. When you're seven I think you – well, you accept things. And soon forget them maybe?'

'But surely your father – if he was away such a lot, he couldn't have brought you all up single-handed, could he?'

'We had Mamma's sister here, Tant Marianne – she became Peter's nanny. She was wonderful.'

'Ah, so your baby brother – did he . . .?'

'Peter was fine. He knew only Marianne, of course – has no memory of Doris. Peter suffered the most, I suppose – and yet in another way, he didn't. We loved him and cared for him. Everyone loved Peter. It can sound strange, but I think he's coped best of all of us. Dear Marianne, she was brilliant. Cared for the whole family, all those years – till long after Pappa went, in fact.'

'And this aunt – she had no family of her own?'

'She never married, if that's what you mean. We were her family, I think.'

'Yes, of course. I can understand that.' My question was tactless. 'You were very brave.'

'I don't know if you can call it that. You can't be so aware at that age, can you? I wasn't, in any case. Only trying to make myself useful, if it was possible. As I said, we were well cared for. And loved. Really loved, you know? And we had enough money. Pappa was no great salesman, but the shop was successful for a while. Beside the antiques he had the ebony carvings and the other wood things from Kenya – they were something different, people liked them.

'Later, sadly, they seemed to lose interest, even for the African stuff. And Pappa, he wasn't so young as in the beginning – hadn't the same energy. At the end it was downhill – he must sell the Valstad shop. When he returned to Hörnvik, summer '94, it was like he made a retreat, really. Nobody wanted his stock, so he transported it all here. You think it's crowded now: you should have seen it then! Bits of it went, later, and then Cecilia . . .' Her voice trailed off.

'He brought everything here? Surely he couldn't expect to . . .?'

'Ah, that was Pappa!' She laughed. 'He had the idea to sell stuff from the house. Well, as it turned out he didn't sell more than a handful of things. Although I think he'd have made ends meet, if he'd had a little more time.'

'More time? Oh, of course.' I should have remembered: her father had died in early 1999 – barely five years after selling the shop. 'So what happened to you and your sister and brother when he died? You'd have been – what, twentyish?'

'I was almost twenty-one. We got by.' She broke off. 'I'm sorry, Guy, it's all a big sob story. I sound hopelessly screwed up.'

'You sound incredibly normal to me.'

She sighed. 'It's as if I owe it to the family to take care of things now. Can you understand that? If only I could be better organised. You've seen what a mess the place is.'

'No, don't say that. Sure, there's a lot of stuff – I wouldn't call it a mess.'

'You English – so polite!'

It was late; the last bus left at six. Helena insisted on accompanying me back to the stop, with Snuffi as bodyguard. As we left I noticed a lumberjack type of coat and a man's cap thrown over the hat-stand. Out on the riverside path she stared across to the other bank with almost an orphaned look. Now the sun had dropped behind the hills there was a coolness in the air; I offered my jacket, but she shook her head. I longed to reach out and hold her close.

'You know, Helena, I'm sure you could breathe a bit of life back into that antiques business. No, really. You've got enough to fill several shops up in the attic. If you wanted to, that is.'

She grimaced. 'I've thought about it, of course. But it's not as simple as that.'

'Well, if not the antiques, those paintings of yours, then – and all the sketches? I'm no expert, but I bet you could do well with them. They're really professional, you can see they are. Outstanding.' She seemed pleased with a little praise. 'That yacht picture, for instance.'

'Which one?'

'You know, with the winch. The blue yacht?'

'Ah. The girl with the purple headscarf.'

'All that wind and sky – I love it.'

'I'm glad.' She pushed the dark hair back from her eyes.

'Helena, what I'm saying is: please let me buy it.' Why did it feel so difficult to say? She stopped and looked at me, unsmiling.

'You don't want that.'

'It's Segelholm, isn't it. How much would you think of asking for a frame that size?'

Helena stared away, fixing her eyes on the little bridge. 'You can't want it.'

'*Can't?*' This was baffling; could it really be simple modesty on her part? 'That's what I'm saying – I do want it! Truly, it's a lovely picture.' Up to that moment I'd not thought of buying anything so substantial, but all at once I could foresee long melancholy evenings back in Bay Leaf Close, dreaming tender dreams of Lammland; the watercolour would look superb over the mantelshelf in the living-room. 'Of course, if you've a particular reason for not selling it to *me*, that's another . . .'

'It's not you, Guy.' Her smile was full of sadness. 'You're a nice person – much nicer than me, I'm sure. But I can't sell right now, that's all. Not to anybody. Can you accept that?' She read my winded look. 'I'm sorry.'

We walked on a few paces in silence. 'Well, if you feel . . . Of course I accept it. Absolutely – it's your work and no one else's.'

By the time we reached the road Helena was shivering, though still adamant she would wait; Snuffi stretched himself out, flattening the wayside flowers. We stood somewhat tongue-tied, Helena glancing alternately down at her hands and beyond the trees for the bus. It trundled into view at last and I thought she might let me kiss her on the cheek, but she turned away. As the bus gathered momentum I watched her slim figure recede; another little wave, with the patient Labrador standing alert at her side, and she was gone.

All the way back Helena's beautiful, troubled face haunted me. Listening to that account of a young family touched by tragedy, no one could have been unmoved by the simplicity and courage of her bearing. Yet the story, and the manner of telling it, left a sense of far, far more still to be told. That she should have confided so much to me felt such a privilege, it stirred the sharpest longing to hear the rest.

Astonished by the range and sensitivity of her sketches and paintings, too, I fell to wondering what she could do to promote them. *I can't sell right now.* Did that mean only the blue yacht picture, or the whole collection? And apart from her art: what about the mountains of furniture, all those African curios? The place would burst if she didn't start getting rid of some of it. In any case, repair costs and upkeep must be astronomical – even if she did have a man helping out. We'd not touched on financial matters, but it had to be to her advantage to get on with selling a few things.

It's not as simple as that. Why not? What was to stop her advertising her pictures at the Valstad tourist board, for instance, and using the house as a base to start with? Hörnvik was hardly ideal for setting up a business, but people have cars. My brief viewing hadn't begun to take in all the oil canvases, but if the watercolours were anything to go by . . .

As for the picture of the blue yacht: it existed, it held a deep appeal for me, and Helena needed to sell things. Offering to buy it that afternoon had felt like the most constructive way of helping her get started. In my naivety – on the slow bus-ride back to Segelholm to pick up the bicycle – I still believed it could only be a matter of persuading her somehow, never doubting she'd have a change of heart once she knew me a little better.

In other words whatever she'd asked me to accept, I hadn't really accepted at all.

Lying in the *stuga* that night, enthralled by Helena and everything in her amazing house at Hörnvik, my sleepless mind seemed to wander those congested spaces and passageways, wondering at all the strange treasures hidden away there.

In every limb I still ached from so much unaccustomed cycling and swimming; my emotions, meanwhile, already ached with something else.

28

Campsites and hostels abroad aren't always the most restful places. On a couple of evenings that week, despite my preoccupations elsewhere, I joined a well-mixed company by the river at Emsäde. It's easy to fall in with other people's whims on holiday – doing things none of us would ever dream of back home; besides, it could have looked offensive not to show willing. Someone had a portable CD player; I found myself reluctantly co-opted into riverside tango lessons by housewives from counties along the Göta Canal, all of whom went to evening classes and could cook a mean steak.

Festivities reached a climax on Friday night, the *brännvin* being addressed with as much dedication as the barbecued sausages. While pensive husbands drank themselves, if not quite under the table, to a much reduced elevation above it, their wives scouted the twilit riverbank for temporary substitutes. Among these smart ladies in end-of-season mood, I seemed to present as good an object as any for fond farewells.

To my extreme relief, undampened by the late-night carousing, they were set to leave en masse at eight o'clock sharp next morning, planning to cross the entire mainland in a day. I awoke with a right royal headache to hear them warbling away outside in their sing-song dialect; it would have felt antisocial not to wave them off. Seeing me at the *stuga* door, several ladies wanted to plant a valedictory kiss on my cheek, along with a smudge of evidential lipstick. Minutes later their minibus was bouncing away across the grass, three mascara'd faces smiling enigmatically through the back window.

Once up, there seemed no point in going back to bed again. Not long afterwards the warden, finding me nursing a sour coffee in the bistro area, ambled over to say there was another call at reception. As before, my first thought was of Georgina, although by this time – given that she'd already made it crystal clear what she thought of me – there was no earthly reason to suppose she'd ring back.

It was a thrilling surprise when another voice came on the line.

'It's me again. D'you fancy a little trip to Fusum?'

'Helena! What – today?'

'Yes, today.'

'What about you – haven't you got things you need to do?'

'I'm all right. The shops have open all weekend – it's enough time tomorrow. I thought you might like another day out, that's all. It's OK Guy, don't if you don't want to.'

'Of course I do.' Guilt over Georgina metamorphosed into exhilaration. 'I'd love to.'

'You've not been up the east coast, have you? We might visit that pottery on the way back – we missed it last weekend. And we could talk – you've heard all about me, I thought you could tell me about you for a change. All I've had so far is the boring stuff about Castles.'

'Thanks very much!'

'Why don't you take the bus? You can still make the nine-thirty. I'll be in the garden.'

An hour or so later I found Helena weeding the slope in front of the house.

'It's going to be hot again. Are you OK to cycle? You can borrow Ulf's.' She led me round to the yard, eyeing me side-ways. 'You're a bit shorter, but we can put the saddle down.'

'Who's Ulf?'

'My boyfriend.'

'Not that chap fixing the roof?'

'That's him. He's done a lot of work on the outhouses. Half the beams were rotten.'

The ones in the cycle-shed looked pristine. 'Good to have someone on hand.' What else could I say? It felt odd, borrowing Ulf's slimline racer. He seemed dauntingly athletic; I had to wrench the saddle well down to sit on it. 'Are you sure he won't mind?'

'He won't mind.'

I wobbled around the yard, mastering the trick of staying on. Perhaps it would be easier on the road. As we set off northwards the sun was already beating hot on our backs; it was a relief to feel a breath of air against the skin.

'We'd better not be too late back, had we? Your friend might need this.' I caught her up on the gravelled incline out of Hörnvik.

'He's not likely to today. He's at work.'

'Ah – so where does he . . .?'

'Valstad. He's a projectionist – little cinema on Älvatrappan. It's about the only one on the island that's any good. Well, you can go to *Storsalen* on Vasagatan, or *Stjärnan* – they show all the Hollywood blockbusters. Lindhem has another, but that's a horrible flea-pit.'

'He sounds pretty versatile.'

'Well, Ulf's not only strong in the arm.' She smiled at the road-side thistles. 'He practically runs that cinema – means doing a lot of other things beside working the projector. I like strong, clever men!'

'What sort of films does he put on?'

'All sorts. French ones sometimes, and Swedish, of course – Yngve Feldman, people like that. Ulf doesn't want to show just any old thing. He likes arty films.'

'Right. And what about you?'

She frowned. 'Some aren't so bad. It's not everyone's cup of tea, is it, those intellectual things?' We exchanged what felt like a look of empathy; it was hard to gauge where she might place Ulf and me on the scale of intellectuality. 'To be honest I'd rather have a straightforward love story any day, wouldn't you?' She brushed the dark hair from her eyes.

'They can be OK, I suppose. When they're not too predictable.'

'Ah, no, that's the part I like.'

'What, lingering embraces and walking into the sunset?'

'Not specially that.' The frown reappeared. 'But I like it when you know from the start everything's going to turn out right. Of course it can be lots of disasters along the way.'

'I don't see how you can know, then.'

'You just *know*, that's all! I do, anyway.'

'So he travels in from Hörnvik, does he?'

'Ulf? He's living in town at the moment. We could drop in one day, if you like. You'd like him. You're a little bit similar.' Her comment intrigued me, though I wasn't sure what to make of this supposed affinity to such a matchless all-rounder. How would he react to my making off with his bike for the day – and Helena too, come to that? She and Ulf weren't actually engaged, as far as I could gather.

Helena shaded her eyes against the light bouncing off another lake. 'Anyway, tell me about you. What do you do back in Dorset – in the evenings, for instance? I'm sure you've got all sorts of wicked secrets.'

'Me? Normal things. Pubs and so on. Wintersham's pretty dead, but you can get to Bournemouth. There's a big ice-rink now, and a dance place.'

'Great. You like dancing?'

I'd never been to the ice-rink, and only once dancing, over a year ago. 'I don't mind.'

'You've got a girlfriend?' Helena's directness was a little unnerving.

'I know a few girls, of course I do.'

'Anybody special?'

'Not really. There's a girl at work, she's not been there long. We've been out once or twice.'

'What's she like?'

'She's very nice. Keen to get on, though, career-wise.'

'And you're not?'

'I wouldn't mind earning a bit more eventually. I'm happy enough as things are at the moment.'

'What's it like at Emsäde?' Helena's breathless changes of subject were part of the excitement of being with her.

'The campsite? Buzzing, in the last twenty-four hours!' I tried to give her a flavour of the recent revelries. 'Anyway, this Ulf: so you'll introduce me sometime?'

'Sure, we can do that, next time he's free. Ulf gets the odd day off – like when he's fixing the roof – nothing regular. It's that way in the cinema business – late night shows, matinées and so on. It's high season – tourists get plenty to fill the day, then they're at a loose end in the evenings. He can be there all hours.' She glanced at her watch. 'Right now he's probably asleep. As I was saying, the projector's not the only thing he takes care of. He and Johan are supposed to share the work – that's his partner – but Johan never does a stroke, so Ulf drafts programmes, orders films, does the accounts. Even cleans the place out most times – you name it.'

The coastal road to Fusum is full of unexpected bends round grey-shingled inlets. I was growing a little less wobbly on Ulf's lightweight bike, even balancing a map on the handlebars as we went. Helena thought it would help orient me among the rivulets and chalk quarries; we stopped once to swim in another abandoned one that was now a deep, dark-blue pool.

With my pulse quickened and every muscle taut from the cold shock of the dive, I watched Helena slice through the water like a dolphin, then fling herself down panting on a cushion of moss to sun-dry her swimsuit. Even more than our disjointed, butterfly conversations, that lithe, shapely body – stretched out beside but not touching mine – made me catch my breath.

29

At first sight Fusum looks like any other Lammland waterfront with a scaweedy jetty and a few fishermen's cottages, but there is a ferry; we watched it sidle away carrying three cars on the diagonal crossing to Stenö. The tiny island lay shrouded in haze under a cloudless sky. Along the quayside black wooden shacks exuded a prickly smell of smoked herring.

Helena had kicked off her sandals. 'Do you want to swim again, Guy? I shouldn't have stopped you the other day.'

'I'm not used to all this exercise!'

'We could catch the next ferry over to Stenö. Or just do nothing?' We stood absorbing the tranquil beauty.

Cycling back was strenuous in the heat, so it was good to break off and escape into the cool pottery. Dawdling between shelves of half-glazed ceramics, I had my eye on a pale blue bowl and a pair of goblets. 'What do you think of these?'

'Are you buying them now? Could be tricky on the bike.'

Having spent a good ten minutes tying them on, much to Helena's amusement, we cycled side by side for a few kilometres.

'You're a puzzle, Helena.'

'What makes you say that?'

'You know what! Those pictures of yours.'

'Ah. Here we go again.'

'I'm serious. You know you're talented. You do all these marvellous sketches and paintings, yet when I want to buy one you say you can't sell it.'

'You're right, it's crazy. It's my way to be, that's all.' Her distinct Swedishness seemed to close in again.

'And that great big house of yours – stuffed with antiques. They must be worth a small fortune.'

'What if I like it that way?'

'Oh, come off it, Helena – what do you live on, for heaven's sake? Don't say serving coffee to tourists.'

'I'm trained as a nurse, if you want to know.'

It was depressing to think how little I knew about her. 'So what's the waitressing for? Don't they pay you enough at the hospital?'

'*Musica?* That's only a filler for the summer.'

'So you don't nurse here? Where then? On the mainland?'

'Till three years ago, yes. Uppsala, since you ask. Anaesthetics. I loved it. Uppsala was a good place for me – I was nearly seven years there. Nurses are paid well in Sweden, fortunately, so it was easy to save. What's to spend it on, in a hospital? You haven't time anyway.' The image came to me of Helena in starched uniform, bustling about with her sleeves rolled up.

'What made you leave, then, if it was that good?'

'You don't give up, do you! I had – well, a kind of breakdown.'

'Oh. I'm really sorry, Helena.' My clumsiness shamed me.

She pushed ahead up the long hill. 'It wasn't so bad. Ulf's been great.'

'You two met in Uppsala?'

'No, no, Ulf's never left the island. He's a *Lammlänning* to his fingertips. We've known each other – well, it feels like always. Family ties, you know? His father used to help Pappa with the house. The way Ulf does now, for me – funny thing, really.'

We reached the top of the incline and started free-wheeling downhill. Helena looked across, sudden distress in her eyes. 'Being in Saint Gottfrid's wasn't funny, though. It's the psychiatric hospital in Valstad. That's when we became, you know, closer.'

At the bottom of the slope we dismounted, wheeling the bikes along the grass verge. 'I was five weeks there. That was a horrible time – horrible. Can you imagine – when your world's in pieces and you feel all split? But things get better – slowly. Somehow it changed the way it was between us. Ulf, he was a lifeline. For months afterwards I was supposed to be – what do you call it?'

'Convalescent?'

'Convalescent, that's right. Ulf came often home to me in Hörnvik. We'd spend hours, talking and talking. For a long time that's all we did, believe it or not. Ulf had time. He couldn't get so much work.'

'And then he became a bit more than just someone to talk to?'

She glanced back the way we'd come. 'He became a boyfriend, yes.' Her eyes had something like a doomed look. 'Once I was home, and could start getting through the days, he'd offer to do things for the house – which was great. His father was a builder, he grew up with it. Ulf has an eye for things that need doing. Big jobs too, sometimes – the roof, and so on. I paid him for the work. And then we – continued from there. In the end he moved out to Hörnvik to be with me.' Her expression lightened. 'I didn't think he'd ever get a regular job! Before *Inblick* he was most of the time unemployed, doing only local jobs, when he felt like it. For cash.'

'*Inblick?* Hang on, I know this.' I'd seen it in a brochure, after the talk with Herr Pålsson. 'Swedish for *insight*, isn't it?'

'Well done. That's Ulf's cinema. It's a proper job there now, so of course he can't do so much on the house.'

The air had begun to cool; Helena was leading the way up yet another lengthy gradient.

'You never said your real job was nursing.'

'Well, yes, it should be.'

'Must have been such a difficult time for you. Three years ago? I imagine by now, you . . .'

'OK.' She stared ahead, as if absorbed in the pink-tinged clouds near the horizon.

'Helena, if you feel this is all just me prying, please say so. I'd hate to disturb you or break in on your privacy.' And yet she'd stopped pedalling again and was drifting to a standstill, waiting for me to draw alongside – as if she'd guessed what I would say. Having come so far, there seemed no point in hiding my honest reactions. 'You mustn't think there's any pressure on you to talk – not unless you're certain you want to. I was wondering, that's all: it isn't as if you've got endless resources, is it? Not many people have.'

She was close to tears now. 'I get by. But you're right, in the long run it's up to me to get myself back, do what I'm trained for.' She looked up at the sky, exasperated. 'At least, I think that's what I should do. Only – I keep putting it off. I'm not sure.'

'Not sure you're ready to go back?'

'Not sure I want to be a nurse for ever.' She stood brushing her fingertips across the seeding grasses at the wayside. 'Other people's lives always look so simple, don't they. How do people know what they really want? That's something they didn't teach us at my school! You're not supposed to pick those, by the way.'

My hand had found a patch of tall white daisies, their delicate petals encircling each yolklike centre. Without thinking I'd pulled one off. 'These? Why not?'

'*Prästkragar.*'

'Don't tell me. Pressed Crabs?'

'*Priests' Collars*! They're like what the priest wears – you know, in church.' She touched her throat.

I pictured Mats Carlsson in his priestly uniform. 'Dog-collars.'

'They're protected – only on Lammland. Many wild flowers are, in fact. We're rather organised about conservation here, in Sweden.' The impersonal note crept into her voice again.

'But these ones are everywhere.'

'That's because we've looked after them!'

'All sounds a bit parental to me.'

'Of course not. Common sense, that's all.' Her glance darted among the bushes. 'It should be wild strawberries here too, if we look. Them you *are* allowed to pick.' She propped her bike and crouched down in a tangle of undergrowth.

'You were saying you didn't know what to do with your life.'

'How does anybody know?' She put a tiny bright dot of straw-berry to her lips.

'It's a bit like being on a train, isn't it?'

'Is it?'

'You're on this train, hurtling towards some destination – you've got no idea where. You've been on it for ages – all your life, perhaps. Suddenly, I suppose you think: what's to stop me getting off?' I watched her rise quietly, tasting the sweet berry 'Then one day you see other trains out there. Lots of them. All rushing in different directions. A few more years pass. Then another time – it seems almost too late now – you think: maybe I could get on one of them instead. Where would it go, Helena – your other train?'

She knelt down to look for more strawberries. 'I have all these nice artistic longings, you know? Well, you've seen. The trouble is I'll never make ends meet with painting and drawing. You must be realistic, don't you? It's far too late for all that – hopeless. I need a real job.'

'But that's the whole point – it's not too late. Realistic's not the same as fatalistic, is it? If we don't believe in our dreams, we're finished. You'd have to get yourself organised, that's all – start producing pictures on a regular basis. If you meant busi-ness, that is.' She reached up and held out a miniature straw-berry to my mouth; I leaned towards her. The ripeness exploded on my tongue.

Helena stood up, lips pink with strawberry, so close I could feel her sweetened breath. 'You know, Guy, now when you're here it's as if I'm starting to think again. But – I can't explain – right at the moment it's still too early. Maybe it's a kind of artistic block?' She turned back to her bicycle.

'All right then, if that's the problem – why not start with the other things?'

'Other things?'

'You've said it yourself – all those pots and pans and kettles.

It's not as if you'll ever need them. Plus the furniture – you can hardly move, up on that landing. What are you going to do with it all if you don't sell it?'

'Chuck it in the sea, I expect.'

'That's your *Inner Child* talking.'

'My what?'

'You're a nurse, you must know – that stuff about roles? Your *Child* is the bit of you that wants to rebel against your *Inner Parent*. Defying authority: that feels good! Up to a point it's a positive force – where creative impulses come from. But it can get out of hand. In the long run it's best to realise our *Parent* might be wise about some things. Like not picking *Priests' Collars*, for instance? Eventually we have to develop a third part, our *Adult*. That's the tricky bit.' It was a pet subject of mine; I could hear how pompous it sounded.

She was quiet for a minute. 'Well, that's all very nice. What if I'm not cut out to be an antiques dealer?'

'Helena, I'm sorry. I didn't . . .'

'You and your pop psychology. You think you have all the answers, don't you? What to do with my stuff, how to straighten out my personality. Advice is so easy. It was that way in Saint Gottfrid's. Like walking a tightrope across some deep gorge – with crowds of people standing the other side, shouting *keep your balance*! It's not always so simple.'

Helena had bumped her tyres back onto the road; soon we were on the long flat coastal sweep into Hörnvik.

'Helena, please forgive me, I was . . .'

'No, Guy, it's me.' She sighed. 'I didn't mean to sound so sharp. Of course you're right, I know you are. And I need someone to say tough things. You've been really sweet – I'm glad you're here.' She smiled again, mouth and chin tearfully compressed.

Near the house we dismounted; leading the way across the bridge, Helena stopped once more. 'I've talked far too much. You don't want to hear all my problems.'

'Try me.'

'I'd talk to Ulf, only he never seems to . . .'

'Helena, forget Ulf for a minute. It's me listening to you now.'

She looked up as if in shock. 'I know it's irrational, but I can't part with anything in the house at the moment. Family things, somehow they're . . . They still feel too precious. They're my – what do you call it?'

'Inheritance?'

'Yes. Well, ours.'

'Yours and . . .?'

'Oh, it must all sound so crazy. But it's more complicated than you think. You wouldn't understand.'

'I'm trying to, Helena.'

She half-smiled. 'People talk of healing, moving on. Well, I haven't. I can't. Not yet – for all sorts of reasons. I know it's not good.' I reached out and touched her arm. 'Thank you for today, Guy. It feels – safe, with you.' For a brief second she moved close and hugged me at the waist. 'Can you be patient with me – let me feel what I'm feeling for a while? Not ask too many questions?'

'Of course. No rush.'

Whatever secrets still lay behind those sad eyes, she clearly wasn't ready to disclose them as yet. For all I knew it could take months to fathom everything that tormented her; the sand in my hourglass was fast running out.

30

'Helena – is that you? What are you doing today?'

'Well, since you've rung me at work I'd have thought that was pretty obvious.' This was the first time I'd taken the initiative to phone her; the uncompromising tone was growing familiar.

'Only I'm in Valstad – *Musica* was in the phonebook.' It was hardly an excuse for ringing in the middle of Monday morning. 'There's a nice little fish restaurant, down by the harbour – you know the one? I thought perhaps tonight, after you finish . . . Could we meet for dinner or something?'

'OK.'

'Are you sure, Helena? I wouldn't want to . . .'

'No, it's all right. In fact if you're in town . . . Maybe I could swap with Nina and get off early this afternoon.'

'Won't she mind, at short notice?'

'It'll be OK. She owes me one from last week.' A clatter of dishes sounded in the background. 'Listen, why don't I meet you there – say about two? We can call it lunch – if you can wait that long?'

Wanting to see her again had dispelled all other thoughts. Near the marina, a tangy whiff of seaweed and fish-based lunches hung in the static air; I sat on the sea wall and watched the sparkling yachts shifting in and out. Life at Emsäde had brought me close to breaking-point. Since the exodus of the Göta Canal group I'd endured a wave of rowdy twenty-something males newly arrived from Gothenburg, keen to fish among the bulrushes and brutalise everything they caught. The whole of Sunday had slid past in a meaningless blur.

A fleeting kiss dabbed my cheek from behind: with a joyful tremor I recognised the herbal fragrance. The simple *Musica* outfit, minus apron and money-pouch, set off Helena's dark-haired grace as she shaded smiling eyes. Up on the restaurant terrace we were shown to a table overlooking the forest of masts. At anchor beyond them lay the giant ferry from Vyborgshamn, sleek and white against a horizonless infinity of blue.

Lunch was a leisured affair of chilled avocado followed by a prawn salad for Helena and marinated salmon for me.

I was trying to sound calm. 'Are these caught locally, do you suppose?'

'Mm? Norwegian, probably.' She squeezed a slice of lemon on her prawns.

'You know, Helena, I'll go up the wall if I stay another night at that ghastly campsite.'

'Emsäde? I thought you liked it.'

'The place is fine. It's the people.'

'All those sexy housewives?'

'It wasn't really like that! Anyway, there's a new lot now – much worse than last week. Lads in their twenties from the mainland.'

'I'd have thought you'd have plenty in common.' She forked an innocent mouthful of salad, gazing out to sea.

'They're on some fishing trip – though it's a moot point what they're fishing for. They get tanked up every night and discuss their exploits at full volume till two in the morning. I'm shattered.'

Helena looked at me more sympathetically. 'Well, I think you've done well to hold out all this time. Are they staying long?'

'About a week, I think.'

She considered for a moment. 'Why don't you move out?'

I smiled. 'Any suggestions?'

143

'Well, it's one place you could go.'

'Don't tell me you've got some friend with a spare room.'

'I might have.'

While my curiosity accumulated she browsed the desserts. 'You could stay with Ulf.'

'Ulf? What, in Valstad? He's not likely to want me, is he? Anyway, does he have space, then?'

'Ulf lives in a little house off Värmlänska Gränden. I say "lives in" – it's empty most of the time. He sleeps there sometimes, and in theory he uses the kitchen, but that's about it. He has a funny little boxroom – you could camp there. Small, of course – better than where you are now, though, by the sound of it.'

'Are you serious?'

'You'd get a lot more privacy.'

'So – OK, say I wanted to stay there: what would Ulf think?'

'We'd have to ask him nicely, wouldn't we.' She gave a small, ambivalent smile. 'Think I might try the crème caramel. D'you want one?' The waitress took our order.

'Are you certain about this, Helena? I mean – d'you really think he'd be up for it?'

'Ulf? Can't see why not. He's always been quite isolated. A little company – could do him good.'

'Seems a bit presumptuous.'

'Not really. Anyway, it's no harm asking, is it? You can pay him some rent. Nobody minds money, do they? How much longer will you be here?'

'Wouldn't he find it a bit – funny?'

'Why? I told you, he's hardly ever there – even at night. Dozes in the projection room most of the summer. Ulf keeps very funny hours.' She raised a knowing eyebrow. 'That's the cinema for you.'

We finished our crème caramel and stepped into the dazzle of sunshine; the day was set to get hotter still. In the middle distance half a dozen water-skiers criss-crossed the outer marina with godlike assurance, the sea under them acquiring strange solidity. I had my old *Leitz* zoom camera, and managed to get Helena into one or two shots: she looked ravishing in the loose oatmeal skirt and a cotton blouse of pale magenta. Toward the horizon lay the island of Kungsö, a shimmering azure silhouette.

'Look, Helena – it's as if it's hovering above the water.'

She stood shading her eyes with slim fingers. 'Heat-haze.'

'The sea's so flat. You'd think you could walk out there.'

'It'd make a nice composition – can you see? All those boats and the harbour in front, and the lighthouse that side.' She closed one eye and held out an appraising thumb.

'Why don't you then?'

But she only smiled and turned away.

The more I thought about returning to Emsäde, the more attractive the idea of 'camping' at Ulf's became. Would it not look a little provocative, though? Besides, Maja might ring the campsite and find me gone; she might be ringing today, for that matter. Well, I couldn't stay forever. But if I left Ulf's number with Herr Wittberg, would he pass it on to her? It all felt rather precarious.

'You're quiet.'

'I'm wondering if this is a good idea.'

'What, going to Ulf? Why wouldn't it be? Don't brood so much, Guy. Anyway, you still haven't told me: when are you leaving? It's not so long now, is it?'

'Not till the middle of next week. Let's see, that's' – the horror of it hit me – 'ten days, I suppose.' Ten days, including today.

'Well, then.' Helena obviously wasn't the least bit bothered; why should she be? Perhaps staying at Ulf's wasn't such an issue: if he was OK with it, what was there to lose? At least it would get me away from the Casanovas in the *stuga* next to mine. And if Herr Wittberg let me down, I'd find some other way of contacting Maja – there had to be people still around who knew her.

'OK. Where can I get hold of him?'

'I can talk to him if you like. He could be at the house right now. In fact, why don't we go take a look?'

'What, now?'

'He might be in, he might not. You never know with Ulf. He could be having breakfast – he could be just going to bed. He's forever re-jigging the programmes.'

'I thought cinemas started the same time every night.'

'It's depend what films come his way in the post, and what audience he thinks he can attract. Come on, let's try our luck.'

We toiled back up the hill in the oppressive heat; even carrying the camera was an effort. Värmlänska Gränden runs north to south below the medieval cathedral, its black onion towers silhouetted against a perfect blue sky. From here you look west over a scatter of bright ochre rooftops sloping toward the sea. Turning downhill again onto a covered stairway, Älvatrappan, we were immediately at Ulf's door. A cat stepped into the shade and rubbed its grubby white head against our ankles. Helena had a key.

I was terrified we'd disturb Ulf in bed, catching up on some dire sleep deprivation. Tall and narrow, the house seemed to be built into the side of the rock on several levels; the internal arrangement of rooms appeared oddly upside-down. Helena led me down a tortuous spiral to the basement and pushed open a door. Ulf's bed stood eloquently unmade; in the twilit space a clutter of programmes and film reviews lay next to an alarm clock. Upstairs in the kitchen a half-eaten can of tuna gave the house a less-than-fresh odour; Helena slipped it into the fridge. I followed her up another flight to the boxroom she'd earmarked for me. Next to the low camp bed a side window opened out over a tiny rectangle of garden, with a glimpse of the covered steps that form a short cut from the cathedral to the harbour.

'Well, if he's not here, it's only one place he can be.'

'How far is it?'

'Two minutes max. Come on. He's probably clearing out last night's junk. You wouldn't believe what people leave on the floor.'

'Won't he mind us invading him at work?'

'He'll say if he does. Ulf's up-front about things like that. Why don't you leave the camera here, Guy? We can pick it up later.'

Outside, the tiled roof gave merciful shade to the worn stone steps. Halfway down we reached the side entrance of *Inblick*; next to it a startled Ingrid Bergman was gazing up at shadowy Bogart. My pulse skipped a beat as Helena's hand found mine, drawing me inside. She banged the door shut behind us, instantly eclipsing the outer world; for a few seconds we seemed to float in the hollow blackness. From our left came a curious rustling and faint intermittent *splat* noises. Rows of seats began to materialise below dimmed wall-lights. A large, bearlike head of black hair rose out of the gloom next to Helena.

'Hi.' The deep bass voice resonated. He flicked another bullet of chewing-gum into a black polythene bag; I noticed an odd farmy smell about him. Straightening up, the bulky figure towered over us both, rather less athletic than I'd imagined, one enormous hand resting on the back of a seat. The strong, silent type. Instinctively I shifted away from Helena, but she appeared unbothered.

'Guy, this is Ulf. How are things?'

'Oh, you know.' He seemed scarcely interested in either of us, keen to get on with his chores. 'The usual mess. What you two been doing?' The 'up-front' manner was not reassuring.

'Us? We've had a nice lunch, haven't we, Guy? They're water-skiing out near the marina. Fantastic weather.'

'Some people has all the luck!' His tone was a little less gruff. Helena had shuffled along the row to his side and was quite tenderly stroking his hand.

'Uffe, listen, we need to ask you something. Guy has nowhere to stay. He's got some business – something he must do on Lammland. We've – well, we had this idea. How would it be if he stayed over at the house?'

'We?' For a moment her diplomacy seemed headed for the rocks.

'Don't be that way, Uffs. You know you're never there in summer. It's only for a week.' She threw what felt like a complicit glance in my direction. 'Guy's in a fix, so I thought . . .' Ulf looked at her, then across at me. After a few seconds he seemed to soften.

'OK. Yeah, he can stay if he like.' He stroked his stubbly chin.

I rushed to soothe his feelings, whatever they might be. 'That's very good of you, Ulf. Look, if you're not happy, I can . . .'

'It's all right. Welcome.'

'Well – thanks a lot, I really appreciate . . .'

He stooped under a seat to prise off another gob of chewing-gum. Ulf didn't do gratitude.

31

'Jump in, then, Guy. Or d'you want to kiss the warden goodbye first?' Helena had that excited, rather wild look. The thought of kissing the unshaven Herr Wittberg – who, it must be said, wasn't very gruntled by my sudden departure – made me laugh out loud. Asking him to pass on Ulf's number if Maja phoned hadn't gone down too well either. As I threw the hastily packed rucksack into Helena's car, the sweetness of deliverance from Emsäde mingled with a sense of embarking on a chancy venture from which there was no turning back.

Beyond the coastline to our right the mainland ferry glided towards a horizon tinged red by the sun's dwindling disc.

'Would you like me to drive for a bit?'

'Guy, I like driving. Besides, you're not used to the car; it'll be dark soon.' Helena's concentration – and the glasses, which I'd not seen before – gave her an older, more assertive air. She occupied her tanklike Volvo with an army commander's authority.

'You'd normally be off home by now, wouldn't you? I feel bad – taking up half your day.'

'It's no problem. Once Ulf said yes, we'd have been silly not to strike while the iron was hot. As it happens I promised Nina to help lock up tonight. That gives me' – she glanced at her watch – 'about four more hours to kill. Anyway, don't want you vagabonding round the island without an escort, do we.'

'I can look after myself.'

'Ah. Well I can tip you out in the harbour if you'd prefer?'

*

I can't remember the exact sequence of events when we got back to the house, but that evening changed everything. We organised the boxroom and tried to tidy up downstairs; daylight was all but gone by the time we'd finished. It seemed ages since the prawns and marinated salmon. Helena made herself at home in Ulf's kitchen, first throwing out the half-eaten tuna which smelled even worse than before. She'd found a tin of ham in the cupboard and sent me off to locate a tin-opener. We sat quietly at the kitchen table, chatting over a cold supper. By the light of a single candle, I shared out a bottle of beer between the two new ceramic goblets, keener on catching the mood of the moment than on keeping them as gifts.

Whatever we talked about, it was nothing too deep – antiques again, selling houses, water-skiing; we didn't revisit any of the sensitive matters Helena had aired on our cycle ride. She sat, chin in hand, with all the simplicity of a little girl. As darkness gathered I think we both felt a sense of oneness and peace. In the candlelight her profile was relaxed and serene: she looked beautiful. Eventually – it was well after dark – she said she'd better get back to *Musica*.

At the door she seemed to hesitate, turning as if to say something else. Then she lifted her face, half-smiled and kissed me thoughtfully on the mouth. It was over in a moment, but as she looked up with pleading eyes, I felt a new dimension to her presence, and to myself.

32

Lying awake that night, my thoughts disintegrated into chaos. The kiss had seemed to be Helena's initiative, but in all honesty I'm not even sure of that: neither of us chose to make it happen, exactly – it just happened. Yet it felt like utter recklessness, on the very day of moving into Ulf's room, even to contemplate some kind of involvement with her.

Was that what I was contemplating? The fact was I'd be leaving the country in little over a week. And what of Georgina? I'd not even told Helena so much as her name – nor vice versa: what kind of sense did that make? In their different ways they were both of them lovely, irresistibly lovely women. Up until that moment the idea of being able to feel love for more than one woman at the same time had always seemed madness to me. Besides, all this was more than likely a complete misreading of Helena. Was I not still hopelessly ignorant of how things were done *here in Sweden*? National differences in body language, and so on – these are notorious quicksands of ambiguity. Perhaps the kiss was Helena's way of showing simple affection – showing *solidarity*? Why should it be anything more dramatic than that?

And yet, tossing and turning on the dreadful camp bed (a big step down from Emsäde, as it turned out), I could think only of Helena's loveliness, of that heart-stopping kiss. There was no point in telling myself this journey to Sweden was for a particular purpose, from which it was folly to get distracted: since Maja's last phone call, Edward and his elusive relatives had already slipped to the periphery of my attentions.

I must have drifted into a doze at last. In erratic dreams Helena was untying a rowing boat, urging me to take the oars. For some reason she wouldn't get in. Instead she calmly pedalled her bike out to sea alongside me. I was terrified of knocking her off it with a careless stroke.

When dawn came it was a relief to throw aside the twisted bedclothes and take a shower. There was no sign of Ulf: he must have decided to sleep over in the projection room. In the following days it became clear he would do this more often than not. I pictured him pottering about with lenses and reels of film in the semi-darkness. There was something shadowy about Ulf – a sense of things left unsaid. The thought of him walking in on us the night before, as could so easily have happened, made me break out in a sweat.

He and I hadn't begun to discuss practical arrangements. That morning I could pad around his kitchen before sunrise as if I owned the place, rooting out yoghurt and flakes for a solitary breakfast; it would be only fair to replace the ham and other supplies as soon as the shops opened. The footfall of early tradesmen passing up and down on the covered steps outside gave me anchorage in some kind of human world, albeit a chaotic one.

My first instinct was to phone Helena – we had to meet and have a proper talk. Tuesday was one of her days off. It would have felt wrong to try ringing her before nine; then, having eaten and tidied up, I thought better of it. Might she ring me? Waiting would be the stronger thing to do. Ulf's phone lay guarded by spiders in a dark corner, obstinately silent; did it even work? I made coffee, and around midday ate the remains of the ham, not daring to go out. I was just washing a plate when the phone rang at last.

'Oh hello, Guy. Is Ulf in? I'm – phoning from home.' Her tone was perfectly level and sensible, almost as if surprised to find me there. She wanted to talk to Ulf. Why else would she ring his house?

'Helena! He's still at *Inblick*, I think. Did you want him? How are you?' I tried to swallow the storm of emotions in my throat.

'All right, I think. No, it doesn't matter now. Are *you* all right? Guy, I can't cope with this. Sorry, this is . . . I don't know what came over me last night.'

'Helena, I love what came over you!' She gave a quick, fractured laugh; it was audible in her voice that she'd been crying.

'Let's not be – unwise, Guy. You must understand. I – I don't know where I am with you. Or Ulf, or anybody, really. It's all – a muddle.' Her voice grew fainter. Had she really meant to address all this to Ulf rather than me?

'Helena . . .'

'Guy, we can't go on like this, it's . . . It's not right.'

'What's not right? What do you mean, *right?*' *Rightness* was risky ground, to be steered clear of. 'We've got to talk, Helena. Let's meet up, we . . .'

'You've been really sweet, Guy, but this is crazy, you know it is. You've got your life back in England, you'll be off again by next . . . Anyway, I'm . . . We've got to stop this right now. For one thing I can't do it to Ulf, he's . . .'

'Do what? Listen, Helena, let me come over. What about this afternoon? I haven't that many days left.' Did it disturb her even half as much as it did me?

'No, Guy, that's not possible . . .' A curious, formal note kept creeping in, as if she were trying to remember a script learnt by heart.

'Helena, I've got to see you. *Please.* Or shall we meet somewhere in town?'

'No! No, nowhere else, it's impossible, we . . .'

'You keep saying what's impossible and what's not right, but whatever happens we need to *decide* about things, don't we? It's what grown-ups would do.' This made her laugh, briefly and painfully. When she laughed I knew we were communicating.

Panic drove my thoughts now, desperate to head off absolute closure. 'Tomorrow's Wednesday. You're at *Musica*, aren't you? Meet me after work. I know, why don't we meet at the cathedral? Please, Helena. Do it for me. Just this once.' Pleading felt like a new, terrifying language. There was a long pause. 'Helena, what happened last night . . .'

'Don't, Guy, please. I can't – I don't know.' Then – sensing my anguish, perhaps – she almost whispered: 'It was a lovely kiss. I – I really like you, Guy, but let's not . . .' At the end of her endurance, she added: 'I – need to think. Don't call me.'

'Helena, just a minute, we can . . .'

'I'll see you, Guy.' She rang off.

For the next hour I waited by the phone in case she should call back. Might she think again about meeting at the cathedral? She hadn't exactly refused. Then the silence and the separation drove me out. All I could do was walk round and round inside the perimeter of the city wall, through the sweltering afternoon, caught in an endless circle of doubt and longing.

Helena had told Ulf I had 'business' on Lammland: well, that was true enough. Staying in Valstad meant I was even rather well placed for it; there had to be a way of getting information to Sofi without putting pressure on her. Yet the events of the last twenty-four hours had blotted out all thoughts of the Chandler estate. I could only visualise Helena in those narrow passages at Hörnvik – perhaps wandering into that childhood bedroom right now, subsiding on the patchwork counterpane, touching the rag doll . . .

Ulf was having supper when I got back. It was a shock to find him in, and apparently rather pleased to see me.

'You want soup?' Along with the Swedish accent his English carried an inclusive Hollywood twang. He waved at a saucepan that had boiled over, plugging his mouth with a hunk of bread. Through it he mumbled: 'What you been doing today?'

'Just – walking around. It's a nice town.' I sat and poured a little soup.

'Bread?' He looked straight at me, pushing the loaf and the knife across the table.

'I'm not very hungry. It was hot out there.'

'Well, yeah, I know. Be a tourist, it's tough.' The sardonic tone reminded me of Bo-Göran Svensson. Did he already suspect something? 'You maybe must do some different things. You feel for a film one day? We're rerun *Casablanca* this week. Classic black-and-white. A crowd-puller – it's why we choose it, of course. But a masterpiece, in that category. Did you seen it?'

'A long time ago. Forgotten most of it.'

'OK, so – why not? We start two o'clock, weekdays on afternoon. It be great. We must take paid, I'm sorry, but you can get student rate if you want, I'm happy for it . . .' The bass voice gave him an easy authority. He prattled on about films and film stars and the trials of life at *Inblick*. 'We do our best for beat off the big guys.'

'Big guys?'

'*Stjärnan*, most times. It's mean *star*. Near of the harbour – central location, two wide screens. All new movies, they're get first refusal. *Hotel Hotline* runs tomorrow night – you know it, the new Gwyneth Palmer blockbuster? So we're think we try put on thomething classy. You can bank on Bogie – a little magnetism? And of course it's Ingrid Bergman. She's yust perfect. I think people are still a little bit proud of her, here in Sweden! At *Inblick* we can't fight the big cinemas, but we like if we can do matinées on the summer. Catch a few tourists, middle afternoon, before *Stjärnan* open – it's work quite good for us. If we can start pull in regular audiences – small but *discriminate* – you say like this?' Ulf pushed stale bread into the shrinking puddle of soup. His large face exuded satiety and something like artistic zeal.

'We?'

'Johan and me. Johan, he's – kind of a assistant. It's true he don't do a lot of assisting. I think he don't like the cinema too much! Well, I maybe don't pay him good enough.' He grinned. 'You can't blame him for it, can you?'

'There must be more to this cinema business than meets the eye.' My thoughts filled only with Helena, what he said was making little impression. They were showing *Casablanca* – that much I'd gathered. As things stood I might as well live dangerously. 'OK, I could drop by one day, perhaps.' My horror at deceiving him over Helena – if that's what I was doing – now coexisted with the absolute necessity of going through with it.

Around ten Ulf trekked off to work again, leaving me to survive a second night on the atrocious mattress. My body would not lie still. It seemed unimaginable that any order could return to my life ever again. I was plankton on the surface of the sea, tossed endlessly by the currents.

33

Soon after dawn I was peering through the tiny kitchen window at the painful molten orb of the sun rising, as on that first day, over a dark sea to warm the city walls. Helena would be in Valstad this morning: I had to see her. It crossed my mind to ring the café, but what was the point of another phone call? I thought of going straight over there for nine and confronting her – but to say what, exactly? In any case, it would be impossible to talk when she was at work. No, better to show a little patience. I'd will the day away till evening, praying she'd be at the cathedral.

The kitchen cupboard was virtually bare. I scratched together a few remnants of breakfast cereal and, having run out of milk, made do with orange juice. By seven I'd cleaned up and written a shopping list. It was bad enough to be fooling Ulf while living in his house; replenishing his food stocks was the least I could do.

Ulf never reappeared that day. Fixated on seeing Helena, I mooned along the dusty pavements and sat on the sea wall at that same spot, tossing stones into the sighing waves, feeding a packet of biscuits to the gulls. Every hour or so the empty house on Älvatrappan would draw me back to hover near the phone, tormented to think Helena might ring and find nobody in, or get Ulf answering.

The afternoon crawled by. Next to the camp bed Edward's harmonica lay forlorn in its box where I'd dropped it two days earlier: music-making, in my present state of mind, was unthinkable. The shadows were lengthening as I crept out again; it was a two- or three-minute walk to the cathedral. A clergyman in black robes emerged to find me pacing up and down.

'Did you want go in?' He rattled a heavy ring of iron keys, tugging the vast doors shut before shuffling off down the hill. Five sonorous clangs resounded from the great clock. If Helena wasn't here by 5.15, it had to mean she wouldn't be coming; 5.30 chimed, then 5.45. There was nothing for it but to go back and hope she'd ring. *Casablanca* had gone clean out of my head; so had the shopping.

The third night in Ulf's boxroom was no less turbulent than the first two. Sleep must have brought brief respite during the small hours, though, because I never heard him come in. It was still dark when sounds from the kitchen woke me; Ulf was sloping around in search of breakfast from the depleted fridge. Shortly after daybreak he came up and squatted by the bed, suggesting I might like to tag along later and lend a hand with the projector. In other circumstances this would have appealed to me, but I made an excuse. The worst of it was he still seemed genuinely glad to have me around; it felt horrible to be waiting for him to go out so I could ring Helena behind his back, on his own phone.

'Hello?' The sound of her voice made my stomach turn over.

'I know you said not to ring you, but . . .'

'What time is it?'

'Just after eight. Were you asleep? Helena, this is terrible – I know it's none of my business what you do with your life, but can't we at least . . .?'

'Give me a minute, Guy, the dog's scratching to come in.' A strangulated yelp was followed by a clatter of claws on wooden boards. '*Nej,* Snuffi.' Her voice sounded muffled; I pressed the receiver to my ear. 'He's after his pig's ears. If only humans were so easy to please . . .' Despite everything there was still a playfulness in her voice.

'Well, I've made a pig's ear of being your friend, that's for sure.'

'Don't say that, Guy. You've been really nice to me, and I'm grateful.'

'*Grateful?* Don't be daft, Helena. I know how difficult this is for you, and of course it's your day off again, but . . . When you didn't turn up yesterday, I . . . Are you free this morning?'

'We've been through this, Guy.'

'Helena, *please* '

'Besides, everyone knows me in Valstad   somebody's bound to see us somewhere, and talk to somebody. Hörnvik's even worse. It's all right for you, you don't live on an island.'

'Yes I do.'

She laughed. 'Britain doesn't count.'

'Thanks a lot.' The tension was released again. 'All right, then, why don't we try somewhere else? What about Segelholm? I can get the eight-thirty. That gives me – what, twenty minutes?' Ulf's house was beginning to feel like the 'scene of the crime'; Segelholm would be neutral territory.

'Guy, we can't possibly, this whole thing's crazy, I've . . .'

'Helena, what's happened has happened.' I struggled to seem calm. 'We can't just break it off without . . .' My sentence trailed away. It was clear to both of us we could perfectly well break it off without anything else happening ever. There was an agonising pause.

'It's so risky, Guy. What if someone . . .?'

'Right, then. See you at the beach. Same spot? Bye.' This time it was me ringing off before she could say no.

34

The enervating heat of summer was on us again like a great blanket, even at that hour. Just catching the bus was exhausting – or was it the effort of persuading Helena? Bullying, to be more exact. What right had I to dictate how she spent her day?

Trees and flowers dawdled past. At the open window I panted for oxygen in the tepid breeze. Would it be as hot as this back in Dorset? There was sweet, long-suffering George slaving away, not least on my behalf – answering mail, putting in a good word for me with the boss, even dropping by at the flat later to feed Columbus – while I was off on my travels, having a nice lazy summer holiday! There might be some justice in chasing up an inheritance (though extending statutory leave was questionable); but making a move on another woman? Living in her boyfriend's house, meeting her behind his back? Secret rendezvous on sultry beaches – what did all that make me?

Some while later – delusional or not – a more soothing view of things began to formulate itself. This whole adventure with Helena had led me to a lot of ridiculous conclusions: she was, after all, simply a beautiful woman with whom I'd discovered a special, uncomplicated rapport – something more like a brother-sister understanding. These things happen. Could it be that, as an only child, a sister figure like this was something I'd missed – possibly always longed for? It was unique, yes, and wonderful – of course it was – but that didn't excuse the abandonment of all reason, nor the emotional storms of the past few days. All that was pure indulgence: I'd wallowed in imagined feelings, blown everything out of proportion, seen hidden depths that weren't there. It was absurd to think this could turn into some kind of love affair.

Helena was good for me, that was all – and with a bit of effort I could be a genuine force for good in return, perhaps guide her towards a more objective, outsider's perspective on life, her talents, her career. Of course there was no denying the physical attraction, but that was separate from the generous flow of sympathy, of mutual support. It was natural, wholesome – probably a special Swedish thing, too. Was it possible a little Scandinavian detachment and freedom of spirit really had started to rub off on me? As the bus crawled past Emsäde, I glowed with inward composure and humanity.

The moment the beach swung into view I spotted her. Standing in the sun in her sky-blue bikini, the glittering sea at her back, she waved once as I stepped onto the shingle. Detachment evaporated: Helena's loveliness robbed me of breath.

It took a second to realise she was with someone; in the shaded doorway of the boathouse a young lad was sorting morosely through a stack of oars.

'Guy, have you got any money?' Her voice, spontaneous and natural, stirred me like music. 'I thought we could have a boat. Trust me to forget my purse at home! This is Anders, by the way.'

'A *boat*? Don't you want to go for a swim – cool down a bit?'

'We can do that too. Anders needs a small deposit, that's all. We can pay the rest tomorrow, can't we, Anders?'

I proffered a few screwed-up banknotes; he stuffed them uncounted in his pocket, flung a couple of oars into one of the rowing-boats and started manhandling it across the stones with impressive muscles.

We followed him down to the water, the power of the sun on our backs. I stripped off my shirt; perhaps, in shorts, there was a chance of getting a real tan. As we splashed off into the shallows

Helena pointed at a gap in the offshore rocks, passing me the oars to manoeuvre us through to open sea. It was utterly calm, a slight cross-breeze cooling our skin. Helena's was glowing; I ached in every fibre to touch her.

Veering northwards into deeper regions of blue, neither of us spoke. In the baking heat Helena had kicked off her sandals and was sprawled on her front, gazing over the side at the becalmed water, her tanned legs gloriously flung out along the scorched boards. The water lapped against the prow like a friendly cat; it would have been blissful to stretch out next to her, yet – uncertain of her mood – I held back. Not used to rowing, it was a relief to let the oars drift a while, resting my arms along the hot rim of the boat. We followed the curve of the beach toward the forested peninsula; lazy ripples moistened the white fringes of sand, tufts of sea-grass seeking a fragile foothold on rocks and shingle. Helena was running her eye quite intently along the coastline.

'What is it, Helena?'

'Nothing.' Was she worried about being seen, even here? The impetus we might have gained in coming to Segelholm seemed to be ebbing away already.

I picked up the oars again. 'What's wrong? We're not com-municating, are we.' The coastline inched past; we were nearing the headland.

'We'll talk another time, Guy, I promise. This isn't the moment, that's all.' She sighed, eyes shielded, staring out at the almost motionless water. The curve of her lips, so close, half-sad, held me mesmerised for some minutes. Finally the tension fell from me, and I abandoned all caution.

'Helena, I think I'm falling in love with you.' She met my gaze now, the corners of her mouth turned wryly down.

'That's your *Inner Child* talking.' The tip of her tongue feath-ered 'that' and disappeared. Even in reproach her eyes were full of compassion.

This time I didn't try to stop myself, leaning forward to kiss her. She looked at me once with those appealing, resigned eyes, and drew me close.

That timeless afternoon hovers still in my memory. A wondrous vista of possibilities seemed to tantalise me, with Helena at their centre; yet in reality we'd clarified nothing. The elation of physical closeness seemed to bring me no nearer to reading her true feelings, nor to penetrating the dark cloud that overshadowed her personal life.

Turning back at last, the going grew noticeably harder. The breeze had picked up a little; Helena was shivering. Across the western sky another spectacular sunset would soon be unfolding. By the time we reached the boathouse and wedged the keel into the sand, Anders had long gone, leaving us to haul the boat inside.

Helena pulled on a T-shirt. 'Do you want a lift back?'

'I don't think that'd be wise, do you?'

'Ah – so now *you're* the wise one.'

'One of us has to be. If Ulf's in it'll look a bit odd, surely?'

She grimaced, glancing at her watch. 'You'll have an hour's wait for the bus – you've just missed one.' But miraculously, at that moment, it flew into view round the bend of the road. 'Hey, you're in luck – you'll have to run, Guy.'

'Helena, I'll call you. Are you OK to drive home?'

'Run!'

As the evening sky grew darker, my mood darkened with it; the chances of unlocking Helena's private sorrow seemed as remote as ever. Sooner or later, too, Ulf would find out we'd been meeting up. Was there any way we could stop that happening before I left the island?

At that point my mind froze. Leaving the island was the last thing I could bear to contemplate.

35

'Guy? It's Friday – you know I'm at *Musica* all day.'

'I had to ring you.'

'I'm leaving right now.'

'We need to . . .'

'You must think I'm crazy. Well, I probably am.'

'Of course not. We've got to talk, that's all.'

'It'll have to be after work. Could you meet me there?'

'I thought you didn't want anyone seeing us.'

'Can't be helped now, can it.'

'So you've decided to live dangerously too?'

'Isn't that what grown-ups would do?' It was extraordinary having her quote this back at me; I pictured that rueful, heart-breaking smile of hers. 'I've got to go, Guy.'

'See you later. I miss you, Helena.' Just saying the words made my whole body tingle.

The moment I put down the phone, it hit me like a blow to the skull: five days left in Sweden! Stephen had entrusted me with tracing Edward's surviving offspring: somehow I'd got to check the torrent of emotion sweeping me along, finish what I'd come for.

Sofi had been fourteen in that Christmas *Lucia* picture; could she have reappeared in the newspapers more recently? A much larger library stood less than ten minutes down the hill from Ulf's place. Crossing the entrance hall I stepped into a windowless alcove full of humming computers; in contrast to Lindhem, no one here rushed to assist me, but once loaded the identical list of press articles scrolled down the screen.

My initial search simply confirmed her birth in Valstad, 1986; a second hit found her in 2005 at a school-leavers' ceremony, *Studenten* – an old tradition to mark the passing of A Levels, or the Swedish equivalent. Sixth-formers, including girls, dress up in rather fetching sailors' caps; a large photograph had them all looking excited and happy. Remembering Sofi's long blonde hair and finely chiselled features from the earlier cutting, I picked her out straight away in her jaunty white cap with the blue and yellow emblem.

A lady next to me kindly translated the text underneath: guests were invited to the evening celebrations – not unlike what the English used to call a 'coming-out' party. This was the year of Sofi's nineteenth birthday, just weeks before she left the island (in August, according to Maja). Had she invited a partner that evening? Finding a likely lad for her to have run away with could be a promising lead . . .

The next page included an informal group shot: there was Sofi, glamorous in a sequinned black evening dress this time. Next to her stood a tall, slim lad with fair, short-cropped hair, perhaps a year or two older, with a shadow of incipient beard. Wasn't his head bent significantly toward hers? No guest list was given, but I thanked my helpful neighbour and printed out the whole article with the picture. It felt like progress of a sort.

It had gone one o'clock by the time I re-emerged from virtual reality. Back in the entrance hall, thinking to kill another half-hour, I took my coffee across to a vast window overlooking the botanical gardens and sat brooding. Outside, a grey squirrel darted Disneylike down a pine-trunk and up another. The sunshine of recent days was giving way to heavy skies and drizzle; with a grim afternoon in prospect, my thoughts turned to *Inblick* and Ulf's matinée. Perhaps making the effort might placate him a little; in any case I wasn't likely to find a better place to while away the empty hours till Helena finished work.

*

Ulf's hope of attracting a *discriminate* audience – small or otherwise – appeared optimistic, at least as far as the daytime showing went: stumbling to the middle of the dimly lit auditorium and sinking into soft velvet, it didn't look as if he had an audience at all. As my eyes adjusted to the dark, though, a few shadowy heads began to emerge here and there. The place had a comforting intimacy despite the rows of vacant seats. A balding pianist began coaxing snippets of Chopin from a battered-looking baby grand, squashed in below the central dais; I recalled Herr Pålsson's account of its history.

Ulf was nowhere in sight – busy behind the projector, no doubt. A squeaky curtain drew back to reveal the modest screen. After a few stills of local shops and hotels (Ulf had aired his views to me on the more brash commercials), the pianist slunk away and we were straight into the familiar theme-tune and titles of *Casablanca.*

In the safety of the dark cinema, caught up as so often before in that haunting story, I was ready to be swept away on waves of ill-defined emotion. The doomed love affair between Humphrey Bogart and Ingrid Bergman never fails to stir me; suspended in the comfortable embrace of plush upholstery, I could torment and indulge myself with melancholy reveries.

It was so comfortable, in fact, that – drained after so many wakeful nights – I must have slept through most of the second half: we seemed to be back at Casablanca airport in no time. I came round to find Bogie still drawling away in those reedy, weather-beaten tones, while the lovely Ingrid braces herself to follow a noble destiny, with her consummate sense of drama and that perfect, not-quite-tearful beauty. *A kiss is still a kiss* . . . No matter how familiar these trancelike scenes, it always takes me some minutes to come out of them.

Once the final credits began to roll, I slipped along the row to the middle looking for an exit, with nothing whatever in mind beyond getting straight to *Musica.* As on numerous past occasions, it was a little bewildering to discover the place had already emptied of its scant audience. Why do people shun endings? Reaching the last seat and turning away from the rolling titles on screen, I was about to mount the steps when a hefty figure started walking down towards me, silhouetted from behind by the dazzle of the whirring projector. Unable to see a face, it baffled me when he stopped on the step directly above mine, blocking the way.

'You've came, then. You got a bloody nerve.' My freshly awakened brain lurched to identify him: Ulf speaks very passable English but with a rather hissing, Sven-Göran Eriksson style of accent that can sound a shade comical at times. It was as if he'd rehearsed this phrase with some care, but the import of his words seemed to glide literally over my head; too sluggish to pick up on their combative edge, I tried to respond politely to what sounded like the opening line of a joke.

'Oh hi, Ulf. Sorry, didn't recognise you. How's it going?'

'Don't *sorry how's it going* with me.' His voice was pre-cooled, dangerous.

'What?'

'You *bastard*. You are a *shit*.'

'Look, Ulf, what is this?'

'*What is this?*' he mimicked sadistically. 'I'll say you what *this* is.'

I know he put out his big fleshy hand and shoved me hard in the chest. The rest is pretty much a blur. It's not likely he had any actual intention of harming me. Everything was shifting. I remember trying to take a step back and finding only air. There was a sharp jolt to my face, a flash behind the eyes, and blackness.

36

'Hallo? Hör du mej? Vad heter du?'

I opened one eye a crack against the glaring daylight and studied the slim, fair-skinned nose of a woman in her mid-twenties, the blonde hair sleeked back under a surgical cap. My Swedish didn't stretch beyond half a dozen words, but everybody picks up *Vad heter du*.

'Chandler. Guy.' My throat felt sore; I craned my neck to one side, trying to work out where I was, only to be halted by a blinding headache.

'So which one is it?'

'I'm sorry?' The whole room was spinning; it was impossible to keep her still.

'Well, you can be Mr Chandler, or we can skip straight to Guy. I'm Nurse Susanna. Here in Sweden it's normal we use first names.'

Of course – still *here in Sweden*. 'Guy, then. Guy's fine.' There was something wrong with my jaw; my voice sounded funny because my mouth wouldn't open properly.

'OK. Do you know what day is it, Guy?'

'What? What's going on? What are you doing here?' I tried to lift a hand and found it shackled to a drip.

Nurse Susanna took the confusion in her stride. 'Well, Guy, put it this way: I work here and you've been here since Friday.' She gave a split-second smile to show she was on my side really.

'You mean this isn't Friday?'

'Sunday. A few minutes after seven am.' Susanna was used to dealing with people as dim as me. 'You've had a little knock on the head. You've been unconscious a couple of days but you're going to be OK.' I tried to feel pleased. A strand of silken hair brushed my cheek as she leaned across to smooth the sheets. 'But it's good you're awake now. We've made a scan. Now when you're awake I expect the doctor will come soon past again.' She administered another minimal smile.

'You're saying I've been out cold since Friday? That's not possible.' My tethered hand announced an acute itch. 'Can you get this thing off me? I've got to go somewhere.'

'You're not go anywhere right now, Guy,' she countered sweetly. 'We bring all what you need. Number One or Number Two?'

'What is this? I'm not . . .'

'Don't worry over the drip, it's for your fluids. Have you pain? We can give you something.' She bustled off to get a urine bottle. A cautious shift inside the strait-jacket of crisp white sheets brought several old men in neighbouring beds into view, labouring to clear their throats and spitting into plastic pots. One of them waved. This wasn't encouraging.

Having lost the best part of a day and two nights drifting, it seems, between coma and deep sleep, not much would remain in my memory of the next forty-eight hours either. The *little knock on the head* had been a lot more substantial than I realised; it also set off a series of recurrent dreams, spiked, so I'm told, by the morphine – mostly about Georgina and Arctic Mints. We seemed to spend half a lifetime walking around inside one of them, brightly lit – like that Austrian glacier that's been dug out for tourists, where you go right inside and it's like an ice palace.

I do remember being wheeled to a different floor and having my chest squashed against a photographic plate: apparently I'd caught an infection, which can happen when they intubate you during a coma. My brain, meanwhile, had given up on any world view other than the horizontal, sending out distress signals if I got even the slightest ambitions to verticality. On the return journey from the X-ray department, bits of the recent past did start coming back: flashing lights, a bumpy ride, and the tuneless *nar-nar nar-nar* of the ambulance. Before that, nothing at all.

The white strait-jacket beckoned: my one desire was to go back to sleep. Helena was expecting me at Casablanca airport on Wednesday, but Georgina was still here; in fact she was on top of me, paralysing all movement. We weren't inside the glacier any more. She was feeding me Arctics out of a Castles filing cabinet. It was no use trying to spit them out: she kept poking them in again. She knew I had to be at the airport by four thirty but she wasn't going to help.

Down the middle of the ward Edward's relatives were lining up to see me. Aunt Tilly stood between the beds, waving *Dog-collars* from the roadside, plaited in grasses and flowers; near the back Ben and Dad waited, cracking jokes. They were all queueing for my funeral: it seemed so rude to keep them waiting. There had to be a way of getting a clean shirt on under the bedclothes – it wouldn't do to be seen in the coffin without one. I was dying to see Sofi, but she hadn't arrived yet. Would she be too late?

*　　*　　*

'Are you awake, Guy?' Helena was putting white and yellow flowers in a vase by the bed. What a lovely thing it is to be a man and get daisies from a woman! It had never happened to me before; gratitude made me weep.

'*Dog-collars?* I thought you weren't supposed to pick those.' I was still talking through gritted teeth, but – unaware of the morphine keeping me on a high – it didn't bother me.

'Maybe I'm not quite such a good girl as you thought.' She had that mischievous twinkle in her eye. 'Anyway, I told you, not *Dog-collars,* they're *Priests' Collars.'*

'Same difference.'

'I thought you wanted to know the proper names of things.'

'Helena, I've got to get out of here. There's nothing wrong with me.' Right on cue I was contradicted by a fresh coughing fit.

'Steady on, Guy. That's not what the doctor seems to think, is it? You've had a bad crack on the head. At *Inblick*. Don't you remember?' She stretched across to kiss a little patch of unbandaged cheek. 'Two cracks, actually. You must have knocked yourself right out. D'you usually do that kind of thing in cinemas?'

'P'raps I should go more often.'

'You're concussed, so you're bound to feel a little bit emotional. You can't be moved yet, but it's not too serious. A few more days, that's all.'

'*Days?*'

'They've done another check on your lungs. They're clearing up fine. The doctor thought at first you might have a hairline crack to your jaw, but it's just very bad bruising. I can tell you, you don't look quite your normal handsome self!' I trawled up the other, untethered hand from inside the covers. 'No, don't, Guy. The bandage is for the gash near your eye. Should come off in a day or two.'

'Helena, I can't stand much more of this. They've given me nothing to eat since I got here – apart from some mashed-up vegie stuff. I could disappear any minute.'

'I don't think so, Guy. Look on the bright side: at least you won't have any permanent scars. *Casablanca* – can you remember that?'

'*Here's looking at you, kid.*' Perhaps my mind hadn't gone altogether. I was looking straight into her eyes at those soft brown speckles. She seemed calm but excited, smiling at me and squeezing my fingers. It was such a lovely, intimate moment, it would have been a pity to sour things by telling her Ulf had pushed me. Humphrey Bogart winked; he'd never tell anybody.

When I woke up again Helena was gone. Nurses were flitting about serving breakfast. What ever happened to supper? Not that it made any difference: I could ogle the fresh croissants and cheeses

171

all I liked: still unable to open my jaw beyond a few millimetres, the only thing coming my way was a mouthful of puréed fruit.

'Now, Guy: what day is it?' Susanna settled herself with her clipboard to ask more silly questions. My brain cells didn't want to talk to each other; 'As Time Goes By' tinkled in the background. She said Helena had come again the previous evening and found me asleep. I started to say she couldn't have, because we'd just met at Rick's in downtown Casablanca, but Susanna had already gone.

It must have been late on Thursday afternoon when they finally unveiled my face and gave me something solid to eat. It still hurt too much to chew, but it was comforting to cram in narrow bits of lemon cake, washed down with milky coffee. They tasted fantastic after all that reconstituted cabbage, or whatever it was.

By that point, levered daily into a bedside chair and back to bed again, I'd already started to take more interest in things; my cough was easing and the headache had dulled to an irksome background throb. The ache was also my undisclosed secret about Ulf. Who would ever believe he'd pushed me? I couldn't think Ulf was likely to admit it himself, so in the end it would be my word against his.

Ulf was a different kind of animal from me in almost every conceivable way. Films were about the only thing we had in common – that and, of course, Helena. I was sure his reaction at *Inblick* must have been sparked by discovering we were going out together, but couldn't think how or when he could possibly have found out about us. It made little difference anyway: no doubt as far as he was concerned, anyone interested in Helena spelled trouble. For me the incident had cast him in a new light. I've said *Inblick* means insight: if nothing else, it had given me some into male Swedish aggression.

37

Another night came and went.

'Good-day, Guy. Arm please.'

'Susanna, what day is it?'

'You tell me.'

'*I* don't know, for chrissake. Why would I be asking?'

She flicked her syringe, waiting for me to offer the appropriate biceps. 'Don't be that way, Guy, it don't suit you.'

'You mean it don't suit *you.*'

'Friday. You've missed breakfast.'

'What? What time is it? I've got to go.' I lowered a foot to the cold lino.

'Now that's enough, you're not go anywhere today.' She strode manfully round the bed to poke it back.

I'd registered *today.* 'Susanna, when d'you think they'll let me out of here? What has the great doctor said?'

She left this unanswered long enough to show she still didn't care for my attitude. 'Doctor Arvin thinks he maybe can release you on the weekend.' *Release* said it all. She jabbed her needle in. 'But don't you be getting cheeky with me, Mister Guy, or I'll tell him you've had a relapse.'

*   *   *

'Guy?' Helena dropped a book on the bed. 'You might like this – Laurens van der Post. It's all I could find in English.'

173

'Christ, Helena, how long have I been here?' The slanting sunlight told me it was late afternoon; I hadn't really been asleep.

'A few days.' She leaned over to kiss a freshly exposed area of chin. 'The nurse says you're awake more now – that's good. You're doing fine.'

'Well I don't *look* fine. They let me see in the mirror this morning – with the bandages off.'

'What, the black eye? That's nothing – you'll be back to normal in no time. In fact,' she brought her mouth to my ear, 'it looks as if we may have you out of here tomorrow.'

'What – back to Ulf's?'

Helena laughed. 'I don't think so, do you?' She must have been thinking of the plundered fridge and the uncleared beer bottles: there was no way she could know he'd assaulted me. 'I thought you could come and stay at Hörnvik for a bit.'

'Hörnvik? But my boat leaves Wednesday.'

'I'm afraid that was the day before yesterday, Guy.'

'Good god, was it? Nobody tells me anything in this place.'

'The ferry people have offered a part refund. You're in a box called *special circumstances.*'

'Is that good?'

'Better than a wooden box, surely.' Helena seemed poised to take full charge of me: who was I to argue? 'Doctor Arvin says you can probably be moved tomorrow afternoon.'

'What time d'you want me ready?'

'Nina's asked me to do her Saturday shift, so I could pick you up straight after work. A week or two *convalescent* – you'll be fit as a fiddle. We can always get you on a flight – September's a lot easier.'

September? The thought of embarking on a new month with her was thrilling. I'd left Castles at the tail end of July on ten working days' leave: just imagining Sidney's reaction made my hair stand on end.

'Are you sure you've got the space, Helena? That house of yours – looked a bit pokey to me . . .'

She did her mock-serious frown. 'Well, we can pitch you a nice tent in the garden if you like – or you *could* make do with the big south-facing bedroom. What's it to be?'

'Mm, that's a tough one.'

'After that we'll have to see how things go, won't we. When you can travel home, and so on.'

'*As time goes by?*'

'*You must remember this* . . .' Her lips brushed my forehead.

How could I forget? *A kiss is still a kiss.* Suddenly a whole Indian summer was opening out before me in glorious panorama: I wanted to dance for joy. The accident at *Inblick* had miraculously up-ended my hourglass and set it running again. Sidney would have to wait. As for Georgina: at that moment it was far too difficult to think about her.

Only one other cloud remained on my horizon. 'Helena, about Ulf, is he . . .?'

'Don't worry, Guy. Leave Ulf to me . . .'

*　　*　　*

Concussion had rendered me abnormally compliant. The next afternoon Susanna wheeled me to the lift and proffered a walking stick. This was puzzling till I tried to stand: my legs seemed to have been on a trip to Mars. Beyond the entrance there was a freshness in the air for late August. Susanna waved to us as Helena swung the Volvo out of the drive; somewhere behind the engine 'As Time Goes By' was still playing. Helena was chattering on about laundry and spare blankets: I was in for the long haul. The prospect filled me with unalloyed bliss.

38

Lying in the south bedroom one morning the following week, savoury vapours of fresh soup wafted up to me from the kitchen. Now the jaw swelling had reduced, it was becoming a lot less uncomfortable to practise the harmonica again; 'As Time Goes By' was still on my brain, the half-notes breathlessly out of reach as I struggled with its plangent cadences. The role of patient was growing familiar – with Helena as nurse this time. She pulled off an apron as she came in, drawing open the blinds.

The dazzle of daylight stopped me in mid-refrain. 'Something smells good.'

'Celery and swede this morning.'

'If it's Swede on the menu, you'll do me fine.' I nibbled at her little finger; she pulled away.

'Are you getting up today – or d'you expect to be served up here for the next couple of months?'

'Ah, I get it. Give me five minutes, then. S'pose I ought to make the effort.'

'Wouldn't be a bad idea. You should start getting out more.'

If she showed a little sternness, it was for my own good. The bang on the head had disoriented me: Helena offered the necessary structure.

Down at the kitchen table she studied my technique with the scalding soup.

'Aren't you having any, Helena?'

'You know, Guy, you won't want to hear this, but Ulf is really sorry for what he did.'

I put down the spoon. 'You *knew*?' So much for keeping secrets.

'Of course. Why wouldn't I? I was terrified when he rang and said you were hurt.' Her eyes brimmed with sudden tenderness. 'I never imagined he'd do something like that – that he'd have such a strong reaction.'

After the morphine-enhanced euphoria of recent days, it was a shock to realise I'd misconstrued all this. 'Well, no one's that predictable, are they.' She and Ulf must have met up sometime in the past week, with me lying concussed; they'd picked things over. What had they said about me?

'If it's any comfort, he's learned his lesson. To be fair to Ulf, though, he says he never meant to push you so hard. And he admits it was a silly place to do it.' She stroked my hand, as if afraid of provoking me.

'Does he now? You sound very keen to make excuses for him.'

'Oh, Guy, of course not. He should never have done it – he knows that as well as you and I do. But you can't put all the blame on him, can you?'

'Can't I?'

'I can understand you feel angry, but the fact is he couldn't possibly have known you'd get such a bad injury. He really never meant to harm you, you've got to believe that. It was just – well, it was a very unfortunate accident.'

'*Unfortunate*?' I could fume all I liked over Ulf – venting my anger at Helena was pointless and destructive. Her rueful look said it all. After a minute she touched my cheek.

'How does it feel now? Still painful?'

'I'm all right.' I kissed her palm, treasuring the moment of closeness; being with her made up for any hurt. 'What puzzles me, Helena, is how he managed to find out about us. We were the soul of discretion, weren't we? Of course I suppose anybody could have . . .' A horrible thought surfaced. '*You* didn't tell him, did you?'

'Of course not. I thought you trusted me.' She drew away. 'In any case, it was no need, as things turned out. In fact I wish we *had* told him. Hiding the fact we were going out together – that was the worst thing we could have done.'

'So someone . . .?'

'I meant to say. That afternoon at Segelholm – you know, when we took the boat . . .'

'What about it? Ulf was at work, he'd have no way of . . .'

'I should have told you. Anders is Ulf's brother.' She probed the grainy tabletop with supple fingertips.

'*Anders?*' Suddenly it felt as if the whole island had eyes. 'You *knew* that, and you went ahead and . . .?'

'It was terrible – you're right. The thing is, I should never have come in the first place. But then – well, you didn't exactly leave me a lot of choice, did you?' Her eyes met mine now, strong and challenging; it came back to me with deep embarrassment how I'd coerced her on the phone, hanging up before she could refuse. 'When I got to the beach and saw Anders, it was as if – well, I'd got to go through with it. You know that sentence – it's Heinrich Böll – about *hiding behind a naked face?* Except that really you can't hide, can you? Not here on Lammland, anyway. You can't stop people – they see things, they talk. But it was all my fault, even before that – I should never have suggested you to stay at Ulf's. Once you were there it was inevitable he'd find out and be upset.'

For a minute I was lost again in her troubled eyes. She leaned forward and ran a finger along my ten-day beard; the swelling had all but gone. 'You know, Guy, you must have twisted sideways in mid-air, somehow. Doctor Arvin thought the corner of the seat probably hit the side of your face. Then your head hit the floor – or the edge of a step – because you got that huge bruise, up here at the back. That's why you were concussed. But he said you were lucky the seat caught your jaw first – maybe slowed you down a bit.'

'*Lucky* doesn't feel quite the word.'

Helena bit her lip, stroking my hair with tentative fingers. 'No. I'm sorry, Guy. That was tactless.'

She looked pleadingly at me, as if waiting to be forgiven. I reached for her hand again; it should have been me begging forgiveness.

39

The following afternoon Helena phoned from work to say she had to do a late shift for Nina. At regular intervals all day Snuffi had been clamouring for his walks, towing me out along the river-bank. Still somewhat dependent on Susanna's walking stick, it was good for me, though I soon tired.

After supper I lay on the sofa listening to the rustle of leaves outside and the clock ticking in the hall; it seemed to clear its throat before chiming each quarter. Hearing it strike eleven was worrying: Helena should have been home a good hour ago. Could she really still be serving coffees at this time of night? Some unplanned celebration, possibly – or a group of friends could have turned out from one of the late cinema shows and decided to make a night of it. Perhaps Ulf would be with them – *Musica* was only minutes from *Inblick*. He had to have a social life some-time, didn't he? The fact he and Helena had once been child-hood playmates, coupled with later events, must have made the relationship very special. Helena wasn't inclined to go into their current feelings for one another; I tried not to speculate.

At last her key was in the door and she was receiving Snuffi's frantic welcome before giving me the warmest hug. Despite the long drive on dark, winding roads she seemed in an animated mood. After a bite to eat she said why didn't we talk a little while, and led me back to the sofa, subsiding on the rug at my feet.

'You're an odd fish, Guy.'

'Me? Why?'

'I've said it before. I know next to nothing about you.'

'Yes you do – Dorset, Castles: you've heard it all, haven't you?'

'That's not you as a person, though, is it? I didn't even know your name till you ended up in hospital. Ulf got *Chandler* from your passport.'

'He called the ambulance?' Up until then I'd given little thought to Ulf's prompt action following my fall. 'You know, it *was* good of him to let me have the room. I've not exactly made life easy for Ulf, have I?'

'That's a nice thing to say.'

'Some police officer came on the ward one afternoon, by the way, asking about the "incident" – did I want to press charges, and so on. To be honest it wouldn't have crossed my mind.'

There was a lengthy silence; she leaned her head back against my knees, frowning up at me. 'Guy, truthfully, why did you come to Sweden? It wasn't just for a holiday, was it?'

It felt important to tell the full story now, starting with Ben's funeral and all the events and emotions that stemmed from it, right up to Maja's two phone calls and what I'd gleaned among the computer records. 'And you were asking about that girlfriend – you know, the one at Castles? Well, we've been out a bit more than once or twice. Only I don't know if she is any more.'

'Working at Castles, or your girlfriend?'

'Put it this way – she's not all that pleased with me at the moment.'

'Oh, and why would that be?'

'Helena, I'm trying to be absolutely honest with you. I've not been very fair to her, that's all.'

'And does she have a name too, this girl?'

'Georgina. D'you want her surname?'

'Georgina will do! I assume she knows you're out of hospital?'

'Not yet, no. We – haven't actually talked about the accident.'

'You've not *told* her?' Trying to explain about George made me realise just how much of it was still utter confusion to me: why on earth hadn't I rung her? Helena shook her head as if to clear her thoughts. 'OK, so you came in search of your uncle and ended up looking for his granddaughter. How far have you got?'

'Well, that's the problem – as I said, not having taken down Maja's number . . . Now Philip has died, I've got to get the message to Sofi. The question is how.'

'Sofi Chandler? Why didn't you say?' Head tilted back, her innocent eyes gazed upside-down at me.

'Don't tell me you know her.'

'I do, as it happens. Well, did.'

'You *knew* Sofi?' I caught the faint smile on Helena's lips. This was the first time we'd touched on family matters since the accident: without my surname, she couldn't possibly have made the connection. 'So how did you two . . .?'

'I'd been a girl at Lindhem School long before Sofi started. Some years after I moved to Uppsala, the new headmistress invited me back to give a talk on nursing to the Final Year students. Right in the front row sat this lively girl, bursting with questions – you couldn't miss her! She cornered me afterwards, and then we met up again and got to know each other. I think I put her off nursing in the end . . .' Helena's eyebrows lifted. 'Is she so important, then?'

'Ben's estate can't be distributed till all his beneficiaries have been contacted. Sofi has to be one of them.'

'And what kind of estate would that be – money? Property?'

Why was she pursuing this? 'There's all sorts – including a big house. All his assets have to be realised first. I think Stephen's trying not to get us too excited just yet.'

'Us?'

'Us, the Chandlers. All Ben's relatives.'

'And are you?' The hint of amusement was in her eyes again.

'Some of us are, I expect. Up to a point.' She sat waiting for more. 'What, have I said something?'

'So, give me an idea – are we talking big numbers here?'

'It could be pretty substantial. Uncle Ben was a shrewd old

bird – and a dab hand on the stock exchange, apparently. Stephen talks about these five-figure sums. Once I've got word to Sofi, Ben's solicitors should see their way to making equal payments to all his siblings, or their offspring.' I wanted to make it clear this concerned the whole family, not just me; and yet – reclining among the linen cushions – I couldn't help a certain pleasurable anticipation. 'We could each get – ooh, I don't know, thirty or forty thousand – possibly more.' From the dark woods across the river an owl hooted as if in mockery.

'Pounds?'

'Yes, pounds.' I was still trying to make light of it, but a sudden coolness overlaid her manner.

'I see. D'you want another coffee?'

'So, what about . . .?'

'Mm? Black or white?' She got up to fetch cups.

'You know what I mean, Helena – you said you knew Sofi.'

'We've talked a lot tonight, Guy. I'll tell you another time.'

'What's wrong with now?'

'It's no immediate hurry, is it?' She hovered by the coffee machine, yawned, then suddenly switched it off. 'Second thoughts, it's late, I'll have to turn in – Nina's not well, I said I'd cover for her again tomorrow. Are you staying up?'

The next morning, strolling by the river with Snuffi in the cooler air of early September, it dawned on me how all that keenness on contacting Sofi must have sounded. Now Helena knew a good slice of the Chandler cake might be coming in my direction, no doubt I appeared motivated by pure greed. I tottered around all day thoroughly ashamed of what seemed my grasping nature.

40

The fading black eye gave me a jaundiced, reproachful look. Helena was right: I needed to get out more. Late on Friday afternoon, a fortnight after the accident, I was hobbling about in the garden with my stick; Helena had left early. From the front of the house you descend between clumps of pampas-grass and sea ragwort through an improvised rockery, where shrubs mingle with small boulders and shingle running down to the riverbank. Snuffi, nose to the ground, trotted ahead, pleased with himself; among the undergrowth there could be small spiders or sometimes the odd frog to play with.

Up river the sun was sinking in amber magnificence against a dappled sky. Watching a seagull swoop to the water's edge, white feathers tinged with orange light, I didn't hear Helena's car pull up.

'Wonderful at sunset, isn't it?' She was suddenly at my side. I moved to give her a hug, but she'd bent down to greet Snuffi. 'Do you have a house, Guy, back in Dorset?'

'Nothing so grand, I'm afraid. Later, perhaps, when things are more settled . . . Mind you, agency work has rather put me off.'

'An apartment, then? A room of some sort? You must live somewhere.'

'I've got a small flat, on the outskirts of Wintersham.'

'Shared?'

'No, just me. Well, and Columbus.'

'A friend of yours?'

'You could say. No help with the rent, sadly – carries his own accommodation! Columbus is my tortoise.' Half expecting the usual strange look, it was refreshing to hear her unaffected laugh.

'That's a sleepy sort of pet, isn't it?'

'He hibernates, of course. This year will be his fourth winter with me.' I'm actually very fond of Columbus, and a bit sensitive to sarcasm, which for some reason tortoises seem to attract. People tend to think they're slow, lumbering creatures, cooped up in their shells most of the time – whereas in fact it's surprising how fast they can get about, once they've come awake.

'He'll be missing you.' Her tone was perfectly sincere.

'Mm. If tortoises get that far?'

'I don't see why not.'

'They're nice creatures. Did you know they've been around since long before we came along? Two hundred million years – and they can live a lot longer than us, if you treat them right. I like that.'

'Ah, me too. Fair treatment.' She turned towards the house.

We climbed back up to the front porch. Near the steps a long horizontal crack in the wall of the basement happened to catch my eye.

'Helena, have you noticed this? Looks as if the whole ground floor could do with a spot of underpinning of some sort.' I ran the walking stick along it, judging the width.

'Ah, right, we're back to the Estate Agent bit now, are we? You may not think so, but it's pretty clear even to me what needs doing.'

'Helena, it's not a criticism, if that's what you think. I was only trying to . . .'

'Well you can save your breath. You're here to get your strength back, aren't you? Not rake up problems about the maintenance – or are you offering to take them on yourself? Work off some of that fortune you're sitting on?'

'What do you mean? All I said was . . .' In my dismay I almost tripped on the bottom step, saving myself awkwardly with the stick. How could she react like this, when things had seemed so harmonious only moments before? 'Anyway, I'm not sitting on anything yet! Listen, Helena, the last thing I want is to cause trouble. If I've said the wrong thing, it was bad and I'm sorry.'

She held the door open. 'I'm sure you mean well, Guy. None of it helps much at the moment, that's all. It'd be easier for both of us if you just got on with getting fit and let me get on with my chores.' She picked up a basket of washing and was squeezing past. The comment about the house must have caught her on a raw nerve. Had I outstayed my welcome? I would have to tread a lot more warily from now on.

In the living-room the 'Moonlight Sonata' lay open on the music stand; I'd practised bits of this as a boy. The piano sounded muddy and out of tune. I was trying to pick out the first few bars when Helena came up and put her arms round me.

'Guy, I'm sorry. It was horrible, talking to you like that.' Her hair smelled sweetly of pine essence; my fingers lost their way on the keys. 'I don't know what makes me say these things. You're right about the cracks, of course. So much needs doing – and it's lovely you're interested. The trouble is I've no money whatever at the moment for things like that.'

The C sharp minor chord decayed mournfully; I released the pedal and turned to kiss her downy cheek. 'You've had a tough time, Helena. I can see what you must think – all this money that's supposed to be coming my way, and so on. It's not what I . . .'

'No, Guy, you've got that all wrong.' She stroked my forearm, frowning. 'I was only – it was convenient to let you think it was like that. Honestly, I'm not the least bit bothered. You can have a hundred million for all I care.'

'Pounds?'

'Sure.'

'I may not get quite that much . . .'

'Well, I hope you enjoy it, whatever you get. It's your inheritance and you've a right to it. Believe me, I know what that means.'

She drew me over to the sofa again, taking up her favoured spot on the rug by my feet. I leaned forward to hold her close, her long soft hair nestled against my face.

'You know, Guy, the beard suits you – you should keep it.'

Shaving had been problematical after the accident; now the conspicuous stubble was something of a novelty. I sensed a fragile restoring of trust. 'Helena, what's really gone wrong? You've got so much you could do here. I can't see why you don't . . .'

'Guy, you wouldn't. You don't know what's happened.'

'Tell me.'

'Oh, it's all so *complicated*. It's too painful.'

'If that stopped people talking they'd never say anything, would they?'

It was as if I'd slapped her. For a minute her gaze rested on the 'Moonlight Sonata'. 'Even the piano needs more love than I can give! It's a comfort, though – to have you here, hearing you play; the harmonica, too.' She looked into my eyes. 'Let's talk over supper, shall we? I think the vegetables are done.'

Helena lit candles and we sat down to a fine piece of grilled plaice. 'It's a long story. I don't know where to start.'

'Well, there's one thing puzzles me. That afternoon cycling back from Fusum, talking about the inheritance: you called it "ours". And yet, when it comes to the house and all that's in it, I get the impression you're the sole owner. Aren't you?'

Helena stared out at the darkened river. 'You know about my sister, don't you. Cecilia and I carried on mothering Peter, really, long after Tant Marianne left – those years when Pappa was still so busy at the shop. Actually, we were the lucky ones: by the time he died Cecilia was twenty-five, I was nearly twenty-one; whereas Peter – well, can you imagine? On top of being motherless, he was only fourteen when we lost Nils. He's had a lot to cope with.'

'Nils – that was your father?' I thrilled at making another

connection. 'But I've been in the shop – that antiques place on Holmgatan? Jansson's!' It's a common enough Swedish name; I'd not thought twice about it being Helena's.

She smiled. 'Pappa learned the trade inside out, working along-side Grandpa.'

'Don't tell me. Isak?'

'You have been doing your homework.'

'Edward worked with him too – years earlier!' The odds against her family having anything to do with my uncle seemed phenom-enal: if the world was a small place, Lammland was microcosmic.

'I've told you Pappa always dreamt of moving back and trading from this house. Cottage workshops – you've seen them around the island: everything from furniture to sheepskins and ceramics. But to be honest the dream wasn't going anywhere. For one thing the roads weren't what they are today: who would drive out all the way from Valstad on a mud-track just to look at a few bits of furniture, even antique ones? And when he died so soon after-wards . . .'

She covered her eyes a moment; I reached across the table for her hand. 'Nils left equal shares to the three of us, so everything should have been plain sailing – would have been, but for Martin. That was Cecilia's first husband. He'd lost his job a few weeks before. They had a smart apartment in Söderköping, very expensive: suddenly they couldn't afford it. So they moved in here.'

'What – took over the house?'

'They had two children by then, Annie and Birgitta – super kids, in their teens now – so their need was greatest. They were a proper family, weren't they? It can seem odd, looking back, but at the time it felt like the only solution, you know? De facto posses-sion, or something – that's what the lawyer called it.' She looked down, as if unable to meet my gaze. 'So we had no formal distri-bution of Nils's estate.'

'Now I'm lost. What do you mean – *formal?*'

'Because of de facto or whatever, his assets weren't divided up.'

'You must have got something, surely?'

'Cecilia got the house and I got access to part of Nils's money – liquid assets, they call it.'

'But you can't say that's *equal shares*, can you?'

'Can't you? I don't really know what's meant with *equal*.'

'It means everybody gets the same, I should have thought!'

'Yes, but who was to say I wouldn't take out my full share in a few years?' Still she wouldn't look up. 'Cecilia and Martin had their lawyer – they weren't keen on a lot of meetings and legal stuff, so . . .'

'I bet they weren't! In any case, why should it have been you moving out?'

'That's not really the way it was, Guy.' Helena raised pleading eyes. 'I'd just finished my auxiliary nurse's course – the job in Uppsala was starting on 1 October. I was all set to share an apartment with some other student nurses.'

'What about Peter?'

'Peter was still a minor, of course, so he stayed on, with Cecilia and the girls. After all it was his home as much as theirs, wasn't it? As it happened, Martin was gone soon afterwards. I don't think he ever really loved her. Martin had the image, the fast Saab: he got fed up with being out here in the wilds – you could see it coming. So then Peter had the run of the place, with Cecilia and his two little nieces – who loved him to bits, of course. We all did. When he turned eighteen he moved out to technical college in Valstad.'

'So what happened about his inheritance?'

'Like I said – he was a minor.'

'But that's years ago, isn't it? How much has he seen of his share?'

'He got free board and lodging in Cecilia's family.'

'Helena!' It felt hateful to pursue her, yet it would have seemed wrong now to let the subject rest. 'Am I missing something here? Of course Cecilia's your sister, but her behaviour and Martin's sounds horrendous. Surely they should have arranged a buy-out of your share and Peter's – didn't you ever challenge them?'

'The fact was Martin had left, so he wasn't there to be challenged, was he? And Cecilia – well, my nurse's salary was coming in, so money wasn't a problem.'

'So you never even took the cash! And Peter – did he get any?'

'At his age he didn't need much. Cecilia had the two girls, she'd got to try and scratch a living from what was here in the house. Things happen, Guy. At the time you don't question them.'

'So – just a minute, I still don't follow. What's Peter doing now?'

At that exact second there was a sharp knock at the door. Whoever it was had dispensed with the gentle bell.

For an instant Helena's face had a wild, startled look. A fork clattered to the floor as she got up.

'That'll be Ulf.' She looked strangely at me.

'*Ulf?* What's he doing here?'

'You weren't to know, Guy, I'm so sorry, I was coming to that too. If we'd had more time . . . I'll explain everything. He's . . .' The knocking came again, more insistent still. 'Trust me, Guy, can you? That's all I'm asking.'

Right then, *trust* felt like a word in a foreign language.

41

It was pitch black in the yard; I stumbled out, wrenching the door shut. The prospect of meeting Ulf again was intolerable: I'd literally fled the candlelit table and dashed through the back kitchen while Helena let him in at the front. She would think me utterly mad, but I've always had an instinctive horror of intruding on other people's private space; I couldn't be in the house with them a moment longer.

In the moonless night brittle swatches of hawthorn clawed my face as the twisting path led me round the side of the house. At the river I turned towards Hörnvik village and crunched along the towpath, shivering in a thin jacket and trainers. As I drew closer to the bridge a solitary lamp cast its unearthly glimmer over the muddy banks. A peaceful toad sat contemplating the universe from a wet stone, his undivided existence in graphic contrast to the turmoil of mine.

Nothing made sense – Helena's life, my own feelings, Ulf. Why had he come to her this evening? The answer to that looked shockingly simple. How in the world, then, throughout the past three or four weeks, could Helena have been so kind and loving toward me?

All our tenderest hours were poisoned now. Her good intentions had been beyond question; yet how much of the truth about her relationship to Ulf had she kept concealed? The mental crisis she'd gone through some five years earlier still cast its shadow: what could have provoked it? Ulf's support at that time must have been crucial – indeed it was all too easy to imagine her vulnerable dependency, in that moment of anguish, igniting his passions.

Given those circumstances, no doubt it was inevitable he and she would form a powerful, lasting bond, the truth of which Helena – in precisely the compassionate, heart-warming spirit that made it impossible not to love her – had done her utmost to shield me from. Was she not simply trying to break it to me tonight, in the gentlest way she knew how? I'd learned to my cost, too, something of the explosive temper that lay dormant beneath Ulf's stolid exterior. It wasn't something to risk stirring up a second time without good reason.

I must have walked for two or three hours, back and forth along the cold riverbank, turning Helena's story over and over in my mind. No other person's life had ever come into quite such sharp focus for me as did hers that night. Even if our relationship was doomed to fail, I ached to help. Beyond a quiet despair over my feelings for her, I was baffled by her legal position which, from the little I'd gathered, struck me as deeply unjust – though it was hard to pinpoint any deliberate wrongdoing against her. Cecilia appeared to have obstructed her rights in their father's estate; yet if that were true, how could Helena since have moved into the family house? Had she not become – as looked to be the case – its sole owner? And if so, what lay behind the apparent paralysis that prevented her confronting its urgent problems – and along with them her own deepest desires?

More confusing still was the mystery of her brother. Peter would be a young man of twenty-three by now: why had he apparently failed to intervene in the inheritance dispute – if not to claim his own share, then at least to defend Helena's? That he'd been a minor at the time of Nils's death had surely to be an irrelevance.

The even more basic question stared at me: where was Peter now?

*

Retracing my steps at last, I stole to the rear of the house. By that hour there was a hardening frost in the air; the yard stretched cold and empty before me. Among the darkened first floor windows a single light burned in Helena's bedroom. Shunning all thought of what it might mean, I rushed to the back entrance from where I'd fled, reaching out in panic to try the handle.

It was locked. What foolishness, to have expected otherwise! I daren't go back and ring at the main door, with the hideous risk of breaking in on some private moment of passion. My heart beating in deeper grief at every step, I tiptoed along the walkway round plant pots and barrels of climbing ivy, keeping close to the back wall.

Built onto the north-east corner stood the large glazed conservatory that I'd not been into before. The door opened at a touch. Darkness formed an opaque wall before my eyes, but the air seemed a degree warmer in here. It struck me I could possibly avoid going into the house altogether by passing what was left of the night in this sanctuary. Ulf would be gone in the morning – he'd have his Saturday night performance to set up, if not a matinée as well. With him away, Helena might perhaps think to offer some explanation about the two of them.

Stepping forward, my shin hit a low edge: focused by pain, I fumbled the surface of a wide coffee table and found a box of matches next to a small hurricane lamp. I lit the wick and made out, in the soft yellowish glow, a tattered sofa against the house wall, the brickwork faintly warm to touch. Piled at one end was a heap of pungent sheepskins; the wool felt a little damp, but might give enough warmth to bed down.

Rustlings beyond the windowpanes told of restless nocturnal activity in the animal world; the wind whispered in the trees. I blew out the lamp and lay shivering for a while, the night's upheavals drifting through my head, and slipped at last into fitful sleep.

Waking with a lurching shudder, I'd hit the stone floor, sheepskins flopped on top of me. The inner wall had lost its residue of warmth; the conservatory was freezing. Dawn, filtering through the aspidistra leaves, seemed to pare down every thought to its starkest essentials. *The cold light of day.* What was I thinking of – an explanation from Helena about Ulf? How absurd. And even more fundamentally: what was I doing here, loitering at her house, as if trying to will into existence some miraculous reversal of the natural order?

Yesterday's dreams were gone. Today it was time to face reality: all my searches and hopes on the island had come to nought. Worse than that, I'd rushed in where there was no place for me; in my naïve clumsiness I'd been proved a vain fool.

There was only one route by which to cut through the agony: I'd accept the inevitable. I'd make a clean break.

42

Sweeping up the sheepskins, I hobbled between sinewy tendrils to the door. Out in the yard the small matter of luggage came to mind: all my belongings were still in the first-floor bedroom where I'd spent those first days of blissful ignorance – letting myself start to believe, despite the hurdles, that Helena and I might one day be together. Now once more her relationship with Ulf loomed rocklike between us.

If there was no avoiding one last encounter with them, at least it could be brief. My watch testified baldly to the time: 6.05 am. With aching limbs I slipped round to the front steps and pulled at the bell. The mournful clanging was followed by a deathly silence. In desperation I banged on the door and called her name: still no sound – even Snuffi didn't stir. Where was everyone? It seemed improbable they could have gone out already. Searching the ground floor in vain for an unlocked window, it came to me that Helena might keep a spare door-key in one of the rear outhouses.

There were half a dozen shedlike structures: a wood store next to a disused garage, the bike-shed, a workshop full of chisels and half-made chairs – Nils's handiwork, no doubt. Another promising door, its timber redolent with tar, gave onto an outside loo with the English message *God's Belief Is My Relief.* Still no key. I stepped across to the last outhouse.

Painted white and set back close to the chalky cliffs, its bulk and sturdiness in the early morning sun were striking. My imagination ran ahead: an art studio? So much about Helena remained an enigma. Could her 'artistic block' have been no more than a white lie – guarding the privacy of her work, carried on with single-minded passion in this secret workshop, perhaps at night? Fulfilling her creativity, building a portfolio year on year – a unique opus. One day she'd reveal it in triumph to a dazzled world!

Expecting the outhouse to be locked, it was a surprise when the tall wide door opened without effort onto a shady space filled with the smell of fresh wood varnish. In the narrow crack of sunlight, as the door swung to behind me, my glance fell on the sleek lines of a large yacht. Canvas sails neatly furled, the pale blue prow suspended above my head, I looked in astonishment along her keel balanced a foot or so clear of the floor on wooden blocks. It's hard to say whether I was more breathtaken by the size or the sheer beauty of this discovery.

Mounting the few steps onto a platform rigged up along her entire length, I ran a hand over the smooth dry planks, sniffing the fresh pine and a tanginess of salt water. Albeit in pristine condition and lovingly polished, there were signs she'd been in active use on the open sea, though perhaps not recently. It was tempting to hop over the side right onto the gleaming deck, but I held back. Another half-dozen steps toward the stern brought me level with the cabin. I peeped in at the tiny stove, a wash-basin, and a neat bunk in a recess made up with clean navy-blue blankets.

'*There* you are. I thought we'd lost you.' In the doorway Helena's slim figure was silhouetted against the outside brilliance; seen from above, her dark hair sparkled. Snuffi padded in to sniff at some bales of rope, his flaxen coat steaming in the beam of sunlight. 'We didn't like to look in your room earlier in case we woke you. What've you been up to?' Her voice sounded indecently normal as she looked up at me with those wide, innocent eyes.

'What *I've* been up to?' Despite her loveliness I couldn't keep the sour note from my voice. 'Looking for *you*, if you want to know. There didn't seem to be anybody in.'

'Oh, that's awful. Have you been up long, then?' She sounded sweetly at one with the world. 'Snuffi always drags me out around daybreak. Sleeps on my bed – it's not much peace after about five. We've been right out to the rocks, haven't we, Snuffs. It's lovely down river this time of day. I left the back door unlocked till about midnight, did you . . .?'

'I slept in that conservatory thing, actually. Well, tried to.'

'What, out here? You must have been frozen.'

'Not really. Those old sheepskins, they . . .'

'You're crazy! You should have woken me.'

'Well I hardly think you'd have welcomed *that*, would you.'

'Yes, I would.'

This butter-wouldn't-melt pose of hers was unbearable. 'Helena, I don't know what's going on and frankly I don't *want* to know, but as far as I'm concerned . . .'

'What d'you mean, *going on*?'

I glared, infuriated she should try and keep up this front with me. 'You've made it pretty obvious.'

'Made what obvious? Honestly, Guy, you've lost me now.'

'You and Ulf, for God's sake.'

'Ulf? What are you getting at?'

'Oh, come on, Helena, it's quite clear what's going on.'

'Nothing's *going on!*'

'Oh, right.' The words curdled as I spoke them. 'So he just dropped by on the off-chance, did he?'

'Yes.' Her tone was dangerously self-possessed. 'Yes he did, since you ask. He does that now and then, as a matter of fact. I've told you, haven't I? Ulf does a lot of work around here.' Was she saying I ought to have done some by now? 'He came again last night, to discuss things. Well, he rang earlier, in the morning – I meant to tell you. In fact we could have done with you, there's no end of stuff to sort out. What with your accident, though, neither of us knew how long you'd be staying – and we could hardly expect you to know, could we? Anyway, what's this all about?'

'Oh, I see. So between you you've been working out when you'd be shot of me. Well you needn't worry, Helena, I'm not hanging around this place a minute longer than I have to. In fact you'll be glad to know I'm leaving right now, as it happens. You've made it clear I'm an embarrassment. You and Ulf, we all know you're this great big item, but it was him pushing *me* over, remember, not the other way round. I'd have thought . . .'

'*Big item*? Oh, Guy, for heaven's sake! Is that what you really think? Use your brains, can't you? Like I said last night, I was going to explain everything. We could both have, if you'd given us half a chance. Marching off like that – wherever did you go?'

The outrageousness of all this anger at her, and the sheer stupidity of everything I'd thought and said, began to dawn. Helena's responses were all the more compelling for their guileless simplicity: 'We were worried. I thought we ought to ring the police, but Ulf said you'd be all right. He'd gone by about ten. I fell asleep with a book. Snuffi woke me eventually and we went to bed.'

'So are you saying . . .?'

'Come back in the house, Guy. You must be overtired – though I've got to say, it's all your own silly fault. Why don't I make us some scrambled eggs and coffee? We can talk over breakfast.'

The matter-of-fact tone put me to utter shame. My sleep-starved brain, bewildered and mortified by these realisations, was in no state to do other than acquiesce.

Back in the kitchen Helena sat waiting for me to return to some sort of normality. We finished eating and Snuffi came and laid his muzzle on my knees again, gazing up with twitching eyebrows as though imploring me to see how misguided I'd been.

'He loves it when you tickle his ears.' Charmingly down-to-earth this morning in plain top and canvas slacks over the Lammland clogs, Helena had somehow resumed her placid, Saturday morning mood despite my ghastly blunder. 'And it's his brushing day today – isn't it, Snuffs? Where's your comb?' The dog obviously knew what would happen next, leaping up to lick her chin as she settled him out on the front steps. She started combing the tangled pelt with vigorous, rhythmic strokes, as if to remove the last traces of my outburst at the same time.

'Helena, all those crazy things I said – it was unforgivable. I'm so sorry.'

'Forget it, Guy. I'm only sad you could even think that way.'

I joined her on the steps; the Labrador, tongue lolling, panted in a trance of pleasure. We watched the blizzard of soft whitish dog-hair drift over the river like translucent snowflakes.

'Snuffi was Cecilia's, originally. We get rabbits and foxes and goodness knows what around here – he loves it. Getting a bit old for hunting now, though, aren't you, Snuffs.' At the name he got up, fidgety for another walk, only to slump back in a shadier spot to wait.

'Tell me, Helena: if Cecilia was so settled here, what made her move out?'

'I was talking about Martin, wasn't I? None of us could see what she saw in him – that rather dominating, impatient type, you know.' He was after *space*, more than anything. It was true the house had this cramped, congested feel; all Pappa's chests and sideboards – it was hopeless up on the landing! So they started to get rid of the bigger things. That made sense, in a way.'

'What do you mean, get rid of?'

'Auctions, most times. It was plenty of demand. Some pieces dated back to the nineteenth century – lovely things. I remember a wonderful old sea-chest from our great-grandfather, with this marvellous date, 1845, painted on.'

Once more I was shocked at all that Helena had – so it appeared to me – been cheated out of. Cecilia had been no fool when it came to business. It seems she had the gift of stirring covetous-ness in those with money to spare, drawing a fine line between *junk* and *antique*: depending on who was after it, any piece could invoke her deepest scorn or rise to dizzy realms of pricelessness, hinted at with rolling eyeballs and a finger to the lips. 'People just opened their wallets. It was all fairly profitable.' Helena gazed at a flutter of gulls swooping over the headland.

'For them, you mean.'

'Yes, for them – why not? Those things could fetch a good price.'

'Which you missed out on?'

'Well, you can say that. But I've told you, my work was in Uppsala, it was my life there. Of course I knew what was happening in Hörnvik – at some level. It was easiest to pretend it didn't bother me.'

'But now it does.' She looked at me, then stared out across the water for a long time.

'Yes. Maybe now it does.' Behind those soft, tired eyes her torment was obvious. 'In a way. Because ... All the time – in that way you're right – all the time it wasn't only Cecilia's inheritance they were selling, was it? It was mine and Peter's, too. That's what hurt most. Still does.' Her voice choked with emotion. 'How could they?'

I touched her shoulder; she drew my hand stirringly over her breast. 'You and Peter never said anything?'

'It would have felt so callous to complain. I used to come and visit at Easter time, or Christmas. All I wanted was to make it as easy as possible for everyone. You know, it's strange: I got more and more to feel it was – well, that it wasn't my home any more. That I was an intruder.'

'*Intruder*? Helena, that's ridiculous.'

She turned and looked into my eyes, struggling with her tears. 'Of course. But a married couple, you know? There's a weight about that – a dignity, and a solidness. Mr and Mrs Söderman – Martin and Cecilia, with their two girls. How could I match that – I was only a single person, wasn't I? And Peter, well – he was still a boy.'

'But you didn't need to match it. Part of the inheritance was yours – yours and Peter's. That's all there was to it.'

'That's all true. That's why I find it – difficult to forgive Cecilia these days. So very difficult.' Her woeful eyes showed what it cost her to articulate this. I wanted desperately to strengthen her in a new, more resolute view of things.

'It was plain wrong. After all, you were a part owner.'

'Technically, yes.'

'Not just technically.'

'No. No, not just technically.' She wiped a tear. 'But really Martin made her do it. They had a roof over their head, but they had no other way of income, except what Cecilia had been left in the house . . .'

'What the three of you had been left.'

'What the three of us had been left. To be fair I think she was angry with Martin – and herself. Deep down she must have known it was all wrong. Wrong towards Peter, wrong towards me – and towards Nils and Doris, in the end.'

'So did she divorce this Martin?'

'Martin had a heart attack. It was the last thing anyone expected – 2001. He wasn't very old, I can't remember . . . Cecilia's situation was desperate.'

'I'm sure. This great big house to run, and with two youngsters . . .'

'That wasn't all. It turned out Martin had been totally stupid with money – all these shaky investments. Left her a whole string of debts she'd known nothing about. Selling off Pappa's precious stock was a habit she'd got into; it seemed quite natural to go on doing it. More furniture, in the beginning – coffee-tables, cake-stands – things she and the girls couldn't use. The house was deteriorating, and of course Peter was another mouth to feed, till he went to college. He got a job on the ferries after that.'

'I meant to ask about Peter. What kind of job?'

'They always need people. You know – stewards, and so on. The Valstad-Vyborgshamn service – the way you came.'

'And he's still with them?'

Her fingers tightened on my wrist. 'Nobody knows exactly what happened. Peter – went missing.'

I stroked her cheek. 'Helena, I had no idea.'

'It's all right, I've been through this a thousand times.'

'You mean he was lost at sea? One of the crossings?'

'No, not the ferries. You saw the yacht.'

'The yacht out here? So that was . . .?'

Helena leaned towards me, controlling her grief. 'She was always Peter's yacht. Is. He and Pappa built her together, here in the workshop. They were so proud. Peter brought her back each winter. We keep her maintained – well, Ulf does. I think she's well cared for – she's here for Peter. Waiting for him. He liked to sail off the north coast; the wind's a bit more exciting up that way. It happened in the summer, three years ago. A bad storm.' She dabbed her eyes again. 'People think it can't happen in the middle of August, but they can spring up any time of year – the Baltic's so unpredictable. But Peter could handle a yacht, Guy, he was good. Nobody could see any reason why he should . . . I'm sorry.' She wept quietly. 'We've sat too long. Let's move.'

'You must be exhausted.'

'It's not that, Guy – I want you to know everything now. Why don't we give Snuffi his walk? He's waited long enough.'

43

Nosing along the riverbank, tail aloft, the dog would stop and sniff the fast-flowing water, half-daring himself to jump in. Helena ran after him, laughing, but was soon back at my side, intent on getting the rest of her story told.

'Cecilia's my sister and I love her, but I doubt we ever really understood each other. Some people seem to do all the suffering, don't they! Even over Pappa, it's as if her grief was stronger – more *significant*, you know? Then losing Martin; and when Peter went . . . You had to tiptoe round this triple bereavement of hers, which was somehow so much worse than what anyone else was going through. It sounds harsh, but I think Cecilia's always had a blind spot for other people – their needs, even their bereavements.'

'Have you never had it out with her about the estate?'

'It was obvious the *equal shares* business wasn't settled, but as time went by it became more and more difficult to challenge. Maybe she did suffer more – I'm not saying she didn't. Cecilia always had a kind of hopelessness about her. That was something men, in particular, could find appealing.'

'She married again?'

'Eventually. She met Gösta Sörensson in 2005. We'd all had a traumatic year. First Peter going missing – that was August. Then in early October Ulf rang me – Cecilia was organising another auction. I was frantically busy with exams. I wouldn't normally bother travelling back for a thing like that, but he said this one was different.'

'Was it?'

'At first sight you wouldn't think so. Ulf met me at the airport – we were here about ten: one of those nice sunny, innocent-looking mornings. Word gets around in a place like Hörnvik. People often start browsing shortly after dawn – you pick out what you fancy, line up your bids for later. I noticed more of the smaller stuff this time, but – piled on little stands out in the yard – it didn't look like much. Some of those brass coal-scuttles and pokers, you've seen them in the hall? Mirrors and fire-screens – all sorts.

'It was strange, all those familiar things up for sale, but – knowing Cecilia's situation – it seemed unavoidable. Then I came across a hoard of necklaces and rings. She'd raided Doris's jewellery. Something inside me snapped at that point.'

'I should think so.'

'I spotted her, sorting out straps and saddles and other horsey things. She should get a piece of my mind this time! You could see the shock in her eyes to see me – she had no idea I'd turn up – but it was a big crowd, I couldn't come to her straight away. Then Ulf was there, pulling me over to the big workshop.'

'Where the yacht is?'

'People were still talking about Peter. He'd been in some trouble with the police: an Algerian had slept in his room – an "illegal", so they said. The *Allahanda* had an article – that made Peter a hot subject. It's a lot of curiosity on an island this size – morbid or otherwise – so it was natural people should wander in and have a look. Lots of yacht owners live around here: they like to make comparisons.'

'You mean – it was in there then? I don't follow – if Peter . . .?'

'Peter's yacht had been blown onto that sandbank at Guldstranden, a few weeks before.'

'So who found it?'

'The police checked her over. The main sail was still up. They think a freak wind might have caught him before he could get it down. She was lying on her side, very silted up – even the sail – but perfectly intact, which is what makes me think . . . Marvellous, really. That very fine sand. If you have to get shipwrecked it's the ideal place!'

'And there was no trace of him?'

Helena hid her face for a moment. 'The police towed her back to Hörnvik. It's hard to explain, Guy, but it's a comfort, to have Peter's boat here. Ulf cleaned her up, bless him. Anyway, the auction: it should begin any minute. Ulf wanted to tell me something, but Cecilia called everyone in front of the workshop. She made a little speech, thanking everyone. She said how much Nils would have enjoyed a day like this – which was all nonsense. He'd have hated it.'

'She tried to . . .?'

'And not even a mention of Doris! Well, that's Cecilia – she can be that way. The auction man from Valstad – very professional, with his little hammer – he opened the bidding. People were making offers – cheap things in the beginning. None of us would ever have any use for all those coal-scuttles; it didn't bother me.

'You could see he was working up to more expensive stuff. Then – we hadn't even started on the jewellery – somebody was shifting about behind the auctioner's stand: no one I knew, just this smart-looking business type from Stockholm. It was Gösta Sörensson. He'd been put there to open up the workshop. For the yacht.'

'The yacht?' It took a moment for the truth to dawn. 'You mean . . . They wanted to *auction* Peter's yacht?'

'Whether Cecilia had really thought it through . . . But you could see it made a lot of sense financially.'

'But Helena, that's terrible. She had absolutely no right.'

Her tears flowed freely now. By this time the confident Labrador (Helena never used a leash) had piloted us across the bridge into the woods.

After a minute she continued, her voice trembling:

'You could feel a false excitement in the air – all those people standing round, and through the doorway that innocent boat, Peter's boat, beautiful, you know? Shining in the sun. Everyone seemed to know what should happen – except me. That was the horrible part. I couldn't think. The bidding goes often slow in the beginning. After a few minutes it was two serious bidders, settling in – not local people, faces I'd never seen. They were ready to put up bigger money. Everything seemed – well, arranged, you know?'

'Rigged?'

'Yes, rigged – really I think it was. They were making offers around the seventy, eighty thousand mark. It sounds a lot, but in *kronor* that's a fraction of what such a yacht is worth. People became restless; some wandered off to look at trinkets again. Then a young couple – I can't say if they were "rigged" as well – they offered a hundred and twenty thousand. They hung on a little while, bidding up, and then it was Gösta, calling over from the workshop. He bid two hundred thousand. I felt so ill – as if I should faint. It was a nightmare.

'Then Ulf, he jumped suddenly up on a chair. He took a breath and shouted *STOP!*'

'Ulf? He stopped the auction?'

'He's such a quiet person – I'd never seen him that way before. He stood and spoke, quite loud and clear – calm as can be. Ulf's way to speak, it's so homey: the slow Lammland dialect – people trust him. He said he wanted that everyone should listen. He said it was a pity, but this auction wasn't legal. All the property belonged to the estate of the apparent owner's parents. Yes, he said *apparent*! The way he used it – no sarcasm at all – it sounded like a legal term. Calm and objective, you know? That was the clever part – something you can't dispute.

'The auctioner, he looked shocked. He wanted to say something, but Ulf he carried on, firm as a rock. The *apparent* owner was subject to a misunderstanding, he said. It was unfortunate, but in fact this whole auction was based on misunderstandings.

With due respect to Mrs Söderman – Cecilia was speechless, she couldn't believe it – the right to sell rested with her deceased parents, whose estate must still be legally distributed. Much as he regretted to inform us – that was so neat – the sale should now stop. Everyone were respectfully asked to leave.'

'Good for him!' Even I thrilled at Ulf's coolness in a crisis.

'It was a deadly silence. In a little while people started to shuffle away, very orderly. Nobody wanted to look at each other or talk; they saw something was up, and they left. When everyone was gone Cecilia asked Ulf and me into the house. Something must be done. Ulf said he should get a lawyer, to look at different options. All the fees could come from the estate, but Cecilia, she should have nothing more to do with selling or dividing it up. She was astonished, she didn't try to argue any more. Ulf said he'd drive to Valstad and we could go in at the office – what's it called . . .'

'Solicitor's?'

'Solicitor's. As we crossed the river, I saw Gösta this side, sitting in his car. He was waiting to go back to Cecilia, after we'd gone.'

'They'd already met?'

'Not before that day – Gösta had seen the auction in the *Allahanda*; he loves sailing and he's rather wealthy, so I'm sure his interest was perfectly genuine. You could think Cecilia manipulated him, but I think it was a real affection. Gösta, he was smitten from the first moment. I didn't think it should work, but they're rather well suited, in fact. You can say he saved her. Financially of course, in the beginning: it's lucky he's a millionaire – well, in *kronor*! A week before Christmas they married and moved to Stockholm; the girls are in school there now – Gösta gets along so well with them.'

Having led us on a well-learned circuit to the southern tip of the estuary, Snuffi was cutting back to the bridge.

'After my exams I left Uppsala and moved in here – at New Year. Snuffi stayed, of course – this was always his home. But I was in no state to care for anybody or anything. For months Ulf took care of us both.'

'That's when you got ill?'

'I'd been at a low ebb for months. Things piled up. You might not think so, Guy, but it happens to a lot of people.'

'At least you had somewhere to live. You were de facto this time.'

'That pleased Ulf! He'd expected trouble, but Gösta and Cecilia, they followed everything the solicitors proposed. We got a proper valuation of the whole estate this time. It was agreed the house should be put in my name. I'm paying off Cecilia's share over thirty years – less what she sold. Peter's too, into a trust. But isn't it strange – to get ill just when you'd think your problems should be over?'

'The unfairness, surely – all the fighting.'

'Any plans I might have had seemed finished: studies, nursing, painting . . . Even now it's still too fresh – too raw. Later, maybe, it can be possible to do something again – with small steps. I never believed in depression before, but it creeps up when you don't expect. The therapist says I've given myself no time for grieving Pappa. That's a part of it, I think. And when we lost Peter . . .'

'Of course. When someone's gone missing like that – trying to come to terms . . .'

'Terms?' The hurt in her eyes flared once more; too late I realised my blunder.

'Helena, I'm so sorry, that's not . . .'

'What would you know of *terms*? People love to talk that way, but it's not the point, is it. Why should I come to terms with something only because people say it?' She stopped, staring hopelessly out at the empty skyline. 'Strange things happen on boats. What's to prove he died? You hear cases where . . . For myself, I've never really believed it. People lost at sea are turning up all the time. OK, so they've not found Peter. What does that mean? Why *wouldn't* they find him, if he was dead?'

We'd re-crossed the river and were near the house. 'If it hadn't been for Ulf, I could have killed myself. He saw me through the weeks at Saint Gottfrid's – and the months after. *Emotional Crisis*, the medical notes said. I got through – well, Ulf got me through. And Snuffi, of course.' She bent down to scratch behind his fleshy ear; he darted up the steps.

*   *   *

We spoke little more that day. Although no words of mine could ease the pain of loss, it was moving that Helena had at last been able to unburden herself with such openness. As for Ulf – despite having put me in hospital with concussion barely two weeks earlier: his humanity and his courage on her behalf now commanded even greater respect. *Firm as a rock*. I wandered around the garden and the outhouses, chastened by these revelations.

Helena had poured scorn on my assumptions about their relationship; yet the awesome bond between the two of them filled me with an abiding uneasiness that was only deepened by her harrowing account. It was something even the extraordinary candour she'd shown me that morning could not altogether dispel.

44

Helena was back at *Musica* on Monday. She had her job: it was high time to start thinking about mine. In fairness to Sidney I'd left her number on his answerphone at Castles, but to date that was as far as I'd got. Having promised to give her a break by making supper, the late afternoon found me rummaging in the attic for a carafe to decant wine into. A collection of rather fine ones had caught my eye; they'd enjoyed their own moment of glory some years back, when Helena had taken them as the subject for half a dozen still-life oils. The artistic paralysis that had since gripped her made a depressing contrast with the vibrancy of these compositions.

On the point of taking the best of the carafes downstairs, my glance fell once more on that same lovely yacht painting I'd asked to buy. I ran a hand over the billowing sail, its roughness evoked by a criss-cross of whites and delicate browny-greys.

'Guy?'

'Up here.'

Helena put her head round the door and stood in bare feet, dangling a pair of sandals.

'I've been so dim, Helena. It's Peter's yacht, isn't it.'

'You couldn't have known before. Anyway, I'm glad you do now.'

'I love seascapes. You know, I do understand about all the inherited stuff, but your own pictures – they're a different matter, surely? In a place like Valstad they'd be snapped up in no time.

Not this one, of course – that's special – but some of these others? You could at least ask in one or two of those little art shops – or let me do it. See if they wouldn't exhibit a few?'

She surveyed the row bleakly. 'I doubt it.'

'Well, I bet you could ask a damned good price. You wouldn't need many. These still-life frames, for a start.' She looked away, but I could see she was pleased. 'Have you thought about trying any new stuff at all?'

'Not yet.'

'The time has to be right, I understand that. The subjects must be endless, though: the sea's always fantastic around here; and what about further inland – those marvellous church ruins at Rävlingbo, for instance?'

She sighed. 'You're right, Guy. Nothing gets done if you don't make the effort. The thing is, I need some sign of Peter. I've – never stopped hoping. Can you see that? If only I knew he was – somewhere.'

A few minutes later we were sipping our wine in the darkened kitchen.

'There must have been a big search at sea, presumably? It does seem strange they never located him.'

'The lifeboat was out from Fusum, and a helicopter from Valstad. A police notice appeared in the national press, too. It seemed a remote chance, but Ulf said Peter might have made it across to the mainland. Personally I don't see how he could have done. You might not think so, but I'm quite realistic. Ulf wanted to give me something to hope for, I think. And yet – in spite of all that – I still don't believe Peter's dead, don't ask me why. Someone who might know more is Sofi.'

'Sofi? Why do you say that?' The agonies of the last few days had driven out all thoughts of Sofi.

'We never got back to her, did we. Sofi and Peter were in love.'

'In *love*? What – Sofi Chandler and your Peter? You mean – in a relationship? But – that's astonishing!'

'Is it? You've seen yourself, Guy – Lammland's quite big, but the population isn't.'

'But that would mean your brother and my . . .'

'She's your uncle's granddaughter, isn't she? What would that make her – your second cousin, or something?'

A whole new segment of family jigsaw was falling into place: the Chandlers and the Janssons, inextricably linked! 'She'd be a first cousin once removed – I think that's right. And second cousin to my children, if I had any.'

'And have you?'

'Not yet . . . Have you?'

'What if I had?' Her bold glance shook me to the roots.

'But Helena, you should have said.'

'About Sofi and Peter? I've told you now, haven't I? You were so smug over that fortune you're expecting – maybe it didn't make me feel like telling you before.'

'You know how sorry I am about that.'

Her eyes were suddenly full of tenderness. 'Yes, Guy – and it's me who's been difficult. I'm sorry – I should have told you.'

'Well, this changes everything.'

'Does it? In what way?'

My impulse was to say it gave us common cause in making sense of the past, but I was wary of suggesting anything so glib. 'It's – it takes a bit of getting used to, that's all.' We sat in silence for a moment. 'So how did they meet?'

'At the marina in Valstad – some yachting event. The trouble was her father. He didn't really approve.'

'Philip? Why ever not?'

'Things haven't always been sweetness and light between the Chandlers and the Janssons.'

'Ah, no – I heard something about that. But that was ages ago, wasn't it, when Edward worked with Nils's father? Some business about a piano – the one that went to *Inblick*?'

'Well, yes, but that was only the original spark. Nils told us the whole story once. Grandpa Isak wasn't happy being dictated to by an Englishman – a foreigner. That's how he saw him, I'm afraid – and it seems your uncle could be pretty obstinate, which didn't help. You're right, it was Edward who caused the argument with Isak, but it's like all family disputes: it's gone on so many years, most people have forgotten who or what started it. That's why Sofi and Peter had – well, a difficult time. Having the yacht was great, though. It meant they were independent, they could get away.'

We finished our peaceful meal with no traumatic interruption this time.

'So do you think . . . Later, when Peter's yacht was washed up . . .?'

'I've thought about it a lot, Guy, of course. You'd expect Sofi might at least know something. But at the time it was very little communication, unfortunately, and since then . . .'

'What do you mean, *communication*? You must have talked with Sofi's parents?'

'Not directly, no.'

'No? Why was that?'

'We were never in touch, that's all. I guess this family feud thing runs deeper than any of us realised. You'd think those feelings could be buried, wouldn't you? I can't explain it any better.'

'But if Peter had a relationship with Sofi, the police would be bound to interview her, wouldn't they? At least find out if she . . .'

'I don't think anybody told them.'

'Nobody told the police about Sofi? Why on earth not?'

'I guess her mother had her reasons – she's not on the island any more, is she. It wasn't for me to interfere. I did read in the papers Sofi's father died later that year. I liked Sofi, but that didn't mean I had anything to do with her family.'

'So which summer was it she went away? Were she and Peter living together by then?'

'No – although I'm sure they would have done if they'd had

their way. Apart from all the problems with her father, Peter had to work round the ferry timetables – anti-social hours. Sofi was still renting a room with an old schoolfriend from my year, oddly enough – Fanny Tinderman. Peter used to drive across from Valstad to see her.'

'And where did Fanny Tinderman live?'

'Lindhem – along the coast here. Had this sweet little cottage, five minutes from the school. Still has, in fact. Sofi had another friend in her year who used to sleep over too, Annalena Carlsson. Fanny and I were that much older, of course, but we'd all meet up sometimes. Fanny would brew coffee and we'd lie about giggling half the night.'

The Carlssons: all these connections made my head spin.

'Do you think she'd have a clue about Sofi?'

'Fanny? She might have.'

45

I was hoping we might go and see Fanny together next morning, as it was a Tuesday, but Helena had other ideas. Our talks seemed to have fired a clearing-out impulse in the basement.

'Why don't you go by yourself, Guy? You can take Ulf's bike – work those legs a bit. I think I'd better do simple domestic things today. Must get into Hörnvik later for some washing-powder.'

'You're sure there's nothing I can do?'

'It's fine. Say hello to Fanny – you'll find the address in my diary. One of those wooden houses, up the hill near the harbour.' She flashed one of her unforgettable smiles and asked me to buy bread and a few groceries in Lindhem, which offers somewhat more choice than Hörnvik. 'Oh, and you'd better come and look where the key is – in case I'm out when you get back.'

By the front steps Helena lifted a flat stone and picked out the key. It was hardly top-rank security. 'You see? You needn't have camped out in the yard.' The memory of what I'd done and said was excruciating. I think we were both emotionally drained. This was my eleventh day at Hörnvik: looking after me inevitably created certain burdens; perhaps it would be as well if I went to Fanny's alone.

Lindhem is on a circuitous route to the south, following the east coastline with its many inlets and bridges over tiny streams. Not half an hour later I was at the general store in the high street. Cool and airy with an aroma of smoked bacon, it was pleasant to wander round the shelves picking up cheese and apples. By the till stood a rack of fresh rye bread; I slipped an extra loaf for Fanny into the pannier before wobbling away again up the hill. The cottage sits above the main street on a steep lane facing the sea, so you look out over glittering yachts and rowing-boats bobbing in the harbour.

At the top of the flower-lined path a woman with a glossy mane of chestnut hair, dressed in faded jeans and a loose white shirt, was opening the door.

'Fru Tinderman? Guy Chandler – I'm a friend of Helena's.'

'Ah. The Guy who stopped one of Ulf's punches and survived . . .'

'Oh, that! I wouldn't put it quite that way.' It was disconcerting to think Helena had already passed on this much about me. Had they been having a good laugh at my expense?

'Well, I've been dying to meet you. Fanny.' She held out a strong hand. 'Come in, Guy. Sorry about the mess, I'm in the middle of something.'

'I've bought bread. Can you use a loaf?'

'That's so kind! I love rye, don't you?' Fanny's English sounded like her natural mode of discourse; she gave me a good feeling of acceptance. The living-room was strewn with magazines, some with bits cut out; she looked a little stressed. 'It's my scavenging day today – I work for *Lindhemsbladet*.'

'I guess there's not always a lot going on in a place like this?'

'Ooh, we have our moments – you'd be surprised.'

I could imagine Fanny being a very good journalist – intelligent and alert to the unexpected. She was also gorgeous to look at. There seemed to be nowhere to sit apart from the chaotic sofa; Fanny transferred an armful of papers onto the table and joined me. The room had an informal, open-ended feel that put me in mind of student quarters.

'I gather Sofi Chandler lived with you for a while. I'm a – distant relative of hers.'

'Gosh, are you?' If she'd already heard this from Helena, she didn't show it. 'Sofi had a room here for about three years. What did you want to know?'

'Helena talked about that time, when you used to meet up, but I'd be interested in your angle.'

'It's not much to tell. Everything was very easy – we were a little group of friends. We'd go places sometimes at weekends; d'you know the south part of the island, Guy? Lovely beaches, all the campsites; sailing too, sometimes.'

'Helena talked about Peter's yacht. It's Sofi's time with him that interests me.'

Fanny's initial willingness to chat gave way to reticence. 'I'm sure your interest is perfectly proper, Guy, and I understand about family research – one of my sisters is doing the Tindermans. But I did promise Sofi not to talk about her and Peter, and I'm not going to start now. Sorry.'

For the moment, that sounded final. 'Fair enough, Fanny – a promise is a promise, I've every respect for that.' Beyond the window, a tall white yacht drifted across the harbour far below us. 'Sometimes, though . . . don't you think sometimes there can be new factors that crop up?'

Her lovely hazel eyes searched my face. 'Like what?'

'I mean, you're obviously a good friend of Sofi's and I wouldn't want to disturb that in any way, but . . .'

'But?'

'Well, look at it from her point of view: it really is in her interests for you to tell me what you know. I believe, if she were listening this minute, she'd want you to tell me.'

'Oh, really? And why would that be?'

So I went through the whole saga of Ben's estate. From where I was sitting, I said, Sofi looked like the missing link. My family needed to contact her – otherwise I'd never have tried to pursue any of this. The inheritance could also mean a substantial sum of money for Sofi – perhaps change her life. My only source so far was her mother, and of course it had been very remiss of me not to get Maja's number. On top of that, the accident at *Inblick* had disrupted and delayed all my searches; things were becoming quite urgent. 'You're my last hope, Fanny.'

'Am I?' She looked as if she thought me a tiny bit big for my boots. 'Maja will ring you again, won't she? If it's just a matter of getting the information to Sofi, it can't be so hard to . . .'

'If it were that simple, then yes.'

'Why wouldn't it be?'

'Well, from what Helena has told me, it's not at all clear what happened the day Peter disappeared, is it. Helena couldn't say whether he and Sofi . . . Even the police never put two and two together, did they? I don't know – supposing she actually was with him?'

She gazed straight into my eyes. 'It's Peter you're really hoping to trace, isn't it.'

Since Helena's revelation about her brother and Sofi, there had been little time to think out the implications. It's true the best chance of discovering what had happened to Peter that summer would now seem to be through locating the girl he'd fallen in love with. Under Fanny's penetrating look, the dilemma this put me in began to crystallise. On the one hand lay the tantalising possibility that some clue from Fanny might help unlock the mystery of Peter's disappearance. On the other, to set out specifically to find Sofi would stand in direct conflict with her declared wish – conveyed to me by Maja – that no one should learn of her whereabouts.

Passing on news of an inheritance through her mother was one thing; physically tracking her down – which an attempt to follow Peter's trail would make unavoidable – was something else altogether. Fanny was adamant about keeping her own promise to a friend; on the face of it any move on my part to find Sofi would likewise amount to a betrayal of both Maja and her daughter.

And yet all I could think about was the desperation in Helena's eyes: *I still don't believe Peter's dead, don't ask me why.* Nothing would give me greater joy than to be able to resolve that uncertainty.

With Peter as a new focus and motive for the search, then, couldn't this be the right course after all? And if, by some miraculous chance, it should lead to finding him alive and well, who would be rash enough to suggest a young woman's wish for privacy – however justified and reasonable – ought to override such a mission? If I could ever do that much for Helena . . .

Fanny's silent look, meanwhile, pointed up the contradiction I was now inviting. Having solemnly agreed promises between friends were there to be kept, here I was – not ten minutes later – trying to persuade her she should break one.

'You're one of Helena's oldest friends, Fanny: you must know what she's been through – what she's still going through? If there's anything you can tell me, anything at all, I need to hear it. For her sake. *Please.*'

For a long time Fanny stared out over the sunny harbour.

'Have you been out on the quayside here, Guy? I've been cooped up in the house all morning, why don't we wander down?' She moved to clear the magazines. 'I always think better outside. Let's take your bread and some cheese, and I'll make coffee.'

Reading my look of disappointment, she turned with a sympathetic smile. 'It's all right, we can talk some more about Sofi, if you like. As long as you . . .' Her glance was sharp this time. 'I won't be quoted on any of this, Guy. OK?'

I nodded, grateful but subdued. Beyond the good friend to Sofi, she was the cool-headed journalist again now.

46

Silhouetted against the gleaming water a couple of pipe-smoking fishermen squatted over a muddle of nets. We sat on the wooden quay, feet dangling. Though Fanny had shrewdly homed in on my dream of tracing Peter, the chance that I might do so by actually finding Sofi – if it could be done without offence – was exciting in its own right. Not only was there now real urgency over the inheritance, but after so many weeks as custodian of Edward's harmonica, it would feel far better if I could meet her and hand that over in person too.

'All right, Guy. You can have my version, for what it's worth.' Fanny sliced helpings of cheese while I cut into the loaf. 'But if you think I can tell you where Sofi is, I'm afraid you're out of luck. All I know is, she was expecting to meet Peter the day he disappeared.' She narrowed her eyes against the sun, the mass of red hair shining.

'So they *were* together!'

'Ah, just a minute. That was the *plan*. Peter had this big motor-bike, you see. A Davidson, something like that? I must say it suited him. He was this tall, good-looking guy. I mean, really good-looking – everyone fancied the pants off him! Used to drive here straight from Valstad. Only it was different that day.'

'In what way?'

'He'd told Sofi he wouldn't come direct to the house this time. I knew something else, too: she'd packed a bag the night before – she didn't know I'd seen her. I guessed Peter wanted to spring a surprise of some kind. It wouldn't be the first time, but Sofi was rather secretive about him – because of her parents, I'm sure. The less *they* knew, the better. Her father, anyway; I think he found it hard to let go – that *little girl* thing, you know? She'd only just left school, of course, but she was nineteen; Peter was twenty. He loved sport, so you'd imagine her father would like that. I don't know if he thought Peter wasn't academic enough.'

'Helena talked about problems there.'

'Sofi didn't want to say where they were going, but – well, I got it out of her in the end. He planned to take the yacht out from Hörnvik, so they'd arranged to meet at the beach.'

'Guldstranden, wasn't it? Helena took me up there a few weeks ago. Amazing place.'

'Yes, but you've seen – it's not ideal for landing a yacht, is it?'

'No?'

'Well you couldn't sail straight in, could you? All that flat sand – miles and miles of it. You'd run aground. Nowhere to tie up, nothing.'

'So you think they must have had somewhere else in mind?'

'Not necessarily. You know that narrow strip of sand – runs way out under water into the strait? He wouldn't need to land: she could have walked right out along it, waded a bit, tossed her bag across to the yacht, then swum the last few metres. I know she had her swimsuit.'

'Sounds feasible – assuming the weather was OK.' I was reliving that long hot day, cycling there with Helena.

'Exactly. Except that it wasn't.'

'Ah. No, of course.'

'That wasn't going to stop her, though, was it? She was so full of him, it was painful!'

'So – if they'd arranged this special rendezvous . . . You think there was more to it than just a little holiday?'

'I'm a journalist, Guy. You don't jump to conclusions.'

'Yes, all right, but surely . . .? If they'd actually *decided* to disappear together – that would have saved everybody's feelings, wouldn't it?'

She took a bite from her sandwich. 'I really couldn't say. Not that I haven't thought about it, naturally. It did cross my mind . . .'

'Yes?'

'Well, this is all speculation, of course. It seemed to me they could have planned some big romantic tryst thing, you know?' She gazed across the sun-drenched bay. 'Have you been over on Stenö, Guy? It's tiny, but Helena and I knew a place on the west side, with a marvellous old chapel ruin. Maybe – just maybe – they could have organised a marriage ceremony. Peter was like that, full of ideas; he was all for the spur of the moment. They were well suited that way, really. It was something nomadic in him – for Sofi that was exciting.'

'You mean they might have decided to – kind of elope?'

Her elusive smile appeared and vanished. 'Whatever. It's a longish trip up the east coast here, but he might have done it in a couple of hours on a good day. We'd had weeks and weeks of these endless hot days and gentle sea breezes. Great yachting weather, in fact. You get to think it'll go on forever, don't you?'

'Obviously it didn't.'

'The morning started fine enough. Peter's ferry was due in from Vyborgshamn at midday – that's when his shift ended. Things change so fast along these beaches – you can get a storm right out of nowhere. I remember I was writing this big feature on swans for *Lindhemsbladet* – had the radio on here all day, putting it together. The gale warnings didn't even start till around noon – Sofi had already left. She went everywhere by bike, so she wouldn't have made it before three at the earliest – it's a good twenty kilometres to Guldstranden. Peter had to drive to Hörnvik first – the yacht lived down at that little jetty during the summer. Sofi called it his favourite place on earth. But I guess he'd have reached Guldstranden by late afternoon – if the weather had held, that is.'

Fanny brushed crumbs into the water. 'Sofi came home long after dark. I'd gone to bed early, not expecting her back. She was exhausted. I tried to make her eat something, but she was in a bad state. She'd waited hours at the beach, she wasn't sure how long: it was no sign of Peter. The wind had got a lot worse – a full gale out of the north-east, which is always bad news.

'We both imagined all sorts of things. Once past Fusum he'd be caught in that narrow strait – you know, between Guldstranden and Stenö? The currents are vicious up near Nordspetsen, and with the gale driving him west it'd be impossible to turn back. Sofi and I talked it over most of the night. We didn't dare think of him getting wrecked out on the headland. If he cleared that, the wind could carry him straight on into open sea again. Eventually he'd reach the mainland – though it's a big *eventually*.'

'But he'd have been sighted long before that, wouldn't he?'

'You'd think so. I made Sofi as comfortable as I could and phoned the police. I lied a bit. Because of the family situation it felt better not to mention Sofi.'

'You didn't *mention* her?'

'I know, I should have. Naturally they wanted to know my connection to Peter, so I pretended he was *my* boyfriend – it was all I could think to say!'

'Which meant they never even talked to Sofi?'

Fanny shook her head, grim-faced. 'I said we'd arranged to meet at Guldstranden, had anyone reported a yacht in trouble? They started inquiries – I think they were phoning half the night. The Fusum lifeboat went out around midnight, but it was pretty hopeless in the dark. About two in the morning the police rang back: they'd had no reports of anyone in trouble – one or two sightings of craft up the east coast in the afternoon, that was all. The helicopter couldn't take off before dawn. I tried to tell Sofi it'd be a simple explanation and he'd be safe, but neither of us could sleep. Then shortly after four she did nod off. I couldn't stand it any longer: I scribbled a note and took the car up to Guldstranden.'

For a minute Fanny stared out to sea again, reliving that troubled dawn. 'It was cold and dark. The sea was still rough, and yet the wind had dropped almost completely. All you could see were these white waves surging across – quite eerie. But the minute I swung the headlights onto the beach, it was obvious.'

'The yacht?'

'She was lying a little way out in shallow water – on her side, at a funny angle. Apart from that she looked so normal, as if . . . The police were there, measuring, writing things down.'

'You told them who you were?'

'I didn't even get out of the car! Panic, I suppose. They had all my details, it's mad to think you can avoid them, but I was worried I'd say things Sofi and Peter wouldn't want them to know. It seemed easiest to turn round and drive straight back. How crazy was that? I needed time to think – get my head clear. I drove fast back to the house – doing well over ninety through Klosterbo.'

'Kilometres?'

'Which is crazy – the limit's fifty. It's a wonder they didn't pick me up just for that. When I got back, Sofi was gone.'

'Wasn't there a message of some sort?'

'Nothing. She'd taken her things and left. I was angry at that – it sounds stupid now. I hadn't slept and I couldn't cope. Sofi was in an emotional state, naturally – but so was I! I couldn't imagine where on earth she'd go. The only person I could think to phone was her mother. Maja knew nothing at that stage, so it was horrible for her, although she did ring back, later that afternoon, to say Sofi had phoned. Not that she'd given much away to Maja – only that she was safe, that was about all we knew.

'Maja said Sofi denied all knowledge of what had happened to Peter. I didn't know what to believe. Could he have broken it off? Maybe that was what we were supposed to think. I was honest with Maja, I poured it all out about pretending to be Peter's boyfriend. I thought she'd be furious, but she was really cool. Maja's a nice woman – we became friends for a time. Lost touch since, unfortunately; she can be very reserved.'

'That's the bit I can't understand – apparently she and Helena have never spoken?'

'Ah, no – I've tried to steer well clear of all that. Family business of some sort? This was before Sofi's father died, remember. I played go-between, up to a point, telling Helena exactly what Maja had told me, but it felt wisest not to say any more. Helena was in turmoil about Peter – still is, of course. We discussed it, over and over. She couldn't believe he'd ever abandon Sofi, and frankly nor could I. It seemed too much of a coincidence they disappeared the very same day, but with no facts to go on . . . All I know is, Helena's never given up hope.'

'And you?'

'You know my answer to that.'

'Sorry. You're a journalist.' We stared into the shimmering water. 'And you've no idea where Sofi might have gone?'

'Nobody has, apart from . . .' Fanny glanced back at the rows of white shiplap cottages. 'The thing is, her mother knows she's safe, so it wouldn't surprise me if she knew a bit more than that. I wouldn't dream of pressing her, though. And I'm *certain* she'd never tell you, Guy, no matter how important it is. Maja's sworn to silence and she'll stick to that.'

'Sofi seems to be surrounded by secrets.'

'I think she's had to protect herself.'

'And nothing at all came to light about Peter?'

'The fact the yacht hadn't fully capsized, and the way she lay on the beach, made the police think he could have been trying to turn her round when she hit the sandbank. Or trying to beach her – which I think is more likely. Either way, he must have been blown overboard. Even with a life-jacket they say your chances aren't good once you're in the sea, but – well, it wouldn't be quite so cold in August, would it, and Peter was strong. The gale would have been driving him towards Nordspetsen. You could never get ashore there – it'd be suicidal on those rocks. And if he managed to stay clear long enough to be swept right round the headland, he'd have the north–south currents to cope with. In fact it's rather shallow down the west side, but of course it's open sea.'

'And near big shipping lanes.'

'Quite. Some vessel could have picked him up off that coast, maybe. For a long while that was our best hope. Although, after all this time . . . The police file is still open, but they don't seem to think he could have made it to land once he'd missed Guldstranden.'

'But you think otherwise?'

'To be honest, Guy, I don't know what to think. The general assumption's taken root on the island that Peter drowned. For want of any other signs, I suppose . . .' Despite the journalistic objectivity, Fanny's agitation was obvious.

We tidied away the remains of our lunch.

'You'll keep all this to yourself, Guy, won't you? It's not going to help Helena, and unless . . .'

'Of course. It's odd, though: hasn't Sofi ever tried to contact you? Being close friends, you'd think . . .'

'I've had nothing apart from what Maja's told me. I don't know that she ever actually reported Sofi missing, in fact. The police looked for Peter's motorbike in Hörnvik, although they never found it – which is very odd, it must be there somewhere. They interviewed me, of course. I played safe and kept to the same story. One policewoman, she was the worst: *So, Miss Tinderman, you'd arranged to meet Mr Jansson at the beach. And how exactly were you planning to do that?* In the end she must have seen I didn't really know anything, even if she didn't believe me. I'd done nothing criminal, so that was that.'

'And the boat itself – no clues?'

'The police phoned Helena a week or so later – they'd drawn a blank on all the forensics. They released the yacht and had her towed back to Hörnvik.'

'Ghastly for her.'

Fanny gave me a long, sympathetic look. 'Helena's been through a lot, Guy. You seem to understand her.'

'Perhaps. We've not known each other very long.'

'That's not what counts, though, is it? You speak the same language.'

47

All the way back from Fanny's, cycling those verdant lanes, I reran the sailing disaster in my head. Could Peter somehow have survived it? It was clear he'd been swept overboard: supposing, against all the odds, he'd made it to land eventually? I tried to work out what this version of events might look like. The idea of his drifting west all the way to mainland Sweden seemed fanciful – although that of being sighted from a ship perhaps less so. Was it feasible he could have got ashore earlier, somewhere on Lammland?

Despite the impossibility of landing a yacht at Guldstranden in any weather without grounding it, that beach remained the one point on the whole north coast where a man could conceivably swim ashore in heavy seas. But then – it would still have been daylight – surely *someone* would have seen him? He'd have been cold, wet and exhausted. Even if no one saw him land, you'd expect him to have been spotted on the road – hailing a lift, say, or even getting on a bus. Yet Fanny had said no sightings were ever reported. Could he have reached land somewhere else? The signs weren't good.

As you approach the southern edge of Hörnvik the road runs close along the shoreline. There's the jetty that Fanny mentioned. It stands in tranquil isolation, a fragile structure poised on stilts above the lapping water. I dismount, prop the bike alongside and walk out on the boards. In my mind's eye a blue yacht rocks quietly at anchor, its proud mast drawing circles against the sky. As I listen to the slow, hushed shifting of shingle beneath, the soft rise and fall of the waves is like the sighing breath of a friendly spirit. Peter's energy seems to hover in this peaceful, well-loved spot. *His favourite place on earth.*

Looking out to the horizon, I'm assailed once more by visions of the storm he was caught up in. Fanny's account prompts various scenarios. I picture the yacht rolling in heavy seas, and this same fit young man in his twenties, battling to haul down the mainsail on a deck lashed by drenching waves. She keels over, Peter is hurled into the water. Assuming he's wearing a good life-jacket he can only be carried westward by the wind and the current. If he's swept beyond Guldstranden, right across the wide estuary, he'll be straight up against the steep rocks at Nordspetsen. It's unthinkable anyone would try landing there – or survive being driven onto them. If he's to clear that headland he'll have to get himself far enough north; perhaps, clinging to some buoyant thing, he can do it.

After that, if he carries on drifting further and further west, he'll soon be in a stretch of open sea that even a ferry takes three or four hours to cross. Any close encounter could be fatal. But he's a strong swimmer: can he get himself south instead, tucking in tighter to the shore again, and try making landfall somewhere on the west side of the island? He'll have strong currents to contend with here too – but could they even run in his favour? How long can a man last out in these conditions? Might some other small boat be in the area?

But there's no other boat. No one has seen him, and no reports are ever filed of his body being recovered, here or on the mainland. I've returned full circle to the dark mystery that has tormented his family for three years: Helena's brother has vanished without trace.

Crossing Hörnvik's little bridge at last, I pedalled back along the river. Fanny thought Helena and I spoke *the same language.* If only! So many unanswered questions: this envelope of silence.

The conviction was now strong that, if I could just reach Sofi, she would provide the key to what had become of Peter. And yet – for all the talk in recent days of the vivacious young student who'd captured his heart – I was no closer to finding her than finding him. How much of their story might Sofi have kept secret, even from her mother? And what would Maja herself have kept from Fanny? She'd disclosed only that her daughter was some-where safe; this made Sofi's whereabouts a mystery, so to speak, of a different order.

It struck me then: Sofi's grandfather had emigrated from England. Might her connection to Edward – my original reason for coming to Sweden – be significant? Could she, in her maturing teens, have become aware of something like an English dimension to her identity – a sort of ancestral homing instinct? The idea of Sofi on a quest for her Anglo-Saxon roots seemed plausible.

Feeling under the flat stone for the key, I turned it in the lock and called out. Silence: perhaps Helena had met someone in the village. At that moment the phone rang in the kitchen. I tossed the basket of shopping on the table and rushed to pick it up.

'Guy? It's me again. Am I glad I've caught you!'

'George? Are you all right?' Georgina's voice sounded a tense note that I'd not heard before, but she was in full command of herself – focused, as she'd have put it.

'It's sort of complicated, I can't explain it all over the phone. We're in – well, a tricky situation at the minute. We're doing everything we can, I'm trying to keep things going, but it's . . . It's quite urgent, Guy. Can you come straight away?'

'What? What do you mean? What's happened?'

'Like I say, there's a bit of a crisis in the office. We're working round the clock, but . . .' There was no trace of the irritability that was so familiar to me. 'D'you think you could travel today?'

'*Today?* What is this – what's going on? Surely Sidney . . .'

'Sidney's died, Guy.'

I was looking stupidly at the phone, the way people do in films

– as if it had perversely chosen that moment to malfunction. *Died?* An image came to me of the somewhat galling but thoroughly innocuous Sidney: bumbling about his office, shuffling papers around a forgotten cup of cold tea. How could this affable, well-meaning man not still be there – tidying his desk, stroking that reptilian throat, doing the things he always did?

'You mean – *Sidney?* When did all this happen? Is he . . .?' It felt like a kind of fiction – something she'd correct in a little while.

'He had a stroke. Last Saturday. It's all very sad, of course it is. At work. People die that way – it happens. There's nothing anybody could have done. Only that's not what I'm talking about. Right now, Castles could fold altogether.' She sounded phenomenally rational; it was difficult to believe she was the same person I'd sometimes thought of as rather too narrow and fixated on work. For once I tried to listen to her properly. 'We're picking up the pieces – or trying to. I'm handling most of the paperwork but . . . We need more help, Guy. Trevor's here of course, he's been great, but there's just too much. At this rate we'll never get through in time, and with all these – you know, creditors, baying at the door virtually . . .'

'So – hang on. Are you in charge, then? What about Head Office, haven't they . . .?'

'It's pretty much just me – for the moment, anyway. Who else is there? For all the good Head Office have been, we might as well . . . It wouldn't be so bad, only there's been all the funeral stuff as well.'

'Funeral? But that's for Sidney's family to worry about, surely?'

She gave a faint snort. 'Put it this way: they're not exactly rushing . . . Listen, Guy, I know it's an awful lot to ask, but we haven't got much time. Couldn't you get yourself on a plane or something? The next flight, whatever. Don't worry about the money, we can cover that somehow. With our sort of debts it's really not going to make that much difference. London will have to bail us out anyway if they want us to carry on – which they're *saying* they do. If you could just *come*, Guy, I'd really appreciate it. And I'm sorry about your holiday, if that's what it is – really I am. No expense spared, though – think of it that way, if you like.'

I knew it would never have occurred to Sidney to offer this kind of largesse, straight out of Castles' till – certainly not in these straitened circumstances. A baffling wave of old affection for Georgina came over me, and a genuine concern for her situation. *Do the decent thing* . . .

'Give me a few hours, George. I'll ring you. Are you in the office now?'

'I practically live here.'

She rang off. As I turned back to the table to pick up the basket of shopping, there was Helena's note under it:

Guy,
Gone into Valstad. Big insight!
Ham's in the fridge.
Talk tonight?
Love H.

Seeing the bald scribbled message, all my unspoken dreads and suspicions of recent days came storming back to the surface, this time with irresistible force. Hadn't Helena that very morning said she was planning only *simple domestic things*? Tuesday wasn't a Valstad day! What else would be a *big insight* if it wasn't *Inblick* and Ulf?

He must have rung . . . She must have driven . . . They must be . . .

Where before everything had seemed ambiguous and unre-solved, suddenly there could be no other rational explanation. The faintest small voice whispered to me: *O ye of little faith*, but it was too late: bitterness and resentment, distorting and vilifying, were already entwined snakelike around my thoughts.

Before awareness of a decision even dawned, I'd rushed upstairs in panic and was bundling clothes into the rucksack. Ominous shades of the past seemed to stalk me, but the little world of Hörnvik I'd shared with Helena was imploding: I had to escape or be destroyed by it.

Beside all that, Georgina's predicament was dire. She was a plucky woman, her call unequivocal: she needed help and I owed it to her. If I went straight to the air terminal there should be a good chance of a flight to Arlanda that afternoon, and with any luck on to London later. As I pelted out over the bridge, one of the 'new' double-deckers was pulling up at the bend outside the village.

'*Valstad, tack.*' A glossy-haired driver in his early twenties took the fare with a yawn; I hauled myself upstairs. With starved lungs screaming for oxygen, I sat gulping air by the open window.

There's a short stretch, as the bus toils up to the big T-junction out of Hörnvik, where the corkscrew inclines make the upper deck sway sickeningly from side to side. Near the top of the hill an overhanging pine branch clawed the roof; there was a long drawn-out scratching and squealing. As if in swift retribution for my untimely departure – and all the follies of a disastrous stay on Lammland – a twig catapulted in and stung me on the cheek-bone.

48

Ten minutes later, staring opaquely out, I realised we'd turned right, not left, onto the main road. Instead of cutting south-westward straight across the island to Valstad, we'd embarked on a vast detour in the opposite direction, anticlockwise via Fusum round the giant arc of Guldstranden. Later, ambling down the west coast, we'd call at places like Segelholm and Emsäde ahead of our final approach to the 'capital'. It was doubtful we'd be there much before nightfall.

To make matters worse there was to be an unscheduled wait at Segelholm to connect with the Vandringe service, delayed by a minor accident. Pulling up near the beach in the late afternoon with a promise to give us a shout when it arrived, our offbeat young driver with the sleeked-back quiff propped his feet on the steering-wheel and sat combing himself with a Cliff-Richardy, summer-holiday air. There was little choice but to join the handful of passengers wandering down to kill half an hour at the water's edge.

Suffused this time in the fervid glow of a dying sun, the beach brought back agonised memories of those precious hours spent here with Helena. All at once, recalling how she'd scoured the coastline, the truth came to me: she must have been distraught over Peter. Our ill-fated rendezvous had happened weeks before I knew anything of her tragic loss; only now could I guess at the desperation she must have been going through. With strong north-easterlies blowing on the day of Peter's disappearance, at least he'd have been in the lee of the land on this side. A glance at the little island map seemed to support the alternative scenario: given the atrocious storm, his last chance of getting ashore on Lammland, once beyond Nordspetsen, would have been to swim south and try for one of these west-facing beaches. Some hundred yards or so from the shore lay the jagged reef, in black silhouette against a crimson sky. It hardly looked an ideal landing-point – but perhaps it was feasible? Doubtless Helena had made the same deduction.

'Hello, Mister Nice Guy.' The strident young voice, instantly familiar, came from a slim kneeling figure in a yellow swimsuit not twenty yards away. Her blonde hair, matted and dark with seawater, hung over the wind-blown surface of a rockpool. Waving, she hopped off her rock, every bit as self-possessed as on that far-off day at the Löwensten's house. A small gesticulating crab dangled from her fingers.

'Angelica! What are you up to?' By way of an answer she sauntered barefoot towards me, hips swaying, and with a giggle thrust the crab in front of my nose. It twirled an impressive array of claws.

I like creatures that have their skeletons on the outside, and wasn't fazed. 'Oh, sorry, I can see you're busy.'

She brushed a little sand off her crab, not showing she'd hoped for a bit more of a shudder. Hiding my griefs, I fought for something else to say. 'You know, Angelica, I was thinking: you really have got a nice name.'

'Well, you would say that, wouldn't you, Mister *Nice* Guy.' She gave her most sullen scowl.

'No, I mean it. Perhaps you've got a little bit of angel in you.'

'No I haven't,' she said sharply. 'Not the littlest bit. That's a lot of sh . . .' She stopped herself.

'You could have. You've got that – floating look, sometimes.'

'I *haven't*. I'm horrible.'

'Ooh, I doubt that.'

'You don't know me.'

'No, of course.' I held up a hand against the glowing sun to see her better. 'But from the little I know about angels, I should think you'd make a reasonable one, anyway.' It would have been nice and simple to leave it at that, but she glared again.

'You don't know *nothing* of angels. You've never seen one.'

'Well, that's true. Nor have you, though, if you're honest, have you?'

'Yes I have.'

'Oh, I see.' Her look censored my smile. 'Ah, yes – you did say, last time. So where . . .?'

'Here, on the beach.' Her tone softened a little.

'This beach? OK. And what did she look like? Was she all done up in a long white robe, with wings and everything?'

'It was a *he*. Actually, angels don't have sex,' she said knowledgeably. 'They only sit around or play harp – looking down on humans.' Her expression said I was just the kind of human they looked down on.

'How can you know he was a he, then?'

She drew a thoughtful arc in the sand with her toe. 'He had a beard. Like yours.'

'Ah, right. I'm not an angel, though, am I? What makes you so sure he was one? Couldn't he be just a man?'

'Because he was walking on the water.' She said it without hesitation.

'Was he!'

'You don't believe me. I can tell.'

'I didn't say that.'

'You don't, though, do you?' She dumped herself on the sand, dejected. I knelt down and looked into her face; it was clear this mysterious angel had inhabited her thoughts for a very long time.

'Yes, I do, Angelica. Really.' There was a part of me that could say it truthfully: told with such conviction, it seemed almost too tall a story to have made up.

Her cornflower-blue eyes stared into mine. '*Really?*'

'Really. It's – rather surprising, that's all.' Angelica was a very special person – why shouldn't she have had an unusual experience of some kind, here on the beach? 'All right then. What did he look like?'

'Well, to start with he was all wet, naturally, that was from the sea.' She splayed articulate fingers, still holding the crab. 'It was very rough, very big waves. He walked off the sea and went away on the road. That way. He looked very cold.'

'What was he wearing?'

'I think he had normal clothes, I can't remember. Maybe also a life-jacket, I couldn't see so good. It wasn't so strong daylight.'

'Did you speak to him?'

'I was in the woods, up there. I watched him. I was scared.'

'I'm not surprised. It seems strange, though, doesn't it? How can a person walk on water?'

'Not person: angel.'

'All right, angel. How can they do it?'

'They just do it, that's all. You can't explain *everything*. Some things happen that way. He had a pole, so it was easier.'

'A pole?' I've come across some good liars in my time – quite a lot of them among the younger offspring of Castles' clients – but her plain, factual tone was hard to resist.

'He balanced with it, you could see it was for that. He walked in off the sea, like this,' and she dropped her crab to get up and demonstrate. Eyes shut tight, head erect, she held an imaginary horizontal pole at waist height. Feeling the way with her toes, she took a few delicate steps across the wet sand, concentrating on perfect balance and poise. When she opened her eyes again she had a look of triumph. 'Like Houdini. Fantastic. He walked on tightrope over Niagara Falls, you know? It's in our English coursebook. Anyway, *that's* how angels do it. I don't care if you don't believe me, I've *seen* him.'

'Angelica, I believe you.' She looked at me for a few seconds in torment, then beamed her radiant smile; I found myself smiling back. 'And I think Houdini's great too. When did this all happen?'

She sat down again. 'In the summer. I always come here. You can do it in seventeen minutes from the house, with bike.'

'You mean – this summer?'

'No, silly. It was for years and years ago. Mamma and Pappa wasn't here, it was wet.' Angelica couldn't be more than eleven – twelve at the most. At what age might she have started cycling to the beach alone? 'It was summer, but windy and cold. It's no problem with rain, I've got a big hood.'

Now I was transfixed. 'Not – not that summer three years ago – with all the gales and storms?'

'What if it was?' She was fed up with the subject now. From the road our own Cliff Richard gave an ear-piercing whistle: the Vandringe minibus swung into view.

Thinking back, I remember that as the exact second when, in the hourglass of my mind, the dwindling sand ran out. It meant those precious, irretrievable days of living on Lammland had come to an end. More than anything I wanted to believe there'd be a next time; it was the same feeling as wanting to believe in angels. 'I've got to go, Angelica. It's been good talking with you. You've given me a very interesting idea, actually. Perhaps we'll meet again one day? I'm going home to England tonight, but I'll be back.'

She pouted sceptically. 'When?'

'It's hard to say. People make promises, don't they, but they don't always keep them. I can't say I've kept all of mine, I'm afraid.'

'Mm. Mr Not So Nice Guy.'

She picked up her crab and padded back to the rockpool to rinse it.

'Angelica . . .' Her tangle of hair was already bowed over the rippling water; I felt a surge of fondness and regret. 'Can I – is there anything you want? You know, from England – next time I come?' She stood up and shook her dripping fingers, considering.

'A book.'

'A book? Is that what you'd like? What sort of book?'

'On Houdini. His escapes – how he's done them. I can't find nothing about it here in Sweden.'

'Really?' At last – something England might offer that couldn't be had *here in Sweden* . . . 'All right, then. A book on Houdini – a proper one, with all his escapes. I'll see what I can do, shall I? Goodbye now.'

She stooped to retrieve her crab. The bus hooted raucously. Angelica didn't do goodbyes. I sprinted back as Cliff Richard started his engine.

Part III

GUY'S WORLD

49

The first flight I could get on left shortly after seven next morning; I'd rung Georgina and spent a rough night on a bench at Valstad airport. Out on the sunny tarmac the quaint little twin-engined plane waited like a child's abandoned toy. With a sense of unreality I dragged myself up the steps, knowing all the tender hopes that meeting and falling in love with Helena had raised in me were dashed. No doubt my leaving would be the utmost relief to her, and to Ulf. What could she possibly make of me – and of this headlong departure? I'd not left so much as a note. She'd once called me *deterministic*: now again it was as though fateful patterns of the past were repeating themselves. Would I be forever running from the place where I most wanted to be?

A couple of minutes after take-off, banking at a giddy angle over the Baltic, the tiny porthole afforded a view of the entire northern half of Lammland that filled me with bitterest regret. In the far distance lay the pale smudge of land called Stenö, its rocky shoreline overlooking the narrow strait at Guldstranden. Amid the sea's deep shimmering blue ran hazy turbulences, perhaps signalling the powerful currents that stream constantly round those shores.

Craning a painful neck sideways, I could survey the barren headland of Nordspetsen and the western coast, its beaches softly fringed with lapping waves. There was the tree-lined river and the little campsite at Emsäde, and, yes, a glimpse of the church spire at Segelholm, nestling in toy-town miniature among trees behind the strip of shingle and the straggling reef, barely visible offshore. An even fainter pencil-line, curious in its symmetry, ran straight out into the sea at right angles to the sandy beach. Some underwater feature, no doubt; I was too downcast to give it proper thought.

Ears cupped by the drone of the engines, I peeped around me at dark-suited executives tapping soundlessly on their laptops; this was the business-class shuttle to Stockholm. At five thousand feet the sweetest imaginable stewardess served tubs of vanilla ice, then announced our estimated time of arrival at Arlanda in that homely Lammland dialect with its lilting, nasal overtones. My heart, meanwhile, had been left far behind on her native island.

*   *   *

Nevertheless out of sheer exhaustion, having transferred to the British Air jet and crammed myself into the niggardly space allotted me, I began to long for home. All memory of the remaining journey has gone, up until the surprise of seeing Georgina at the Arrivals barrier, flapping a lacy handkerchief. Heathrow is a long drive from Wintersham, so I was specially touched.

'Over here, Guy! Give me that, we'll get a trolley. Love the beard!' She gave me a quick kiss on the mouth as if we'd parted only yesterday, seeming not to notice the awkwardness and guilty despair that shadowed me. Her hair had grown a neat inch longer and, if I wasn't mistaken, a chocolatey hue lighter.

She bustled me to the car, her head tilted confidentially towards mine. Still in shock at the brisk resumption of such closeness, I slid into the seat beside her to be greeted by the sweet aroma of Arctic Mints: she'd not cracked the addiction. Popping one in her own shapely mouth and another in mine, she manoeuvred the car out into the maëlstrom of taxis and airport buses.

'I thought it'd save time if I picked you up – though goodness knows how I made it after today's antics. Anyway, this way I can fill you in as we go. A lot's happened since you left.'

'I bet.' Lulled by Georgina's familiar presence, it was easy to leave practicalities to her. How could I ever explain all that had happened to me since leaving Dorset? Listening to the energetic account of her life in the intervening weeks, I was only thankful she wasn't expecting a blow-by-blow account of mine – or at least, not yet.

'One thing I've learned these last couple of months, Guy: if you do a job like mine, not everything's stated in the job description.'

'No, I'm sure.'

'Like picking up dead bodies, for a start.'

'Christ, George, don't say it was you who actually found him?'

'Well, I suppose that's not *so* surprising, is it? I'm the one who's been traipsing in at weekends to help him with his paperwork. He's not been on good form – well, obviously. Head Office are talking bankruptcy. It's not nice.'

'I can imagine.' She didn't snap back at me for this as she might have done a few weeks earlier.

'They wanted to call in the Receivers straight away, but I've managed to stall them. I still don't think it'll to that, personally.' She pursed her lips and jabbed the hooter at a Belgian juggernaut. 'Not if I get my way, anyway.'

'Which I'm sure you will.'

She grinned. The new responsibility suited her; George's resourcefulness was something you had to admire. 'The other thing is the Chandler estate. It would have to come through now, wouldn't it, just when we're into debt management. Not that I'm complaining, mind. Just what we need at Castles, really.'

'Chandler? How do you mean?'

'Haven't you heard? Your Uncle Benjamin, of course.'

'Ben? You mean – Castles are handling his house?'

'Well, we're not there yet. Should have the rights of sale in the bag this week. One step at a time.'

'I thought Turnhams were doing it.'

'Turnhams are furious, of course – thought they had it sewn

up. I do take a bit of credit for that, if I say it myself. Managed to persuade your Uncle Stephen we'd shift it quicker at Castles. Which we will.'

'Stephen? Hang on, how did you come to . . .?'

'Wasn't that hard, to be honest. It's about keeping your eye on the papers, that's all. He's in the phone book – it's not rocket science. Since we're within striking distance of Dipsey, I thought why not go for it?'

'So – you've talked to Ben's executors and everything? Their name's gone out of my head.'

'Chalks & Conroy. I'm seeing them again first thing tomorrow. I'd have asked you along, only – well, we can't, can we.'

'Can't we?'

'Don't be daft, Guy. Conflict of interest, obviously. Sidney would've had a fit. Mind you, I have thought of another little chore you could do, if you like.'

'Oh?'

'Someone's got to go out there and check the place over. If we do get it on the market we'll need all our blurbs and specs ready pretty smartish. Any delay and Turnhams'll make mince-meat of us.'

'You want me to do the survey?'

'Well at least you know the way there! To be honest, I'll have to do it myself if you don't. What do you think?' Georgina had so much on, I said I'd be happy to, although privately the thought of going into Ben's house filled me with some trepidation. The go-getting look in her eye hadn't changed. 'Nice fat contract, if we pull it off. I'm hoping it'll cut a little ice with London, too.'

'I should think so. Good for you!'

'Well we'd never survive on Wintersham sales alone, would we? That Frickleigh one fell through, by the way.' She acceler-ated past a small army of tanks heading for Bovington. 'Anyway, I'm expecting us to go on the market with Uncle Benj early next week – if Chalks has completed his side, that is.'

'You mean he might not have?'

She shrugged at the motorway.

Dusk was falling by the time we'd nudged our way into Dorset. There's a strange intimacy about returning to England after a period abroad, like slipping back into old clothes; this time Georgina was part of an uneasy if beguiling familiarity. She looked tired, though she wouldn't admit it, so I was pleased when she accepted dinner on me at the Coach and Horses in Wimborne Minster, it was the least I could do.

We raised our glasses.

'This is thank you, George – for everything. Especially feeding Columbus.'

'No problems.' She sipped her Perrier water modestly. 'He sure can murder a dandelion. So what've you been up to all this time? Chasing those Danish mermaids?'

'I was in Sweden, actually.'

'Same difference. I must say you're cool about taking time off.' She made a geometric incision in her steak. 'Most people wouldn't have the nerve. You'd only been here – what – a couple of months? Then you waltz off for seven or eight weeks! Not that I blame you, Guy, honestly I don't. It's your life. Actually I'm glad for you. Doing a few things you really want for a change.' She chewed doggedly; this was a new, rather surprising Georgina.

'Well, it's nice of you to look at it that way. I know you've had far too much, George. I've not been very ... Disappearing like that, when you were up to your eyes – I feel really bad. Not that that's any use.'

'Hey, forget it. You weren't to know, were you? None of us could. People don't just drop dead every day – where'd we be if they did? It was *Just one of those things*,' she sang à la Cole Porter. For a second the buoyant mood felt almost disrespectful; it had never occurred to me her feelings for Sidney might have been rather less warm than mine. 'You know, Guy, I do like the beard. And you look quite tanned. What's that mark on your cheek?'

Nothing could have lifted me out of my wretched state that evening, but her attentiveness was oddly comforting; where she could have harboured festering resentment, which I'd more than deserved, there was nothing of the kind. In the soft lighting she looked good herself, in her eye-catching red suit and the white muslin scarf loose at the neck.

'Hats off to you, though, George. Handling all that red tape from London, plus the business with Sidney – I don't know how you've managed . . .'

This came out a bit wrong; perhaps it was the second glass of wine. In an inside pocket my fingers closed on the little gift from *Janssons* antique shop. It would be hard to describe the ineptness I felt, taking out something so personal for her now; yet at that moment it seemed the only thing to do. 'George, I wasn't sure what to get you . . .' Passing the box across the table felt an oddly theatrical gesture – like play-acting the person I'd been that day in Valstad all those weeks ago.

Her eyes flashed a look of complicity, but when she took out the necklace it was with unfeigned delight.

'Guy, it's fabulous! I *love* amber. *Thank you!*' She leaned forward to bestow a feathery kiss on my cheek, then put the necklace on straight away. Our little 'scene' was done: she did look lovely.

There was no way to explain what I felt; and yet somehow, in a kind of frantic revolt against the events of the past two months, I wanted to put everything straight between us, once and for all. 'What I meant to say . . . I've been thinking – you know, the way we left things? I'm really sorry, the fact I never – that was terrible . . . George, are we . . .?'

'What? Oh, Guy – you're such a worry-guts! No harm done, is there? It's over and done with. Don't worry, I perfectly understand.'

She may have done; to me, all was bleakness and conflict.

50

Being with anyone – even with Columbus – served only to accen-
tuate the unbearable distance that now lay between Helena and
me. Next morning – doubtless heightened by Coach and Horses
house wine – the traumas of the past forty-eight hours caught
up with me in the form of a splitting headache. Sidney had always
been a stickler for punctuality, though, and it would have felt
unworthy to be late now he wasn't here to scold me. Trevor was
out, appeasing the bank. I pulled up a chair next to Georgina's
and tried to help her through a mountain of strident post and a
little judicious accounting, for which she would periodically sweeten
my mouth with an Arctic.

'Rather you than me with this lot, George. All these noughts
– I'd never cope.'

'It's only money, I always say. You all right, Guy? You look a
bit rough – here, have one of these. I don't go anywhere without
them.' While I swallowed a Perdamol she initialled the printouts
with the lightning flourish of her GG and slipped her jacket on.
'Right: Mr Chalks, here I come. This time of day he's bound to
offer me coffee and biccies, so that'll save time. You ready?'

The idea was we'd drive round to Chalks & Conroy together,
and then – being still carless at that stage – I'd take her little
Paris Vector on from there to Dipsey.

She parked expertly on double yellows in Wintersham High
Street.

'Are you sure you're OK to walk back, George?'

''Course I am. Just go – you'll have your work cut out measuring that place up in a day. Good luck!' She gave me a light
peck on the cheek and banged the door shut while I crunched
first gear.

Always having travelled by bus to Dipsey Marsh before, I'd never
personally undertaken the maze of blind crossroads and hairpin
bends to get there. Dorset's famously tortuous lanes, often allowing
one-way traffic only, give an apt meaning to what Ben liked to
call his *neck of the woods*. Pulling up in his drive – now little more
than a patch of weeds – the smell of mud took me back to
tadpoling with him as a boy, in the pond beyond the vegetable
garden; both were long gone.

Georgina had given me a full set of keys, but an old habit led
me round to the side entrance. A bit of khaki sleeve snagged the
door. For a ghastly moment I had visions of Ben's frail body pros-
trated across the Dutch tiles – his ancient army greatcoat had
slid off the hatstand that still stood sentry there. Easing past into
the musty alcove, the familiar reek of Old Shag met my nostrils.

When life feels unendurable, practical jobs can give some sort of
orientation. Measuring all the rooms and features of a house that
size, not to mention going round everywhere with a humidity
meter, is a substantial task. I'd learned a few short cuts on the
training course, but this was, as it happened, my first surveying
assignment for Castles; it had gone six in the evening by the time
I'd finished. It was a relief to drop into Ben's old armchair and
pack away all the kit in readiness for the drive home.

Doug and Tammie had already cleared most of the rooms
upstairs, but in the silent living-room everything was still just as
he'd left it. It was humbling to sit here now Ben was gone, touched
by memories of the kindly soul behind that rasping, military voice.
By the fireplace stood a shelf of encyclopaedias, along with a
fine twelve-volume set of Shakespeare I'd never looked at before,
with one or two marked passages.

'For in that sleep of death what dreams may come . . .'
This wasn't quite what I'd have associated with a one-time soldier like Ben. Nor was the bundle of mouldering letters, hidden away near the floor – including several from an old flame that I tried not to look at. It was most stirring for me, though, to come across an envelope in Dad's large unmistakable hand.

> The Willows
> The Banks
> Wareham
> 7th December, 1959

Dear Bennie,
I should have penned you news of life here long ago. Away from Mother and Father at last, the freedom is a boon – even if it leaves me, as you predicted, a tad homesick for company and comforts!

First, to business: herewith a Postal Order, sum of 15 shillings, trusting you'll put it towards our 'Edward Fund'. With a permanent position at the farm now I should manage a monthly remittance.

Given Father's loving kindness to the rest of us, his attitude to Edward seems perverse. Father lives by his own code, doesn't he? – albeit, if you ask me, an outdated one. (Reason why it has such a hold on him?) But it's good – no disrespect to Father – that we can give Ed a helping hand. Who knows? With a spot of monetary (not just moral) support, he could yet come up Trumps in the end.

There followed a few lines about the work and some domestic news of Christmas preparations. All this happened years before I came on the scene, but it evoked such images of our old house, and trips out with Dad to the dairy farm where he'd first helped milk the cows as a teenager, that I sat dreamily recalling childhood days.

*

Nightfall was sudden. Tunnelling through fog in the labyrinth of dark lanes, I stared into the beam of the headlights, still moved to think that Dad and Ben – neatly sidestepping grandfather Mark's callousness – had kept faith with Edward throughout those early years in Sweden, even helping finance him behind granddad's back. How ironic, though, that while they – unbeknown to Tilly – were sending Edward money orders, Eddie was posting discreet sums back to Mark and Isobel! That mutual loyalty – and scrupulous discretion – must have been the pride of our family, not to say the hallmark of their generation.

Bang! I jabbed the brake too late, helpless as the car slewed sideways across the lane. In the veering headlights the stern of a large white yacht gleamed above a trailer, now sidling lamely into a concealed entrance, one light extinguished. Heart in mouth, I followed at a crawl round a long driveway.

Ahead the other driver was already parked, running a hand over the yacht. He waved calmly and walked back, gesturing to me to wind down my window.

'All right, mate? Ya look kinda shaken. Lucky ya weren't accilerating.' Stunned, no words would come to me at first. He glanced forward at his dangling tail-light. 'Few scretches on the boat – Ar can git thet seen to. Y've cl'pped ma w'ng, thet's all. Your vehicle looks fine.' He opened the door for me to stagger out, half leaning on him. 'Hemmond – Kin. Thet's short for Kinneth.' He offered a large warm hand. 'Look, matey, no b'g worries. Wanna come in an' chet about it?'

Sitting in his spacious kitchen, I gathered he'd spent the day down at the coast and was bringing the yacht back to the house for the last time that season.

'Beck home, o' course, we can sile all year round – Christmas Diye, if ya like!'

'Home would be – Australia?'

'New Zilland.' He picked up a leaflet with a view of Auckland. 'Hev ya got tin minutes? Plinty more p'ctures upsteers.'

'That's really kind, I'd better . . .'

'Ar'll git thet tea. Look as if ya could use one.'

While he pottered I glanced through the panoramic beaches and hiking trails of North Island.

'Mr Hammond – Ken, I'm so sorry about all this, I . . .'

'No worries, matey. What w'th the fog . . . Can heppen to inyone.'

'You'll bill me for the damage, won't you. Can I give you my . . .?'

'Nah, forgit it. Ar can f'x the light m'self. The yacht – well, it's paintwork, thet's all. Metter of fect theere's someone down at Gullworthy – l'ttle workshop under the cl'ffs. Plisant chep, does all ma maint'nance. He's choice!'

'Well, at least let me arrange it? That much I owe you.'

'Well, if ya feel thet way . . . Thet's decent of ya. Till ya what: ya can mintion it to him if ya go thet way? No b'g penic, mind – he can come an' f'x it sometime. He's done thet kind o' th'ng before.'

I finished the sugared tea and got up; he jotted the workshop address on the leaflet and stuffed it in my pocket. 'Hev ya toured New Zilland? Not to be m'ssed. You take keere, now.'

*　　*　　*

'Hi Guy, it's Doug.'

'Who?' I'd been out cold all evening in front of the television. Columbus hadn't emerged from his shell since I got back.

'Cousin Douglas? Dad said you were back from your travels. I gather you had some sort of prang out there.'

'Sorry Doug – I wasn't quite . . .'

'You on your own, Guy? Only I hear things are moving fast. We need to talk.'

'What, Ben's stuff, you mean?' All I needed right then was sleep.

'Looks like the house'll go on the market any minute – you're in on all that, though, aren't you? We've got to know where you're at, Guy, obviously. What happened in Norway, and so on.'

'Sweden.'

'It's no good over the phone, Guy. How about tomorrow night – the Black Ram? Dad's up in Scotland this week, otherwise he'd . . . Tilly's not been too well, I expect you know.'

'No, hasn't she?' Events had put me out of touch; the thought of Tilly in her cottage made me want to cry.

'Dad said to keep him up to speed our end, that's all. Fliss and Tammie thought it'd be easier if we had a little tête-à-tête, you know, just you and me. Must say I'm curious about this Edward dude – sounds like you're the horse's mouth on all that too?'

Tossing and turning that night, as every night now, my mind seethed with chaotic dreams. Ulf had given me a bit part in one of his sci-fi movies: I was boarding a spaceship in slow motion, the airlock hissing shut behind me. Within the reddish glow of a sleeping compartment Ulf and Helena were making soundless love. He looked up in mock surprise. ULF really stood for UFO: he'd journeyed from another galaxy, somehow using up all the precious oxygen in the process. Inside the suffocating chamber I made Herculean efforts to reach Helena; Ulf put out a casual foot and prodded me in the chest.

Later, Dad was there again, still urging me to *do the decent thing*. I was trying to explain about sheep and Lammland, but he couldn't hear me.

I woke to the sound of the alarm hammering at my eardrums. Time to face another day at Castles.

51

Georgina's assertiveness could be a bit much at times. After seeing Mr Chalks she'd gone straight ahead and booked me in the following Monday to see Mr Conroy, who was handling the rest of Ben's Will. I hadn't asked her to. No doubt a couple of months earlier I'd have told her where to go, but her thoughtfulness since my return, if a little overwhelming at first, was beginning to grow on me. Released from keeping an eye on Sidney, she seemed to be on a mission to sort out my life instead.

Back in his office on Friday morning, we ploughed through the blizzard of aggressive letters and emails. But for Georgina's strenuous rescue bid, there's no doubt Castles of Wintersham would have been wiped off the real estate map for good. Later she put me onto sifting recent house offers (all far below the asking price) – part of a survey she'd launched on Castles' performance over the past three years. I was still so tired I hardly knew what day it was. My eyes kept wandering to the clock, as if knowing the time would restore some anchorage in reality. *Musica* always filled up around one – or was that already an hour ago in Sweden? Helena would be jotting orders on her little pad, whisking away the empty plates, re-emerging in the sun with fresh salads and sandwiches. Dark hair blown by the breeze, loose clogs scuffing the flagstones . . .

'So where are you at, Guy?' To save time Georgina had suggested lunch at the Swan and Thistle. She scooped another neat forkful from her shepherd's pie.

'Mm?'

'You were miles away.' She looked faintly amused. 'What really happened out there? You've not told me the half of it.'

'In Sweden? Haven't I?'

The last thing I wanted was to deceive or hurt her, and if anyone had the right to a comprehensive account of events in Sweden, it was George. Once I'd worked my way back into office routine I fully intended to tell her everything, but as yet – however cowardly – I still couldn't come straight out with the truth about Helena. This meant as far as the Chandler search went there were safe sources and dangerous ones: people like Herr Wittberg, Herr Gellerstedt, the Carlssons and Maja were safe; anyone and anything closely connected to Helena or Ulf were not.

Fanny's story was a positive minefield, but with George now to some extent involved in Ben's estate – and if anything rather inclined to take my side over the inheritance – I owed her at least an outline. She took a sharp interest in the part about Sofi, which of course made it unavoidable to bring in Peter as well. It must have been obvious there were gaps, but – watching me with that quizzical expression – she confined herself to the odd polite question.

'So how did you get to hear about this Fanny person? Was she . . .?'

This brought me so close to mentioning Helena that I must have blushed scarlet, but George had the sun straight in her eyes and seemed not to have noticed. 'Oh, you know, you pick up bits here and there. So – what about you, then, George: you'll be staying on in Dorset for a bit, won't you – now they've made you a Big White Chief?'

'What – just 'cos of a little bit of promotion? No fear!' We'd reached the cappuccino stage; Georgina nibbled her complimentary mint chocolate with a show of nonchalance.

'Hardly little. So what's next – Area Coordinator? Or are you still pining for the Big Outdoors? Australia, wasn't it?'

She gave me her nicest smile. 'Maybe I'm over that.'

'That reminds me.' I felt in my pocket for the Auckland leaflet, which had gone right out of my head since leaving Ken Hammond. 'Sorry, George – *dreadfully* sorry. I meant to say first thing this morning, only you were on the phone.'

'Say what?'

'I owe you a huge apology. The thing is – well, I had this little brush last night, with another vehicle.'

'*Brush?* What – in my car? Now he tells me!' She aped shock and horror.

'It was bad and it shouldn't have happened. This is awful, George – I'm not quite functioning at the moment.'

'You're telling me.'

'It's all right, though, honestly – the car, that is. It's fine, as it happens – hardly a scratch. It was his tail-light, that's all. And the rudder housing, or something . . .'

'What are you talking about?' I was skimming the leaflet, turning it over. The name pencilled on the back stared at me: *V Jansson*. 'What is it, Guy?'

'Nothing, he's written the . . .' This was extraordinary. I looked again. Or was that *P Jansson*? Could it really be Peter – here in Dorset? The notion I might have stumbled on a lead to Helena's brother at last thrilled me to the core.

'Someone you know?'

'It's just possible . . . This might be Sofi's boyfriend.'

'So she could be . . .? Guy, that's marvellous!'

It was all I could do to hide my real feelings. The only thing I'd told George about Peter was that he'd disappeared the same year as Sofi – evading all reference to his family background. There was no way I could go any further into his identity yet, or the true implications of finding him – if indeed it was him. It would certainly make sense for Sofi to have brought him to Dorset in search of Edward's roots. We chatted some more about Gullworthy and where the maintenance workshop might be. George got quite animated: she thought I should definitely 'check it out'. Then, as we were leaving, she offered to drive me down there.

257

'That's so nice of you, George. Have you really got the time? All these Affairs of State, you must be . . .'

'Gotta take a break sometime, haven't you – I could do with a day out. What about Sunday?'

This was more than generous; she'd been slaving away seven days a week, so it would mean a rare moment of relaxation for her. The irony was – for reasons I still couldn't bring myself to divulge – that where George assumed our prime aim was to find Sofi and (much to my advantage) settle the Chandler inheritance, I could think only of finding Helena's brother.

*   *   *

'How's the 'research' going, then, Guy? Dad told us you'd been off scouting for that Edward character – get anywhere?' Hot and dishevelled, Doug reached the bar right behind me, shedding an anorak. He listened attentively as I talked about the trip. 'Mm. Pity he's dead – sounds a fun sort of uncle. So this son of his, Philip – did you meet him?'

'Turns out he died in a skiing accident three years ago.'

'Blimey. All seem a bit accident-prone, don't they.'

We ferried our drinks to a table.

'I did talk to Philip's wife. We know Ben's Will can't stretch to non-blood relatives, but they had a daughter, Sofia – Philip's share has to go to her. She's a first cousin once removed to us.'

'And where would she be?'

'Ah well, there's the rub. All we know for sure is, she's been in a relationship with the brother of someone I met while I was out there – someone I've got to know quite well.'

'Oh, I see.' He was giving me a discerning look.

'Pure fluke it all came out. We were just talking one day.'

'Like you do?'

'Like you do.'

'Nice, is she – this girl?' He drew a thoughtful draft from his tankard, watching me from the corner of his eye; I'd not even said it was a girl.

'Yes. Yes, she is, if you're asking. Very nice.'

'You've fallen for her, haven't you.'

'Don't be daft.'

'All right, Guy, I get it. Don't worry, my lips are sealed.' He wiped the froth from his mouth. 'So, this Chandler girl, Sofia? Where d'you reckon she could have got to?'

'Nobody knows apart from her mother. And she's not saying.'

He surveyed the other drinkers. 'So mum's keeping mum. Shouldn't be that hard to track down, though, should she? Have you tried a search under *Sofia Chandler* on the Internet?'

'Actually she might not even be a Chandler any more.'

'Ah. So – the brother of the girl you . . .' Doug was putting it together fast. 'Come on, Guy, spill another bean. What's his name?'

'Peter.'

'Peter what?'

'Jansson. We don't *know* they're married. Nobody really knows anything.'

'No, but if Sofia's quit the scene like you say, my guess is she'll be off with him somewhere.'

'That's what I'm hoping.'

'So, any clues on this Jansson character?'

'You're not going to believe this: he could be living locally.' Doug lowered his tankard.

'What – Wintersham? No kid!'

'Not quite. Gullworthy.'

'*Gullworthy*? Are you sure?'

When I told him about Ken Hammond's yacht and the repair business, Doug gave a Stephenish belly-laugh. He drained his pint. 'Well, if Sofia's living locally she can't be using the name Chandler, anyway.'

'How come?'

'Dad and I did a big trawl of all the local Chandlers soon after you left – went through the phone books for Wintersham and surrounding districts, as far out as Winkley. There were quite a lot of us, including a couple in Frickleigh. No Sofia, though.' Fanny's marriage theory for Sofi and Peter seemed to be holding up. 'Tell you what, Guy, I've got to go over to Dipsey next week. Fancy a little trip? We could go the coast road and look in at Gullworthy.'

'Ah, that's nice of you, Doug. Someone's offered me a lift today, as it happens. Girl at work – the one doing the house sale. We're popping down there Sunday; she likes driving.'

He grinned. 'You're a crafty sod, Guy. Dad mentioned you had this little number at the office. Aren't you two, like – an item?'

'We were, I suppose.'

Another thunderous laugh: 'You don't exactly live in a monastery, do you!'

'All right, we still get on. Nothing serious.'

'That's not what Dad thinks. Has these visions – you know, love between the filing cabinets? I dunno, all these lovelies swooning at your feet. What with the one in Norway . . .'

'Sweden. Anyway you're both well wrong this time, I'm afraid.'

I've always liked Doug, but at that moment it was more than I could bear; nothing could convey the gaping abyss inside me.

'Sorry, Guy, didn't mean to be mean. Anyway – so she's helping you track this once-removed cousin of ours and her famous boyfriend, is she?'

'She might be.'

'Well, let's know how it all pans out. Down at Gullworthy.'

52

Early Sunday morning, hearing Georgina's triple hoot from the street below, I grabbed a coat and dashed down two flights – ricking an ankle in the process. Outside, it was breezy but sunny; on a day like this Helena would be walking Snuffi by the river, or racing him up onto the cliffs. In the car Georgina started telling me the latest on Ben's property sale, but I wasn't really listening; after a while she gave up. In our separate worlds we stared at the road, chewing her perpetual mints. At last we were turning off on the winding track down to Winkley Sands.

'All right, Guy – it's your day, how d'you wanna do this?'

'How do you mean?'

'Well, would you rather get the business out of the way first, or shall we sun ourselves for a bit and then look for that work-shop thing?'

'I'm easy. What would you rather do?' I knew she'd have it all planned out, and she had.

'Only it's supposed to blow up windy later on. The forecast said rain. It's so nice at the moment, isn't it? We'll miss the sun altogether if we don't grab it.'

I'd not thought of getting the weather forecast. In my state of mind it was too much effort to think ahead about anything.

Gullworthy Cove is not that easy to get to in a car, and when you do there's nowhere to put it, so our best bet was to park at Winkley and walk there via the beach. The tide was on its way out, leaving the sand soft and glittering, like toffee; the sun was already beating down. Georgina had taken off her white cardigan and flung it over her shoulder.

My ankle was still sore, but once we were on the move I forgot it; deep inside, meanwhile, another part of me was crying out to be taken care of. As we hobbled across the sloping sand she half-turned, clasping my wrist and supporting me in a snug, sideways embrace. This is going to sound terrible now, but it was like being drawn back into an obsolete mode of being: somehow – I can't explain it any better – the familiar old *habit* of George's physical presence, the reassuring warmth of her, seemed to take me over.

We must have tramped half a mile or so. George's bare, fine-haired arms felt nice and warm, and smelled of that lemony soap which I liked; yet all the while the closeness of her body was magnifying Helena's absence, Helena's tormenting distance from me, like a constant ache of separation. At the far end we sat down for a rest, leaning back against the rocks. Monday felt a long way off: tracking down Sofi ahead of my appointment with Mr Conroy didn't seem quite such a burning issue any more.

I honestly don't know how it happened but we ended up in a kiss: there was the taste of that familiar mouth again, fresh and minty as in the days when we'd first got together. Everything was sweet and yet desolate, all in one breath.

Beyond the west end of Winkley Sands, if it's low tide, you can walk right round the headland into Gullworthy Cove. I'd done it dozens of times. The tide hadn't long started going out, so we weren't going to get cut off. I told George it was easy, but she was staring out to sea with that funny helpless look. There was something appealing about her when she was like that. We had another big kiss. I could tell she enjoyed it, and within that confined, remembered intimacy so did I, at the same time as the pain of what we were doing cut right through me.

'Come on, George, round this way.' I went ahead to show how to balance and pick your way between the rockpools. The wind was quirkier down here. A few yards out the glistening boulders threw up cascades of dazzling white foam; you could see mini-rainbows. Trying not to topple, I was in a sudden déjà vu moment – right back at Segelholm standing on the rocks, smelling the sea and the wind-blown pines. A second later Georgina started wobbling towards me, looking petrified. She lunged forward and grabbed my arm. We laughed. The sun was really hot now.

Then I thought of the Whimsies. They're the caves at Gullworthy, round on the other side. They're so tucked out of sight, a lot of people don't even know about them, but it's an extensive system of interconnecting caverns and – if you go far enough in – a lot of underground pools; plus some dark spaces where nobody goes, ever. You see bats sometimes. They're charming creatures, but it's so dark, some people find them frightening. You can go in two ways: the first is a proper entrance, biggish, with steps and railings, but I like the smaller one further on – an old haunt of mine as a boy. I had a memory of these nice flat rocks, well above the rockpools, a few feet inside the cave mouth. On a sunny day it's dry enough; the tide takes several hours to go out and come in again, so it's quite safe. They say someone forgot the time and drowned in there once, but that doesn't happen these days.

The other thing was – unless we were unlucky and bumped into a school party or something – we'd be well out of sight. I've already tried to explain how it was between Georgina and me. The truth is I'd never have thought of her in that way any more if it hadn't been for the knowledge that, however unimaginable, I'd got to forget Helena.

None of us gets more than one chance at life; just then, mine was in catastrophic breakdown. Helena was gone out of it forever, and there was absolutely nothing I could do about it. Most of us have a sort of self-preservation instinct; in the end there's an element of sheer survival. Losing Helena left me with no choice but to try and move on. I truly believed if only George and I could manage to draw on that moment together – if I could put everything else out of my mind and break with all that had happened – then perhaps it would be thinkable to start looking forward, start getting through the minutes and the hours again. It sounds crazy, but George could be the person who would show me the way, so I thought. She'd be the one to 'cure' me. It was foolish, and selfish too, I know it was – and you could say manipulative; I'm not denying it and it's not something I'm proud of.

We lay in the sun for a while outside. We were both lightly dressed for September, but it was all right. After we'd cuddled a bit longer, I said why didn't we move inside the cave a little way, and she got up and went in. Once we were there, though, it was much chillier than you'd expect. By the time we'd found somewhere dry to lie down we were shivering; George let me caress her some more, but she was tense and goose-pimply. She was really sweet, although sometimes I caught a watchful, frightened squirrel sort of look in her eyes. There was a dripping sound coming from far inside; now and then it was as if you could hear voices, a long way in.

After a few minutes we moved out in the sun again. My head felt all jumbled up. Georgina was edgy, but she still wanted to hold hands, which made me feel accepted and somehow humbled.

'Never mind, Guy, it's made a day out, though, hasn't it?' George's optimistic gloss on things only heightened the desolation. Her down-to-earthiness, something that would always peep out behind the chic and the glamour, was one of the things I liked most about her, and yet it irked me that she could talk that way, mid-morning, as if the day were as good as over.

Not long afterwards she spotted a seagull with about a foot of line caught in its wing. She started trying to creep closer, tracking it across the rocks.

'Leave it, George.' The bitterness of everything seemed to suffocate me.

'Well someone needs to do something. He could die otherwise.'

'We can't do anything, it's pointless. He'll be all right.'

'Oh yeah? You think he's gonna shake it off all by himself?'

'He might do.'

'He might not!'

'So what, then? You can't keep going round rescuing things, it's daft. Anyway, it's happening all the time, it's not as if you can stop it.'

She stopped and smiled. 'That's not what this is about, is it?'

'What's that supposed to mean?' People love to talk about what everything's *about*, but it nettled me that she could use such a glib phrase, not having the first idea what I was going through – as if you could read a person's feelings like some child's story book.

'Poor Guy.'

'I don't know what you're on about.' I stomped off down the beach; the wind was making me shiver again, standing between the rocks watching the water seep into my shoes. Georgina came up and put her arms round me.

'Don't be miserable, Guy. I do like you, you know.'

'Do you? You seem pretty fed up with me.'

'*I'm* fed up? Hark who's talking.' She looked away along the cliffs.

'I'm sorry, George – I don't know what's the matter with me.' I tried to put my lips to her cheek, but the warmth had gone out of us.

'I thought we were just having a nice day out, weren't we? Don't be so mopey! You need to get a bit more real, that's all.'

'What d'you mean, *real*? What about?'

'Us, of course.'

'You've lost me now.'

'It's obvious, isn't it? Of course we get *on* all right, I'm not talking about that. Well, we rub along, anyway. It's no big deal – we like each other. But let's face it, you and I haven't got that much in common, have we.'

'Haven't we?' It was infuriating she should start this sort of conversation when moments earlier we'd tried to be in a safe, personal place together. 'I thought we had!'

'Like what, for instance?'

'Oh, come off it, George, don't act all dumb. You know you wanted to as much as I did.'

'Ah, well that's just it, isn't it.'

'What?'

'Now you're only talking about sex, aren't you.'

'Am I? All right then, perhaps I am, but it's you who said it, not me.' The seagull had taken off, calmly trailing his line. Georgina had that look, as if to say she knew best – well, she did as a rule. A tanker was crawling along the horizon. She stood gazing out to sea with her neutral, perfectly innocent little smile.

'Look, George, yes, for goodness' sake, of course you turn me on, what's wrong with that?'

'OK, so what else is there?'

'What else?'

'You said we had things in common.'

'Of course we have – why are you denying it all of a sudden?'

She stayed motionless, studying the tanker. 'You still haven't given me a "for instance".'

'Oh, for God's sake, George . . .'

'Just give me one example.' She turned her head and looked straight at me with those deep blue-green eyes; the shapely chin jutted upwards.

'All right: houses, then, if you like. We talk about them all the time, don't we?'

'Do we?'

'Leave it out, George, you know bloody well we do. You're the one with the big career at Castles, aren't you?'

'Oh, am I? Well if I am, maybe there's reasons. As a matter of fact I'm trying to earn a living, in case you hadn't noticed. *Some* of us have to.' Was this a dig at the inheritance? 'You know, Guy, you ought to start doing a bit more serious planning. Or have you given up on adult life altogether since that Great Big Adventure of yours?'

'What Great B . . .?'

'Oh, I get it: you're banking on Uncle Benjie to bail you out.

Well I wouldn't count too many of *his* chickens yet a while, if I were you.'

So it *was* about money; the indignation welled up like nausea. 'Of course I'm not *banking* on him!'

It was shameful of her to talk like that – how could she begin to understand any of it? I'd loved Ben and I missed him: those things were real. It was true I should have gone and seen him a whole lot more when he was still around, cared for him far better – him and the rest of the family. I regretted it all bitterly, but that didn't alter the connection I felt to them – and it had nothing to do with the estate. 'Anyway, how did we get onto this? You asked me what we had in common: well I've told you – houses.'

She turned away again. 'We're estate agents, Guy! It's our *job* – what else would we talk about?'

'Oh, shut up, George! So that's all off limits now, is it, everything to do with work? If that's the way you think, you're not likely to find much in common with anybody, are you? We all have to work, for chrissake – it's a third of our lives, or something. If you leave all that out . . .'

'I'm not leaving anything out, Guy. You are.'

My blood was up. 'Leaving out? What then?'

She lifted her eyes to mine with perfect self-assurance and uttered the unanswerable word:

'Love.'

Later, climbing the chalky steps all the way up onto the cliffs, she took my hand again. The tide was on the turn and the sun had gone in. Up here the wind was much stronger; a sudden gust almost knocked us off our feet. A vast mass of black cloud was rushing in from the south-west. The first heavy raindrops spattered our faces.

'There's no need to get so worked up, Guy. It's just facts, that's all. We like each other, we've *said* that, and OK, we turn each other on sometimes, I'm not saying we don't. Be honest, though, you can't stand me when I'm doing my own thing – being myself

– can you? And – don't take this the wrong way, Guy, it's nothing *wrong* with you – I can't stand you either, most of the time.'

'Oh, great. So what's the bad news?'

'We're talking properly now, aren't we? I should hope we could at least do that without you taking umbrage. The thing is, you're different since you got back from that Danish island.'

'Swedish.'

'Swedish. You don't have to sulk.'

'I'm not sulking.' It felt as if she were taking me apart under a microscope. 'Anyway, how am I different?'

She gave my arm a pally squeeze. 'This is gonna sound awful, but you're – well, you're more grown up. Not a lot, but . . .' She said it with such a rueful look, it was impossible to be angry any more.

'I thought you said I'd given up on adult life.'

'That was the planning bit – it's true, you need to think more long-term. And you've still got sex on the brain all the time – like most men, if you ask me. But there's more to you now.'

'Thanks a lot.'

'I'm sorry, Guy. I knew you wouldn't like it.'

'I don't – I need to hear it, that's all.'

'There you are, you see?'

'What?'

'You've said it – you want to hear. You never really did that before, you know? That's how you're different: you're hearing the bad news as well as the good.' Her bitter-sweet smile lingered.

A minute later she turned to me again. 'Did you meet someone, Guy, while you were out there?'

Up ahead were benches, a few yards from the edge. We sat down, huddled against the gale, staring out over the sea. The clouds rolled lower still; we were getting drenched.

'George, everything's gone wrong, I . . .' The tears came like a tidal wave. Without a word, George turned and held me, very tight and safe. I still had a lot of growing up to do, but she was right: something inside me had started to change.

53

By this time there was a proper squall whipping in over the cliffs; we'd be soaked to the skin if we stayed any longer. Heads bent against the gusts, we squelched across the turf. Through horizontal sheets of rain the contours of Gullworthy Lighthouse hovered above the void.

Georgina had the inspiration. 'Come on, they should still be open. At least it'll be dry in there. We can sit it out till this lot eases up.'

'What about the workshop?'

'What?'

'You know, Peter Jansson.'

'Oh god, sorry, Guy, I'd forgotten all about him. Don't worry, there should be time on the way back.'

I'd spent numerous summers in and around Winkley as a youngster, but never been inside the lighthouse. Drawing near the white-and-red striped building, we were soon shielded from the gale by its reassuring bulk. The heavy iron door opened with a querulous squeak, the impersonal metallic space receiving us with hollow echoes. Across from the entrance a large table offered damp bundles of curling sepia postcards. Beyond the battened windows trees lashed the air, the wind's roar curiously muffled in here. It can't have been much after five, but darkness was closing in fast, the afternoon curtailed by the sudden storm. There seemed to be no one about.

'Have you been up before, Guy? It's great at the top. Come

on, we might as well now we're here.' She led the way up the unlit spiral.

There were ninety-five steps to the first landing; my legs felt leaden. 'How much further?'

'You can't be tired already! All that cycling in Sweden – thought you'd be in fine form. There's another floor after this one, then another, I think. Or is it three more?' She towed me across the landing to the next flight. 'You wait – it's worse going down.' She was off again, with me panting at her sinewy ankles. A distant clank made us stop and listen. Was it only the wind making the ironwork strain and creak like an old steam engine?

At the top a blast of wind and rain whistled through an open doorway. For a dizzy second, glimpsing ominous skies over a black horizon, I could have been looking out across the strait at Nordspetsen, the sea whipped up in furious ranks of tossed whiteness.

We were about to step through and walk round the main lamp when a burly keeper in a navy-blue jersey appeared, blocking our way.

'Can I 'elp at all?'

My eyes drew level with the lifeboat logo on his barrelled chest. 'Sorry, we were . . .'

'Lamp's orff limits now, if that's what yer after.' He towered over us, rain dripping from his nose, scowling at the horizon. 'Wouldn't git 'er goin' before six as a rule, but it's kickin' up a bit rough tonight, see. No good waitin' till nightfall wiv this lot closin' in, is it?' He faced us again and added more kindly: 'Sorry 'baht that. Why doncha pop back termorrer? You can still 'ave a look from top landin', if yer like – down one from 'ere. Should be aada see 'er flashin' in a minute.'

George was right: going down was worse – you could feel it in the back of the legs after the first few dozen steps. Nightfall or not, it was almost pitch black now on the narrow staircase; whatever the lighthouseman's expertise with the lamp, internal lighting wasn't a priority. Georgina let me go first this time, growing more giddy with each clanking circuit round the endless spiral. As we reached the top landing, glad of the brief respite, a livid flash from outside told us the main lamp had started beaconing at regular six-second intervals. Blinded for an instant, I hesitated. All at once in the gloom I sensed somebody else there. Surely we'd not passed anyone on the way up?

Six long seconds elapsed again, and in the next fleeting beam I glimpsed, at the head of the stairs opposite, a pair of young lovers locked in a passionate embrace. Under the spell of their presence I froze: two people absorbed in the moment and in each other, their bond clear and compelling.

Georgina emerged behind me. The two looked across, startled, the girl pulling a shawl closer round her neck. Her partner, somewhat taller, was still tenderly enfolding her in a protective, almost angelic pose.

'Oh, hi.' The deep voice resonated in the hollow void; another flash from outside lit up the head of short fair hair and a striking Jesuslike beard.

Georgina slipped past me and started heading across to the downward flight. 'So sorry. We thought you could get right up to the lamp. Not tonight, apparently!'

'No problems.' He shifted to one side, making room as she descended into the darkness. 'It's not our normal place to make love,' he added to me with easy humour, 'we yust – couldn't help.'

I stopped again, transfixed. The girl flicked her head and frowned, brushing the flaxen hair from her eyes.

'Come *on*, Guy,' Georgina called briskly from below.

In the awkwardness of the moment I wavered, unable to speak. The next flash lit up the young man's quick frown.

'*Guy!*' Georgina's tone was sharp now. 'We've got to *go.*' The blackness filled my eyes once more as I shuffled past them.

54

On the motorway juggernauts deluged the windscreen with water.

'You're sure it was them? Why didn't you . . .?'

'George, how could I? You saw, they were . . . In any case, I didn't say I was sure.'

'So? You could have asked, couldn't you?'

'Oh, just leave it, George. I can come back another day.'

'All right, be like that.' She sat hunched over the wheel, peering through sheets of rain. It was pitch dark now, but in the beam of oncoming headlights I could see the hurt in her eyes.

'George, I'm sorry, that was . . .'

'Don't mind me, I'm just the chauffeur! I thought we came down here to find them, that's all. It's not been much of a day otherwise, has it?' The events of the past few hours hung over us; we drove on in silence to the steady beat of windscreen wipers.

A little later she sighed and turned to me. 'I didn't mean it that way, Guy, I'm . . .'

'No, you've every right to be cross. All the same, thanks for today – and everything else, George. You've been . . .'

'Any time.'

The thought of having found both Sofi and Peter together at long last was stunning, even if I'd hoped and prayed for nothing less. Surely it must have been them? I had a sudden joyful image of Helena, in the kitchen at Hörnvik, taking the phone from the hook – her tears of relief, struggling to grasp that she was hearing Peter's living voice:

'*Peter*? Är det *du*?'

Yet in the same moment I knew this had to be pure fantasy on my part. What possible basis was there for thinking he would have rung her with the good news? He'd been gone three years or more: if he intended to get in touch, he'd have done it long ago, wouldn't he – if not the moment he and Sofi reached England safe and sound, then at least as soon as they'd got their bearings and found somewhere to live?

Lying awake that night, the ghastly truth sank in: Helena must still be languishing, distraught and inconsolable, in total ignorance of her brother's survival. My knowledge of Peter was scant, apart from Fanny's impression of an impetuous, somewhat rootless young adventurer. No doubt that had counted for something in his appeal for Sofi – leaving home, risking everything for the man she loved. Helena had described him as a virtual fugitive; but from what? There'd been trouble with the police over an illegal immigrant; or was it, as Fanny hinted, Sofi's family and her father's disapproval that he was running from? Helena had also intimated how deep the Chandler–Jansson feud ran; these seemed more likely reasons.

When sleep came it was sporadic and short-lived: in the early hours I woke again with a pounding heart, furious at Peter Jansson. Being an adventurer was one thing, but how dare he vanish in a storm at sea and then wait years without telling anyone he'd survived? Keeping his family in the dark – and above all Helena, who had endured such anguish over him for so long!

If only I'd stopped to think, up in the lighthouse. Why hadn't I challenged him point-blank there and then?

Well, I'd got his address now – plus a little outstanding business to settle, as it happened, for a yachtsman from New Zealand. Aside from that, I still needed to talk with Sofi in person – hoping and believing, in the circumstances, she might forgive the intrusion. By daybreak I was ready to walk to Gullworthy if necessary and have it out with Peter Jansson once and for all.

55

Professional commitments, not surprisingly, didn't quite allow me to do that. It was Monday morning. Mindful of Georgina's heavy workload in what was to be my first full week back from close on two months' absence, taking yet more time off wasn't an option. There was also the small matter of Mr Conroy: resourceful George had made sure the appointment slotted neatly into the lunch-hour. I daren't overrun it.

Legal business takes for ever; anything to do with inheritance is the worst. The fact that I was about to produce what looked like the last missing link on the Chandler family tree seemed not to make a blind bit of difference. Given Peter and Sofi's likely pennilessness, it would have felt good – irrespective of my current feelings towards him – at least to help bring her inheritance to quick fruition. Unfortunately no force in the universe was going to hurry it up; Mr Conroy was not a man to take short cuts.

Back at the office Georgina, having finished the day's correspondence, had turned to publicity notices again.

'Type these up for me, Guy, would you? They're due for the *Extra* Wednesday.'

'Extra Wednesday?'

'The *Wintersham Extra*? You're still not quite with it today, are you. I've heard of jet-lagged, but keep *up* for goodness' sake.'

She passed me half a dozen sales blurbs, with room specs and prices. Ben's was among them – based on my own handiwork – but it hardly interested me. At the computer keyboard my fingers had forgotten how to spell. Wintersham and everyone in it felt as if they were the other side of a misted window, with me peering out, wondering where we were. Helena would be at *Musica* again today. There would be fewer visitors now. Loading her tray, wiping down the empty tables, turning chairs upside-down ready for closing . . .

Helena in her world: there was no place in it for me any more. Nor would there ever be.

After the day at Gullworthy Georgina and I virtually gave up talking about personal things. The wrongness of the relationship had become excruciating to us both; by mutual consent we'd abandoned any physical contact. Not that the attraction wasn't still there: the long-limbed beauty, those thoughtful eyes, that smiling, sensuous mouth. Yet all the while hers was the wrong smile, the wrong beauty; I pined for another.

In the office we circulated at a safe distance, trying to find some negotiable ground where we might coexist with a minimum of embarrassment. It was easiest to take refuge, as I'd always done, behind a façade of banter – still playing the hapless bachelor, telling her my 'case' was 'terminal', and so on. Nonetheless I knew how hurtful my actions had been, although for her part Georgina wouldn't allow any feelings to disturb the poised, outwardly radiant persona that made her so well suited to take on Sidney's mantle.

Where the emotional connection had run its course, these cheery, sexless asides were now all we had, as she'd have put it, in common – apart from the inevitable houses, that is. Over them she remained my clear superior, and always would; I still had the greatest respect for her cleverness in snatching Castles back from the Receivers' unwelcome attentions. For that we were all in her debt.

A dismal autumn stretched before us. On Saturday nights I'd sit warming a pint of Diamond's in the Black Ram; cousin Doug would often drop by. His live-in girlfriend of seven years' standing had recently thought better of it, and him, and gone off with a plumber from Swanage, who thereby incurred Doug's deepest wrath. Like me Doug now appeared aimlessly single; we'd commiserate in a pathetic fog of alcohol, looking for what might seem the funny side. In reality we were each adrift in our own private world, with no landmarks to steer by.

It would have felt like a betrayal, though, to start discussing Helena with Doug. I let him more or less reconfigure the whole Swedish experience, too numbed to protest – going along with his silly fantasies of 'Scandi maidens' and 'sex goddesses'. Behind the beer-driven crosstalk, meanwhile, I was fighting to retrieve some semblance of rationality.

Everyone has the right to choose. Helena had not, in the end, chosen me – it was as simple as that. Looked at this way, the whys and wherefores were all beside the point. And yet, bit by bit, some of Doug's venom must have begun to percolate into my system. Perhaps I was seeking the line of least resistance – and finding the lowest level. Deep down, in my lion's den of emotion, prowled a jealous resentment that threatened to consume me. Helena hadn't just chosen someone else: she'd chosen Ulf. Why him, of all people?

Big, heavy-limbed Ulf, the roof-fixer, renovating the beams, painting the outhouses. Ulf the breadwinner, in charge at the cinema, single-handed: running the projector, masterminding the programmes, cleaning the auditorium. And Ulf the defender, standing on a chair, scowling through black hair: with his sweaty, no-nonsense determination he'd stopped a whole auction in its tracks for her sake. You couldn't argue with that kind of grit – it was plain for all to see. It came to me that I'd admired Ulf's sheer physicality, his stamina and his courage from the moment of our first contact. Admired, and feared.

Anyone could see he'd done an enormous amount for Helena. Correction: done *everything* for her. It wasn't just the practicalities: since early childhood he'd been a mainstay of her psyche – of her sanity, even. Was it not Ulf who had gathered her up, ravaged by grievous loss, and helped her rebuild her life? He'd supported her when she needed him most. Time and again Ulf had *proved* his strength, his faithfulness – yes, his love. That, ultimately, had to be why she'd chosen him – her *lifeline*. How could anyone ever compete with all that?

Was that what I'd hoped to do, then – compete? It was, of course; but at the beginning, in the breathless thrill of being with her, it never once occurred to me to think in those terms. With her unerring honesty Helena had made clear from the outset how things stood. Those innocent, appealing eyes, hiding nothing: *my boyfriend*. And yet, in the earliest days, her relationship to Ulf had felt like a harmless 'given' – something that, while known to us both, we could somehow leave to one side. For me, even in that very first encounter with him at *Inblick*, he seemed barely to figure as a significant presence in her life. I'd already started to fall in love with her – how could it have been otherwise?

That's your Inner Child talking . . . It was wonderful when she started to pick up on my words: mocking, yet at the same time affirming my approach to things. Or was that another fatal misreading: had I missed a more literal, too painful truth? Was it, in fact, childishness – of the kind so patently exposed in recent days by Georgina – that would become Helena's overriding image of me? *A kiss is still a kiss* . . . But if it was true that her feelings were really engaged elsewhere, then the warning signs must have been there, surely, right from the start. Why hadn't I seen them? Try as I might to recall our conversations, any actual signals she may have given as to what she and Ulf felt for each other were now gone from my memory.

About Helena and me, on the other hand, I'd sensed (imagined?) such a rightness: it had seemed inconceivable that her relationship with him could in any way measure up to that! Her smile, her voice, her quick laughter had torn down my defences. So open, so warm and welcoming – if this was how I remembered her in those first hours spent together, must it not have been so? Lulled by that certainty, each day lost in deeper love for her, all thought of serious contest had been subdued.

Instead, the cherished hopes that germinated in me as time went by – like those hardy clumps of wayside daisies, all over the island – had taken nourishment whenever and wherever they could find it. From the moment I first met Ulf, for instance, it had struck me how oddly assorted he and she appeared. To my watchful eye he looked altogether too large and lumbering for Helena: alongside her lithe, graceful movements, her intelligence, her quick flashing glances, he cut a rough, rather clumsy figure. Not that he wasn't sensitive and articulate in his way – cultured, even, when it came to films; but his was an earthier, more ponderous presence than hers, mentally as well as physically.

Well, what they felt for each other might be no more complicated than the attraction of opposites. Who was to say Ulf couldn't be exactly what Helena needed? There was no doubt (my next sour thought) he was exactly what her house needed . . . That job on the underpinning wouldn't wait for ever: my guess was Ulf would be on it by this time. What changes would they have made since I left? Doubtless he'd be staying over more often at Hörnvik now.

Staying over – what was I thinking? He'd have moved in there for good. As for the tiny house on Älvatrappan, so convenient for *Inblick* – yes, he'd want to keep that on for a while, but there was no comparison with hers at Hörnvik, to which her commitment was absolute. They'd be taking it all in hand together: the house, the garden, perhaps very soon creating that proper art studio for her at the back . . .

Would they? Would he ever truly grasp that side of her – the artistic need, the inner drive to self-expression? More crucially: could he ever *love* her for it, as I did? Somehow it wasn't imaginable. If it had been – that's to say, if I could have seen him as a genuine rival for her soul; if, indeed, I'd ever felt myself to have been properly *defeated* in love by Ulf – then it might have seemed conceivable to let go. That, in any case, would have been the courageous, the manly thing to do.

But it was no more in my power to do it than to stop loving her.

My unchanging belief was that Helena's art formed an indispensable core to her existence – and that she needed a companion who could help her reset that artistic focus. Did he have the patience – no, the *vision* – to foster her creative reawakening? I was convinced he hadn't. Given that deficit, how could she ever be happy with Ulf? The question wouldn't leave me now. It wasn't jealousy that gripped me so much as a paralysing sense of injustice. Where before Ulf's innate goodness and steadfastness had seemed to earn and deserve her love, I could no longer see them as sufficient. And so, pointlessly, I yearned for her.

Each day became a renewed battle to put the two of them out of mind. People around me provided some distraction, as did the work; aside from earning a living, in fact, I could see no other point in carrying on at Castles. The nights, meanwhile, were indescribably worse: then the tide of hopelessness and self-loathing would engulf me. Hadn't I myself been the greatest disruptive force in Helena's life? My actions and words had caused her nothing but pain. The only solace was in the thought of having made a clean break – leaving her relationship with Ulf to heal quickly, if it was capable of healing.

Abandon all hope, ye who enter! I tried to tell myself there was no alternative any more but to face the reality of a life without her.

56

One small thing, nevertheless, still remained that I could do for Helena – the last thing I'd ever do for her. Was it the finality of this, then, that made me put it off so long? Of course work inter-vened: Georgina, it must be said, proved an inspired leader around whom the whole Castles team now rallied in a way that would have been unimaginable during Sidney's reign. For a while, too, even my weekends were spoken for – by Doug and his precious garden shed, as it happened (I knew a bit of basic carpentry and he'd asked for help).

I got away at last one Saturday in November, taking the early train down to Winkley. Having shunned confrontation all my life, this time – watching the Dorset hills and barren fields of stubble filing past – I was fired up. I'd say my piece to Peter, make him see how unforgivably he'd prolonged Helena's distress: he'd be forced to end it!

A heavy coastal mist hung low over sand and shingle as I crunched westward below invisible clifftops; there, close to the dripping rock-face, lay the huddle of sheds and huts that was home to him and Sofi. They lived in a funny little loft with dormer windows above the repair workshop.

The young woman who came to the door was more assured, more mature-looking than I'd visualised her. It was clear at once she was heavily pregnant. Holding a scrap of sandpaper, her loose smock marked with lines of dust, she'd been lending a hand with the unfinished yacht's hull now suspended on its side in the middle of the floor. A smell of hot glue and planed wood hung in the air. She pushed the long fair tresses back from striking blue eyes.

'Sofi Chandler?' As I said the name she touched her lip in puzzlement, searching my face. Her partner came and put a shielding arm round her, the trim auburn beard and worn jacket giving him a somewhat monkish air. There was no mistaking the couple Georgina and I had passed in the lighthouse. For an awkward moment they eyed me guardedly, but once they heard who I was, and recalling that afternoon, Sofi introduced Peter and asked me in. The diffidence soon melted away, and I was invited to share a simple lunch. While he set out a third place on a pair of sack-covered tea chests that served as a table, she began ladling soup, turning spontaneously to me:

'Your father was brother to Grandpa Edward? Wonderful! He visit sometimes, from the north, when we was live in Vätshamn. Wonderful – a wonderful grandpa. He bring always his banjo, sing English songs – "My Blue Heaven", "As Time Goes By" and so. I was fifteen when Edward die – but it's long time since.' She paused a moment, staring absently.

It's disarming to be with young people very much in love – brushing wood-shavings off the makeshift tablecloth and clasping hands across it, gazing into each other's eyes. In that kind of atmosphere no one wants to introduce a jarring note; as we sat enjoying our meal, it felt right to start with the good news. Nothing specific was yet settled over Ben's Will, but Sofi was entitled to know she was in line for a substantial inheritance from her great-uncle. Talking in general terms about what she might expect in the fullness of time, I couldn't but be touched by her look of joyful anticipation.

'Oh, and there's something else.' I slipped the harmonica out of its box.

Sofi gave a puzzled smile. 'From great-uncle Benyamin?'

'Not exactly – it was your grandfather's, in fact.'

Intrigued, she took the little instrument gently in the palm of her hand. Turning it over, she felt the silvery case and smooth edges, tested the little button at one end; she wouldn't put it to her lips. 'It was in Benyamin's house?'

'He wanted it returned to Edward. It's a bit late for that now, obviously, so . . .'

'You mean – it's for me? Grandpa – he want that I should get it?'

'It belongs in your family, of course – you're the person to take it now. I heard about your father, Sofi – I'm so sorry.'

She frowned, giving me a direct look. 'It's OK, Guy. We're together, Peter and me,' she held his arm, 'we manage.' There was a pause; she looked down. 'This thing – *munspel*. It's a mouth-organ?'

'It is. You can also call it a harmonica.'

'Harmonica. Of course – *munharmonika*. It's a very fine one. Guy, I wouldn't know what I shall do with it.'

'Play it, of course.'

'It's too hard! I'm not musical. Do you play, Guy?'

'Not really. I've only . . .'

'Go on! Play something. Please?' She passed it back and clapped her hands girlishly. They sat watching, willing me to play.

I blew a few random notes and stopped. 'Are you sure?'

'Do it – play for Grandpa.'

Throughout the weeks in Sweden there was only one song I'd managed to get anywhere with, and even then not the whole thing. I cupped the harmonica, trying for the proper Larry Adler hand-shape. The first few lines of 'As Time Goes By' are easy enough. To my ear, knowing this had once been a favourite of Edward's, the song had acquired a special resonance; it was uniquely evocative now, playing a few bars to his granddaughter. I felt honoured.

For anyone familiar with the film, of course, the lyrics can't fail to evoke *Casablanca*, with its compelling black-and-white cameo of unrequited love. So much the more hauntingly for me, there-fore – after *Inblick* and all the events flowing from it – they would forever conjure joyous, irredeemable moments with Helena. *You must remember this* . . . I reached the middle section with its tricky key change, faltered, and gave up. Sometimes the simplest cadence will get straight to me: for a second I had to turn away.

It was hardly a demonstration – I'd not even begun to master those poignant semitones. Sofi and Peter clapped anyway, saying they loved it. We went back to our meal, but I could see Sofi had been moved by the simple little tune.

'You know, Guy, you look so natural when you play – on the harmonica. You should have it.'

'No, I couldn't possibly – it's yours. It was your grandfather's, it's in your family. You've a right to it.'

'I'd like that you have it.'

'It's not all that difficult, Sofi – honestly, you'll be far better than me, once you've . . .'

'Guy, I insist.' She fixed me again with that steady, serious gaze. 'Really.' There was a powerful self-possession about Sofi; her mind was made up. More than ever, too, I realised how much the harmonica had come to mean to me.

'Sofi, that's so generous. It's a lovely thing, I'd be very happy, as long as . . .'

'That's settled then, no more discussion. Have another bit of bread?'

Before I left, inevitably, she wanted to ask about Sweden. It was hard to know how to answer. After weeks and weeks with no word of anybody on Lammland, the whole episode was beginning to feel more and more unreal. It was still beyond me to confide in anyone the real truth of what had happened, but I tried to relay what little news I could of Helena, and a few things Fanny and Maja had told me – most of which they knew already.

In an effort to change the subject I asked how they'd found their feet in England. Sofi gave a bubbly account of initial struggles in London and the move to Gullworthy – she'd been adamant they should go there when she realised it was close to Edward's birthplace. Peter, however, was saying nothing. It wasn't surprising he didn't want to talk about being swept overboard and surviving heaven knows how many hours in a rough sea, but I had expected a little more animation over the family he'd left behind, not to mention the baby now on the way.

'You've landed on your feet here, then, Peter, haven't you – boats being your strong point? Fine workshop. How do you like the work?'

'Yes. It's a nice yob.' He studied his roughened palms, as if baffled at my interest.

'There's another small job waiting for you, actually.' He looked up with a defensive little movement, but when I told him of Ken Hammond's yacht near Dipsey he seemed pleased, promising to follow it up. 'I expect you're busy. Do you get time for other things at all? You know, out and about – meeting people?'

'Friends, and so, yes. We meet sometimes – not every days. It's different.'

'You must miss home, surely.' I thought I saw a chance. 'Have you talked with Cecilia? Helena?'

'No.' He said it without discernible emotion of any kind. It felt like a solid wall of resistance against my chest.

'No? Your sisters? Why ever not?' He lowered his eyes; I went in grim pursuit now. 'I should have thought it's about time, isn't it? I can't speak for Cecilia, but Helena's worried sick about you – you must know that, surely.' He looked pleadingly at Sofi, as if expecting her to come up with an excuse for him. 'Don't you think you owe it to her? She's your *sister*, for God's sake. At least tell her you're *alive*?'

His English was poorer than Sofi's, but he must have grasped what I meant. The name *Helena* passed between them a couple of times, and then she flung it at him a third time with what sounded like reproachful, questioning sarcasm: *Helee-ena*? Suddenly it wasn't me confronting him any more: Sofi was doing it for me. Peter's face creased in distress – for a moment I thought he was going to cry. The next minute he was talking back at her in rapid

Swedish. All I could catch were occasional names: *Maja* once or twice, and an emphatic *Cecilia*.

Sofi turned to me. 'Guy, please. You must excuse Peter. His English – he's not learn it on school. And he have so many problem – with the Swedish emigration and so.' She glanced round the workshop. 'He don't speak about it, but here in England, he haven't a work permit. He's work "black", if I can say so. He get his money, no questions. We can live – and it's the baby coming, of course. So it's better he don't talk with the Swedish emigration. He owe the tax also, for his last job – the ferries company. It's another problem: Peter, he don't leave the ferries in the right way, with all papers and signatures, so it's better they doesn't find him now.'

'Yes, but surely – the family, his . . .'

'He know what you mean – OK, yes, it's terrible for them, but listen me: he *was* in contact. He write Helena a postcard.'

'A *postcard*?'

'I know, it's strange. Peter, he's that way now: it's pain him but he can't do no better. He say it's not possible do more.' She looked exasperated, as if sharing my anger. 'Peter, he . . . You must understand, it's not so easy . . .'

'*Easy*? You think it's *easy* for his sisters, not knowing where he is, not knowing he . . .?'

'But Guy – they *know* it – yes, know he's alive. He have write till Helena. Cecilia also. Of course it's for a long time ago – oh, three year, about – but it's mean he done what he must do – he's tell them he's safe, he's well. If Helena she say Peter haven't send a message, it's not true: she have hear of him, here in England.' She met my eyes with a look of entreaty.

My fury at Peter's negligence turned to disbelief. *Strange things happen on boats, Guy . . . If only I knew he was – somewhere.* Helena's honesty had been absolute: she'd heard nothing from him. If she'd had news, she'd have told me.

Sofi caught the bewilderment and pain in my face. 'I'm sorry, Guy, I don't know what Helena have say you, but Peter, he *have* send it, I know. But he can't talk with his family right now. He have many problem,' she repeated. 'It's mean – number one – he must make a life *here*. Later, maybe, it can be possible he talk with them again? When he feel himself ready?' Watching Peter, sitting there tugging at his threadbare sleeves, I had an inkling of his torment.

On the journey home, staring out at a grey, autumnal landscape, the sudden memory came to me of Tilly's single heart-rending card from Edward in Sweden. What is it that drives a man to leave his loved-ones, perhaps never to return? *A clean break* . . . Everyone needs approval, the support of family or friends; Edward must have felt he'd lost that. Peter likewise, it seemed: the need to get away, to sever all links, may have seized him with something like panic. His position with the Swedish authorities, especially over the unclosed police file, remained dubious. Like Sofi, he'd sacrificed everything for the love of his life. Now, strong in the knowledge of her at his side, it looked as though neither his beloved yacht in Hörnvik, nor a rightful share in the Jansson estate, nor indeed his sisters could tempt him back till he'd established his own independence and identity. In his way – much like Edward – Peter was a man of honour.

People lost at sea are turning up all the time . . . *Why wouldn't they find him, if he was dead?* Could Peter's card to Helena have gone missing in the post, then? Or was I simply naïve to think that, having received it, she'd have been incapable of keeping the fact from me?

My painfully rehearsed broadside at Peter had misfired in the end. That being the case, what was to stop me ringing Helena myself, to be reassured she had news of him?

But at that point my mind coiled back to the bleakest truth of all: my own reassurance in these matters was neither here nor there. Any call from me now would be a violation of her privacy, and Ulf's. Their life was none of my business any more. Whatever feelings Helena and I may once have had for one another: that was then. The fledgling love I'd so desperately wanted to believe we shared was part of a world that no longer existed.

57

The frosts came and even the Treen froze over; Columbus got fed up and went into early hibernation. We settled in for a long, hard winter. Dorset – despite global warming – was shrouded in snow; as memories of that second visit to Gullworthy receded, my emotional life seemed to ice up as well. Each evening, office hours done, I'd slip away in the dark without talking to anyone. Christmas had come and gone; Stephen and Zoë asked me to join them for New Year's Eve, but I couldn't face family life or anything resembling celebration.

Georgina continued a heroic campaign to stabilise the firm, unsung by anyone at Head Office; in retrospect we all cherished Sidney's humanity (more than we'd ever done while he was still around). By February Trevor, well-meaning as ever beneath that rather crude exterior, was regaling me once more with the delights of annual holidays in Perranporth:

'You know, Guy, you ought to come down sometime. Nice bit of bikini on offer – you'd be well in, single lad like yourself. Healthy instincts – know what I mean?' I tried to imagine *not* knowing what he meant. But where once I'd been irritated by his hang-ups and his sciatica, I now felt only sadness for him. Something else had changed too: none of his remarks struck me as the least bit funny any more.

Eventually a tentative spring got under way. Columbus – just when I'd forgotten all about him – came alive again. Spring and summer are his peak time for out-of-shell experiences; having missed most of last year's, I wanted to keep an eye on him.

Sometimes he'll stop and meditate for minutes on end, stock-still, that gnarled, primeval head elevated on the wrinkly stalk of a neck, eyes misted, as if the proof to Fermat's Last Theorem has that moment dawned. He lives in this Parkinsonian time warp – it's like something out of *Awakenings*. Another day it'll be no more than a pause between bites from a never-ending lettuce-leaf, or a little rest en route to the balcony.

One morning it hit me that I'd still done nothing about Tilly. My emotions might be in limbo but there was no excuse for not passing on what news I had of Edward and his family, so I made myself sit down and write a letter. Ringing her would have made for a more personal touch, but the deafness wasn't getting any better and I was terrified she might mishear and think he was still alive. The story about Philip and Maja wasn't easy either, but in the end I found a form of words that I thought conveyed it all to her quite gently. Of course when it came to Sofi and Peter things remained very uncertain, but there was an element of hopefulness now: surely it would raise Tilly's spirits to know Edward had had a family, that his delightful granddaughter had returned to his native Dorset, that I'd met her and her partner, and that they were expecting a baby.

I was about to seal the envelope when I thought of the flowers. Recalling Edward's bunch of anemones that Tilly had kept all those years, I opened a drawer and pulled out the spray of *Dog-collars* I'd snatched from the hedgerows that day cycling back from Fanny's. Their flat white petals were a little withered but the centres still glowed sunny yellow with a sweet, fresh smell; I dropped a couple in with the letter and went to post it, feeling I'd at least done one small thing for someone I really cared about.

At the end of May Georgina bought a big pot of lilies for my birthday. Everybody was so nice to me – I couldn't think I'd done anything to deserve it. In private my wordless grief could bring sudden tears; somewhere deep inside, frozen regrets were thawing. The lilies blossomed over and over; the new lino was full of petals and pollen. As spring gave way to summer I busied myself with practical things – cleaning out the gas fire, painting the kitchen. Churchgoing has never been my thing, but one Sunday morning I called into Saint Leonard's in Frickleigh; the theme of the sermon was Renunciation. For a second it felt as if there might be some sort of life ahead eventually.

June and July dragged on, hot and hay-feverish; annual leave was due again, but I couldn't decide where to go. Then one Saturday morning in the first week of August, listening to *The Four Seasons* and thinking I ought to do some housework for once, there was a call from Giles Conroy:

'Mr Chandler? We need your signature on a few documents. Could you pop into the office one day next week?' I'd not given a thought to Uncle Ben or the inheritance for months. Chalks & Conroy had transferred their operation to Throgmorton Street in the City (Edward's old hunting-ground): *pop in* meant take the train up to Cannon Street.

I cleared it with Georgina and took the Wednesday off. The previous day Columbus had gone walkabout in Bay Leaf Close and been trodden on by a neighbour, which meant having his broken leg pinned – and a phenomenally expensive overnight stay at the vet's. Crammed among the morning commuters staring through an unwashed window, it suddenly came to me: whatever the cost, I'd got to get out of Castles. The job didn't suit me, and I didn't suit it. I'd never get used to saying 'build' instead of 'building', or telling people I 'had concerns' when really I was fed up to the back teeth – things like that. There had to be something else I could do. Journalism had always appealed; then again, a patchy record at a provincial estate agent's was hardly the best springboard for launching a dynamic new career.

The business with Mr Conroy went smoothly enough. Ben's

house had a buyer: it sounded as if we might see an actual distribution of the estate at last. Afterwards I bought a paper and sat in a sandwich bar off Hanover Square scanning the jobs page.

I'm sitting there wondering whether to fork out for another chicken and mayonnaise sandwich when I notice this chap in a well-worn sheepskin jacket looking at me. The resemblance to Ulf is uncanny. It's even more uncanny when he lumbers over, John Wayne fashion, and stands leaning on the back of a chair.

'Hello, Guy.' It's the same old quiet, neutrally polite tone; he feels more like a ghost than a real person. The faint agricultural smell has come with him. 'What you doing here?'

'Ulf? Good god. Well, I have to be somewhere.' What I'm thinking is, what the devil are *you* doing here? Given the rarity of my London trips, it's outrageous bad luck, bumping into him like this. 'How are you?' How he is is the last thing I'm interested in. He pulls out the chair and slides into it as if there's never been a shadow of a problem between us. After months of telling myself I've got over all those petty resentments, they're already coming furiously to the boil again.

'Fine. Yust fine. I have holidays now – two week. It's my first visit here in England. It's a nice country,' he adds with an air of generosity.

'Where are you staying?'

'I'm stay here in London.'

His speech sounds more foreign than I remember. Waiting for me to ask something else, he drums peacefully on the table, looking out at the traffic as if to say this is his home now. I can feel my smile getting more and more cardboard. He offers no news, no plans. I'm desperate to ask after Helena but the idea of hearing him talk about her is insufferable. Another dread assails me: might he try and invite himself down to my place in Wintersham? Could Helena even be with him now, here in London? The pressure of his presence grows; my smile has died. Some perverse part of me insists on bringing things to a head.

'Look, Ulf, I've got nothing against you personally, but – well, we don't exactly get on, do we? It's not as if we've got that much *in common*, is it.' I've borrowed Georgina's phrase; he takes his time bringing his gaze round to me again.

'What are you try to say, Guy?' He raises his eyebrows pleasantly.

'I'm not *trying* to say anything! I just don't think we can sit here and chat like a couple of old buddies, that's all. As if nothing's happened.'

'Happened? Oh, that. It's in the past, Guy.' He looks out of the window again. 'In any case, I never said we was buddies.'

'That's not the point, is it. Don't be such a *jerk*.' He ignores this, watching a bus go by.

Insults aren't going to help: I've got to pull myself together. 'OK, Ulf, I'm sorry, that was way out of order. Let me say this: *I understand how things are*. That's all, really. *I understand*.' When it suits him he graces me with his sleepy eye contact. 'We all realise you and Helena were together long before I came on the scene – since you were kids, from what she's told me. I know you still are. She's explained how much you've done for her, what you mean to her. That's all clear, Ulf, and believe me, I *accept* it.' I feel myself groping for more of a saintly stance. 'As far as I'm concerned, good luck to you – both of you.' Saying it seems to exhaust me. Why has this had to happen? My face is turned almost to the wall. 'It's just that Helena and I, we were . . .' The conversation is doomed. The very fact of calling her by her name feels like sacrilege. What *am* I trying to say? 'Oh, this is useless. I can't explain – least of all to you. Why would you want to hear it?' I'm wishing he'd drop through the floor.

He muses for a moment, stroking his moonlike face. 'I'm sorry if you feel in that way, Guy. All I say is hello, I have holidays, how are you, and already you're spit fire on me. What is with you English?'

'*English?* That's got nothing to . . .'

'You talk such a lot of crap, Guy. I'm sorry for it, but it's that way. You always done, I think.' He ruminates on this with detached amusement. 'You don't never *understand* thomething, do you? Can't you see the facts?'

'*Facts?*' Now my pulse is racing. 'Oh, I can see the facts all right. OK, what does it matter if you know: I was in love with Helena, all right?' I'm forcing myself into the past tense. 'I really *loved* her, but we both know she was involved with you all along, don't we? And always will be, by the look of it. Like I say, good luck to you. I don't know if you've got enough space in that tiny imagination of yours to twig it's created a little stress for me, that's all. Is that so hard to get your head round? If it is, frankly I couldn't give a . . . Now will you just shove off and let me get on with my life?'

He looks out at the traffic again with a knowing smile, as if he's tried to share a joke with me that I simply don't get. 'OK, Guy, have it in your way. You can carry on be a – what you call in English – a bloody idiot? Do it – it's not a problem for me. I leave you in your precious life, without try explain about Helena.'

His arrogance is breathtaking. '*Explain?* You think you can *explain* her? Oh, of course – she appreciates your finer points, doesn't she. Can't say I've noticed them myself.' In fact his far-reaching virtues are all too clear to me: I'm digging myself into a deeper and deeper hole. He smiles back, sphinxlike. I'm thinking: we've got to end this before one of us does something stupid – it's sure to be me this time. 'All right, Ulf, I'll say this much, if you like: I was grateful for the room, OK? I mean it. That was very nice of you, so thanks a lot. But don't think it gives you the right to come here and gloat!'

Now he throws his head back and laughs at the ceiling. I'm not sure he even knows *gloat*. Several people glance across at our table.

'You think I come here yust for bug you? You *are* a idiot, Guy,' he repeats factually. 'More of a one than I had think. I don't come and look for you to tell it. It's yust happen I run into you – it's a chance, that's all. So I think – maybe I tell it, explain him some facts? At least try – one more time?'

'What? You still think you've got things to *tell* me?' And yet there's something in his unruffled tone that compels me to listen. 'All right, then. Run it past me if you must – whatever it is. What makes you so clever and me such a *bloody idiot?*' My fury makes him even slower to answer.

'OK. I can try. For begin with, you got that all wrong with Helena and me, Guy. We was together a lot of years, yes. We had thomething – what you call *in common*. We liked each other.'

'*Liked?*'

'Yes, liked. Why not? It's possible, you know. Even for a man and woman. We work together on a lot of things. It's what matter sometimes. The roof, on the backside – it was fall down – did Helena told you about it? I fix it. I fix a lot of things. I work on the yacht, Peter's – clean it. Helena, she plant potatoes, some beans – I'm digging the ground. All that vegetables – the celery soup? You must remember this – or did everything go out when you get that bang on the head? I was do a lot of things in the house, also. Helena, she pay me sometimes – I must live, don't I? We get close, later, yes, sometimes I sleep there, but . . .'

'Ulf, I don't want to hear it. It's not my business and anyway I don't care what you . . .'

'No, of course – that's it, that's your problem, isn't it?' He stabs a finger at my chest. 'You really *don't* care for nothing, don't you. Why can't you yust *listen*, for a change?' He spits it at me; I have no choice. He pauses. 'I was for Helena – what it's call? – her *rock*. That's how she call me. It's what I *was* for her. Not any longer. It's different now. Helena, she have no more need of me. She's stronger, Guy. Strong – and it's because of you.' I stare at him: now he's talking complete gibberish. He adds: 'I have my girlfriend, she live with me now, since a month. In Valstad.'

'Your . . .? Helena, you mean.'

'No, *not* Helena! You're not *listen*, do you. Where is your ears? Let me tell you it. Helena, she never has *loved* me. You see, that's all inside your head, Guy, she never loved *me*. I was there only for protect her. Some women, it's a need, you know? I was for her like a bodyguard, in that way. Like at *Inblick*, that day – when I push you? It was for Helena – it was yust instinct. I don't knew who you was. How can I know? Yes, you was share my apartment, sleep on my room, but you was a stranger. So when I push you it was for protect Helena. That's all what I wanted. Ever. Helena, she was alone in that time, she need of someone. Not any longer.' His gaze, full of sudden compassion, is directly on me. I can't even recognise him. 'I'm sorry you get hurt, Guy – your head, and so. It's was terrible, it shouldn't happen, it yust *happened*. How are you now? OK I hope.' He stops, examining his big work-rough hands. 'This is say sorry, Guy. I've lose my temper, I shouldn't done so, I don't meant it. But it's not mean what you think! It's *all wrong*, what you think. *All*.'

I stare at him, speechless. I feel as idiotic as he thinks me. Now he's looking almost tenderly at me. 'It's you, Guy. She love *you*. Why you can't accept it?' A second later the tenderness gives way to amusement. 'You English – so civilised. You love your complicate feelings, isn't it? Most of all you love hurt yourself – so much self-torture. It's the Marquis de Sade all again, I seen on films! You're do it right here, today. It's what you're do best. Of course you English, you're better in all things. We Swedish, and so – we're yust *foreigners*. But when you come in our country it's *you* the foreigner, Guy. So you can get hurt sometimes. It's happen. But I say you: Helena, she love you. In Sweden maybe we don't talk so much of feelings – it's our way to be – but she have say me this. Of course I know it already, from the beginning. She was talk always of you. You was in her mind, from the first days.' He leans back, resting from the effort. 'What you do now, it's your business, Guy, I don't speak of it. But don't say me it's not true, because it's that way and you can't change it.'

Ulf's words are like a second crack on the head, rocking my world even more than the first. In a single flash I grasp what's happened. It's as if up until this moment I'd wanted him to be the immovable, unseeing villain in this drama – wanted it to be *his* slow-ness of thought obstructing Helena and me, *his* dark presence standing between us. Yet in all these months the blindness has been mine. Through this single unplanned, unwanted encounter in London, I'm seeing clearly for the first time.

Kindness, coming from Ulf, has swept away the last vestige of my delusions: I stare at him in astonishment, all feelings and faults stripped naked. The way I've behaved has been more loathsome and mean-spirited than he's ever been to me. Despite my insensitivity and rudeness, he lets me buy him coffee. I try to apologise. I'm ready to confess to whatever charges he cares to level at me; but the strange thing is he doesn't even want to. Blame isn't in Ulf's vocabulary.

We talk for another half-hour. He would like to know: have I heard from Helena? He thinks I should have done. My head tells me everything he has said is true, but it's too fresh, too extra-ordinary to take in. Pain and hope battle within me. Ulf asks for nothing, but I give him my Wintersham address, which he writes in the palm of his hand; we promise to contact each other.

Eventually he saunters off to buy fancy knickers in Oxford Street for his new girlfriend. When he's gone I realise people are staring at me. Ulf has dissected the exact truth: I'm a *bloody idiot*. The thought is exhilarating.

Some time later, wandering bewildered, I find myself on Oxford Street too. There's something I should be looking for. Where would be the best place to find a book on Houdini?

58

No answer! Why no answer when I phone? In dismay I check the number: it's cruelly correct. Has she sold up at Hörnvik? Nothing can undo the past. The day I walked out of her life, Helena was lost to me forever. The tone rings on.

*   *   *

There has been only one time when the shadow of despair hovered over my life in this way. Like anyone else I've known events that have shaken me, prompted disturbing dreams, full of pain and loss. Yet none resembled the one that came a few days after that shattering confrontation with Ulf in London.

In the beginning I'm nowhere at all. There's complete darkness; it's as if the universe hasn't started up yet. I'm hovering above water; a while later, my body is submerged in it. The cold is immense, like nothing I've ever experienced. But then the cold isn't quite what I myself am feeling: it's someone else's sensation. There's a woman in the sea; I know who she is but I can't say her name. She is far, far out of reach, because we are not two people here together. This makes no rational sense, but she is completely alone, and I'm a nothingness – except that I am also her, seeing and feeling what she sees and feels.

Black droplets, barely visible, fall from her fingers as she reaches out to part the water. Glassy contours of darkness lap her cheek, waves closing cold on neck and shoulders. The sea feels colder moment by moment; the warmth of her being seems to hang in the balance. The solitary challenge, pitting herself against cold and current: the swim before dawn, on the black night-side of the island, is something she returns to each summer. Flinging herself free of the shore, she senses rather than sees the rocks and shingle glide away in whispers behind her. She strikes out further; the land grows remote.

My skin is joined onto darkness and water; my skin is the water. Invisible ripples parting around lips and chin; I'm sucking in black air. The cold numbs the hurt in my feet, scoured by sand, a myriad crushed shells. Two arms, stretching, dipping – they're part of my body, yet separate from me. Blackness encloses my spirit, ice-cold.

How long? Time is unmeasured. The sea absorbs the dawn like diluted ink. Each second tiny increments of light are creeping in around her – photons from the vacuum of space. Cold. Her waist and thighs are flowing with coldness. The reef slides closer, inch by gradual inch, the gap dwindling. At last she touches the shadowy rock and hauls herself up onto its unyielding, biting hardness. Scratching and pressing into her wet legs; she scarcely notices the knifelike edges. *My rock.* Panting, shivering, she listens to her pounding heartbeat. The dark shoreline stretches faintly grey against the glimmer of a dawning sky.

Abruptly now her mind (and therefore mine) is seeing – imposed on the filtered greyness – the motorbike. It lies on its side, waiting. *I've found Peter's motorbike.* Since that distant day it has lain under a sparse blanket of pine needles and moss, lost among trees, not two minutes from the jetty. *Peter's favourite place on earth.* She's dragging it upright on sagging tyres, propping it against a gnarled trunk. Solid, steadfast: a sign of life.

Later, in the infinite slowness of advancing daylight, she can breathe slower breaths, taking in fresh good air. She stands, the dawn breeze drying her skin. She's ready to swim back.

59

It's 3.30 am. Sleep has deserted me. Shreds of dreams, half-remembered, dart away at the edges of recognition. It's deathly quiet outside – no rowdy celebrations this time. The reception desk closed hours ago, but its neon sign shines on. The harsh light is oddly comforting, as if keeping at bay the childish dreads of the night.

Herr Wittberg is away on leave, but his young assistant has given me last year's *stuga* once more. Deep shadows loom behind the wardrobe and the tiny writing-desk, where I've tried to compose a letter to Georgina tonight. Tried and failed. She's a lovelier person than I ever deserved, and I wronged her. Her dauntless sincerity has helped me see so much that has gone awry in my life – and even more that has to be changed for the future.

As for Helena: nothing I say can make amends for leaving her the way I did. That must have seemed callous indifference. It's without expectation I've returned here: only to know she's well, and safe, and, as far as possible, happy.

More urgently than the chance meeting with Ulf in London, my strange sea dream has awoken me to the truth of Helena's life throughout these long months. Whatever my doubts as to Ulf's real grasp of her creative being, I'd never for a moment thought to question that she was safely back with him: cared for, supported, and loved. The bitter reality – all the while I've pictured the two of them coping, renovating the house, planning a future together – is that she's been in a cold, dark place, betrayed and alone.

It would be the simplest thing in the world to phone from here, in the morning. The thought makes my heart race, but shame at all I could and should have done – in another country, oblivious of her plight – fills me with misgiving.

The confines of the *stuga*, the closeness of a summer's night, are stifling. My return to Emsäde is like rewinding the film of all last year's upheavals. Still half-dreaming, it's as though I hear the whirr of the projector, glimpse the flickering image of those events on the blank walls; Ulf's massive presence, too, is almost palpable, here in this room.

Regret drives me from the bed. The sea and the winding coastal roads, vivid in sleep-drunk fantasy, seem to beckon. Fumbling in shadows, I dress and splash a little cold water on face and arms. The warden has allocated me the use of a bicycle: will it wake someone if I take it out at this hour? The door creaks; in the much cooler air outside I'm glad of a windcheater. As an after-thought I pick up a towel, feel my way across the bumpy turf. It's loose and sandy underfoot; once, several million years ago, this was a beach.

Beyond the corner of the main building the grounds lie in pitch darkness. There's a good smell of earth and river water; it's been raining, just as in this season last year. At the sheds I unlock the rear wheel and clip the rolled towel onto the rack. Blindly I swing myself across the frame and push forward into the black void, flicking a dynamo switch for the lights.

On the rutted path the headlamp flashes a thin, tremulous beam, its eerie circle lighting a glimmer of mud: the sluggish river to the right, a slippery bank to the left. An overhanging birch gives me a spiteful thwack to the temple, a smear of blood moist on the back of my hand. Within seconds I'm levering the wheels up onto the gravelled main road. As if somnambulant, I turn left. A trillion stars arch overhead, flung in reckless magnifi-cence across a black cosmos.

Pedalling, pedalling; the ache in my legs is like sexual desire, but my mind dawdles still between dream and waking. Another story, another old film spools forward: Sofi, lying sleepless in the pitch-dark hours of early morning. Etched on her mind are the deserted sands, the pounding seas, the endless vigil in fading light. She won't believe Peter has drowned. Fanny, the friend who tends and loves her like a sister, has taken the car back to Guldstranden. Sofi clings to her fragile life-raft of hope.

In a parallel frame I watch a young man, bedraggled, on the Klosterbo road. Shivering from hours in the sea clutching some debris, through sheer toughness and resolve he's reached land. His energies are all but spent. Only knowledge of the girl he loves sustains him.

A solitary car pulls up: one of the loggers from the coastal forest, perhaps, driving home in the small hours. The trail of cat's eyes lights their gleaming way through the night. Few words are said; it's not the custom to question strangers. Daylight tinges the eastern sky; a change of gear marks the slow climb to the village: Lindhem. Peter raises his arm as the car draws away. A few more steps; he taps at a window. Sofi is there, weeping. They embrace, drinking the reality of being together.

Later, they'll steal away unseen. Haven't they forfeited precious time in a family dispute not of their making? Peter's few belongings are on the ferry. They're holding hands in the empty cafeteria; staff, seeing him, step quietly past, smiling. From Vyborgshamn they'll head due west to Gothenburg for the midday Harwich sailing. A new life in England: the land of her grandfather's birth.

Some weeks later, working in a Soho restaurant, Peter picks up a magazine: there's a vacancy in a West Country boat-builder's yard. They'll face months of virtual poverty, but they're resilient and they're in love. One day Sofi has joyful news: the prospect of a child inspires them.

My pace has slackened. At last the yellowy beam flickers over glistening pebbles. Unseen waves whisper: Segelholm. In darkness my wheels pitch straight onto crunching shingle.

Higher up, near the trees, a bike can be safely left. From here the downward slope of the beach brings me to a stretch of firmer sand; it's soothing to pad barefoot now over the soft, gritty ridges, a million granules resisting and enfolding my soles in cool moisture. Sea and sky are conjoined in unifying blackness; a slight breeze blows from the land. Faint reflections of stars dance on the water's shifting surface.

I turn and climb toward the trees. Finer, drier powder under-foot, laced with tufts of sea grass: I'm back among the dunes. A dusty mound trips me. Stumbling into the hollow behind it, I'm cocooned on all sides by a ring of sandy hillocks sprouting wisps of grass. Curled up here under the windcheater, the night breezes will pass me by. Sleep comes in an instant, deep and obliterating.

60

I wake chilled to the bone, my left side numb. A breath of wind rustles the pines; overhead the sky has grown minutely paler, the horizon darkly visible for the first time. The offshore reef lies silent, a smudge of deeper blackness against indeterminate black-grey. Nearer the shore tiny ripples traverse the surface; the sea breathes in sleep.

Despite the grief inside me there's nowhere I'd rather be, nothing I'd rather be doing than watching the break of dawn in this place. The charcoal rocks are outlined at last with the crystal clarity of an artist's sketch. My eye follows the luminescent horizon as it sweeps round to the northern headland, where a slow incremental greenness is warming the dark foliage. I'm gazing in that direction when a slight movement out to sea seems to catch the left edge of my vision. I turn back and stare straight at the reef, already textured darkest brown and black against the steel-grey water. Nothing. A seagull, perhaps. I continue watching, not expecting anything, when all at once it happens again. There *is* something out there. *Someone.*

Now I can hear too: someone's getting into the water. A sudden belated splash and a trail of telltale whiteness: he's swimming – swimming towards me. For a strong swimmer the conditions are perfect, though the sea must still be very cold. I scan the mesmerising ripple of waves, straining to see. With agonising slowness he draws away from the rocks; the stretch of water seems immense, wider than anything I'd ever attempt in semi-darkness.

Near the horizon the sky is absorbing light, tinged already with what in a few hours will become that unique Scandinavian blue of late summer. Eternities pass. Tiredness bears down on my drowsing eyes; for a moment, unable to resist, I close them.

When I look again the swimmer has widened the gap from the reef. The bulk of the distance to the beach still lies ahead, but he's a little closer.

Or she? For a few seconds I'm unsure. Something in the style – alternating the vigorous crawl with a rhythmic, painstaking breaststroke – seems to suggest it. Yes, there's her white swimsuit – why didn't I see? Doubt evaporates.

In almost the same instant I know it's Helena. Joy, fear, disbelief and affirmation shake me at once as the knowledge takes hold. It *must* be Helena! Her arms gleam in the radiance of dawn, lifting and dipping as she swims her deliberate crawl, then reverts in a moment to the forward-lunging breaststroke, parting the water seamlessly beneath the surface. Is it an effect of the light, or is her pace slowing? The distance to be covered looks vast, unrealistic: how can she ever reach the shore? I'm willing her, in an agony for her to manage it. Her fatigue is in my bones, as if the exertion draws on my energy even as it saps hers. She makes an odd move to one side; can it be deliberate? Perhaps one of the powerful currents is dragging at her body: tendrils of panic clutch at my chest, impelling me forward. I'm sprinting down the slope, I've thrown off coat and shoes, I'm dashing across the margin of wet sand.

The impossible happens, halting me at the water's edge. I'm watching her rise up out of the sea. No, this can't be happening . . . For split seconds she's balanced out there, as if kneeling, prayerfully close to the surface. The next instant she stands erect, her white-clad form complete above the shimmering waves. She raises both arms outward to shoulder height, balancing, then steps forward. Helena is *walking on the water*. Seeing fuses with believing:

momentarily I seem to witness the miraculous, caught inside its enveloping wave.

Wonder comes first; secondary to it is confusion, the mind's struggle for understanding. An unseen structure, no more than a few fingers' breadth beneath the tideless sea, bears her solidly up, carrying her in a perfect straight line to the safety of the beach. Her walking – athletic, yet measured, like a reflective walk home – can only be along a causeway of some kind, inches below the surface. Though my baffled vision identifies it, the marvel of the moment is with me still.

Man-made, judging by its straightness: a wall? Rough, nonetheless, and narrow, dictating the outward stretch of her arms in the effort of balance. Now I'm back in Valstad's museum – those age-old ridges to shelter fishing-boats, for centuries thought to be natural in origin: this one was even visible from the air, that morning last year; a time remote as a sleepwalker's dream.

Even as I wait in tremulous expectancy, I see another figure – bearded, poised Houdini-like with an oar – emerging from an angry sea at this selfsame spot. Under the trees a young girl watches: in this exact second, her wonderment is mine.

With that I stand quietly in the first light of dawn, the sea-spray stinging my legs, as Helena steps the last few paces out of the water, mouth half-opened in her breathlessness, and to my joy I can hold her. Huddled against me, she draws hungry breaths. Her cold, wet limbs are trembling. Pulling the coat around her shoulders, my fingers touch her beautiful ear still streaming with water. She stumbles a little, and I support the close, precious weight of her body, salt tears on my face. At the little nest among the dunes she flings herself down.

I'm trying to dry her hair and back. Little by little, resting out of the wind, the shivering subsides and she breathes more easily, but in her face are etched the shock and pain of all that's happened.

Through the grass-topped dunes we watch the warming advance of daylight. A Seaways shuttle plane soars in the cloudless sky to the south, glinting orange from a sun that, where we lie, has yet to show itself. Seagulls dart and dive along the shoreline against translucent blue. Close to the rocky outcrop, black-capped wagtails are pecking in the grit.

For many minutes she stares in silence at the horizon.

'Helena, I'm so sorry.' Words can't right those wrongs – my unconscionable departure, the loss of faith – nor wipe away her months of loneliness and anguish.

I gaze at the reef, awed by the mystery of her coming out of the sea. 'It's early. You've come here in the night, in the cold – what makes you . . .?' I touch her fingers, not daring to draw too close.

She turns to me, frowning. 'To swim, that's all. Just for a swim.'

'It was pitch-dark out there.'

'I don't mind the dark. It's good to swim before dawn, in the summer.' Chin in hand, she watches birds flitting to and fro. 'I must try to heal the past; it helps me do that. You've not been here – how could you know?' Her tone is bruised and embittered. In another time the conjunction of our two lives, at this exact moment and place, might have seemed fortunate; now I'm beyond hope, other than that of laying open my sorrow. The separateness yawns between us.

We listen to the hushed swell of the sea; her gaze shifts along the skyline.

'The dawn's such a special time. Promises of a new day . . . I love to watch the sunrise, don't you?' Subdued by exhaustion, she drops forward, head resting on her arms.

'You always come to Segelholm – there are beaches nearer home, surely?'

'Segelholm has something – don't you feel it? For me it's the best place. It puts me together, when I'm all split and sleepless. I've told you, I like this side of the island. My favourite beach, I

305

suppose – and of course . . .' She breaks off and looks along the shore, one hand held up against the reflected brilliance of sea and sky. 'Walking on the ridge – that's special too.' Her eyes are full of sudden tears. We lie silent, watching the first rays of sunlight glint on gentle waves.

'Helena, there's something else. Peter and Sofi . . .'

'I know.' She raises herself a little and for a second rests a finger on my lips.

'So he . . .? Sofi said he wrote, I wasn't sure if . . .'

'We've talked on the phone – not long ago. I'm so happy for them.' A momentary, private joy infuses her voice.

I lie quietly beside her, thankful she's been freed of this burden. 'Watching you out there – for a minute you seemed to be walking on the water.'

She brushes away the tears; her brows lift with the hint of playfulness that I love. 'Not quite! It's a kind of cheating, isn't it? I like to swim out to the reef, but it means I can always come back along the old wall – not get too exhausted. Me and my rock . . . It feels safe, sitting out there.' For a moment she leans her head against mine.

'I thought Ulf was your rock.'

'Oh, Guy!' I feel her quick smile against my face, but the desolation in her voice has returned. 'Yes, well . . . For a long time he was, I suppose.' She draws away once more. In her eyes are reminiscences of half a lifetime shared: years of companionship and trust.

'Helena, I only want to tell you . . . I *know* what I did, how bad that was. Thinking back – your kindness when we first met, then after the accident, all those weeks . . . Now, coming here again, I'm – I know how much it must have hurt, leaving you that way. Ulf talked to me, he made me see, he . . .'

'He said he met you – in London? You weren't too pleased to see him!'

'I was such a fool, Helena. Everything was wrong in my head. But you had a life with him. It *worked*, you were . . .'

306

'We had, yes. Not any longer. Ulf has his own life now, he has someone . . . I'm glad for him.'

'It was something solid – you had someone to rely on. I destroyed all that.'

'No – not destroyed. That's something you can't blame yourself for. It couldn't stay like that for ever – we both had to move on. But when you left – in the way you did, Guy – yes, it's true, I was hurt. I'm still hurting.'

We lie listening to the sounds of morning. Birds call; the sea whispers its secrets. Some while later, Helena rests her head on my shoulder once more. Now she sleeps, and I hold her, the warmth of her breath on my cheek.